Praise for The Paul Manziuk & Jacquie Ryan Mysteries

Shaded Light: The Case of the Tactless Trophy Wife

"Ontario police detectives Paul Manziuk and his new partner, Jacqueline Ryan, make an odd team—he's white, an abrupt, patronizing veteran, while she's a recently promoted, vivacious black woman—but... the two rub elbows and tempers to captivating effect...."

Publishers Weekly

"Detailed characterization, surprising relationships, and nefarious plot-twists provide ample diversion… Recommended."

Library Journal

"A recipe for murder and mystery that simmers slowly and emits an enticing aroma reminiscent of earlier delights...."

The Charlotte Austin Review Ltd.

"Reminiscent of the best Agatha Christie had to offer... You have humor, complications, and characters so real that you can just about touch them and smell their sweat."

Midwest Book Review

"An admirable first outing for a pair of detectives readers will look forward to hearing from again."

The Mystery Read

"[The author] works every twist imaginable in her modern c meets-police-procedural.

I Love a M

Glitter of Diamonds: The Case of the Reckless Radio Host

"A master of plotting, [she] seeds her tale with concealed clues and innuendoes that keep readers guessing until the very end."

Library Journal

"A finely drawn police procedural written in the style of Georgette Heyer, long considered queen of the British mystery genre."

The Suspense Zone

"The investigation is fascinating to watch as the police follow the clues and eliminate suspects one by one.... An exciting baseball whodunit."

Midwest Book Reviews

"A modern-day whodunit, much in the style of the classic Christie novels.... I had to stay up all night to finish it."

Armchair Interviews

"Although this reviewer very seldom watches a baseball game... it's possible for someone like myself to enjoy the story."

Hidden Staircase Mystery Books

"Baseball. There are few things that say lazy, hazy summer days than hat sport. But this book is anything but lazy or hazy—and is one hell a read. A Christie-style mystery, this one does a good job of it."

Mysterical-E

ses are loaded, it's the bottom of the ninth, who is on first, I w, keep reading to find out the answer in this nicely done ystery."

Book Bitch

humour, the story-telling is edged with compassion, are well drawn. The story is baseball, the language d entertainment of professional sport and the nd-up triple."

The Hamilton Spectator

SHADOW OF A BUTTERFLY

THE CASE OF THE HARMLESS OLD WOMAN

Paul Manziuk & Jacquie Ryan Mysteries by J. A. Menzies

Shaded Light: The Case of the Tactless Trophy Wife
Glitter of Diamonds: The Case of the Reckless Radio Host
Shadow of a Butterfly: The Case of the Harmless Old Woman

Short Stories by J. A. Menzies

"The Case of the Sneezing Accountant" (A Manziuk & Ryan Short Story)
"The Day Time Stood Still"
"Revenge So Sweet"
"They Can't Take That Away from Me"
"Dying with Things Unsaid"

SHADOW OF A BUTTERFLY

THE CASE OF THE HARMLESS OLD WOMAN

A PAUL MANZIUK & JACQUIE RYAN MYSTERY

J. A. MENZIES

MurderWillOut Mysteries

Markham, Ontario

Shadow of a Butterfly: The Case of the Harmless Old Woman

ISBN: 978-1-927692-10-3

This novel is a work of fiction. Names, characters, and events are the product of the author's imagination, and any resemblance to actual persons, living or dead, is purely coincidental. The city of Toronto, the Toronto police, and any other entities that seem familiar are not intended to be accurate, but come totally out of the author's imagined fantasy world.

MurderWillOut Mysteries is an imprint of
That's Life! Communications
Box 77001 Markham, ON L3P 0C8
Email: connect@thatslifecommunications.com
http://www.murderwillout.com

Printed in Canada

Library and Archives Canada Cataloguing in Publication

Menzies, J. A., 1948-, author
Shadow of a butterfly : the case of the harmless old woman / J.A. Menzies.

(A Paul Manziuk & Jacquie Ryan mystery)
Issued in print and electronic formats.
ISBN 978-1-927692-10-3 (pbk.).--ISBN 978-1-927692-11-0 (epub)

I. Title.

PS8573.I53175S54 2015 C813'.54 C2015-902482-X
C2015-902483-8

Dedication

For my grandmother, Alice May MacDonald.
Whenever she came to visit us, she left Erle Stanley Gardner's Perry Mason books where I could find them.
Without a doubt, those books had a strong impact on what I currently read and write.

Major Players in Order of Appearance

Paul Manziuk: A frustrated cop who misses his former partner and can't quite figure out how to work with his prickly new partner

Jacqueline Ryan: A fledgling homicide detective who's beginning to wonder what she really wants in life

Mary Simmons: A former children's singer who longs for excitement

Lyle Oakley: A character actor who takes life as it comes, even when it includes dead bodies

Ingrid Davidson: An elderly wife and grandmother who is passionate about crocheting

Hilary Brooks: A former ballerina and a recent widow

Naomi Arlington: The ambitious young administrator of Serenity Suites

Audra Limson: The rather unhappy manager of the twentieth floor of Serenity Suites

Catarina Rossi: A retired stage actress who fully enjoys her amplified life

Olive Yeung: The excited new assistant for both staff and residents

Nikola Vincent: Catarina's long-haired new husband who's young enough to be her son

Frank Klassen: A bestselling author who is hard at work on his next book

Violet Klassen: Frank's wife, who has always taken good care of him

Patricia (Trish) Klassen-Wallace: The only daughter of Frank and Violet

Ben Davidson: Ingrid's husband, and a much-loved former talk show host

Kenneth Harper: A second-career tenor looking at the end of the road

Elizabeth Carlysle: A jazz singer and teacher who feels the walls closing in

Norm Carlysle: Elizabeth's husband, a portrait artist who, despite his age, is in high demand

Derrick James: A nurse and physiotherapist who loves elderly people

Scarlett Walker: The cook for the twentieth floor of Serenity Suites, and a budding author

Dr. Granger: The medical doctor who looks after a number of the residents

Map of Serenity Suites

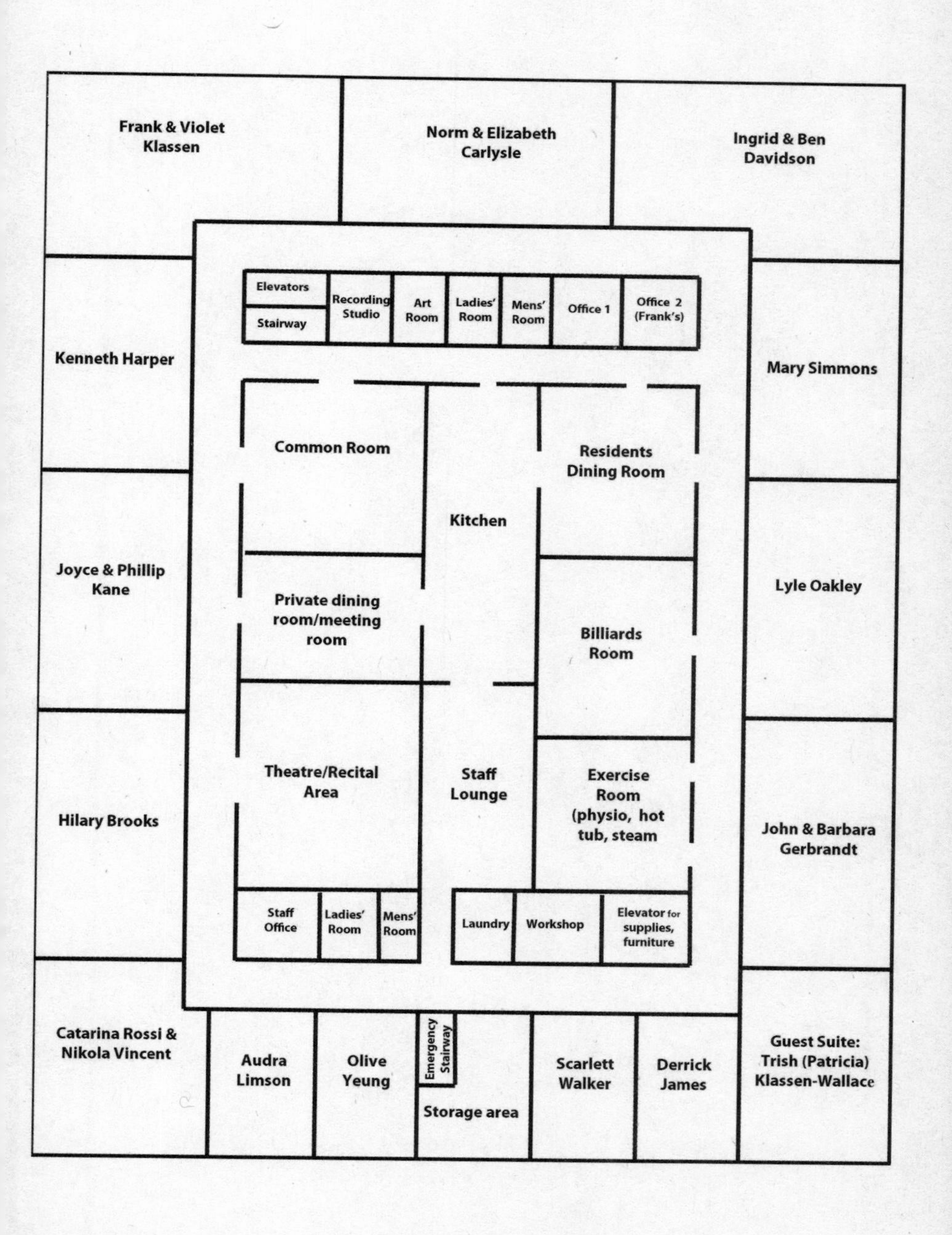

Prologue

In each action we must look beyond the action at our past, present, and future state, and at others whom it affects, and see the relations of all those things. And then we shall be very cautious.

—BLAISE PASCAL, French mathematician, philosopher and physicist, 1623–1662

Detective Inspector Paul Manziuk raised his eyebrows at his boss, Superintendent Cliff Seldon, seated behind the desk in his office. "You want me to what?"

Seldon repeated, "I want you to let Ryan take lead on your next investigation. Find out what she's got."

"She's not ready."

"Why not?"

Manziuk stepped back from his position in front of the desk, leaned against the closed door, and took a deep breath. "Because she hasn't had enough experience."

Seldon smiled. "I'm asking you to give her experience."

"I know, but—"

"When, in your opinion, will she be ready? Next week?"

Manziuk stared at his boss. "Are you serious?"

"Dead serious."

"I don't understand. She's been in homicide for a little over a month. She's just beginning to learn the ropes."

"She's smart. She learns fast."

"Is there an agenda or something I'm missing?"

"Of course not."

"You want to have her on display," Manziuk said in a flat voice. "Just because she's a black woman."

"Not on display. We have high hopes for her, and we want to make sure nothing impedes her progress."

"And I want to make sure she learns how to do a good job."

"That's why we put her with you."

The men locked eyes. Both were in their mid-forties. Seldon had taken the fast track to leadership while Manziuk thrived on hands-on involvement in cases. Of course, this meant Seldon got to call the shots. Finally, he said, "I'll give you another month to get her ready to take the lead role on an investigation."

Manziuk moved closer to the desk, placed both hands on its pristine surface, and leaned toward Seldon. "Are you blaming me that Woody never went beyond detective sergeant? Do you think it was my fault he was content to be my partner all those years?"

Seldon neither flinched nor moved back. "No one is blaming you for anything. We simply believe that Detective Constable Ryan has a great deal of potential, and we want to make sure she goes as far as she's capable of going. That's it."

Twenty-eight-year-old Detective Constable Jacqueline Ryan sat alone in a busy sports bar, drumming her fingers on the top of the cherrywood table.

A little while ago, she'd been in the middle of an intense discussion with Armando Santana, the Toronto baseball player, originally from the Dominican Republic, whom she'd met on a case and been dating for several weeks. Now he was at a large, round table in the back corner, surrounded by a pack of adoring fans.

Armando finally slipped onto the stool across from hers. "Jacqueline, I am so sorry. I would never have stayed to talk, but the guy whose birthday they were celebrating, he just got out of hospital after an operation for brain cancer. It was hard to sign and run." He picked up his menu. "So, what are you going to have?"

"Most of their stuff is deep-fried, but I think there's a grilled chicken salad I can eat."

Armando winced. "I am *so* sorry. I should have picked a healthier place."

"True. And not only because I don't eat junk food."

"I know. I need to eat healthier. I am trying. Really!" His brow furrowed. "The bad thing is I did not even think about it for one second. When you asked me where I wanted to go, I remembered coming here a few times and liking it, and I never even thought past that. Just habit—that is all. I am truly sorry. I will try to do better."

Jacquie laughed. "Next time I won't ask where you want to go."

They gave the waiter their order.

Jacquie sat back. "You had something you wanted to ask me about?"

Armando leaned forward, resting both elbows on the table, and cleared his throat. "So, this is it. Some of my friends on the team and I have rented a place in Hawaii for a month at the end of the baseball season. Basically all of November. We have done this a few times. There is a villa right on the ocean beach on the island of Kauai, and it is very beautiful there. The villa is pretty new and very nice. It has five huge bedrooms, a pool, a hot tub, a gym, and several acres of land with trees and flowers. Nearby are golf courses, tennis courts, walking trails, a wildlife refuge, and shopping malls. And of course you can go surfing and sailing in the ocean. Or just relax on the beach. Jacquie, will you take some time off from your job and come to Hawaii with me?"

Jacquie started to speak, but Armando extended his left arm to put three fingers on her lips. "I know exactly what you are going to say. You can't do it. But, please, think seriously about it. I will pay for everything. And if it is about loving your job, surely you can take one month off."

He took his hand away and looked at her with pleading eyes. "So tell me, would you like to come?"

Jacquie smiled. "I'm not sure I'm the type to lie around on the beach."

"Oh, yes. I am not the lying-around-relaxing type either. We can keep busy."

"You'll be off golfing or something with the other guys."

"If I am gone, you can go shopping."

"I don't do shopping."

"There will be wives and girlfriends there. You might like them."

"I don't do girly chitchat either."

"Play tennis. Golf. Swim."

"Maybe I could manage that for a week. But not a month."

The waiter brought their food.

Jacquie continued. "There's a bigger issue. We've had some cups of coffee and a few meals, taken some walks and had some interesting conversations, but I'm not ready to make any commitments."

"A couple of the rooms have two beds."

She looked at him.

"You could think about it."

She nodded, not sure what else to say. As she began eating her grilled chicken salad, she caught herself almost—but not quite—wishing her phone would ring, calling her to a murder victim.

Part I

The human understanding is like a false mirror,
which, receiving rays irregularly, distorts
and discolours the nature of things
by mingling its own nature with it.

—SIR FRANCIS BACON, *The New Organon* (1620)
in James Spedding, Robert Ellis, and Douglas Heath (eds.),
The Works of Francis Bacon (1887–1901), Vol. 4, 53–55.

One

"Lyle, I think Ingrid's dead."

Glancing up, Lyle Oakley sighed.

Mary Simmons nodded her head, with its halo of snow-white hair, stuffed a tissue up the sleeve of her blue cashmere cardigan, and leaned closer to peer into the still face of the stout, grey-haired woman who was slumped over in an easy chair.

"She's asleep." Lyle went back to his newspaper. He was seated on a leather recliner two chairs over from Ingrid's. He'd enjoyed a short post-lunch nap and was finishing up his perusal of the four daily papers. He'd just arrived at his favourite journalist's column in the sports section of the *Toronto Daily News*.

Lyle, Mary, and Ingrid Davidson were the only people in the common room of the twentieth floor of Serenity Suites, an exclusive condominium for seniors in downtown Toronto.

"I'm pretty sure she's dead."

Lyle glanced over again. Ingrid's eyes were shut, and her head was tilted back in an awkward position. The blanket she was crocheting for a newborn great-grandchild, along with skeins of pink and white wool, had spilled from her lap onto the hardwood floor.

"She isn't breathing."

After shaking his head, Lyle removed his reading glasses, folded his newspaper, and stuffed it down one side of his recliner before pulling himself to his feet. He shuffled over to stand behind Mary, his head above hers. "She's sleeping. Look, you can see her chest rising just slightly."

"You're too old to be looking at women's chests."

"Well, *you* look!" He shook his head as he moved back to his chair. "Always thinking the worst and then acting as if *I'm* in the wrong."

"I just thought the way her head's tilted over like that, she looks unnatural."

"Yesterday you were positive she was dead because her hands were blue."

"Well, they *were*. They still are. And you know people get cold when they're dead. Besides, most of her is well-layered, so I'd have thought her hands would be, too, and not have such thin skin and big veins."

"You just want something exciting to happen."

"That's not true at all." Mary moved away, her soft pink bedroom slippers making a whooshing sound as she struggled to keep up with the walker she tended to push ahead, then catch up to and push again. Just one of several reasons why Mary reminded Lyle of the Red Queen in *Through the Looking Glass*.

"I need a mirror," she said. "That way I'd know for sure. Because she could be dead. Any minute now. Could be." Mary threw the last words over her shoulder as she left the room.

Lyle carefully lifted his wonky knee into place as he sat down in his chair. He put his glasses back on, picked up his newspaper, and spent a couple of minutes finding his place.

But before he started to read, he glanced over the top of his glasses at the sleeping woman. Mary was probably right. One of these days Ingrid *would* be sitting there dead, and it might be hours before anyone noticed.

He shook his head and returned to the sports section of the paper. Maybe getting old was better than the alternative, but there were aspects of it he hated. Like not being surprised when people you knew died.

Hilary Brooks, a recent widow, sat rigidly on a gold brocade wing chair in the sitting room of her condo on the twentieth floor of Serenity Suites. On the matching chesterfield across from her sat Naomi Arlington, the administrator of the building, who was young enough to be Hilary's granddaughter. Not that anyone would assume such a relationship between the two women. In addition to the glacial nature of both their body language and their speech, their appearance bore no similarities beyond the fact that each was dressed in the manner she felt most likely to intimidate the other.

Naomi looked every inch the young professional in her two-piece navy business suit with a frilled white blouse and red heels that had to be four inches high. Her beautifully made-up face reminded Hilary of a porcelain doll, and her long blonde hair, which Hilary was positive was dyed, was pulled back in an attractive chignon.

Hands clasped as if in supplication, Naomi spoke in a voice that was anything but supplicating. "I'm very sorry, Hilary, but according to the agreement your husband signed, ownership of the condo cannot be passed on to his heirs. We're very sorry for your loss, and we really hate to ask you to move, but we've already given you over two months to find alternative accommodation. I explained in my letter that we'll be putting the condo up for sale on Monday, August 25th, and you'll have to leave by September 30th at the very latest. As you know, we have a waiting list of people who want to move in, so the sale will be completed quickly." She came to the end of her undoubtedly well-rehearsed speech.

"Grant meant for me to live here, and I see no reason why I should leave. I qualify to live here."

Naomi's words were smooth and clear and, to Hilary's ears very final, implying that only a fool would to try to argue with her. "The agreement of sale clearly states that on the death of the owner, the Serenity Suites Corporation has the right to sell the condominium. Any profit will be split 75/25 between the owner's estate and the corporation."

"And that would make perfect sense if Grant hadn't left a widow who wants to stay here and who qualifies in every way." Hilary's voice was low and well-modulated, with just a touch of a British accent. "So you're going to have to explain to me exactly why it is you think I should leave."

Naomi shifted in her seat. "It's my job to see that the sales agreements are upheld. I have no authority to make any changes or amendments. The board says that—"

"Tell the board," Hilary interrupted in the same well-modulated tone, "that I have no intention of moving out, and that if you try to sell my condo, I'll have my lawyer file a lawsuit accusing the corporation of racial discrimination. I don't really think they want that kind of press, do you?"

Naomi pressed her rosy lips together.

Hilary rose from her chair, her long purple caftan billowing out around her. She grasped the silver knob of the black cane that had been leaning in wait against the right arm of her chair. "Now, if you'll excuse me, it's time for my nap." She walked to the archway between the living room and the front hallway, and stood there waiting.

Naomi made a few notes, closed the black leather portfolio on her lap and carefully set it into her matching briefcase, and stood up. She walked past Hilary into the hallway and opened the door. She turned to the older woman. "I'll be talking with you again." And shut the door behind her.

Hilary muttered, "Whatever." A moment later she brought her left hand up to cover her mouth and chin. After the feeling of queasiness passed, she shouted at the closed door, "I shall not be moved!"

Back in her living room, she opened the French doors leading onto her balcony. For some time, she stood at the railing and gazed out at the lush, green trees in the Don Valley. Within a couple of months, they would be glorious shades of yellow, orange, brown, and red. She loved this view, loved this condo—even loved herself these days. And no one was going to make her move. She called out to the valley, "They're not getting rid of me so easily."

Hilary had moved into Serenity Suites with her fourth husband, Grant Brooks, who knew Ben Davidson, one of the original residents. The day they'd moved in, both Hilary and Grant had quickly realized that no one, with the possible exception of Ben, had been aware that Grant had a wife whose ancestors had been born in darkest Africa. Nothing had been said; it was more what hadn't been said. That night in their pillow talk, Hilary and Grant agreed that if the powers-that-be had been aware of Hilary, they wouldn't have approved Grant's application. The next morning Grant asked Hilary if she wanted to leave.

"No, honey, there's always something. Or somebody. We'll just have to change their way of thinking. Been doing that all my life."

"Fine. But if you ever decide you want to move out, all you have to do is let me know."

They'd moved into Serenity Suites almost a year ago. For the nine months Grant was alive, they'd had each other, and nothing else mattered. But one horrible afternoon in May, Grant dropped dead from a massive coronary while they were in the elevator descending to the ground floor.

Since then, Hilary had found her life very difficult. Most of the other residents had known each other for many years. Even newer ones knew at least one or two of the group. But she not only hadn't known any of them when she'd moved in, but as the only non-Caucasian resident, she stuck out like a sore thumb. And if for no other reason, that made her want to stay.

Why shouldn't she have just as much right to live here as anyone else? She fit the criteria. At seventy-five, she was certainly old enough. She was in good health and didn't require much care. Grant had left her with enough money, so that wasn't an issue. The final qualification residents of the twentieth floor of Serenity Suites had to meet was a connection with the arts. Well, she had that. So stay she would, come hell or high water.

Her intercom beeped, and a woman's voice said, "Hilary? Are you okay?"

"Come in, Audra."

Audra Limson, the petite Filipina manager of the twentieth floor and one of two registered nurses living on the premises, joined her on the balcony. Audra's smile was as much a part of her style as her floral scrubs and her sleek ponytail. But right now, she looked grim. "I saw Ms. Arlington leave. Are you all right?"

Hilary gritted her teeth. "I'm very angry that I have to go through this, but I'm fine. And I have no intention whatsoever of letting those people win."

"She still won't listen?"

"No, but I can't really blame her. She's just doing what the board members tell her to do. They're the ones I have to convince."

"I'm so sorry about all this."

"Nothing I'm not used to."

"Would you like anything? A cup of tea? Some brandy? A shoulder to cry on?"

Hilary smiled. "You are for sure the best nurse I've ever known. But I'm okay, honey. Don't worry about me."

"I sure hope I have half your strength when I'm seventy-five."

"Don't wish for that, honey. Way you get strength is by going through all the storms and struggles. Either you give up and stop trying and just get swept away, or you get strong. Mostly I'm just too stubborn to let anyone get the best of me."

"Well, you keep being stubborn. I'll see you at tea." She gave Hilary a quick hug and left.

Hilary smiled. Maybe the residents didn't accept her, but the staff sure did. Curious how all the live-in staff were minorities: Audra; Derrick James, the other nurse, who was a mix of black and East Indian; Scarlett Walker, the cook, originally from Nigeria; and Olive Yeung, the young assistant, of Chinese and First Nations ancestry. The staff not only accepted her, but did what they could to make her feel this was her home.

Hilary once again mouthed the words, "I shall not be moved." Crazy, but in spite of everything, she felt safe in this odd community.

"Olive, pull those hangers over. Maybe it's fallen behind." Catarina Rossi, who owned the corner condo next door to Hilary's, stood in the middle of her bedroom watching Olive Yeung, the young woman recently hired to do odd jobs for both the staff and residents, look for Catarina's missing blouse.

At twenty, Olive was just over five feet tall. Her straight black hair was cut in a short pageboy and parted in the centre. Her skin was olive, and her cheekbones were high in her rounded face. As usual, her brown eyes glowed with interest as she turned to Catarina. "Nothing on the floor. And I don't see anything that looks like it on the hangers. There's a gold brocade jacket and a gold sweater—but no gold blouse."

"Oh, this is maddening! I particularly wanted to wear it tonight."

"I can look through the hangers again. Maybe it's got something else hung over it."

"Oh, you darling, please, would you? I so want to wear it!" Catarina moved over to her mahogany dressing table and perched on the black velvet seat of the matching chair. She checked her short burgundy hair in the mirror and began applying make-up. "I look like a ghost." Picking up a crimson blush, she applied it liberally to her cheeks. She added lip liner and poppy-red lipstick to her lips, making them slightly fuller. "Sorry to make you work so hard, but my poor old heart was set on wearing that blouse and nothing else."

Olive quickly worked her way through more than half of the large walk-in closet's jumble of hangers for the second time, checking under each item. "Got it!" she shouted, exiting the closet with a gold blouse.

Catarina rose and hurried forward, plump hands outstretched. "Oh, my dear, that's it! I'm so relieved! You're an absolute darling to go to all that trouble just for my silly little whim." She held the blouse up before her and checked herself in the floor length mirror next to her closet. "Yes, it's exactly as I remembered." She smiled at Olive. "My second husband gave it to me a week before he died. And his death was a year ago today. So I wanted to wear it tonight when Nikola takes me out to dinner."

Olive frowned. "You think that's okay? I—I mean, you and Nikola only got married less than two weeks ago. Won't he mind you remembering your former husband?"

With no prior notice to anyone, at eighty-one, Catarina had married Nikola Vincent, her third husband, in a civil ceremony on July 30th. No one knew his exact age, but guesses ranged from thirty-five to fifty.

A former stage actress, whose resumé included long stays on Broadway, Catarina had freely told the residents and staff on the twentieth floor that she was perfectly aware Nikola had married her because of her money. "But," she shrugged, "if money didn't buy some enjoyment in life, what good was it?"

Catarina smiled in response to Olive's question. "He won't mind. I'll look good in it. That's the most important thing."

"Is there anything else I can do for you?"

Catarina swept her arm in the direction of the doorway. "No, darling. Run along. You have been an absolute angel! Thank you so much."

"No problem." Olive left the bedroom and walked toward the front door.

Nikola, a bearded man with long black hair, was sitting on a chair in the living room and strumming a golden guitar with darker, reddish wood on the sides, neck, and bridge, and what looked like a braid of yellow and red around the hole in the middle. Olive stepped inside the room. "Oh, what a beautiful guitar!"

Nikola looked up and laughed. "She was designed by Greg Smallman. And she thanks you for the compliment."

"She?"

"I name all my guitars after beautiful women. This one is Sandy. After the actress Sandra Bullock."

Olive giggled. "So you talk to your guitars? 'Sandy, I don't know if I feel like playing with you today.'"

"Something like that. Do you play?"

"No, but my brother does. I love listening to him."

Nikola set the guitar on a stand. "So were you able to find the errant blouse?"

"Yes, it was under a jacket."

"Good. Catarina hates it when things don't go the way she plans."

"Well, everything is fine, and I'm leaving now. Goodbye."

"Till next time."

Olive had an uncomfortable feeling that Nikola's eyes followed her until she shut the door.

Frank Klassen's private investigator, the intrepid Dusty Metcalf, was stuck at the bottom of an old well in the middle of New Mexico, and Frank had no idea how to get him out. A thirty-two-year-old former rodeo cowboy turned PI, Dusty had starred in each one of Frank's twenty-eight published books.

The author did a few hand stretches. His arthritis was getting worse. Some days it was a chore to type. His daughter, Trish, had suggested he hire someone to type for him, but he honestly couldn't see himself speaking the ideas instead of writing them down. Just didn't think it would work. He'd had to dictate some letters and a bit of one book to Violet once when he'd broken his arm, and he'd hated every minute of it. No, when he couldn't type any more, he'd stop writing. Maybe this would be his last book. Or maybe he'd squeeze out one more. Make it an even thirty.

His cellphone rang, and he glared at it before picking it up to check the display. Everyone knew not to bother him when he was writing. His daughter most definitely knew.

"Trish, what is it? I'm working."

"I'm sorry to bother you, Dad, but I wanted to talk to you when I knew Mom wouldn't be around."

"Well, she isn't around. What is it? I've got a book to write."

"I wanted to ask you about Mom's book launch in September. Since it's her tenth book, I thought it would be good to have a party after the launch. Just family and close friends. I wondered about having it at Serenity Suites. What do you think?"

"What do I think?" Frank began breathing hard. "I think it's ridiculous. It's a stupid cookbook, for crying out loud. She's not a writer. She'll tell you herself she just takes recipes from members of her family and types them up. I don't even see why the publisher thinks they need a launch for it."

"But, Dad, this book is special. She and Scarlett have worked really hard on redoing all the recipes to make them healthier as well as easy for seniors to make. And they've added new ones."

"Well, you do whatever you want, but I'll have nothing to do with it!" Frank ended the call. "Cookbooks! *Plain Food for Plain Folk*. The stupidest title ever! She doesn't know the first thing about writing a book." Frank scowled at his phone. His office across from the residents' dining room was his private sanctum. No one was supposed to bother him here. He was tempted to throw the cellphone at the wall, but it was too expensive. Maybe he ought to break it anyway, and then no one could bother him out of the blue that way.

He had a perfectly good office in his own condo, but he'd discovered that he worked better here, where he didn't have to converse with his wife. For some reason he didn't even remotely understand, when he was in his office in the condo, Violet seemed to feel obligated to stop in and talk to him.

The other advantage of this office was that it was soundproof, which meant he could play his music as loudly as he wanted. Violet wasn't at all partial to his music, which consisted largely of older rock bands like Aerosmith, Metallica, Bon Jovi, and Nirvana.

Well, at least the cookbooks keep Violet busy and out of my hair so I can focus on my work. But people need to remember that I'm the writer, not her! Frank laughed. If you'd told him when he was young that he'd write a book, he'd have suggested you see a psychiatrist. He'd hardly even read a book until he was in his thirties. Scraped through English in school every single year, doing just enough to get through. Got top marks in math and physics. Breezed through university and got a job teaching math at the University of Toronto.

He'd begun writing while in his forties, had his first book published to enormous success in his early fifties, and was now, at the age of eighty, the author of twenty-eight bestselling thrillers, one each year since his first.

The seeds of his writing had been planted one winter afternoon when he was flying to speak at a math conference and his flight was delayed. Bored, he'd picked up a Desmond Bagley paperback someone had left behind on a chair in the airport. Less than three pages in, he was hooked. Later, he wondered why on earth no one had told him there were books like that.

Some years later, after he'd read hundreds of thrillers, he started to write one, just to see what it was like. Of course, being able to write on a computer instead of a typewriter or, horrors, having to do it by hand with his illegible writing, had made the writing possible.

The photo on the back cover of his books had been taken many years ago, but it still adequately portrayed the man. True, grey was sprinkled through his thick brown hair, and numerous small wrinkles surrounded his eyes and mouth, but the intelligent brown eyes and the cleft in his jaw were unchanged.

The real change wouldn't show up in a photo. Frank had always carried himself ramrod straight, but osteoarthritis had gradually made walking both difficult and painful. A man who valued his independence, Frank had finally been persuaded to try a scooter, and he now used that to get around.

Frank looked back at his computer screen. *Back to what matters. And that isn't cookbooks.* He had no idea how Dusty was going to get out of the well, but it would likely involve either an ingenious solution or a seductive woman, or both. Frank grinned. As long as he enjoyed coming up with plots, he'd do his best to keep writing. It was the most fun he'd ever had. Maybe he could even adapt to dictating his thoughts if he absolutely had to. Not to Violet, though. It would have to be one of those mechanical dictation things.

Still very much alive in spite of Mary's concerns, Ingrid Davidson leaned heavily on the wheeled walker she was pushing across the common room and through the doorway, then to the right and along the hallway toward the corner condo she and Ben shared.

At eighty-one, Ingrid was a shrunken five-foot-six, with more than 200 pounds dispersed unevenly over her body. A recent stroke had forced her body to list to the left and caused one leg to drag slightly, which gave her a limp. The walker provided some stability.

Her long, braided, ivory hair and the sweaters and scarves she wore added to the impression of a short squat woman. Ingrid had been tall and blonde once, attractive in a wholesome way, but too muscular to be considered either thin or curvy. Of course, the muscles were long gone now, too. And her eyes, once a piercing blue and usually sparkling, were now pale and rheumy, hidden behind thick glasses that only helped a little. She had to hold her romance novels and her crochet instructions, not to mention the crocheting itself, a few inches from her nose.

Ingrid doggedly kept going until she reached the door to her condo. She mumbled, the software recognized her voice, and the door opened. She went inside.

Ben came out of the kitchen. "Hi, sweetheart."

For most of his life, Ben had been compared to an owl. He had a round face, large ears, horn-rimmed glasses, and hazel eyes that always seemed to have a quizzical, slightly-amused expression. His other notable physical characteristic was skin that tanned easily and held the tan long after its expiry date. But his physical attributes paled in comparison to his deep voice, which had proven to be his ticket to hosting a radio talk show for many years.

In the monotone that had replaced her former voice some months before, Ingrid replied, "Came back because I'm hungry."

"It's almost tea time. Will a couple of cookies do to tide you over?"

She kept moving along the hallway toward the main bathroom and shut the door behind her. She knew Ben would get cookies for her, the special ones for diabetics. Sure enough, when she exited the bathroom and pushed her walker into the kitchen, there was a plate with two small cookies. "That's all?" She scowled.

Ben smiled. "Don't want to spoil your appetite for whatever Scarlett has dreamed up for tea. How are you feeling?"

"You ask me that twenty times a day."

"If I do, it's because I care."

"I'm the same as I was this morning and yesterday."

"Hip hurting?"

She stared at him.

"I assume that means yes."

"Assume what you want. I want more cookies. And why didn't you make some tea?"

Ben gave her an odd look. "It's only half an hour until tea time in the dining room."

"Oh. Oh, yeah. I forgot."

She set the plate in the front basket of her walker and moved toward the living room. "Get me some water then."

With a good deal of effort, she sat down in a green leather recliner. "I can't reach the cookies."

Ben brought a glass of water and set it on the end table next to her chair. He put the plate of cookies on her lap. Ingrid was breathing heavily, and her chest was visibly moving.

Ben watched her take one of the cookies and stuff it into her mouth.

"Why are you staring at me?"

"I might like to look at the woman I love."

"Well, it's annoying. Go away."

Ingrid finished her cookies and drank her water, unaware of the crumbs that littered her bosom, the water that missed her mouth and landed on her jowls.

Tears running down his cheeks, Ben watched her from just outside the doorway that led to the front hall.

Lyle Oakley was still in the common room. After Mary had finally left him in peace, he'd finished the newspapers, had a short nap, helped Ingrid gather up her wool, and then sat thinking about his next job. His agent had called just after lunch to tell him he'd been picked to be in a commercial for a coffee chain. They'd be shooting it next week. All Lyle had to do was greet two other actors, sit at a table with them, drink coffee, and look happy. He quietly rehearsed what he'd say about the job at tea. *Real hard work! I have exactly two lines. But it gives me something to do.*

He heard a noise and looked up. Kenneth Harper, the only other single man on the twentieth floor, had come into the room through the far door. Lyle studied the man walking toward him, the newest resident, if you didn't count Catarina's husband.

Both men were of medium height and slim build. But while Lyle had a full head of steel-grey hair with matching eyebrows and a clean-shaven chin, Kenneth's forehead had expanded to push his hairline back and his remaining white hair was cut very short. In contrast, he had dark grey eyebrows and a thin grey moustache and beard, neatly trimmed.

Both men wore loafers and tweed pants with dress shirts, Lyle's coral with white stripes and Kenneth's a staid eggshell blue. Lyle had a pair of gold reading glasses perched on his nose; silver-rimmed glasses poked out of Kenneth's shirt pocket.

Kenneth paused by a chair kitty-corner to Lyle's. "Do you mind if I sit here?"

"I could probably get you a job."

"I'm sorry?"

"Oh, yes, sit down. Free country. We sit where we like."

Kenneth sat and looked expectantly at Lyle. "You said something about a job?"

"Oh, just thinking out loud. I do some acting, you know. You've got the sort of look they like. Might hear of a role you'd fit. For a commercial or a small role in a play. That sort of thing."

"Well, thank you, but acting's not something I've ever thought of doing."

"Oh, yes, you sing, right?"

"Yes, but I'm pretty much retired now. I just have a few bookings this fall."

"I could sing passably well in my time. For light musical comedies, you know. Nothing serious."

"Oh, I see."

There was a moment of silence, which Kenneth broke. "Nice out there."

"You were outside?"

"Yes, I went for a bit of a walk. Hot, but not too hot. A nice cool breeze off the lake."

"Better enjoy it while you can. Won't be long before winter."

Kenneth picked up a section of newspaper from the table between their chairs. "Anything new?"

"Not much. More murders. Sports news, of course. Some new movies. And so forth. Only thing I saw of interest to me was a new play opening in November. It's one I starred in some years ago. Shaw's *Arms and the Man*. I played the part of Sergius Saranoff once. One of my favourite characters ever. I might give it a look-see."

"Oh, yes. I think I've seen that play. Amusing." Kenneth turned a page. "I understand The Tenors will be here for a few shows in October. That interests me."

"It would," Lyle chuckled.

Kenneth's thin lips curved slightly. "To each his own."

Mary wandered in from the kitchen, where she'd probably been watching Scarlett Walker prepare tea and offering suggestions, all of which Scarlett would have accepted politely and completely ignored.

"Oh, hello, Ken."

Without looking up, Kenneth said, "Mary," and rustled his paper.

Lyle smiled. Although he'd been part of Serenity Suites for only a few weeks, Kenneth had made it quite clear to everyone that he hated being called Ken. Lyle couldn't tell for sure if Mary did it on purpose or simply didn't remember, though he assumed the latter. "Did you find what you were looking for, Mary?"

"No, I don't think so." Birdlike, she tilted her head and stared at Lyle, her forehead furrowed. "What was I looking for?"

"A mirror. My guess is that you thought if you had a small mirror in your purse, you could hold it in front of Ingrid's face to see if her breath fogged it."

"Oh, of course. The moment I left here, it went right out of my head."

Kenneth cleared his throat. "I read an article recently on how the action of moving from one room to another actually affects our ability to remember. I've had it happen myself. Many times, I knew exactly why I was going to another room, but when I got to that room, whatever I was going to do had flown completely out of my mind, and no matter how hard I tried, I couldn't remember."

Mary laughed. "At least you knew you'd forgotten. I didn't even remember I was looking for something."

"What was it again?" Kenneth leaned forward, his face puzzled. "A mirror for Ingrid?"

Lyle cleared his throat. "Ingrid often sits here to crochet and then falls asleep. Mary has several times thought Ingrid had stopped breathing. If a mirror held in front of her nose or mouth became foggy, Mary would know Ingrid was alive. And if not—" Lyle shrugged.

Kenneth looked from Lyle to Mary and back again. "I see." He returned to his newspaper.

TWO

Violet Klassen sat at her desk, writing in a spiral-bound notebook with red and yellow roses on the cover. She wrote a last paragraph, signed it, and set down her pen. *There, I've put the words on paper at last. One day Trish will know the truth. It will be up to her to decide what to do with it.*

That moment of enlightenment was in the distant future, of course, but still, once you'd decided to do something—especially something unpleasant—it was good to get it done.

Another memory came into her mind. Violet leaned back in her ergonomic chair and sighed. Should she write about that, too?

After a few moments of thought, she added a few short paragraphs. Maybe she'd add more details some time, maybe not. She closed the small journal and stood up.

Violet's office was in the southeast corner of the condo she shared with Frank. Besides the two walls of light oak floor-to-ceiling shelves filled to overflowing with books, she had a matching desk for writing, a computer table with two screens, a narrow filing cabinet, and a tall oak storage cupboard.

Right after lunch, she'd asked Derrick James, one of the staff, to bring her the plastic step stool from the kitchen. She opened the storage cupboard and pushed the step stool in front of it.

The cupboard had been custom made to hold mid-sized rectangular plastic bins with white lids. Each of the ten shelves held two bins, side by side. Ten bins were for her cookbooks, one per book, containing original recipes, first drafts, samples of promotional materials, cards and printed emails from fans, and related memorabilia. The remaining bins held business correspondence, personal cards and letters, and other mementos.

When she'd determined to write down everything for Trish, she decided to place her current journal at the very bottom of the bin of the bin marked "First cookbook." No one but her daughter would ever look there. However, that bin was kept on the top shelf, which meant the step stool.

It took only a couple of minutes for her to get the bin down, open it, place the journal on the bottom, then replace the other papers and the lid. It required more effort to put the bin back on the top shelf. Gravity, maybe, or, let's face it, her arms weren't as strong as they used to be.

She got off the step stool, shut the cupboard door, folded the stool, and carried it to the front door. She set it in the hallway where Derrick had left it for her and used the intercom. "Derrick, I don't need the stool any more. Please pick it up when you have time."

That done, Violet went into her kitchen and poured herself a glass of orange juice. Then she took a wine glass from the cupboard and carried both glasses to the bedroom she shared with Frank.

After setting the glasses on her night table, she took a pillow from beneath the king-sized duvet and covered one side of the bed with a blue fleece blanket.

She'd bought the duvet when she and Frank moved into Serenity Suites. Snowy white with pale blue flowers and green leaves delicately embroidered on it. Yes, white was impractical, and she prided herself on being practical. But she'd always wanted one and why shouldn't she have it? However, it was a nuisance. Any mark would show, so she always covered it when she wanted to lie down. Frank never took naps, which was a blessing.

Violet sat on the bed and removed her black slip-on shoes. She took several tablets from a pill organizer on her night table and swallowed them with the orange juice. From the top drawer of her night table, she removed two squares of fair-trade dark chocolate from a bar and ate them, enjoying each bite and licking her fingers to catch any melted bits. Finally, she poured a glass of wine from a bottle she took from between the bed and the night table, and drank it slowly, savouring each swallow.

She then lay down on the bed, positioned her head on the pillow, pulled the other half of the fleece blanket over her, shut her eyes, and went to sleep.

Disgusting! Elizabeth Carlysle stood in the double bathroom she shared with her husband, Norm, examining her face in the mirror. No matter what anyone said about growing old gracefully, having your skin sag in all the wrong places was loathsome. She didn't mind *being* older—that just meant you were still alive—but she deeply resented that, instead of people respecting you for your years of added wisdom and experience, they stopped at the sagging bits and assumed you were worn out and unnecessary. There was something wrong with a culture that valued youth and beauty above wisdom and experience.

Most days she didn't let her aging appearance get to her, but on days like today she saw only the wrinkles on her neck, the thinning of her porcelain skin, the skin that seemed flaccid in spite of the hours she spent each week doing facial exercises, not to mention how hard she worked under Derrick's tutelage to keep up her overall fitness. *I'm getting a turkey neck.*

And really, there was nothing she could do about it unless she went to the plastic surgeon again. Was it worth it? Especially when her husband was so obviously old. And, when you got down to it, not that wise. No, being old didn't make you any wiser.

Having lived a long time and having had lots of experiences wasn't necessarily a plus either. Doing the same stupid things all your life didn't make you any better able to advise others.

She shut her eyes. *Admit it, you hate it here.* She'd thought she'd like it. No responsibilities. No housework or cooking to do. Stimulating company. Time to spend on whatever she wanted. It should have been great, but it wasn't. Was she too young to be in this place, or was she restless for some other reason?

She looked in the mirror again. Her straight black hair, cut in a medium-length bob, contrasted starkly with her pale skin and accented her bright green eyes. She dressed well, and when the occasion demanded, she could wear a dashing, low-cut dress with the best of them. At five-foot-nine, she was still confident enough to wear heels that added another few inches. Anyone seeing her at a distance saw a tall, striking woman they didn't easily forget. It was only when they came close that they saw beyond the prominent cheek bones and the angular but attractive face to the fine lines on the edges of her lips and eyes, the wrinkles on her elegant neck. Well, so what? Maybe she wasn't young any more. She still looked better than ninety-nine percent of the women her age. Or even ten years younger.

Plus, she was an adult, and she could leave Serenity Suites any time she wanted. But where would she go? And would she slip quietly away, leaving Norm safely entombed here, or would she invite him to go with her?

Norm, who, at seventy-nine, was seven years older than his wife, wandered into the bathroom. "Not putting your make-up on again, are you, Liz? 'Vanity, thy name is woman,' eh?" He'd teased her about how much time she spent doing her make-up and assembling her outfit for the day since before they were married, forty-two years ago. She tuned him out most of the time, but sometimes she retaliated. Today, she swung around and looked him up and down.

When she'd first met him, she'd been attracted to his six-foot-two height, his muscles, his unruly brown hair, and the healthy relaxed vibe he gave off. She'd felt there was nothing he couldn't handle, including her.

The man before her had mostly grey hair and was slowly going bald. His head bent forward, and his shoulders were hunched, giving off a slightly defeated vibe. He was wearing his favourite grey sweat pants with baggy knees, a faded blue T-shirt with pink and orange stains mostly on the protruding stomach and chest areas, and moccasins with gaping holes at the tips, where his big toes peeked out.

She sighed. "Well, I *could* let myself go the way you do and run around like a sloppy mess, but for some reason that's never appealed to me."

Norm laughed. "Maybe I *am* a sloppy mess, but it took me two minutes to put my outfit together, so I have lots of time for other things. And I'm very comfortable!"

Elizabeth turned her back on him. "Yes, you have time for so many other things. Like what, exactly?"

"Well, painting, I guess."

"Then go and paint, and leave me alone!"

Derrick James pulled off his camouflage scrubs shirt and replaced it with a sports shirt. He'd already exchanged his black scrubs cargo pants for faded cut-offs. A registered nurse as well as a physiotherapist and personal trainer, thirty-three-year-old Derrick was six feet of lean muscle. His milk chocolate skin glowed with health. Since the beginning of summer, he'd sported a thin moustache and a short beard. He liked the moustache but was still toying with whether or not to keep the beard.

He grabbed a black scrunchie and tied back his medium-length black hair. A week ago, he'd had his mass of tight curls relaxed. He wasn't sure he liked the way it looked, or that it was worth either the time or the cost. Maybe he should just get it cut short. Oh, well, he'd decide that later.

He glanced at his watch. Almost 2:00. Time he was on his way. He hoisted a grey backpack onto his shoulders and left his room.

The staff office he shared with Audra Limson was just to his right. He poked his head in the open door. "I'm off."

Audra looked up and smiled. "Have fun."

He was about to open the door to the stairs when he remembered the step stool he'd taken to Violet's condo. Best to get it out of the hallway before someone tripped over it. He hurried to the other end of the twentieth floor, retrieved the stool and took it to the kitchen where Scarlett was busy preparing afternoon tea. He deposited the stool in its usual spot. "In case you need this."

Scarlett looked up and smiled. "Thanks. I just might."

"What am I missing, and will you save me some?"

In her white three-quarter-sleeved chef's jacket with black piping, black pants, and chef's hat, Scarlett was a striking figure. Tall and sturdy, with sepia skin, a golden brown Afro, and delicately tweezed eyebrows, she might have been intimidating if not for her perennial smile, which included a dimple on each cheek. She was in her mid-forties, just old enough to treat Derrick as a younger brother.

“Of course I will, but it’s a surprise. You’ll have to wait just like everyone else.”

“Okay, I’ll come for it the second I get back.”

She waved a wooden spoon. “Have a good time.”

He laughed. “Always.”

Moments later he was on his way to the ground floor in the elevator, wondering why he never seemed to have time to take the stairs and get some added exercise. But he quickly dispensed with that thought and instead gave some consideration to the question of what Scarlett might be cooking.

At 2:50, Audra Limson was seated in the kitchen watching Scarlett finishing preparations for afternoon tea and Olive going back and forth between the kitchen to the residents’ dining room, setting the tables.

“So how’s it going with you, Audra?” Scarlett asked.

“Good. Just thinking about the weekend. I have to do some serious shopping before fall hits. I’ve lost so much weight that I’m afraid none of my fall or winter clothes will fit me.”

“Poor you!” Scarlett patted her own rump. “I wish I had that problem. Mine is the opposite—nothing fits me because I keep expanding.”

“You cook too well.”

“But I’m cooking healthy food!”

Audra grinned. “And is that all you’re eating?”

“Well, I do like to have my snacks now and then. As you know very well.” Scarlett winked at Audra. “I guess so far I haven’t decided that being thin is worth giving up my comfort food. Maybe one of these days.”

Olive entered the kitchen. “I’m done. Some of them are already seated. What should I do next?”

“I think we’re ready. I just need to boil the water for tea. Take in the milk and cream now. And maybe start serving coffee to those who prefer it.”

Audra stood. “I’ll see who’s missing and round them up.” After checking the dining room, she called a couple of people on the intercom. Violet didn't answer, which meant she was on her way since she was always on time. Lyle didn't answer either but she had an idea where he might be. Sure enough, she found him in the common room asleep in his recliner. She didn't think twice about waking him, because everyone knew Lyle never missed tea.

Actually, unless it was unavoidable, no one missed afternoon tea on the twentieth floor of Serenity Suites, a highlight of the day because Scarlett always made something special, but not too high in calories or fat.

Audra followed Lyle to the dining room and stood just inside the doorway.

Their numbers were down because the Kanes and the Gerbrandts—two married couples in their seventies—had gone on a cruise for the month of August.

The room currently had four square tables, each ideal for four people. While the arrangement wasn't static, people tended to sit at the same places for most meals.

At the table to the left of the kitchen doorway sat Catarina Rossi. Next to her was Ben Davidson, with his wife, Ingrid, on his other side. Catarina and Ben were enjoying an animated conversation. Ingrid, however, was looking around as if not quite sure where she was. Noting this, Audra determined to talk to Derrick about her.

The chair between Catarina and Ingrid was empty. That's where Catarina's brand-new husband, Nikola Vincent, would normally be sitting. Audra sighed. Nikola was getting to be a bit of an annoyance, far too frequently popping into her office to talk to her, for what she felt were usually flimsy reasons. After lunch today he'd stopped by to tell her he had an afternoon appointment and would miss tea, something he could easily have mentioned to Scarlett at lunch. And even if it was necessary for him to tell her, there was no reason it should take twenty minutes!

She was sure Nikola was bored. And why not? He was a relatively young man living in a community of seniors with no job to keep him busy. He ought to have considered that before he married Catarina. One of these days she'd have to tell him to stop coming to her office.

She wasn't afraid of him—he seemed innocuous enough—she just didn't want him wasting her time. Okay, that wasn't true. The reason she didn't want him coming near her was because when he was standing next to her, she had a ridiculous urge to ask him to hold her—an urge that made her wonder if she was losing her mind since she didn't even like the man!

Audra looked over at the table to her far left. Lyle Oakley and Mary Simmons were talking and laughing. Kenneth Harper seemed to be listening. Audra hoped that, after five weeks, he was beginning to feel at home, but she had her doubts.

At the table to Audra's immediate right was Hilary Brooks, alone as usual, with an open book.

At the last table to Audra's left sat Elizabeth Carlysle and her husband, Norm. Frank Klassen was next to Norm, but Violet's chair was empty. Audra frowned. Violet was never late for anything.

As if reading Audra's mind, Catarina spoke in the voice that had let people in the back rows of theatres hear her every word. "But where is Violet? Why is she not here?"

"Don't ask me," Frank said. "I've been in the office writing. She did say at lunch that she had a bit of a headache. Maybe she fell asleep and didn't hear the bell." He put his hands on the table to push his chair back. "I suppose I should make sure she knows what time it is."

Audra walked over to the table and gently motioned for him to stay seated. "That's all right, Mr. Klassen. I'll check on her. If she still has a headache, Olive can take her tea to her."

"I hope Violet's all right," Mary muttered as Audra left the room. "It's not like her to miss tea, even for a headache."

"My, oh, my!" exclaimed Lyle. "Will you look at that! Scarlett, you've outdone yourself! It looks delightful!"

Scarlett had entered the dining room carrying a large silver tray of crystal goblets filled with baked apples, granola, yogurt, and just a hint of maple syrup. She set it down on a buffet standing against the wall and picked up three goblets. "Raisins and pecans in yours, Mr. Davidson." She set a goblet in front of Ben. "Neither in yours, Mrs. Davidson. And you have pecans, but no raisins, Mrs. Rossi."

"Where's Violet?" Ingrid asked in her gruff flat voice.

Ben looked at her. "Audra went to see if she's coming."

"She thinks she's so important we should all wait for her, but I'm not!"

Ben looked down.

Catarina exclaimed at how good the coffee tasted.

Scarlett and Olive continued passing out the goblets.

Audra strode along the hallway toward the Klassens' condo. Violet had probably taken something for her headache and fallen into a deep sleep. But she never missed tea. And she rarely complained of a headache.

Audra called "Violet?" into the intercom. No response. "Violet, are you all right?" Nothing.

Audra checked the door, but it was locked. She spoke into the intercom with her special code, and heard the lock click. The door opened, and she stepped inside.

"Violet, it's Audra." No response.

Her heart pounding, Audra headed down the hallway toward the bedroom. *Please let her just be asleep.*

The door was shut. Slowly and quietly she opened it and took a few steps inside. She relaxed. Violet was on the bed, still asleep. Audra had been sure she'd find the older woman in a heap on the floor, having fallen and hit her head on a corner of the dresser and bled to death.

"Violet." She repeated it more loudly, but Violet didn't move.

Audra walked around the bed and gently shook Violet's shoulder. "Violet!" No response.

Hesitantly, Audra pulled the blanket down a little and felt the carotid artery on the left side of Violet's neck. No pulse. She checked her mouth and throat for an obstruction. Nothing. She pinched a finger. No response.

Running to the intercom, Audra punched in the number for the reception desk, and called out, "It's Audra. Code Blue. Room 20-E. Stat. I'm alone."

A man's voice said, "Help is on the way."

Audra hurried back, pressed the button to move the bed to its lowest position, positioned her hands on Violet's breastbone, and began chest compressions, trying to be fast and hard, aiming at one hundred per minute, concentrating on releasing completely between each compression, and hoping that she was strong enough to keep doing it until help came.

After a minute, she placed her cheek close to Violet's mouth. Still no sign of breathing.

A nurse who worked on the nineteenth floor rushed into the room with a portable defibrillator and manual resuscitator.

Audra said, "She's not breathing. I can't find a pulse." She continued doing CPR while the other nurse bagged Violet. Then the nurse took over CPR while Audra got the defibrillator in place and opened Violet's dress to place the pads. "Her skin feels clammy."

"Give it a try anyway."

Nothing happened, but the women kept working on her, willing her to come back to life.

At last, a voice called into the room, "Paramedics are here!"

As they took over, Audra went out to talk to the two firemen and the police officer who had also responded to the 911 call.

Audra hurried into the kitchen, her hand in front of her mouth. Scarlett stared at her. "What took you so long? Where's Violet?"

The two women looked at each other. Scarlett's eyes grew huge. Audra glanced toward the door to the dining room and quickly shook her head.

Olive came in from the dining room. "Oh, you're back, Audra. Should I take Violet's tea to her?"

Scarlett answered. "I think Violet prefers to leave it until later. Why don't you see if anyone wants more tea or coffee?"

After Olive left the kitchen, Scarlett whispered, "How bad is it?"

"She's in her bed. I thought she was asleep, but she wasn't. She's dead. We tried CPR and the defibrillator, but—"

"I thought I heard some commotion."

Motioning toward the dining room, Audra said, "Do you think they heard?"

"No. I was in the kitchen with the door to the hall open and didn't hear much. I don't think they heard a thing."

"I can't believe she's gone." Audra looked away, tears gathering in her eyes. "She must have just passed away in her sleep."

"Well, that's the way I'd want to go. And she lived a pretty long life." Scarlett frowned. "You're paler than a ghost, and you look as though you're going to be sick."

"Finding dead people isn't what I normally do. Or anything I want to do. I—" Audra put both hands to her stomach and rushed over to the sink.

"Scarlett," said a low voice from the doorway to the dining room. Scarlett whirled.

Hilary was standing there. "Is something wrong?"

Scarlett smiled. "It's okay. Audra—she's not feeling well. I was just going to send her to her room."

"Can I have a little more cream?" Hilary held out a small silver pot.

Scarlett took the pot. "Where's Olive?"

"She's helping Mary look for her ring. She thinks it fell on the floor." Hilary looked over toward, Audra, then back at Scarlett. "Is Violet all right?"

"Ms. Brooks, you go back to your table, and I'll bring the cream right away." The two women looked at each other for a long moment.

"Very well." Hilary said. The door swung shut behind her.

Scarlett quickly put some light cream into the jug. A few residents wouldn't drink their coffee or tea without cream of some sort, and that had been the compromise.

"I'm okay." Audra was leaning against the sink, patting her lips with a towel. "I can't say for sure there won't be more where that came from though." She tried to smile. "I guess it's good I haven't eaten my dessert yet."

"Don't go anywhere. I'll be right back." Scarlett hurried into the dining room with the cream and made sure everyone was satisfied with their afternoon tea. Their compliments confirmed that her maple apple parfait was the hit she'd hoped it would be, especially since it was a recipe she'd created for the cookbook she and Violet had been putting together.

When Audra came through the swinging door from the kitchen. Scarlett raised her eyebrows slightly, and Audra gave her a quick nod and coughed for attention. "I wonder, is everyone finished? I don't want to rush you."

"All but Mary," Ingrid said.

Mary giggled. “It’s just lovely. But you know me. Always last to finish. Talking too much, I guess. And I dropped my ring. Or I thought I did. But I just remembered that I left it in my jewellery case this morning because it was loose.”

“Well, when you’re finished, I’d appreciate it if everyone would gather in the common room.” Audra’s voice was gentle. “There’s something we need to discuss. It won’t take long. Maybe Scarlett can call me when you’re ready.”

Several people murmured, and some began to get up and move to the hallway to the common room.

Lyle offered, “I’ll have another coffee and sit with you, Mary, until you’re finished.”

Scarlett helped Frank move from his chair to his scooter and then walked beside him into the hallway. “Should I go and get Violet?” he asked.

“Let’s just leave her undisturbed for now, Frank.”

“Someone did check on her?”

“Yes, Audra did.”

“Frank,” Audra came up behind them. “Could we have a short talk in your office first?”

He frowned. “What’s this all about?”

“Let’s wait until we get there.”

Audra led the way to Frank's office. Once they were inside, he asked, “All right, what’s wrong?”

“Frank, I’m afraid—it’s Violet. She—she seems to have passed away in her sleep.”

“What?” His voice was loud and angry. “Don’t give me that nonsense. She was perfectly healthy at lunch. You don’t just go and lie down and die.”

“Frank, I’ve been to see her. She was lying peacefully in her bed with a blanket over her, but her skin was cold, and there was no pulse. I tried to revive her, and the paramedics tried, but—I’m so sorry.”

“I want to see her. Did you call for a doctor?”

“Dr. Granger’s on his way. And two police officers are here.”

He glared at her. “Police? Why would you call the police?”

“When we called 911, an officer came. And then a second one. They asked me to keep everyone together, and they said I could tell you what had happened.”

The residents gradually settled into their favourite chairs in the common room.

Scarlett brought in two members of the day staff: Tess Cooper, who looked after all the laundry, and Gulab Brampton, who did light cleaning. They came in each weekday, from early morning until late afternoon. Olive came in with Mary and Lyle.

Scarlett walked over to Frank's office and knocked quietly. Audra opened the door. "Are they ready?" Scarlett nodded. Her eyes went to Frank, who was staring at the far wall.

"I'll go and break the news then," Audra said. "Dr. Granger will be coming up soon. There might be other people, too."

"Who?"

"I don't know. I told the officer who came up with the paramedics that I knew of no reason for her to die so suddenly. So he wanted to talk to Dr. Granger and make sure everything's okay. I'm sure it will only be a formality." Audra left the room.

Scarlett nodded and stepped into the room, her eyes on Frank. After a few moments, he turned toward her. "I need to be out there."

"Audra will tell them."

"I need to be there."

"Are you sure?"

His voice was strong and firm. "Yes."

Scarlett moved aside to let him manoeuvre the scooter through the door. It had taken months for Audra, Derrick, Dr. Granger, and Violet to convince Frank to get it, and now he zoomed around like a teenage boy on a mountain bike.

"She looked very peaceful, as though she was sleeping," Audra was telling the others when Frank and Scarlett came into the room. "There was no sign of distress or pain. She must have simply passed away in her sleep."

There were sighs and exclamations.

"There might be a bit of an investigation—I'm not sure. Dr. Granger will be here soon, and he'll take care of everything." She paused. "Violet was such a nice lady. She'll be missed by all of us. She—"

"Not by me," Ingrid said without emotion. "She was a mouse. Barely uttered a squeak. Never made a comment on her own initiative. Always backed up whatever Frank said. You barely even knew she was here." There was an awkward silence.

"Well, I shall miss her. She was an exceptionally nice lady," Lyle said. "Refined. Kind to everyone."

Elizabeth stood up and walked over to Frank. "Frank, we're so sorry. This is just terrible. We're all devastated." She put her hand on his shoulder and seemed about to lean over and give him a hug, but contented herself with just the touch.

"This is terrible." Norm's eyes had filled with tears and his voice was hoarse. "I—I don't know what to say. So terrible."

A police officer came to the door and motioned to Audra. Everyone turned to look. Audra hurried over and, after a quick conversation, turned to the others.

"Dr. Granger is here, along with the coroner. I'll go and talk to them. I'm sure it won't take long."

Frank coughed.

Audra and Scarlett looked at each other. Then Audra spoke. "Except for Frank, everyone needs to stay in here until I've talked to the police. I'll come back and let you know what's happening as soon as I can. Frank, I assume you'd like to come and talk to the police?"

Ben walked over and clasped Frank's shoulder. "I'm so sorry, Frank. If there's anything you need, you know that we're all here for you."

Frank shrugged and began turning the scooter.

"So terrible," muttered Mary, her eyes filled with tears. "Violet of all people! Life is so unfair."

The firemen and paramedics were gone, but several police officers remained. One of them was talking to Dr. Granger, one of six specialists with offices on the main floor of Serenity Suites. A good-looking man in his early forties, he carried an air of authority that was validated by his expensive grey suits and carefully styled blond hair.

Audra generally felt uncomfortable in his presence, as if she was barely qualified to do her job and any minute he'd find a flaw in something she'd done and have her fired.

When she'd told Derrick how the doctor affected her, he'd called the doctor a pompous ass, but that didn't really help.

Dr. Granger ignored Audra and came close to lean over Frank. "Frank, I'm so sorry for your loss. But, given what we know, I can't help but think this might be the very best thing that could have happened. A simple falling asleep."

"So you'll get these police out of here? I don't want her poked and prodded. And no autopsies."

"I'm sure that won't be necessary." Dr. Granger turned to Audra. "Ms. Limson, I really don't understand why you thought it necessary to create all this commotion."

"I—I thought— Her death wasn't expected. I wanted to try to revive her if we possibly could."

He waved his arm as if brushing aside her words. "Yes, yes, I understand. No, her death wasn't expected; but surely it wasn't *un*expected either. We certainly didn't need paramedics and firemen and police here."

Audra looked down. "I'm sorry. Violet didn't have a Do Not Resuscitate order, so I did what I felt was best."

"Yes, well, I wish—"

He turned as the administrator for Serenity Suites, Naomi Arlington, stepped out of the elevator and strode over to them. She glared at Audra. "What's the meaning of all this? Why are all these people here? There I am in the middle of a meeting with a couple who may want to buy a condo in Serenity Suites, and all of a sudden we hear all kinds of noise, and the security guard tells me there are fire trucks and paramedics and police here. Do you have any idea how much speculation they've caused?"

"Violet is dead. I called for help—Code Blue."

Naomi pointed her index finger in Audra's face. "We have doctors on the first floor. You call them in an emergency!"

"They would have heard the Code Blue."

Dr. Granger looked down. "That's true, but of course most of us are busy. I was at the hospital myself until I got a call from security."

"Whatever. There was no need to call 911!"

Naomi patted Frank's shoulder. "Mr. Klassen, you shouldn't be out here. Let me take you to your condo."

The police officer coughed. "I'm sorry, Ma'am, but you can't go into the condo."

She rounded on him. "And why not?"

Audra said, "Naomi, why don't you take Frank into his office and call his daughter?"

Naomi glared at the police officer. "Are you going to object to that, too?"

"Where is this office?"

Naomi pointed down the hallway.

"That's fine, Ma'am."

As they moved toward Frank's office, a young man came out of the Klassens' condo. Audra's first impression was that he could easily be a college senior who wasn't at all into sports and probably enjoyed parties more than studying. He was about average height, somewhat pudgy, with an abundance of freckles and reddish hair that could have used a cut.

Dr. Granger went over to him, and the two men talked quietly for several minutes. Audra was taken aback when Dr. Granger introduced the young man as the coroner, Dr. Weaver.

Up close he looked slightly older than she'd thought, but still nothing like what she'd have expected a coroner to look like. In a voice that was definitely older than that of a college senior and with an authority that left no room for discussion, Dr. Weaver said to Audra, "Time of death was between 2:15 and 2:45. I've spoken with Dr. Granger, and even though her death was somewhat unexpected, given her age and the state of her health, I have no difficulty accepting his assurance that her death was due to natural causes."

Something in Audra wanted to argue, but she noticed the frown on Dr. Granger's face. "Yes, doctor."

"You did everything you could," the coroner added.

Audra blinked back tears. If she'd only gone to Violet's condo earlier, after she'd found Lyle in the common room, maybe— But he'd just said that Violet was dead by 2:45. There was nothing she could have done.

The death certificate was duly signed. Dr. Granger went to assure Naomi and Frank that an autopsy wouldn't be needed. Moments later, Violet's body was removed, and Dr. Weaver and the police officers left.

When Naomi came out of Frank's office, she said to Audra, "I'll be back up to talk to you." She then punched the down button of the elevator with a lot more force than was needed.

Dr. Granger came out of the office with Frank. As they passed, Audra heard Frank say to the doctor, "I'm fine. There's no need to fuss over me. Go look after somebody who needs you."

With a sigh, Audra smoothed her hair and walked to the common room to tell everyone they could resume normal activities.

THREE

Audra walked into the kitchen and collapsed into the chair at Scarlett's desk. Scarlett turned toward her. "Is everything okay?"

Audra nodded. "Dr. Granger is finally gone. He was the last one."

"How's Frank doing?"

"I checked on him right after Dr. Granger left. He says his daughter is on her way, and she'll take care of everything. And he doesn't want anyone fussing over him. Of course it likely hasn't begun to sink in yet."

Scarlett poured a cup of tea and took it to Audra. "I'm sure he's in shock, whether he realizes it or not."

"And I expect he was raised under the 'men don't show their feelings' philosophy. When Derrick gets back, maybe Frank will talk to him."

"Or he could really be as self-centred as he often appears."

Audra nodded. She took a sip of tea. "This is good. What is it?"

"Darjeeling."

"I like it. Anyway, I expect Frank will be fine. I've often thought he'd be happy to stay in his office night and day and have his meals slipped under the door."

Scarlett smiled. "He never misses a meal, or a snack."

Audra looked up. "Speaking of food, what do you think will happen to the recipe book you and Violet were working on?"

Scarlett frowned. "I never even thought about that! Violet said she sent it to the publisher on Monday, so I assume it will still be published."

"I hope so. It could be the start of something big for you as co-author."

"All I did was give her some of my recipes and adapt some of hers and work with her on the proportions. She did all the writing and whatnot."

"Still, it's got your name on the cover."

"Yes, that'll be nice." Scarlett frowned. "But I'd sure rather have Violet back here with us. Such a nice lady."

"Way too good for Frank."

"He never appreciated her."

"I don't think I ever heard her disagree with him or say no."

Both women shook their heads, and Scarlett added, "I'm sure I don't know what he'll be like without her around to look after him."

Derrick walked into the kitchen, backpack still on his shoulders. "They told me downstairs there's been a death. Violet. Is it true? What happened?"

The two women quickly filled him in on the afternoon's events.

"How's everybody taking it? Have they all gone to their rooms?"

Audra nodded. "I think so. They handled it well, but I'm sure most of them are upset. Including Olive."

"Who isn't?" Scarlett said. "At least when Mr. Brooks had his heart attack in the elevator, he wasn't on our floor. And what's Olive got to be upset about? She barely knew her!"

"I don't know, but she was clearly upset. I told her to go and lie down for a few minutes."

"I assume Her Highness was here?" Derrick grimaced. "Did she say anything?"

"Not much," Audra replied. "She was spitting mad at me when she arrived, but fortunately a nice police officer—I wish I could remember his name—assured her that I'd done everything I should have."

"What did she say to that?"

"She suddenly remembered Frank and took him to his office. I'm not sure he wanted to go with her, but he went. They phoned his daughter."

"Where's Frank now?"

"In his condo. Dr. Granger took him there and told him to rest for a while."

"He okay with that?"

"When I checked on him, he told me to go away and leave him alone."

"So what do we do now?"

Scarlett smiled. "Well, I'm making something light for dinner."

Audra checked her watch. "Yes, everyone will be hungry soon. Derrick, I wonder if you and I should check with everybody, one on one, before dinner?"

"Call on them in their condos?"

"Yes. You could take Kenneth, Lyle, Ben and Ingrid, and Frank, and I'll take Catarina and Nikola, Hilary, Norm and Elizabeth, and Mary. Does that sound okay?"

"Sure, that's fine. I'll change and get started."

"You two do that," said Scarlett. "I'll go get Olive to help me here. Take her mind off things."

Lyle Oakley was coming down the hall when Derrick left the kitchen. "You're back. I guess you've heard our sad news?"

"Just now. You've all had a pretty difficult day."

The two men walked together toward the common room.

"Yes, not what one would have chosen to happen. Or expected. Actually I'd have bet good money she'd have outlived us all. Don't think she ever smoked a cigarette or had a drink of anything harder than milk all her life."

"How are you doing?"

"Well, I'm feeling a bit morose. I expect we all are. But, other than that, I'm fine. Just another reminder that any of us can go at any time. The old Russian roulette. You can sit and wonder who'll be next, or you can just ignore it and hope that, whoever it is, it's not you."

Derrick patted Lyle on the shoulder and watched him head into the common room, where he'd no doubt sit in his usual recliner and finish going through the day's newspapers.

Audra started at Catarina and Nikola's condo. She spoke into the intercom. "Catarina, it's Audra. May I come in for a moment?"

Seconds later, the door opened. Catarina stood there smiling. "*Just* the person I need. What do you think? Is this appropriate to wear when there has been a death?"

Audra stared at what appeared to be a black hostess gown, low-cut, shimmery, and flowing.

"No?" Catarina twirled. "You think it is too much?" She pursed her lips. "I thought so. Come then and see what else I have. Normally I try to stay far away from death, but when it comes to visit me, I have no choice. I must find something appropriate to wear."

Still unable to find appropriate words, Audra followed Catarina into her bedroom. An array of dark clothing was spread over the bed, the dresser, and the slipper chair.

Catarina picked up a garment from the bed. "What do you think of this?"

Audra's expression was answer enough. Catarina threw the long purple skirt to the floor and picked up a short skirt and jacket. "Is this better?"

"I think that might be better." It was hard to tell. The neckline on the jacket looked very low. Would Catarina wear a blouse under it? Not likely.

"You must be thinking me a frivolous old goat. What difference does it make what I wear? But I do not wish to appear unsympathetic. Just because I did not particularly care for Violet does not mean I am not unhappy that she is dead."

Audra didn't speak.

"Ah now I have surprised you again! How can I be so thoughtless as to say I did not like a woman who has just died? But, alas, it is true. And I believe in speaking the truth. Not always, of course. I try not to offend. But I try to be honest when I can. And since it is simply you and me here, I can say it. I really did not like her much."

The front door opened and shut, and a male voice called, "Cat, where are you?"

Catarina dropped the suit and hurried to the living room. "Nikola, my dear, I'm so glad you are back."

The man, who was dressed in torn blue jeans and a blue T-shirt with a skull and crossbones on the front, gave her a quick hug.

"It has been an absolutely horrendous day. Violet is dead. Just like that."

"Yeah, I know. The doorman told me what had happened. And there were some people downstairs in the foyer talking about it."

Audra had followed Catarina out of the bedroom. As usual, she had great difficulty watching the elderly woman embrace the much younger man without thinking how totally inappropriate their relationship was. She'd heard about May/December romances, of course, although it was usually an elderly man with a young woman, not the other way around. But she'd never actually known anyone who was married to a person young enough to be his or her child. Or even grandchild. Surely not. Where did the phrase "boy toy" originate? "I'll get out of your way now. I think that last outfit looked best, Catarina."

Catarina waved her away. "Nikola can decide now that he is here. And although I would prefer not to have to deal with this, I shall be fine."

The door to Kenneth Harper's condo was open a crack. Derrick called out, "Mr. Harper."

"In here."

Derrick stepped into the hallway and then through the archway into the sitting room. "Just wondering how you're doing. Is there anything you'd like to talk about?"

Kenneth was sitting on an off-white wing chair in the far corner near the window, a book open on his knees. He took off his reading glasses. "I've been wondering. Did the police say what killed her?"

"Audra told me it was natural causes."

"But she didn't seem ill." Kenneth's voice rose slightly.

Derrick hesitated. "I agree, but you never can tell."

"I suppose. Lots of things could do it—maybe she had a brain tumour, heart attack, a blood clot. No end of things that can just zap us out of this world the same way we'd swat a fly or step on an ant." He paused. "You know, when I was young, I used to wonder if we were just little specks in someone else's cosmos. Like Whoville in the Dr. Seuss book. Maybe earth is really just a speck of dust—an atom—and all these huge creatures just swat us whenever they feel like it."

Derrick sat on a burgundy leather couch across from Kenneth. "Even if things seem to happen unexpectedly, there's always a cause and effect of some kind. That's why we have investigators of all types, and scientists, as well as forensic people. They follow up to see what really happened, not only when someone dies, but when there are fires or bankruptcies—anything unusual."

"Will there be an autopsy?"

"That's up to the coroner, I think."

"It doesn't pay to get old. You're just gone, and no one cares why."

"I'm not sure Violet would have wanted an autopsy. She was a very private person. I doubt if she'd have liked all the attention."

"True." Kenneth smiled. "You know, I found her quite an odd woman. I can't say I knew her well—I've been here such a short time, and I wasn't around her much—but I never once heard her talk about herself. Only Frank. Always Frank."

"She was very proud of him."

"I'd say she treated him as though he was not only her husband but her god. And he treated her as though she was his housekeeper."

Derrick nodded slowly. "I guess people get into different rhythms when they've been married a long time. It can be easy to take the other person for granted."

"My wife and I were married sixteen years when she died."

"Her death must have been very difficult for you."

"Difficult. Yes, you could say that."

"Mr. Harper, if you—"

"But that all happened years ago. In another lifetime. And right now I'm perfectly fine, and I have a good book to read. So, please, if you don't mind, I'd rather you go away and hover around somebody else."

"Sure you're okay?"

"Perfectly sure. Will dinner be ready soon?"

"Scarlett is working on it."

"Good. I'll read until then."

"Certainly, Mr. Harper. Just call me if you need me."

As Derrick stepped into the hallway, he heard Kenneth mutter, "I don't need anybody."

Audra found Hilary sitting on her balcony overlooking the Don Valley. After a moment's hesitation, Audra took one of the other patio chairs.

Hilary spoke first. "She didn't like my being here, you know."

"Did she ever say anything to you?"

"No, but I knew." Hilary looked up and smiled. "In some ways, I'd rather have the people who *do* say something. Those ones you can deal with. Argue or yell or something. Sometimes you can even change their minds. But the ones who don't say anything—who treat you fairly while looking down their noses at you and silently wishing you'd just disappear—those ones never change. And you can only follow their example and pretend everything's fine."

"So you aren't feeling too sad?"

"I'm just sitting here thinking that Violet is gone, and so are those grey eyes that always seemed to see into my soul and find it wanting." She bit her lip. "Do you know how many times I looked over to find Violet watching me with those eyes?"

Audra shook her head.

Hilary smiled. "No more accusing eyes." She thought for a moment and then tilted her head on one side. "Is it just me? Are the others all broken up?"

"Well, of course we have a few people here who've known her for years, so naturally they'll be more upset. You were in a different position. Kenneth, too. He barely knew her."

"But is anyone else sitting there thinking that his or her life just became better? I doubt it."

"She had a lot of good points."

"I'm sure she did. And her friends will miss her."

Hilary smiled at Audra. "Don't worry. They won't know what I'm thinking, or how much I'd like it if the same thing happened to Naomi Arlington."

It was Audra's turn to smile. "I don't think you can count on her dying of old age any time soon."

"Is that what they called it?"

"Natural causes. But it usually means the same thing."

"That's strange. She came of good healthy Mennonite stock. She told me once that everyone in her family had lived until they were well into their nineties."

"Hilary, you don't suspect anything about her death, do you?"

"Me? What would I suspect?

"No, of course not." Audra stood up. "I'll see you at dinner." As she turned to leave, she paused. "I see you found something suitable to wear. That midnight blue is stunning on you."

Hilary smiled. "Thank you. It's as close to black as I normally get. Unless I want to make like I'm a ghoul or a vampire."

Ben let Derrick in. "I'm glad to see you. Maybe you can help. She won't listen to anything I say."

He led the way to Ingrid's bedroom, where she had the closet door open and clothes scattered in piles all over the floor around her walker.

"Hi, Ingrid. What are you looking for?"

"My black dress. Need it to wear to the memorial service. Don't want to go, but you'll insist. Need my dress."

Ben whispered to Derrick, "She got rid of the dress she's looking for years ago, and it wouldn't fit even if she did have it. None of her clothes seem to fit her these days. It's as if she gains several pounds each week."

Ingrid continued pulling clothes off the hangers and throwing them to the floor.

"Ingrid, forget about that old dress," Derrick said. "We'll get you something new."

Ingrid frowned.

"Ingrid hates shopping." Ben moved closer to his wife. "You've always hated shopping haven't you, old girl? Hated it with passion."

"Can't make a silk purse out of a pig's ear," she muttered.

Derrick said, "What about one of those companies that brings clothes to you?"

Ben snapped his fingers. "Of course. We'll get them to bring in some black dresses and a few other things, too. And we'll get rid of everything here that doesn't fit."

Ingrid looked in the mirror and grimaced. "I'm too fat." She thrust out her chin. "Don't care. Over eighty years old, and if I want to be fat, nobody's business but my own."

"That's right," Derrick said. "It's nobody else's business."

"Violet spent her whole life worrying about her weight."

"She did try to eat healthy."

"Too thin. Everybody thought so, not just me."

"She *was* pretty thin."

"And now she's dead." To Derrick's ears, Ingrid's laugh sounded like the cackle of an old crone. Her voice became animated. "What good did all that worrying about her weight do her? None at all."

Ben held out his hand. "Ingrid, why don't you come out to the sitting room with me and rest for a bit?"

"Violet is dead," Ingrid crowed. "Deader than a doorknob."

Derrick looked around for inspiration. "How about I get Olive to come and tidy up here? Maybe—Ingrid, is there a program on TV you'd like to watch?"

Ingrid smiled at him. "Violet's being fitted for a casket, while old overweight Ingrid is still going strong."

Ben grimaced.

In his most endearing voice, Derrick said, "Ingrid, let's all go out to the sitting room. You can do some crocheting."

"Poor Frank's all alone now." Ingrid smiled. "Or is it poor Ben? You always loved her, didn't you, Ben? Don't think I didn't know. Lots of things I know."

Audra used the intercom to ask if she might enter the Carlysles' condo and received a terse, "I guess you might as well come in," from Elizabeth. Taking a deep breath, Audra stepped inside. From the hallway, she could see Norm sitting in a big leather recliner, head in his hands, shoulders heaving. Elizabeth was nowhere in sight.

Audra hurried to Norm and put her hand on his shoulder. "Norm—"

"I can't believe this. Just can't believe it." He looked up at her, his face wet with tears, his eyes pleading. "Please tell me she isn't really dead. There must have been a mistake."

Audra knelt down beside his chair. "Violet died peacefully, Norm. In her sleep. She looked content."

He shook his head. "She looked fine at lunch today. I remember thinking how healthy she was. Always took good care of herself." More tears spilled from his eyes, which he wiped with the back of his hand.

Audra gave him a handful of tissues from her pocket.

"I just can't believe she's gone, with no warning at all. Gone in a moment."

"I know. It's hard to believe."

Elizabeth walked into the room holding a mug, which she handed to Norm. "Coffee. The strongest thing you're getting from me." She sank down on the couch. "Now that his paragon of virtue is gone, how shall we all survive?"

"I've known her most of my life. Since we were in grade one."

Elizabeth crossed her arms. "Yes, I've heard the story. You, Ben, Frank, Violet, Mary all met in elementary school and became bosom buddies. All through school and into university. And eventually Frank married Violet. So you had to find someone else. And you did. But she died, and you were all by your lonesome again until you settled for lucky me." She fixed a cushion behind her back. "But neither of your wives could hold a candle to Violet, could we? Not in your eyes, at least."

"You don't know as much as you think you do."

"Oh, don't I?"

Norm looked off in the distance.

Audra, who was still kneeling next to his chair, noted that the hand holding the coffee mug was trembling. Concerned that he'd spill the hot coffee on himself, she reached out to take it from him.

"I can do it!" he snarled. "You don't need to help me!"

Audra jerked back.

"Just so you know, I have a class tonight," Elizabeth said. "I have no intention of cancelling it."

"No one asked you to," Norm shot back. "Although I'd have expected even you to show some respect for the dead."

"Even me?" Elizabeth stood up. "I think that's my cue to be on my way. Otherwise I might be persuaded to say something there's a remote chance I might regret." She left the room.

Audra stood and looked down at Norm, who muttered something she couldn't make out.

Elizabeth returned with her briefcase and a light jacket. "I'll be back when you see me."

"You don't need to worry about me. I'm fine."

Elizabeth strode out of the condo.

"Maybe some warm milk instead of the coffee?" Audra suggested.

"I'm fine."

"All right. Call me if you need anything." Audra walked to the door and opened it.

"She was a wonderful woman. Life was never fair to her."

Audra left him to his memories.

"I just came to see if there's anything I can do for you, Mr. Klassen." Derrick studied the recent widower, who was sitting on his living room couch watching CNN. No outward signs of distress.

"My daughter will be here shortly. She'll see to everything."

"We're all so sorry, Frank. Everyone's going to miss Violet. If there's anything you need, just say the word."

"Well, if you have nothing else to do, you can help me get off this blasted couch. Dr. Granger had me sit here and now my leg's aching. I need to put it up."

"Do you want to get into bed?"

"I'm not sick. Just help me move to the recliner."

Derrick steadied Frank as he stood up, and then half-carried him to the brown leather recliner a few feet away. Once Frank was settled to his satisfaction, Derrick covered his legs with a blanket. "Maybe you'll be able to get some sleep."

"I'm not tired. Is there going to be anything to eat? Seems like tea was a long time ago."

"Scarlett's making dinner. I'll have Olive bring you a tray the moment it's ready."

"All right. And make sure you send Trish here when she arrives. If she hasn't eaten, they can bring her a tray here, too."

"Will do. The pager is right here next to you. Call Audra or me if you need anything."

"I don't need a keeper. Never did."

Derrick said nothing.

"Nearly drove me crazy with all her fussing. After fifty-five years, I'll finally get some peace."

"I'll check in on you later." Derrick let himself out.

Audra found Mary on her balcony, wrapped in a blanket on a chaise lounge, crying.

"Oh, Mary." She pulled another chair over and put her arm around the older woman's shoulders. "I'm so sorry for your loss."

Between sobs, Mary murmured, "We were friends all our lives. And now I'm all alone. Truly alone."

It was true. Mary's only immediate family was a distant cousin whom she barely knew and didn't particularly like. After much discussion and debate, Mary had left the cousin a small legacy in her will and entrusted the rest of her money to an animal shelter.

"You have us." Audra patted her hand.

Mary smiled through her tears. "I know, dear. And please don't think for one minute that I don't appreciate you all. The Suites are a godsend for me. You've all become my family." She sniffed. "But Violet was like my real-life sister. What do they call it nowadays? No wait, I know. BFFs. Best Friends Forever." Mary buried her face on Audra's shoulder and sobbed.

FOUR

Twelve days after his wife's death, Frank sat in his living room with his daughter, Trish Klassen-Wallace.

Since the evening of her mother's death, Trish had been staying in the guest suite of Serenity Suites. Her husband and children had come for the funeral but then returned home. Trish had stayed to help Frank adjust to his new life.

An only child, Trish had been born, quite unexpectedly, when Violet was forty and had long given up hope of carrying a baby to full term.

Both Frank and Trish had been surprised to discover that Violet's will made Trish her executor. Their second surprise was in discovering that only the money in their joint accounts went to Frank, while all of her personal possessions, the rights to her cookbooks, and any personal investments went to Trish.

Frank's annoyance lasted only moments. He laughed and said he was fine with the will. He had no interest in keeping any of his wife's possessions. What would he do with them? And he had no interest whatsoever in her little hobby of writing cookbooks. As for her *investments*, that was ridiculous. What possible investments could she have?

Trish spent the first few days after her mother's death planning the funeral and informing friends, family, and aquaintances about her mother's death. She'd then spent a couple of days going over the will with her mother's lawyer and carrying out the duties of executor. The past weekend, she'd busied herself going through all of her mother's clothing, jewellery, and other personal effects. Frank wanted it all out of the condo as soon as possible.

Trish didn't blame him. She'd found the last few days both emotional and stressful. Seeing his wife's possessions every day would no doubt remind him of her and make him sad. And it wasn't as if any of her clothing or jewellery was of any use to him.

So she'd gone through it all and sorted it into things to keep for herself or give another family member, things to offer Mary or one of the staff, and things to donate to various charities.

The next step was Violet's office. Trish had already emptied the desk, but she'd only glanced at the files and the storage cupboard. She was dreading having to sort through her mother's correspondence and photographs, as well as her business files and the notes for the cookbooks. It was the cookbooks she and Frank were discussing now. "The new one is due to come out next month," Trish said.

Frank waved his hand. "Why not just cancel it? Makes no difference now."

"I've talked to the publisher. Mom's books sell very well, and they have no intention of stopping the publishing process. And after all the work involved, I'm sure Mom would want the book to be released. Besides, she gave Scarlett co-authoring credit."

Frank made another disparaging motion with his hand, to sweep it all away.

"Are you saying you aren't interested in any of the details, Dad?"

"Your mother handled all of her dealings with her publisher. I wanted no part of it. I never understood why she had to get into all that nonsense in the first place. As if she didn't have enough to do without testing recipes and writing them up. Always making a mess in the kitchen and having photographers running in and out!"

"I'm not sure why that bothered you, Dad. You never went into the kitchen that I know of."

"Well, she had enough to do without all that."

"I think it's good she found something to interest her. And her books are great. They're more than just cookbooks. They've got a lot of history in them, too."

"Well, then, we agree to disagree. What else do you want?"

"I'm trying to understand what more I can do to help you. I know you hated the business part of writing. Did Mom handle that?"

"I have an agent to do that."

"The agent deals with the publisher, but I'd think you'd still have had to do your own accounting."

"Your mother took care of that."

"I see."

"She didn't do it herself; there was an accountant she dealt with."

Trish thought for a moment. "Dad, have you ever looked after any of the business side of things?"

He leaned forward, eyes glinting. "What are you trying to say? I worked full-time, first teaching and then writing. Your mother looked after the house and the meals and raised you. Why *shouldn't* she look after the business parts? And she never seemed to mind. She liked the fiddly stuff."

Trish sat back. This conversation wasn't going at all as expected.

"Look, is this necessary? I've missed a lot of hours of work on my book over the last two weeks. I need to get back at it before I lose track of my characters and plot lines and have to start over."

"Sorry, Dad. I'm leaving Thursday morning, which only leaves me the rest of today and two more days. I don't want to miss something important. And I need to know if there's anything more I can do to help you."

He closed his eyes. "Trish, I'm very glad you came, and I do appreciate everything. But what I most need is for you and everyone else to just leave me alone so I can write."

"Got it. Okay, Dad. So what I'll do is take Mom's computer and all her files and bins home with me and go through them there. If I have any questions, I can call you, or, if you prefer, I can talk to your agent or your bank for you. But if that's what you want, I'll need power of attorney; otherwise I'll have problems looking after everything."

"You already have it."

"I do?"

"There's a paper some place. Your mother insisted that we both give it to you so you could look after things in case it was necessary. We did it a while ago."

"Oh, I didn't know. Mom never said anything."

"If the lawyer doesn't have it, it's probably in one of her files. I don't know. Just do what you need to do."

Mary was sitting in the common room, ostensibly reading a book but in reality watching Ingrid, who was seated at a short distance. Ingrid had been crocheting but was now fast asleep. At least Mary assumed she was asleep, and not dead. She shivered and looked away. Since Violet's death, she'd had no urge to make sure Ingrid was breathing.

Kenneth came into the room and took the chair next to Mary's. She greeted him with a smile.

Nodding toward Ingrid, Kenneth said, "Does she always come here to sleep? Be more comfortable to have a nap in her room."

"She says she doesn't sleep." Mary giggled.

"Well, at least she doesn't snore."

"True. That *would* be difficult."

"What are you reading?"

"Oh, a mystery. But it's not a very good one. Too much gore and sex for me. Might be okay if it fit the story, but it isn't really needed at all. And besides, calling it a mystery is stretching the truth. What I like about mysteries is the puzzle part. I like to try to guess who's guilty, but I hate it when I solve it too soon. I had this one figured out by the end of chapter three."

"Are you sure you're right? Maybe the author tricked you into thinking you know."

"I wish."

"Have you lived here long?"

Mary nodded. "Since it opened. I knew about it from the beginning, you know. Violet told me she and Frank were moving in as soon as it was built, so I immediately bought a condo, too, and sold my house."

"So you knew the Klassens before?"

"Violet was my best friend from before we started school."

"I didn't realize that."

"I've known Frank and Ben and Norm almost as long."

"Norm Carlysle?"

"Yes. And the funny thing is, back in high school, I actually dated Frank, and Violet dated Norm."

"And Ben and Ingrid?"

"They met when he was in university. She's a year older than Ben. Before that, in high school, Ben was going with another—another friend of ours." Mary frowned. "She died. It was very sad. And then the rest of us went on to university, and life happened, you know. Violet married Frank, and Ben married Ingrid. Norm married a girl he met at university, but not long after they were married, she was badly injured in an accident. She died a few years later. After a time, Norm met Elizabeth, and eventually they married."

"Funny how you all ended up here."

"Yes, isn't it? But now Violet's gone." She looked away. "One of these days, not too long from now, we'll all be gone."

"Nowadays people live a lot longer than they used to."

She nodded. "That's true. I still haven't decided whether that's a good thing or not. With my luck, I'll be the last one standing, having had to watch each of my friends go. Is that a victory or a defeat, I wonder?"

Thanks to Derrick's quick whisper a moment before Dr. Granger had entered the office, Audra had been forcing herself not to smile during the meeting. Derrick was right. In his charcoal suit, lavender shirt, swirly patterned tie, and gleaming black pointy shoes, the doctor did resemble a mannequin in a store window. But as their talk turned to Ingrid's health, all desire to smile left Audra. "She's getting more and more confused every day."

Derrick nodded. "She's talking to you one minute, and the next she either wanders away or starts talking about something completely different, often something that happened when she was younger."

"She didn't recognize me the other day," Audra said. "I brought her a cup of tea she'd asked for, and she thought I was one of her daughters from years ago. She said I was too young to be carrying something hot because I'd burn myself."

"Perhaps she was thinking about something else," Dr. Granger said. "Older people sometimes get lost in their thoughts."

"All I know is that she was wide awake and looking right at me. I'm not sure she knew *where* she was either, but I didn't want to upset her, so I didn't ask. Just said I was Audra and I'd brought her tea. And a few minutes later, she wandered off, leaving her full cup on the table."

"All right. It sounds as though we should do some tests. It could be something simple like a vitamin deficiency. I'll talk to Ben first. Do you think he's noticed?"

"I don't see how he could help but notice."

"I feel sorry for him," Derrick added. "He's such a nice man, but lately he looks so sad."

"He really took Violet's death hard," Audra said. "They'd known each other since they were young."

Derrick tilted his head. "As to that, I'd say Ben, Norm, and Mary all took Violet's death harder than Frank did."

Dr. Granger shook his head. "You don't know that. No one knows what another person is feeling."

"Well, that's how it appears to me."

Audra nodded. "I agree with Derrick that Frank hasn't *seemed* very upset. Well, that's not quite true. He's been upset, but I got the impression it was more that this inconvenienced him and kept him from writing. But Frank's hard to read at the best of times."

"I feel bad for his daughter. Trish is such a nice person, and she came here to help him, but he doesn't seem to appreciate it at all."

"She told me he just wants to write and forget everything else, and he asked her to leave him alone."

Dr. Granger spoke. "Like many men in his age group, Frank doesn't deal well with his emotions. I expect writing is his way of coping."

Derrick grimaced. "Shades of Dorian Gray?"

Audra frowned. "Well, if he writes to get rid of his negative emotions, he must be a really angry person. Have either of you read any of his books?"

Derrick nodded. "I'd say his books might reflect who he'd like to be. A daredevil Indiana Jones or James Bond kind of person. But that's far from who he is."

"To me, they seem—well, 'bloody' is the best word I can think of. He deals in death, destruction, and horror."

"I haven't read them," Dr. Granger said, "but I've seen them. They're thrillers, that's all. And they sell well."

“I just read one,” Audra said, “and that was enough for me. But I realize many people enjoy them. Do you think it’s actually possible that he channels all of his negative emotions into his books?”

“Not *all* of them.” Derrick grinned. “He’s still a pretty grumpy guy most of the time.”

It was Audra’s turn to shake her head. “I don’t know how Violet put up with him all those years.”

Dr. Granger cleared his throat. “Frank will be fine. He’s simply not one to show emotions.” He got out his notepad. “Let’s get back to Ingrid. I’ll order some blood tests to determine whether she has a deficiency of any sort.”

“What about a cognitive assessment?” asked Audra.

Dr. Granger looked at Audra. “Do you really think that’s necessary? Why not wait for the blood test results before we get into tests she might find upsetting?”

Derrick shrugged. “Can’t you just tell her she’s due for her yearly check-up?”

Audra nodded. “I really think it would be good for you to do a complete assessment.”

Leaning forward, Derrick said, “Look, the real issue, which we’re all skirting around, is that Serenity Suites isn’t set up for the kind of nursing she’ll need if she has dementia or Alzheimer’s.”

“Exactly.” Dr. Granger sighed. “Well, let’s not jump ahead of ourselves. There’s always the chance it’s a vitamin deficiency. We likely need to get a pain assessment, too. Pain can cause a whole variety of side effects.”

“Her hip *has* been bothering her quite a bit,” Audra said.

Derrick added, “I’ve tried to get her to do more exercises that might help, but she wants no part of them. Ben tried to convince her to do them, too, but he had no more success than I did. Whatever else may be going on, she’s extremely stubborn.”

Dr. Granger nodded. “Okay, I’ll talk to Ben and get some tests arranged. And I’ll do a simple cognitive assessment myself.”

“I’d like to be there when you talk to Ben if you don’t mind,” Audra said. “After you’re gone, Ben may have questions. If I’ve been part of the conversation, it will be easier for me to reassure him.”

Dr. Granger frowned. “You’re not going to tell me you think Ben is having his own issues, are you?”

"No. I think that intellectually Ben is fine. He just seems kind of sad, but it might have something to do with Violet's death, or even just the realization of mortality it brought."

"Well, I'll have a look through Ingrid's file and see if I can see any pointers there. You can go ahead and do the blood tests right away. She's used to those because of her diabetes. And maybe we should just go and level with Ben about your concerns right now. If there's anything to them, he's probably wondering himself, and maybe doing the tests and knowing exactly where we stand would help him."

Ben Davidson was alone in his condo when the intercom buzzed. "It's Audra, Ben. Do you have a few minutes?"

He activated the door to admit Audra and Dr. Granger.

Ben turned off the television. "I have to stop this. I can spend the whole day flipping from talk show to talk show, and all it does is make me miserable."

"You must miss being part of it all," Audra said.

Ben laughed. "Well, I can't say I miss the research and prep work, but I sure miss talking to different people every day, and being in the 'know,' and, well, just having something to do that felt a little bit important."

Dr. Granger smiled. "Retirement isn't all it's cracked up to be."

"Nope, sure isn't. But I don't expect that's what you're here for. Why don't you both have a seat?"

After a moment, Dr. Granger said, "Ben, I won't beat around the bush. We checked to make sure Ingrid was in the common room before we came because we wanted to see you alone. Audra and Derrick tell me that Ingrid has been having a few difficulties lately. They wondered if it's time for a check-up. I'd talk to Ingrid about it, but Audra and Derrick tell me she's gotten pretty stubborn lately and might just refuse. So we thought it might be better to talk to you first. Derrick is watching to make sure Ingrid doesn't come back while we're still here."

Ben pressed his lips together. "Everyone always said that having a floor that was a nursing home would ruin this place. And now look at what we have." He stood and walked to the window. "Of course she needs a check-up. She has either Alzheimer's or dementia—I'm not sure which. Not much difference anyway, is there? Either one means she can't stay here. We don't have the kind of care she'll need." Tears formed in his eyes. "And what do I do? Let her go by herself or go with her? At least here there are people I can have a conversation with. But how can I send her away all by herself?"

Audra spoke softly, "Ben, why don't we start with an assessment? Find out exactly what's going on. It might not be as bad as you think."

Ben shut his eyes. "I've been putting it off, telling myself it's just another phase. Like menopause, you know. I've been calling it the 'getting old and cranky phase.'" He opened his eyes and turned to look at them. "She won't want to do it. And she won't want to go anywhere for it."

Dr. Granger said, "I can come to see her on Friday afternoon at 4:00."

Ben nodded. "Do you want me to hang around or leave?"

"Let's try it with her alone. Audra will be here with me."

"All right. I'd really prefer not to be here. But you'll tell me the results after?"

"Of course. And we'll cross the next bridge when we come to it; so wait until after the tests are done before you start imagining the worst. There are other possibilities. Audra is going to get some blood tests going right away. We'll check for vitamin deficiencies and a few other things."

"All right." Ben smiled. "I'll put it out of my mind until then." More tears came to his eyes, and his smile disappeared. "You have to realize Ingrid and I have been married for fifty-six years, and my biggest problem isn't that I miss my job; it's that I miss my wife. The person who's living with me right now—she's not my Ingrid."

Kenneth sat at his computer looking for efficient, foolproof ways to commit suicide. They said that once you'd tried and failed, most people didn't try again. And he'd managed to convince himself that the only reason he'd tried the first time was because he was depressed.

He still took pills for depression, but either the pills weren't working any more or there was something dark inside him that was stronger than the pills.

Violet's death was the catalyst for his decision. As he'd thought about it, he'd realized three things. First, now that he was getting too old to travel around the world singing, he had nothing to live for. Second, he had no family or close friends who'd care whether he was around or not. And third, he was too old and too tired to make an effort to change.

As he read what various people said online about how and why they wanted to kill themselves, he felt guilty. Many of these people lived horrendous lives. Compared to them, he had little right to complain. And yet he continued to search. It occurred to him that perhaps his threshold for pain was lower than theirs.

In any case, his mind was made up. And this time he'd make sure he did it right. There'd be no one to save him at the last minute.

"I'm so glad you decided to come here today," Derrick told Hilary, who was doing Pilates on a mat in front of a large mirror in the exercise room. She wore a red sleeveless muscle shirt and navy yoga pants.

"Other than for a short time after the hip surgery, I've worked out every single day for my whole life since I was four."

"That's amazing."

"It was what you needed to do to be a star. That was always my goal—not just a member of the corps, but the prima ballerina."

"And you made it."

"Yes, in a way."

"And you kept on working out after you retired from dancing?"

"I just kept doing what I'd done before. Dancing, too. Only not for an audience. But eventually my hip bones started rubbing on my thigh bones, and there was no cartilage left in between to cushion them, so I hurt all over."

"You haven't lost any of the gracefulness of a ballet dancer."

"The posture and the way of walking is drilled into your brain and imprinted into your muscles. You can't slouch even if you try."

"Was the hip replacement the only consequence of dancing you've had to deal with?"

She laughed and shook her head. "Oh no, I've had sprains, strains, torn ligaments, stress fractures, and a million other aches and pains. But you never stop moving. Don't let anything get seized up."

"Wow! Well, I'm so glad you decided to come and use our facilities and not keep doing your exercises in your condo. Maybe you can inspire a few of our residents who seem to be afraid they'll break if they try to bend."

"I don't think they'll be too inspired if they see me. More likely to remember why they don't want me here."

"Hilary, don't ever think that. They just don't know you, that's all." Derrick tilted his head and smiled. "You know, you can be pretty intimidating."

"Yes, Audra hinted something like that to me the other day, too. No doubt you've been discussing me behind my back."

While Derrick didn't exactly blush, he did look away for a second. Then he grinned. "We want everyone here to feel like this is home."

Hilary smiled. "Well, I've never found a place where I felt I completely belonged, but if it makes you feel better, Serenity Suites feels as much like home as any other place I've lived."

Norm Carlysle made a few small brush strokes and then stood back to look at his portrait of the woman. It was completely unlike anything he'd ever painted before.

The morning after Violet's death, he'd come to his studio to work on the half-finished portrait he'd been painting of his old friend. He'd wanted to paint her for years, but she'd always demurred. It had taken her daughter, Trish, to finally convince her to sit for him.

Anxious to finish Violet's portrait, Norm had barely managed a single stroke before dissolving in tears. The pain was too close. Better to wait until he could paint it with even a small amount of objectivity.

For over a week, he'd painted nothing. Hadn't even entered his studio. And he'd just about gone crazy, wondering if he'd ever paint again. And then on Saturday morning he'd awakened early, come into his studio, taken a brand new canvas, and begun this portrait, leaving Violet's unfinished one waiting on its easel.

Usually Norm only painted people he knew. Most of them sat for him in his studio, although now and then he went to them. Occasionally he'd agreed to paint a busy person, who either sent him a series of photos to paint from or preferably let him come and take the photos himself.

But the portrait before him was totally different. He had no idea who the woman was.

For most of his life, he'd have called her a Negro, or perhaps, if he was being quizzed, a Negress. Now they said African-Canadian, or black. He was never quite sure which was preferable. The woman's skin wasn't anywhere near black. More of a dark caramel colour, rich against her green-patterned sundress. She was young and beautiful, with short black curly hair, a perfect oval face, unblemished skin, a straight nose, inviting lips, and soulful eyes. Half of her face was in the light, half in shadow.

Her face had come to him in a dream. When he woke up, he'd felt compelled to run to his studio and paint her before he lost the image. He thought he'd done a good job of capturing what he'd seen.

He hadn't shown the portrait to Elizabeth. Not that she was clamouring to see his work. But if she saw it, she'd ask him who it was, and for the life of him, he didn't know.

FIVE

Some time after lunch on Wednesday, Trish opened the door to her father's office and poked her head in. "Dad, can we talk for a few minutes?"

Frank was sitting at his desk, staring at his computer screen. "Can't you see I'm busy? I thought you knew not to bother me when I'm writing."

"Dad, I'm going home tomorrow morning. I need to make sure I've packed everything I need to take."

He sat back and looked up. "Well, you've already broken my train of thought. Why didn't you ask me at lunch instead of waiting until I'd gone back to work?"

"I hadn't thought of it then."

"Well, what is it you want?"

"It just occurred to me that you and Mom might have a storage unit in the basement here. Some places do that."

"How should I know? Your mother did all that." After a short pause, he said, "I guess there might be something."

"So, if you did have a unit, you don't know where it is or if you have a key?"

"She did all that."

"Okay, thanks. I guess I'll contact the custodian; then I'll know if I need to look for a key."

"Should have done that in the first place instead of barging in here bothering me."

"Sorry, Dad. How's the book going?"

"As well as can be expected given that people keep interrupting."

Trish shut the door quietly behind her and walked back to the guest suite, deep in thought. How much she'd misjudged her mother! She'd always seen Violet as a humourless worrywart, always checking on details. Now that she'd had a sample of life with her father—well, she just wished her mother were still here so she could apologize. She saw Audra approaching. "Audra, do you have a minute?"

"Sure."

"If you don't mind my asking, is my dad always this bad-tempered?"

"Well, he doesn't have a lot of patience when he's writing. The rest of the time he's pretty good."

Trish frowned. "Isn't he normally writing?"

Audra grinned. "Well, yes."

Trish burst into laughter. "Good one! Actually, I'm staying here to help him, and he just wants me to leave him alone."

"Your mom did a lot of the business side of things, I think."

"I'm beginning to think she did everything!"

"Well, since he's in his office most of the day, I assume he writes his books."

Trish started to walk away, but turned back. "Audra?"

"Yes."

"You don't think he's getting—well, a bit senile, do you?"

Audra thought a moment. "He might be losing some of his inhibitions and saying whatever he thinks a little more easily than he used to, if that makes sense. That can happen as people get older."

Trish considered this. "You're saying he no longer worries about trying to be polite, or politically correct, as they say nowadays?"

"Yes, a lot of older people do that. It's not so much that their personalities change as that they simply stop trying to be diplomatic and say exactly what they think. For some it's a conscious decision. They feel they don't have time to waste on things that aren't important to them any more."

"I would have thought being nice to others was important, but I see what you mean. And I hope that's all it is. I actually came here prepared to insist that he come back with me for a visit, but I think he's better off here with his friends and his routine."

Audra's eyes twinkled. "Yes, I'm sure you're right."

Nikola found the door to Audra's office closed, so he knocked. No answer. He tried the door. Locked. He swore under his breath, then headed to the billiards room.

No one was there, so he set up the balls, chose a cue, and made a perfect shot, breaking the balls and sending three of them into pockets. He then proceeded to put the rest of the balls into pockets, missing only two shots. When the table had been cleared, he set up the balls again and tried some trick shots.

After about twenty minutes, Derrick looked in. "Ah, I thought it was you. Too bad you've got no competition here."

"Oh, Lyle isn't too bad. I'd guess he probably made himself a few dollars taking on rookies at some time in his past."

Derrick laughed. "More than likely. Have you played Ben?"

"A couple of times. He's quite good, except he gets caught up in the conversation and loses focus."

"And I'm a total duffer."

"Well, I'm a duffer at a lot of things myself. I assume you're headed to your class?"

Derrick looked at his watch. "Yeah, and it's five after two. I'd better get a move on."

"You don't happen to know where Audra is, do you?"

"She's not in the office?"

"Didn't appear to be."

Derrick shook his head. "You could page her."

"It's nothing urgent. I just wanted to ask her a question."

"Can I help?"

"No, it was about, er, Catarina. More the kind of thing another woman might know."

"Oh, okay. Well, I'm sure she'll be back soon. I need to run. See you later."

Nikola played a game of one-pocket pool, and then walked back to Audra's office. This time the door was open, and Audra was sitting at her computer.

"Oh, hello, Mr. Vincent. May I help you?"

He sat on the corner of her desk. "Yes, I have a question."

She looked up at him, waiting.

"When do you get some time off?"

"What?"

"Off. You know. A time when you aren't working. I have something I'd like to discuss with you."

"Can't you talk about it now?"

"Not really. I was thinking we could meet for coffee in a restaurant. Or go for a walk outside."

Audra pushed her chair back and set her hands on her lap. "That's impossible."

"Why?"

"If you really need to talk to me, you can do it here."

"But, well, it's a bit embarrassing. I don't want anyone to overhear."

"If you're having some kind of medical problem, maybe you could see Dr. Granger."

"It's not medical. More, a kind of, well, social thing. I need a woman's advice."

He gave Audra a pleading look, one he knew wouldn't work with Catarina but had proven successful with a lot of other people.

"Sorry, you'll have to find someone else to talk to." She turned back to her computer and began typing. "Now, please leave. I have work I need to finish before tea time."

The moment he was gone, Audra stopped typing and deleted the gobbledegook she'd just entered into a form. She pressed her lips together. *Stupid man! Where on earth did Catarina find him?* She'd been, if not happy, at least content here, until he'd arrived.

Last night Olive had commented wistfully that Nikola was handsome enough to be on the cover of a romance novel. Audra didn't read romance novels, and she didn't like either his long hair or his beard, but she couldn't lie. No matter how much she fought it, something about him attracted her. His air of confidence maybe? Those disconcerting eyes that seemed to see everything? She shook her head. *Why am I wasting time thinking about him? I'm supposed to be working.*

Her mind went back to that first dinner when Catarina had brought him into the dining room and introduced him. As Audra shook hands with him, and their eyes met, some kind of electric current seemed to pass between them. Catarina had then announced that she and Nikola had been married the week before while she was on holiday in Italy. Audra quickly let go of his hand, stammered a quick "Congratulations," and left the room.

Later that evening she and Scarlett and Derrick had decided that Nikola was some kind of gigolo who'd married Catarina solely because of her money. Since then Audra had done everything possible to stay out of his way.

She stared at the computer screen. *They're both adults, and presumably they know what they're doing. And Catarina certainly seems happy.*

She forced her brain to concentrate on the words she needed to put into the form and willed herself to forget about warm brown eyes that seemed to see into her soul.

Ben sat at his dining room table surrounded by stacks of photograph albums. For most of their married lives, these had been Ingrid's most precious possessions—the things she'd always said she'd grab if their house were ever on fire.

A month ago he'd hired someone to scan every picture and label them with any information written on the backs of the photos or beside them in the album. The albums had been returned this morning along with a set of CDs for them and a set for each of his children and grandchildren. Now he had to decide what to do with the albums themselves.

He opened an album and looked at the photographs of young children. He smiled. In truth, he'd never been able to tell his kids apart in photos. Ingrid, on the other hand, had known who everyone was, not only which of her beloved babies was which, but who every non-family person was, too, from their oldest son's best friend in kindergarten to the girl their youngest son had taken to his first dance.

But just last week Ben had found Ingrid standing in the living room looking at their youngest daughter's university graduation photo, which had hung on the wall for years. Ingrid had turned toward him and asked why that strange woman's picture was on her wall. Any day now she wouldn't recognize him. *Oh, Ingrid, where have you gone?*

Tears flowed from his eyes and dripped onto his burnt-orange golf shirt. When he'd retired, Ingrid convinced him to start wearing golf shirts, insisting they'd be far more comfortable than the shirts and suits and sports jackets he'd always worn. She'd been right. As usual. *Oh, my Ingrid, I miss you so much.*

Scarlett was busy putting the finishing touches on the Melt-In-Your-Mouth Meringues she and Violet had created for the new cookbook. They'd come up with their recipe by trying out a number of other meringue recipes and adapting the best ones until they had a new one that was better than all the others.

Audra came in from the hallway. "Mmm, something smells really good."

"Sure does," agreed Olive, coming in from the dining room. "I'm going to buy that cookbook the moment it comes out and try to make all those recipes."

Audra smiled. "You like cooking?"

Olive looked wistful. "I don't know how. But I'd absolutely love to cook like Scarlett does."

"Thank you," Scarlett said. "If you mean it, I'll do my best to teach you. I never assume people want to know things, but if they do, I'm more than willing to offer suggestions. I didn't know you had aspirations to cook."

"I didn't know either, but watching you and seeing how much everyone looks forward to your creations have made me realize how important food is to people, especially as they get old. And I love how you're so concerned about making things healthy and not satisfied if they only taste good but aren't good for you."

"Well, thank you, Olive. I'd be delighted to give you some lessons when we have time."

"That would be terrific."

Audra smiled at Olive. "You're really enjoying it here, aren't you?"

"I love it! I really get a kick out of helping people and making them feel good. And it doesn't have to be anything major. Even a small thing can make someone feel better. Like helping Catarina find the blouse she wants, or asking Mary to sing me one of her songs, or telling Lyle how much I like his new shirt." She frowned. "That might sound wrong. I don't mean just flattering them. I really do like hearing Mary sing, and Lyle always looks so well-dressed. I guess what I mean is I like discovering something that's important to them and encouraging them."

Audra put her hands on Olive's shoulders. "This girl is a keeper. Maybe we should try to figure out how to clone her."

Olive blushed. "Anyway, I'll be first in line for your new cookbook, Scarlett! And if I can help you more in the kitchen, I'd love that, too."

Scarlett's smile faded. "That's assuming the cookbook will actually come out. I'm beginning to wonder if it will."

Olive's jaw dropped. "Why?"

"Frank. After breakfast this morning he said no one needs another stupid cookbook, and if the publishers ask him, he'd tell them to throw it out. Then he said he had a good mind to phone them and tell them to just forget about it."

Olive stared at her. "Why on earth would he do that?"

"Because he's a grumpy old man, and he hates it when he thinks someone else is getting more attention than him. Especially if it's his wife."

Audra looked puzzled. "Did Violet ever say anything to you about that?"

"Huh!" Scarlett shook her head. "If you listened to Violet, you'd think Frank could do no wrong. But if you ask me, he's all about himself, and he didn't like anything that took her attention away from him. I think he'd have been happy if none of her cookbooks had ever been published. And if he can stop this one, he will."

As was her custom, Mary went into the common room about half an hour before 3:00, the time for afternoon tea. Ingrid was already there, seated in a brocade wing chair in the middle of the room, chin on her chest, the baby blanket she'd been crocheting resting on her knees. She was wearing a rust cardigan that was buttoned up most of the way. Mary thought she could detect stains on the front. She sighed. Like it or not, Ben was soon going to have to consider putting Ingrid into a nursing home.

Mary chose a recliner near the door, and lay back with her eyes shut. She tried to erase her concern for Ingrid from her mind, only to have thoughts of Violet take its place. She missed Violet so much. Sure, she'd been a bit of a pain sometimes, but Mary knew that inside Violet's sometimes annoying exterior was a good heart.

She heard a noise and then Norm's voice. "Mary, have you seen Elizabeth? I can't seem to find her."

Mary opened her eyes and sat up. "Sorry, Norm, I haven't seen her since lunch."

"I don't know where she can be. Not that many places to hide from me here." He laughed.

"She's not downstairs getting her hair done or something like that, is she?"

"I suppose that's possible."

"Do you need something? Can I help?"

"No, no. I just wondered where she was, that's all. I've been painting, and when I came out of my studio, she wasn't in the condo. So I came out to find her. There was something I wanted to ask her. But I—I'm not sure I remember what it was. I don't think it was anything urgent. It'll come back to me."

"Why don't you sit down? We haven't talked for a while. How are you doing?"

He took a chair across from her. "I've been feeling pretty down for a while. I guess since we lost Violet."

"Her death was so unexpected, wasn't it?"

"Unexpected and unsettling. We all thought she was in such good health, didn't we? That she'd be the one to bury the rest of us."

"You were always fond of Violet. I remember you dated her back in high school, before she started going with Frank."

"That's right. Took her to the prom and high school graduation, and we dated through first-year university. I thought we'd keep going together and eventually marry, but she changed her mind. Right after university was out, she left to stay with her aunt for the summer and help with her kids, who were just youngsters. You remember that?"

Mary nodded. "I went away that summer, too. I was helping at a church camp. That's the first time I was ever paid money to sing. It was wonderful to know I had a talent people would pay for."

"Well, I stayed here in Toronto working in a hardware store. I wrote Mary every week for a while, but she only replied once, in the middle of August, and it was to tell me she wasn't ready to get serious about anybody, and that even if she was, it wouldn't be me. She said she liked me well enough, but only as a friend."

"I never knew that."

He looked away. "It just about broke my heart. I was sure I was in love with her. I'd even started thinking about looking for a full-time job instead of going back to university so that we could get married. Came as quite a blow to know it was all on my side."

"I only had a few letters from her. She didn't say much at all of a personal nature. Just talked about her cousins, the kids she was helping look after. Said they were really keeping her busy, but that she enjoyed it. And then she wrote to say that her aunt needed her to stay on for the fall, so she was skipping first term and starting in January. But she never mentioned you." Mary picked at a thread on her sweater. "When she finally came back, I remember being surprised that you and she weren't dating any more. I thought she liked you a lot."

"When she came back, she was still friendly enough to me, but she treated me like a kid brother."

"The same way Frank treated me."

Norm looked at her and frowned. "That's right! I'd clean forgotten. You and Frank were an item, too. We used to double-date." He tilted his head to one side. "Which happened first? Violet dumping me or Frank dumping you?"

"Maybe *I* dumped Frank."

"Be good for him if you did."

She sighed. "No, when Frank realized Violet was free, he lost no time in switching me for her. The funny thing is that Violet and I remained friends through it all."

"But later on you met someone else, didn't you?"

"Yes, I did."

"There was going to be a wedding, wasn't there? But it never happened."

"I called it off. I guess you'd say I got cold feet. I just wasn't sure I wanted to commit to spending my life with him."

"Huh."

"He married his secretary a year later, and they had three kids the last I heard."

"Did you regret not marrying him?"

"Oh, off and on, I guess, but not really. The truth is I never found anyone I wanted to give up my independence for." She wrinkled her nose. "It was different back then, you know. It's a lot easier for women and men to be equal partners these days." She gave him a searching look. "But you and Elizabeth managed to do that. You're pretty equal."

Norm smiled. "Well, maybe. Or maybe it's easier to just let her be the boss."

Mary snorted. "Let? Right."

Norm laughed.

Mary glanced over at Ingrid. "Remember the agony Ben went through in university trying to decide whether or not he should date a woman who was a year older than him?"

"I do." Norm lowered his voice to a whisper. "Remember her then? Such beautiful golden hair. And her skin so flawless. Glowing with health."

"You sound like you had a bit of a thing for her."

"No, not me. I was never into the athletic type. But I did think Ben was lucky to have found her."

The two of them looked over at Ingrid, slouched in her chair with her chin hanging on her chest, drool and other stains on her sweater.

She's starting to smell funny, too. More stench than smell. As if she'd— Mary looked at Norm, but he didn't seem to have noticed.

"So full of life she was. And now—"

Mary sat forward. "Norm, I think—"

Lyle wandered into the room. "Almost tea time," he said happily. "I can't wait to see what Scarlett has for us. There's a wonderful smell coming from the kitchen."

"Lyle," Mary said, "I know I've said this before and been wrong, but I really do believe Ingrid's dead this time."

Lyle laughed. "Mary, how many times—"

"Lyle, please check."

"I don't have a mirror, so I won't be able to see if she's breathing."

"Just touch her hand."

Norm started to get up. "Mary, you don't really think—"

"Sit down, Norm. Just touch her, Lyle. If you wake her, it's not a problem because it's almost tea time."

"All right, but this is getting silly."

He walked over to Ingrid and reached out to touch her hand where it hung by her side. "Her skin feels pretty cool." He bent to touch her neck but paused with his hand outstretched.

Mary stood up. "What is it, Lyle?"

Lyle stepped back. "Mary, get Audra or Derrick. I believe the Grim Reaper you've been expecting has finally come. But he had some help."

Part II

Kindness is passed on
and grows each time it's passed
until a simple courtesy becomes
an act of selfless courage,
years later, and far away.
Likewise, each small meanness,
each expression of hatred,
each act of evil.

—DEAN KOONTZ, *From the Corner of His Eye*

SIX

Hearing his name called, Detective Inspector Paul Manziuk of Toronto homicide division nodded at the middle-aged secretary and got to his feet. At six-foot-five and two hundred and fifty pounds, he was well aware that he intimidated people by his size alone. But right now he felt like his four-foot-two and ten-year-old self, being called into the principal's office for fighting at recess. It was the first time he'd ever punched anyone, and although the punch had been fully justified, and he'd felt good when he did it, he'd been almost paralyzed with fear during his trip to the principal and the subsequent meeting with the principal and his parents.

Today's meeting was with a psychologist instead of a principal, but it was no more his idea than that long-ago meeting. After his partner's death from a heart attack several weeks ago, Paul's wife, Loretta, had insisted that he see a doctor for a physical. When he'd agreed to that, she'd suggested he also speak to one of the counsellors the police force had on hand to talk about stress and loss and all the nasty things he dealt with on a daily basis.

He'd told her it wasn't necessary.

She'd pointed out that there was a reason the suicide rate among police officers was higher than the norm and that she hadn't signed up to be married to someone who carried everything around until he ended up with post-traumatic stress disorder or worse.

He'd just looked at her.

She'd put her hands on her hips and told him she was well aware that many police officers saw the need for counselling as a sign of weakness. But surely *he* wasn't still living in the dark ages, was he? While he tried to find the right words, Loretta reminded him that some years before, after he'd been involved in a shooting where a police officer and two armed robbers had been killed, he'd talked to a psychologist named Joseph Pazernak. Pazernak had been in private practice and nothing to do with the police force. And Paul had liked him.

In the end, Paul agreed to talk to Pazernak if he was still around. But now, stepping into Dr. Pazernak's office, he wanted to be anywhere else.

The psychologist looked up and smiled. "Good morning, Paul, good to see you again." A slim, black-haired man with a bushy black moustache and gleaming white teeth, he came forward to shake hands. His head just reached the top of Paul's shoulder, but his voice was deep and resonant. "What would you like? Coffee? Tea? Iced tea? A soft drink?"

"Coffee might be good. Black."

"Excellent. We have a great blend—organic, and fair trade." The psychologist walked past Paul into the doorway. "Coffee. Black. And a refill for me, too, please." He stepped back into his office. "Please sit. Anywhere you like. Except at the desk, of course." He grinned.

The grin was contagious, and Paul smiled back in surprise. "You remember what I said—when was it? Fifteen years ago?"

Pazernak laughed. "Well, to be honest, I wrote it down. I mentioned to you that sitting behind a desk gives you power, while sitting across from someone without anything in between is more likely to give you rapport. You said you thought that might help you in your investigations. Has it?"

Paul sat in a large brown leather wing chair. "Yes, it has. I've sensed people are more comfortable when there's no desk." He relaxed and smiled. "Of course there are occasions on which I want the desk between us, too."

Dr. Pazernak sat on a muted peach and green floral couch and nodded. "Of course."

"Nice office." Paul looked around the warm lemon-yellow room with floor-to-ceiling bookshelves lining three of the four walls. The fourth wall was largely window panes offering a view of the tops of trees. One wall had a large aquarium in the centre of its bookshelves.

Dr. Pazernak smiled. "A step up from my old one, eh? I love it. And I think most people who come here do, too."

"It—well, it's certainly not what one would expect."

"Always an advantage, don't you think?"

The secretary came in with their coffee and shut the door on her way out.

Dr. Pazernak made himself comfortable on the couch and took a sip of his coffee. "Ahh. I love this blend." He looked at Paul. "So what brings you here today? Not another shooting, I hope?"

Paul shook his head, then cleared his throat. "My wife, actually."

"How is Loretta?"

"Good."

Dr. Pazernak sipped his coffee and looked with interest at Paul.

"I lost my partner just over a month ago. Detective Sergeant Woodward Craig. He had a massive heart attack. They did bypass surgery. Technically, the surgery was successful, but Woody didn't make it."

Dr. Pazernak was nodding. "I remember seeing his obituary in the newspaper. I was very sorry to see it. Seemed like he was a good man, and a good cop."

"He was also my best friend."

"So Loretta thought you needed to talk to someone about the loss?"

"Well, not exactly. She wanted me to get a full check-up. Make sure my arteries are doing their job. The works. The thing is, Woody and I—we'd been eating the same food and sharing the same hectic, stressed-out lifestyle for the last twenty or so years. She thought I might need to make major changes before I end up in the operating room, too."

"And?"

"I don't have all the results yet, but the doctor said I looked pretty good to him, although I could stand to lose a few pounds, particularly around my middle. And I believe I need to watch my cholesterol."

"So not too bad."

"Yeah."

"And she wanted you to see me, too?"

"She seems to think I'm stressed."

"Are you?"

"Well, I guess it's just hard. So much change."

"You mean losing Woody?"

"Well, yes, but I also have a new partner."

"Ah, of course."

"She's—she's a prickly, uncomfortable young woman, and she makes me angry all the time!"

Dr. Pazernak opened his mouth to speak, but Paul went on, "I know that no one can make you angry. But she comes as close as anyone."

"What is it about her that makes you angry?"

"She thinks she knows it all! But she's inexperienced. And she doesn't know how to deal with people. Too blunt. Plus I find myself constantly comparing her to Woody and thinking how much better he was." He sighed. "The worst part is that the powers-that-be want me to have her ready to take the lead on an investigation by September first."

"Really?"

"Yes."

"Why is that, do you think?"

"Because she's a woman, and she's black, and they want to showcase her—you know, show everyone they're hiring more women and minorities and moving them up the ladder."

"Hmm. That would be difficult." Dr. Pazernak thought for a moment. "How hard is it normally for you to work with a woman?"

"You mean am I a male chauvinist?"

"Well, are you?"

"I don't think so. I know Loretta is way smarter than I am. I truly believe my daughter, Lisa, should be able to do anything she wants."

"So it's not the fact that she's a woman. Is it the fact that she's black?"

"Absolutely not!"

Dr. Pazernak frowned. "You said that with a lot of anger."

"Only because I have strong feelings on the subject. I am *not* biased. Ask anyone who knows me."

"All right."

"Her age?"

Paul bit his lip. “Late twenties.”

Dr. Pazernak nodded. “So, young and probably green. Are you concerned that she won’t be able to pull her weight?”

Paul shifted uncomfortably in his chair. “I suspect a few years down the road she could be way better than me. She’s smart. She’s got a master’s degree in criminology.”

“Ah. What about you?”

Manziuk shrugged. “All I have is a high school diploma. And some courses.”

“So she knows more than you do about some things?”

“She has more head knowledge, but nowhere near as much experience.”

“You’re her boss, right?”

“Technically, yes, although we both report to Superintendent Seldon.”

“Well, let’s look at it another way. Does she have any good qualities? Maybe even some things Woody didn’t have?”

Paul considered the question. “Working with her is different, of course. Woody and I worked together on so many cases that we didn’t even have to think about it. We tended to think alike.”

“I see. Can you think of a time when it’s been helpful to have someone with a different perspective from yours?”

Paul looked down and made a face. “Yes, she’s had a few good ideas.”

“So, aside from the fact that you have to get out of the rut you’ve been in and learn how to work with a bright young woman, what is it you dislike about her most?”

Paul laughed. “Okay, she has a huge chip on her shoulder, and she seems to think she knows as much as I do, but she doesn’t. She can’t possibly! She’s only been in homicide since the beginning of July—not even two months! But she was like this right from the moment we met.”

“Give me a specific example.”

“Well, she interrupts me when I’m interviewing people, as if she thinks I don’t know what I’m doing or I’m too slow to get to the point.”

“Have you spoken to her about it?”

“Many times.”

"Have things improved?"

"A little."

"Have you tried letting her interview some of the people while you watch?"

"A bit."

"Maybe talk it over ahead of time so she knows what you'd want her to cover?"

Paul shifted in his chair. "Yeah, I guess I could do that more. With Woody, I did all the interviewing while he made notes."

"And he was comfortable with that?"

"He hated doing interviews. But he watched and listened and took great notes, and he'd give me his perspective afterwards."

"But she isn't like that."

"Not even remotely."

Dr. Pazernak thought for a moment. "You know, it strikes me that she might still be doing interviews thirty years from now. Have you considered what tools you can give her to help her become as good as you?"

Paul shook his head. "I've never thought of it that way. I guess I've just been trying to survive."

"Can you think about that idea?"

"Yes. Look, I know intellectually that it's an advantage to have a different perspective. She's certainly not afraid to disagree or argue and point out different ways to look at things. While that can be annoying, I know that in the long run it's better than having two people who think the same."

"Think of it as a challenge to keep you sharp."

Paul looked down. "In my heart I know that the real problem is she isn't Woody. Will never be Woody. Is a constant reminder that Woody's gone. And nothing's going to change. I've even wondered if maybe I need to take early retirement. I'm well past my twenty-five years."

"Had you considered retirement prior to Woody's death?"

Paul stared at his left knee. "No."

"Are you dealing with any other changes?"

"Well, I guess this has made me realize that none of us is getting any younger. My dad and mom are in their late sixties. Loretta's parents are even older. They've all been fortunate thus far but, as we've learned, you don't know what might be going on under your skin. No one suspected there was anything wrong with Woody's heart, never mind the complete mess it was in."

"So you think there might be more changes coming?"

"Woody's wife, Arlie, had Loretta and me over for dinner last night to tell us she's decided to sell her house and move to Ottawa to be close to her only daughter. Arlie and Loretta are best friends. I don't blame her for moving, but Loretta will miss Arlie as much as I miss Woody."

Dr. Pazernak nodded. The silence stretched.

"Arlie made me an offer that needs a quick decision. My son Mike is seventeen, going into his last year of high school, and he's been begging us to get a second car. Arlie knew that, so she's offered to sell us Woody's car at a pretty low price, but…"

"But?"

"I don't know. I'm still not convinced we need a second car. But maybe more important, I wonder if seeing Woody's car in our garage every day will only keep his memory alive and raw."

"So you have two decisions to make. The first is, do you need a second car? The second is, is this the right car?"

"Yeah."

"How will you decide?"

"Right now I'm having trouble even focusing on it."

"Have you any reason to think you don't need a second car?"

"Not really. It's just the expense. The truth is *I* need a new car."

"Should you buy the car for yourself?"

He shook his head. "No. Never."

"What does Loretta think?"

"She wants me to buy a new car for myself and also get Woody's car for her and Mike."

"Can you afford it?"

"If we're careful, we can manage."

"Well, you'll have to make that decision, of course, but I suggest the three of you sit down and do a BOAR analysis: benefits of buying the car, opportunities currently available, arguments against it, reasons to wait or defer the decision until later." He paused, and then added, "One other thought. You might consider asking yourself whether Woody would want Mike and Loretta to have his car."

"Right."

"As for momentary feelings of stress, I recommend stopping to take a deep breath any time you feel yourself beginning to get heated. Just keep breathing slowly and deeply until the moment passes."

Paul frowned. "I'll try." *Oh, sure. All I need to do is breathe and I'll be fine.*

"As for what the doctor said, do you have any concerns there? Are there lifestyle changes you need to make?"

"I need to eat healthier. I eat way too much fast food."

"What do you plan to do about it?"

"Loretta offered to make a list of foods I should avoid and foods I should have. I guess I just need to follow it."

"And can you?"

"If I want to enough."

"Then I guess the question is, do you?"

On his way out of Dr. Pazernak's office, Paul imagined what Ryan would say if he changed what he ate. They'd been partners for less than a day when she'd given him a dirty look after he ordered a burger and fries at a take-out restaurant.

Ryan and her salads and grilled chicken and yogurt! If he told her he had to eat healthier, she'd be worse than Loretta, bugging him about it all the time.

He was almost at his car when his cellphone rang. A moment later his mood shifted. Back to work!

On a rare day off, Detective Constable Jacqueline Ryan sat on the edge of her single bed analyzing her small second-floor bedroom. Her conversation with Armando two weeks before had forced her to think about the future.

She was twenty-eight years old, a homicide detective, and she lived with her mother, grandmother, aunt, and cousin. Five women—one of whom was, in Jacquie's opinion anyway, obsessed with her looks—and only one full bathroom. A recipe for disaster.

Fortunately they each had a bedroom. Jacquie shuddered at the thought of having to share with any of them. Maybe Gram, but she'd feel bad for being in Gram's way.

Several months ago she'd decided to get her own apartment. Thanks largely to Armando's pointing out how lucky she was to have a family, she'd come to appreciate them more. She'd realized she liked to come home to people who loved her rather than to an empty apartment. Well, to Gram, anyway. So she'd changed her mind about moving.

But if she was going to stay for more than a few months, she'd need to find some way to make living together smoother. Maybe she'd look on the Internet for ideas on renovating houses. Or check the library for books. Might not be a bad idea to fit some normal things into her life. Not good to think about tracking down murderers all the time. Maybe.

Her mind jumped to Armando's request that she go to Hawaii with him for a month. That could lead to, well, a lot of things. Was she ready to jump into an intense relationship with a man she'd known for only six weeks?

She knew exactly what Manziuk would say if she told him she wanted to take a month off when she'd only recently been promoted to homicide. That she didn't deserve the promotion. That she couldn't take the heat. Not to bother coming back.

So many decisions.

Her phone rang, and Superintendent Seldon himself informed her that her day off had been cancelled.

She smiled.

Manziuk and Ryan met at the front doors of a 20-storey black and gold high-rise east of downtown Toronto, not far from the Don Valley and the lake. Directly in front of them were gold-tinted glass doors with thin gold bars across the middle. The words *Serenity Suites* were picked out in gold above the doors.

"What's up?" Ryan asked. "I was just told to meet you here."

"All I know is that there's been a suspicious death and that someone connected with the place is an old friend of Seldon's and asked for me."

"What is this place anyway? The name sounds like a funeral parlour."

"Seldon says it's a ritzy retirement residence for people who have enough money to afford it."

They stepped toward the entrance, and the door on the right, which was easily wide enough for a golf cart, swung open.

They stepped into a large foyer with a black and taupe marble floor and lofty taupe walls, hung with lively abstract paintings of flowers and landscapes, each with an individual spotlight.

On their left were several closed doors. On the right was a large desk with an attractive young receptionist and a burly security guard in a form-fitting black and gold uniform, looking like a doorkeeper at a ritzy hotel.

Beyond the desk were six elevators, and beside them stood a young police officer. She came forward. "Excuse me, but I'm afraid—"

"Police." Manziuk flashed his badge. The young officer nervously pointed to the elevators. "Ident is already up there, sir. And the coroner went up a few minutes ago."

"Has the building been secured?"

"Yes, sir. We're not letting anyone go to or leave the twentieth floor, and we're taking names of anyone who goes to or from the other floors."

"Are the responding officers still up there?"

"Yes, sir."

"Thanks."

Manziuk walked to the reception desk. "Can you tell me something about the building? How many floors? What is on each floor?"

The receptionist, who'd been sitting with her hands clasped together, looked around nervously for a moment before finding her voice. "Okay. Just give me a second. Today has been difficult." She unclasped her hands and began to speak. Her voice took on a mechanical quality, as if she'd flicked a switch. "Serenity Suites is five years old. There are twenty floors above ground, and five below. This floor and the next one down have businesses, and are larger than the rest of the floors. The roof above the extended area has a large green space with a roof garden and terrace.

"So, on this floor there's a pharmacy with a post office, a card shop, a flower shop, a small grocery store, a hair stylist, several cafés, a coffee shop, gift boutiques, and a twenty-four-hour convenience store. Oh, and a medical clinic. The lower level has a food court, a bakery, several women's and men's clothing stores, a couple of shoe stores, and a number of offices, including a lab, a dental office, a chiropractor, and an optometrist. Below that are four levels of parking. The floor above this one has indoor and outdoor pools, a gymnasium, and other amenities. The other floors are all residential."

Manziuk thanked her, and the woman visibly relaxed. To Ryan he said, "Let's go up."

In the elevator, Manziuk didn't look at his partner as he said, "Let me do the talking for now." Ryan didn't speak, but Manziuk was quite sure she'd rolled her eyes.

Another police officer was standing next to the elevator on the twentieth floor. After checking their badges, he pointed to a doorway down the hall. "They're all in the common room, sir."

This room turned out to be a large cheery place with aqua walls, white crown moulding, rich hardwood flooring, and the most up-to-date ambient lighting. One wall consisted of floor-to-ceiling shelves filled with books, magazines, and DVDs. A second wall was centred by a stone fireplace with a flat-screen television above it. The third featured a well-stocked self-serve bar. A few large scenic paintings enhanced the remaining walls.

Around the room were several cozy groupings of comfortable-looking taupe or brown chairs of various types and sizes. Each had an adjacent side table. There were also four small tables with chairs, presumably for those who wanted to play games. One table held a partially-completed jigsaw puzzle.

Several police officers were standing just inside the doorway along with a worried-looking woman wearing a short pink floral smock with blue jeans.

Dr. Weaver, the coroner, was easy to spot in the middle of the room, his messy red head bent over a heavy-set woman slumped in one of the chairs. He looked up and smiled. "Ah, good to see you. I'm told no one has moved anything."

Manziuk stopped a few feet away. "Is the cause of death apparent?"

Dr. Weaver nodded. "A rather nasty one. And quite unexpected. Of course that's only my opinion."

Manziuk moved closer. "What is it?"

"She was stabbed in the neck, and bled to death."

"Nasty is right."

"There's a knife on the floor next to the chair."

"Did it fall, or could it have been left there on purpose?"

"My guess is that it fell, although I suppose it could have been dropped."

"Is the wound deep?"

"Not terribly. And the knife is rather long, and wasn't in very deep, which is why I think it might have fallen. They're finished with the pictures if you want me to pick it up."

"Let me have a look first."

Dr. Weaver moved out of the way so Manziuk could take his place and observe the body from all angles. The wound was a red slit that gaped slightly. Blood had flowed from it like a small rivulet, darkening the right shoulder and sleeve of the rust-coloured sweater and the arm of the chair, from where it had dripped to the floor. A black-handled knife lay in the blood on the floor.

Manziuk got out his notebook and took a tape measure from his pocket. Ryan helped him take some measurements. During their first case, they'd had a somewhat heated discussion about the fact that, given modern cameras and videos, his sketching and measuring was really no longer necessary. He'd told her to do what she wanted, but this was what he was accustomed to, and since it had helped him notice things he might not have otherwise, he'd keep doing it for now.

He made a quick sketch of the room and the body, while his partner stood a little behind him quietly sharing her observations with her digital recorder.

When they were finished, Manziuk stepped back and nodded to Dr. Weaver. "Go ahead."

Dr. Weaver carefully picked up the knife with latex-covered hands and held it up to the light so all three of them could see it.

It was a little less than a foot long. The handle, encased in black leather with a row of eight diamond-like cut-outs, was about an inch wide. Below the handle, a circular black guard extended out about half an inch. The slightly curved blade was a little more than half the total length. Its cutting edge looked thin and sharp and ended in a point. The other edge was thicker and flat, maybe an eighth of an inch in width. The sides of the blade were smooth and shiny. One side had a design like a long arrow and some other markings.

"That's different," Manziuk said.

Special Constable Irving Ford, head of the Forensic Identification Team, had come over. He shook his head. "Never seen anything quite like it."

"It reminds me of a ceremonial dagger," Dr. Weaver said. "The kind you see in movies."

Ford nodded. "Yeah. Indiana Jones or something."

Ford himself looked as if he could have stepped out of an Indiana Jones movie in which he'd been cast as one of the heavies. He was a couple of inches short of six feet, but his barrel chest, deep voice, and brusque mannerisms, combined with the long scar that ran across his left cheek, masked his true nature, which those who had worked with him compared to either that of a pussycat or a teddy bear.

"That writing or whatever it is—could it be Asian?" Ryan asked.

"Could be," Ford answered. "We'll get on it right away." He took the knife and carried it to the Ident team photographer for further pictures before it would be sent to headquarters for processing and hopefully identification.

Meanwhile, Dr. Weaver called for help, and Ingrid's body was carefully picked up and laid down on a body bag, where Weaver made a more thorough examination. "I don't see anything else. Just the one wound."

Manziuk put on gloves and took a quick look, but there seemed to be nothing more to see. Ryan observed without touching, then nodded to Dr. Weaver to zip up the bag.

Manziuk looked around and raised his voice. "Who was first on the scene?"

A young woman stepped forward. "Me, sir. Constable Sasha Brown. I was a few blocks from here doing interviews with respect to a pedestrian–bicycle accident that happened yesterday. When I got the call, I hurried straight here. I asked the security guard at the main entrance to keep everyone inside the building until we had more people here, and to make sure all security cameras were working and that no recent recordings would be erased. I then came up here and looked for a pulse, but it was obvious the woman was dead. The nurse assured me she was clearly dead when she was found. I then asked the nurse to gather everyone on this floor into one room and keep them together. She chose to use the dining room, and I asked two officers to guard them. We had everyone turn off their cellphones and other electronic devices to make sure no one leaked information."

Manziuk smiled at her. "Good work!"

Brown motioned to the woman in the pink floral smock. "Sir, this is Audra Limson. She's an RN and the manager of this floor."

Manziuk introduced himself and Ryan. "We're with the Homicide Squad, and we'll be in charge of this case."

"I understand. I've sent for our staff doctor and for the administrator of Serenity Suites. They can answer more questions than I can."

Manziuk nodded.

Audra continued. "I don't want to be a bother, but this is a retirement home, and we have a number of elderly people here. They're all in the dining room along with any staff who were on the floor. I wonder if perhaps you could speak with them and let them know what to expect."

"Yes, of course. How many residents do you have?"

"We have fourteen now, but four of them have been on a cruise since the beginning of August. So only ten are here."

"So eleven residents including the deceased?"

"Yes."

"And how many staff?"

"Four live-in staff, including myself. And there are also daily staff. Two of them were here today."

"They're still here?"

"Everyone who was on this floor when Constable Brown arrived is still here."

"I'll need a list of both residents and staff. Plus I want the names of anyone else who came up to this floor today for any reason or any amount of time. Can you get that for me?"

"It might take a few minutes."

"Please make it a priority. We'll also need access to every room on this floor and two rooms we can use: a small room for interviewing people and a larger area for a situation room—a sort of home base while we're investigating."

"I have a master key I can give you. As for rooms, there's a small office just across the hallway from the dining room that might work.

For the larger room, there's a private dining room that's used for meetings and small groups. I can show you both of them, and you can decide if they'll be good enough."

From outside the room, a male voice said loudly, "You can't go in there!"

"Try and stop me, buster," said a woman's voice. "I'm the administrator of this building."

"That's Ms. Arlington," Audra said quickly. "I sent for her."

Manziuk motioned to Brown, and a moment later Naomi Arlington walked into the room and stopped in front of Audra. "What's the meaning of this? Why are there policemen everywhere?"

"There's been a death, Naomi."

Naomi's voice rose. "A death?" She looked around. "Where's Dr. Granger? I told you—"

"I paged him at the same time I paged you, but he isn't here yet."

"I was in a meeting. I can't just drop everything whenever you can't handle things. Now what's going on?"

"Naomi, this is Inspector Manziuk. Inspector, Ms. Arlington is the administrator of Serenity Suites. I paged her after I called 911."

Ignoring Manziuk, Naomi shouted, "You called 911 again? I told you the last time, we have people to take care of everything! If you think we're going to keep you on when—"

"Ms. Arlington," Manziuk said, "Ms. Limson had a suspicious death, so she called for the police. She did exactly as she should have."

Naomi turned to look at him. "Suspicious? What do you mean, suspicious?"

"Naomi," Audra said, "Mrs. Davidson is dead."

Naomi's eyes bulged. "Ingrid Davidson? But that's not possible. She was perfectly fine earlier today. I saw her myself."

Audra shrugged. "Then you agree that her death is suspicious." She motioned to Manziuk. "Ms. Arlington, Inspector Manziuk is a homicide detective. As is Sergeant Ryan."

Naomi stared at Manziuk, then at Ryan, and then at the people in navy blue clothing who were gathered around Ingrid's chair. Her attention wavered as she caught a glimpse of the body bag. She ran forward. "What are you doing? You can't take—!" Catching sight of the blood on the back of Ingrid's chair, she faltered and stopped.

Ryan grabbed her by the arm and held her.

Naomi tried to push her away. "Let go of me!"

"You can't go over there."

Still trying to break free, Naomi gritted her teeth and yelled, "I can do anything I want to. I'm the boss here!"

Manziuk moved in front of her. "Ms. Arlington, for the time being I'm afraid you're going to have to do exactly as we say."

She stopped struggling, and Ryan let go of her shoulders. Naomi pulled out a cellphone and began looking for a number.

"What are you doing?" Ryan asked.

"I'm calling the mayor. She—"

"She'll tell you to do exactly what we say," Manziuk said. "But if you want to bother her while she's in the middle of a special budget meeting, feel free. Or you can calm down and let me explain why we're here and what we're going to be doing over the next day or so."

Naomi bit her lip, put the phone away, and moved away from Ryan. She glared at Manziuk. "You have five minutes to explain."

"Ms. Limson was about to show us a room we can use to interview people. Why don't we go there?"

Naomi turned to Audra. "Where's Ben?"

"In the dining room with everyone else."

"I'll go and give him my condolences and then I'll come." Her eyes narrowed. "You aren't putting them in Frank's office, are you?"

"No, I'm giving them the other one."

She began to walk away, stopped, and looked back. "How did she die?"

"We don't have a definite cause of death yet," Manziuk said, "but she was stabbed."

Naomi's eyes grew wide. She almost said something, but bit her lip. "I'll be a few minutes." She walked off, her head held high.

Manziuk gestured to Ryan, who shrugged and followed Naomi out of the room.

Manziuk followed Audra down a hallway with several doorways on the left-hand side and two on the right to the second last door on the left, which was unlocked.

"The dining room is directly across from here," she said before going in.

"How soundproof is this room?"

"Very. One just like it is used as a recording studio."

"Good."

The office had a black wooden desk with a computer, telephone, and writing surface, a matching credenza against the wall with a printer on it, a black leather manager's chair behind the desk, and a taupe wing chair in the corner of the room near the door. A reading lamp attached to a small table stood next to it.

"We can bring in anything you might need."

"Just another chair. One sturdy enough for me. What rooms are next door to this?"

"The men's rest room is to the right. It rarely gets used. Most of the residents prefer to go back to their own condos. And there's another office on the left. It's virtually identical to this one. One of our residents is an author, and he uses it most days from just after breakfast until dinner time."

"This author is in the dining room now?"

"Yes. But honestly, even if he was in the room, he wouldn't be able to hear you."

"All right. Now, you mentioned another room that was a bit larger?"

"Yes."

"And you said you had a master key for all the rooms on this floor. Let's see that room, and I'd like to have that key for Special Constable Ford so he can get a search underway."

"Of course."

A few minutes later, they were back with the extra chair.

"Would you like some coffee, tea, or a cold drink?"

"If it's made, coffee, please. Black. And Detective Constable Ryan will have water, with lemon if you have it."

"Is there anything else you need from me?"

At that moment Naomi walked into the room. Ryan slipped in behind her. Naomi looked at Audra. "Go back and look after the residents until I get through here. And try not to lose any more of them."

Audra looked at Manziuk. "Is it all right for me to go to the dining room, Inspector?"

"Yes. I'll come in a few minutes."

Ryan followed Audra out.

Naomi turned to Manziuk. "Ben Davidson, Ingrid's husband, wants to talk with you."

"All right. After I've spoken to you and told everyone what to expect."

Manziuk motioned Naomi to the wing chair at the right of the desk and sat across from her on the chair Audra had found.

Ryan came back and took the chair behind the desk. She opened her laptop.

Naomi sat on the edge of the chair as if counting the seconds.

Seven

Manziuk willed his voice to be pleasant, quelling his temptation to tell the annoying woman exactly what he thought of her. *Do what Pazernak said. Get rid of the stress by taking a deep breath.* At that moment, he realized that the receptionist downstairs had done exactly the same thing before answering him. He wondered if she was a patient of Pazernak's, too. He brought his hand up to his mouth as he stifled a grin.

As he inhaled, a second thought flashed into his mind. *Naomi Arlington makes Ryan look like a complacent young woman.* He had to work harder to restrain himself from smiling.

"Ms. Arlington, Mrs. Davidson's body was discovered with what appears to be a knife wound in her neck. Ms. Limson did exactly what I hope you would have done had you been in her position. Her behaviour has been exemplary, and as her boss you should be very pleased. You've trained her well."

Naomi said nothing.

"Now, I have a few things I'd prefer to discuss with you before I speak to the others."

Naomi crossed her arms. "Such as?"

"We need to know more about this place and what goes on here in general, and we also need to understand who the victim was. I assume you're the best person to give me that information?"

Naomi took her time settling further into the chair and crossing her knees. "Certainly. Serenity Suites is a retirement residence for people who are still in good health but no longer want the responsibility of a large home and staff, and who prefer to be with like-minded companions. On this particular floor, everyone is associated in some way with the creative arts. We have an author, a children's singer, an actor, a painter, and so forth. All of them are in their seventies or early eighties."

"The victim's first name is Ingrid?"

"Yes. Ingrid Davidson."

"Had she been here long?"

"She and her husband, Ben, have been here since it opened five years ago."

"How old was she?"

"Ingrid was eighty-one, a year older than Ben."

"What part of the arts was Ingrid in?"

"She wasn't. Ingrid was a homemaker. Ben was a talk-show host."

Manziuk rolled the name around in his mind. *Ben Davidson. Of course!* "He had a national radio program until a few years ago?"

"So I understand."

"I listened to him whenever I had the chance."

"He retired at seventy-five, and they moved in here."

There was a soft rap on the door. Manziuk called, "Come in," and Olive entered with their drinks and a plate of cookies.

As soon as she was gone, Ryan asked, "Have the other residents been here since the beginning, too?"

Naomi shook her head. "Some, but not all of them. Kenneth Harper has only been here a little over a month. The previous owner of his condo moved to Vancouver. Hilary Brooks has been here the next shortest time. She and her husband moved in almost a year ago, but Grant died from a massive heart attack in May. She'll be leaving soon."

Ryan made a note. "Do the residents get along?"

She smiled. "Of course they do! That's the whole idea behind Serenity Suites. You live in a home that's been designed specifically for your needs, among people you know or have similar interests to, rather than stuck in a place that barely suits you, having to put up with strangers you have nothing in common with. And if you think one of our residents would deliberately stick a knife into another one, you're being ridiculous."

"What about the staff?" Manziuk asked.

"We do our very best to hire good people, of course. The residents would complain otherwise. And we've had no complaints."

"Thank you. Is there anything else we should know?"

Naomi stood up. "Just that I *refuse* to believe this is a murder. That's what you're saying, isn't it? Well, I don't for one second believe it, and I deplore the way it's being handled. I want you and all the rest of the police out of this building as quickly as possible."

"We'll keep that in mind." Manziuk stood up. "Now, perhaps you can take us to the dining room and introduce us so we can start interviewing the other people?"

Naomi motioned toward Ryan with her head. "*She* knows the way. And Audra can introduce you. I'm late for a meeting." She walked briskly out of the office.

"What a sweetheart!" Ryan said when she'd returned from walking Naomi to the elevator and watching until it stopped at the first floor.

Manziuk nodded. "I expect the idea of a murder here isn't going to sit well with her bosses, whoever they might be. A big black eye for Serenity Suites."

"Does seem a weird place for a murder like this. Smothering, sleeping pills, substituting medicine I could see. Even pushing someone down the stairs and trying to make it look like an accident. But stabbing an old woman in a room everyone uses seems a bit of a stretch."

"And yet it happened." He stood up. "I guess we shouldn't keep them waiting any longer. Let's see who we've got."

Ryan led the way to a door across the hallway, which was guarded by a female police officer Manziuk guessed was in her fifties. "This is Constable Singh."

"Good afternoon, Inspector," she said. "It's good you're here. Everyone is anxious to know what's happening."

Manziuk nodded toward a male officer standing guard at a set of swinging doors to the right, which he assumed led to the kitchen.

"Constable Miller and I have been making sure no one leaves unaccompanied," Singh said.

"Any difficulties?"

"Nothing to worry about."

"Good."

Manziuk glanced around the room. His first impression was of a pleasant room, comfortable yet elegant. The four round tables were covered in snowy linen, crystal, and fine china. The people who sat at them were, for the most part, elderly, Caucasian, well-dressed, well-behaved, and unsmiling. Only one of the elderly people was dark-skinned. One man and two women looked younger than the rest. Only one person, an elderly man seated at the table in the far left corner, hadn't turned to look at them.

Chairs had been placed against the far wall for the staff. They were dressed in an assortment of scrubs and jeans, and one chef's uniform. All of them were darker-skinned, ranging from warm gold to black. They were watching Manziuk and Ryan with sad faces.

Audra had been sitting next to the kitchen door. She jumped up, hurried over to them, and spoke softly. "Please be gentle with them. They might bluster a bit, some of them, but they're only worried. None of us can imagine anyone here doing something like this. There has to be another explanation."

Manziuk said, "I understand. We certainly aren't here to add to their stress. But we do have a job to do."

Audra nodded, then turned toward the tables and raised her voice. "These are the detectives from Homicide. Inspector Manziuk and Constable Ryan. They'll be looking into Mrs. Davidson's death. I'm sure they'll be very thorough but also respect our loss and be as non-invasive as possible."

A man at the far end of the table directly to the left spoke in a clear, resonant voice. "Manziuk? Good." He stood and came forward. "I'm glad they were able to send you, Inspector. I'm Ben Davidson. It's my wi—" His voice broke, and a sob escaped, but he quickly regained control. "It's my wife's death you're investigating."

Manziuk moved forward, and the two men shook hands. "Thank you, Mr. Davidson. We'll do our best."

Ben nodded in acknowledgement and went back to his chair.

Manziuk raised his voice slightly. "Thank you all for staying here. We appreciate it. We'll ask you to remain a little longer. Constable Ryan and I will interview each of you as quickly as possible. At the same time, some of our team will be doing a quick search of this floor to make sure no one is hiding here and to look for anything that might be helpful to our investigation. Let me assure you that anything we find, or anything you tell us, will be kept confidential unless we discover a connection with this crime."

There was a murmuring in the room, but no one protested.

"One thing I have to ask. After we've gone, please don't go on social media and post details about what's happened today. In particular, don't give names of people involved or show pictures of the people or the rooms. We have to notify all next of kin, and we also need to keep as much as we can confidential."

There were quite a few nods of understanding and a couple of quick smiles.

One of the older men put his hand up. "Do you know whose knife it was?"

Apparently feeling it was time she made her presence felt, Ryan answered quickly. "I'm afraid we can't give you any details just now. The first thing we do is gather every bit of information we can. Later we'll put it all together to try to determine exactly what happened here today."

Manziuk threw her a look which he hoped she'd interpret as "Don't say any more." Her eyes flashed, but she stopped talking.

"We'll start by interviewing each of you, one at a time, residents first and then staff, in the room across the hall. Ms. Limson will decide the order in which you come. Please answer our questions as briefly but as honestly as you're able. We'll be recording all the interviews so that we can refer to them later."

An older woman with burgundy hair and a bright red blouse raised her hand.

Ryan said, "Yes, do you have a question?"

"Officer, you must understand that none of us came here prepared to stay for the afternoon. Is it not possible for us to go to our rooms for a moment, just to get something? The air conditioning makes this room too cold for me, and I need a shawl."

"Ma'am, if it's something that can't wait, one of the officers will go with you. That's the case if you need to use the restroom, too."

One of the women Manziuk had thought looked too young to be a resident spoke in a clear drawl. "I'm teaching a class tonight. I appreciate your routine, but I need to be there. My students will be waiting. So can we get these interviews over quickly, please?"

Ryan said, "Please talk to Ms. Limson, and she can put you near the beginning of our list. Any other concerns?" Ryan looked them over. No one spoke.

"All right," Manziuk said. "I just need to talk to Ms. Limson for a few minutes, and then we'll begin with Mr. Davidson."

As Ryan and Audra followed him out, Manziuk had a quick word with the two police officers. Singh stayed inside the dining room. Miller, a young man with white-blond hair and a rugged look, followed them out and waited just outside the dining room, where he could watch both the dining room door and the door to the office.

Once they were inside the office and Ryan had turned on the recorder, Manziuk said, "Ms. Limson, I'm not quite clear as to your role here. Didn't I hear that you're a registered nurse? Yet my understanding is that this place isn't really set up to be the kind of facility that offers round-the-clock nursing. Have I misunderstood?"

"No, you're correct. My role is that of floor manager and team leader, but because I'm a nurse, I'm also able to give medications that people have trouble with or do other things that the doctor might want done—like changing a bandage or giving a bath. Even giving an IV on occasion."

"So are you on call at all hours?"

"Pretty well. But I do get days off, and if I'm not here, Derrick is. Derrick is a registered nurse and also has a master's degree in physical therapy, so he can do everything I can, and more. They actually like hiring people who can fill more than one role. And if Derrick or I need help, there are nurses on the other floors. We cover for each other."

Ryan asked, "Do you have any suspicions as to who might have done this? Did any of the other residents or staff dislike the victim?"

Audra thought for a moment. "Ingrid was getting more and more difficult, and we were beginning to feel she might need more care that we could give her here. We're not set up to be a nursing home. But she wasn't really a bother. Most of the time, at least lately, she just seemed to be off in her own world. Now and then she'd say something that was really odd and occasionally she was a bit rude, but I don't see how that would make anyone want to murder her.

Most of us just felt bad for her. And everybody likes Ben. The only thing that makes any sense to me is that someone assumed he was helping Ben by taking away the problem of Ingrid's needing more care. Someone who knew how distraught Ben was at the idea of putting her in a nursing home."

Ryan nodded. "That makes sense. Which of the people might have thought that way?"

Audra frowned. "No one, really. I mean, it makes sense in a general way. But while we were in the dining room, I looked at each person in the room, and I tried to picture them doing it, but I couldn't." She looked at the floor and took a deep breath before speaking again. "In case it's relevant in any way, Ingrid was diabetic, and I gave her insulin shots because she wasn't able to do it herself, and Ben just couldn't. He's unbelievably squeamish. There's no way on earth that Ben could have stabbed her."

"Ms. Limson," Manziuk said, "are there any other staff members who might have been on the floor earlier today?"

She bit her lip. "Derrick, of course. He went out at two. As to who else might have come up, we have cleaning and maintenance people who look after the entire building, but I don't believe any of them were up here today except for Jared Wright, who was up briefly. He's the building maintenance supervisor. Lyle had complained about a tap that wasn't working properly, and I believe Jared installed a new one. There are also a few people who deliver the mail and do light shopping and other errands for anyone in the building, and one of them was up twice this morning with the newspapers and then today's mail. But that was before lunch."

"Anyone else?" Manziuk asked.

"One of the doctors might have been up. Six doctors have offices on the main floor. Dr. Granger, the Davidsons' doctor, is one of them. One of the doctors occasionally comes up to see a patient. I didn't see any of them today, though. Ms. Arlington also occasionally pops up to see someone. I didn't see her today, either."

"All right, we'll check. What about family or other visitors?"

"I'm not aware of any visitors today. Well, except Frank's daughter. Frank's wife died two weeks ago, and his daughter came to help with the funeral and ended up staying to go through her mother's things and make sure Frank is okay."

"Frank's last name is?"

"Klassen. Violet was his wife's name, and Trish Klassen-Wallace is the daughter."

"Let me get this straight. Frank Klassen's wife, Violet, died here recently?"

"Yes. It was actually two weeks ago today."

"She died of natural causes?"

"Yes."

"Who was her doctor?"

"Dr. Granger."

"All right. If you think of anything else that might help us, please let us know."

She got up slowly. "Are you ready for Ben now?"

"Yes."

Hearing Ben's Davidson's voice briefly in the dining room a few minutes before had taken Manziuk back to the many times he'd listened to that voice on the radio—a habit he'd caught from his parents, who never missed a show. The voice was still deep, rich, and melodic. He'd never met Ben in person, but over the years he'd seen a number of cartoonists' caricatures of him, virtually all of which pictured him as an owl with glasses perched on large ears. It was hard to put that image out of his mind.

As Ryan settled the older man in the wing chair, Manziuk quickly studied him. He was thin, with tanned, healthy-looking skin. His hair was mostly grey, with a sprinkling of brown. It was balding in the front, creating a high forehead. The combination of that with his rather rounded face, eyes that looked as if they missed nothing, and the brown glasses perched on his rather prominent ears did indeed give him an owlish look.

Ryan took her own seat behind the desk.

Manziuk leaned forward. "I'm very sorry for your loss, Mr. Davidson."

"Thank you. This all seems like a dream. And not a nice dream."

"I understand. And we hate to bother you, but we need to gather as much information as we can before people begin to forget.

I should probably mention that I'm a big fan of yours. I listened to *Ben's Room* whenever I could and really enjoyed it. And my parents never missed it."

"Thank you. I enjoyed every minute of it. It was a privilege to get paid good money to enjoy myself for so many years." After a moment, Ben added, "Just so you know, I asked for you."

"Yes?"

"I've known your boss, Cliff Seldon, for years." He smiled. "Let's be honest. I know everyone: the mayor, the police commissioner— You name the position, I know the person who used to be in it and the one in it now. So I called Cliff and asked him who his best detective is, and he said you. So I asked for you to be put on this case." His smile took in both of them. "Not sure if you consider that a good thing or not, but there it is."

Manziuk smiled.

"So tell me. Is it true? Did someone actually kill my poor old girl?"

"We haven't yet determined the exact cause of death, but there was good reason for us to believe that her death wasn't natural."

Ben leaned forward. "I prefer plain talk. Before the police came and made us stop talking, Norm and Mary told me she'd been stabbed."

"That's right."

"With what?"

"A knife."

"What kind of knife? One from the kitchen?"

"We haven't identified it yet. It didn't appear to be a typical kitchen knife. As soon as it's been checked for fingerprints, we'll show it to a few people and see if they recognize it."

"How many times was she stabbed?"

"As far as I know, only once."

"Where?"

"In the neck."

Ben stiffened. "Whoever heard of stabbing somebody in the neck?"

"It certainly isn't what we'd expect, but a neck wound can kill."

"Could it have been an accident, or do you think the person who stabbed her knew what he was doing?"

"I'm afraid my best guess is that it was intentional." Manziuk shrugged. "Of course there's always the chance it was an accident. But in that case I'd expect someone to acknowledge it. Call for help. Plus I can't think of any reason someone would be wandering around that room with a knife."

Ben nodded. "Nor I, I'm afraid."

"Mr. Davidson," Ryan said, "can you think of anyone who disliked your wife? Someone she had disagreements with?"

Ben turned his head to look at her. "I can't imagine anyone disliking my wife enough to kill her."

"Who benefits from her death?"

Ben looked startled. Then he shut his eyes. "I guess you need to ask these things. No one, really. Everything we own is in both of our names. And when I go our kids will get it all. We have five kids, and they'll share equally." He smiled. "I call them kids, but of course they're well past middle age. And don't go suspecting any of them. They're good people, with wonderful families. Ingrid was an amazing mother and homemaker, and she raised them right. They all adored her. It's only in the past year or so—since she had a small stroke—that she hasn't been herself."

Manziuk asked, "What do you mean by that?"

Ben settled himself in the chair and crossed his ankles. "Lately she'd been forgetting things she'd normally know, and she'd gone from being a generally cheerful person to being vague, short-tempered, and depressed. She didn't seem to want to talk to anyone, which was very unlike her. And her short-term memory wasn't good. Dr. Granger was going to do some tests on Friday to see if she might have Alzheimer's or dementia."

"Was she aware of the upcoming tests?"

"No, Dr. Granger was just going to show up and tell her he was doing a routine check-up. So as not to alarm her."

"You said she was short-tempered," Ryan said. "Did she have words with anyone recently?"

Ben smiled ruefully. "Mostly me. But nothing that would make me want to be rid of her."

"So you have no idea who might have done this?"

"None whatsoever."

Manziuk spoke up. "When did you see your wife last?"

"Right after lunch today, we went back to our condo. She puttered around a bit, and then she got out the bag she keeps her crocheting materials in and left. She liked to sit in the common room and crochet. I think she still liked being around people, even if she didn't want to interact with them."

"What time would she have gone, do you think?"

Ben looked toward the ceiling as if expecting the answer to be written there. "Well, we normally finish lunch at about 1:00, so maybe half an hour later." He smiled at Manziuk. "That's just a guess. I never looked at a clock."

"That's fine. It gives us something to go on. So, when she left, you stayed in your condo?"

Ben smiled. "Full disclosure, I guess. I tend to watch far more television than I should. Mostly the talk shows. I was watching TV in the sitting room of our condo when Audra came and got me."

Manziuk smiled back. "That makes sense. Sort of job-related."

Ben cocked his head a little to one side. "After all those years of doing *Ben's Room*, I was at a bit of a loss as to what to do with my time, which led to too much television watching. Ingrid was never much for TV, but she used to watch some shows with me. However, the last few months she no longer seemed interested. Or, I hate to say it but maybe she couldn't follow them. That might be one reason she went to the common room. She never said anything, but it's possible that my having the TV on bothered her."

"All right. Thanks. Is there anything else you can think of that might help us?"

"No, nothing. I realize what's happened, but I feel as if you're on a TV screen instead of here with me, and you're telling me that you're here in the room with me, but I can't quite take it in."

Ryan spoke up. "I assume your family has been informed?"

Ben turned toward her. "Yes, I called my oldest son. He was going to tell the others and then come over here to get me and take me back to his house, if you have no objections."

"None," Manziuk said. "Just leave us his address. We'll make sure the officer in the lobby sends him up when he arrives."

"Thank you."

"No members of your family were here earlier today, were they?" Ryan asked.

Ben chuckled. "I feel I ought to resent that question, but I'll answer it anyway. No one in my family has been here for over a week. And none of them would ever consider doing something like this, not for one second. They all loved their mother. You can take my word for that."

"All right," Manziuk said. "Thank you." He shot a look at Ryan. "I'm afraid we tend to suspect everybody, no matter who they are, until proven otherwise. It makes things easier for us in the long run."

"Yes, I see that. No prejudices."

Manziuk stood up. "I'm afraid I can't let you go into your condo just yet. But if you'll go back to the dining room, you can leave with your son as soon as he arrives."

"I have no problem waiting with the others, thank you. I'd just as soon be with them as be alone." Ben got to his feet and started toward the door. He turned back to Manziuk. "I suppose if she did have dementia or Alzheimer's, maybe this was a blessing in some way. But for someone to take her life in that way—it's incomprehensible to me. I just cannot understand why anyone would do it."

"Neither can I, Mr. Davidson, but we'll do our best to find out."

"You'll keep me informed?"

"We will. Otherwise I'm afraid you'll tell my boss, and he'll demote me."

Ben smiled. "He said I'd like you. He was right." He took a step toward Manziuk and held out his hand. Manziuk shook it. He then went past Manziuk and held his hand out toward Ryan. As she stood to shake it, he winked at her and said, "Don't let him intimidate you. You hold your ground."

Before she could respond, he was gone, walking tall into the hallway under the watchful eyes of Miller.

Manziuk had been waiting for a chance to tell Ryan to wait until he gave her the okay to ask questions, but after Ben's words, he found himself tongue-tied.

Audra appeared in the doorway, followed by Miller. "Inspector, here's the list you requested. Names and contact information for all of our residents, live-in staff, and day staff. And a map of this floor with the residents' rooms marked."

"Thank you very much. I take it you know that Mr. Davidson's son is coming here today?"

"Yes, I know. Can he come up?"

"Yes. And he can take his dad out. But no one can go inside their condo. Which reminds me, how do we reach the main desk downstairs?"

"Press 0 on the phone on your desk."

"Thank you. Would you send in the lady who teaches next, and then the others in the order you think makes the most sense?"

"Elizabeth Carlysle? Yes, I can do that."

But before Audra could leave, there was a noise in the hallway, and a well-dressed man pushed past Audra into the office. "Are you Manziuk?"

Right behind him was a police officer they hadn't seen before. The police officer said, "I'm sorry, sir. I wasn't sure what to do. I didn't want to interrupt you, but he's the victim's doctor, and he said he can't wait."

Audra said, "Inspector, this is Dr. Granger. I paged him earlier."

Manziuk observed Dr. Granger, a man in his mid-forties, with blond hair that looked dishevelled but had likely been cut, brushed, and gelled by a high-end stylist. He was clearly upset.

"I want to know what's going on. I can't believe what I've been told about Ingrid Davidson."

"Why don't you sit down where we can talk? Ms. Limson, please tell Mrs. Carlysle we won't be long."

"Is it true?" Dr. Granger asked the moment the door was shut.

Manziuk shot a quick look at Ryan before answering, hoping she'd get his silent "do not interrupt" message. Then he gave all his attention to the doctor. "I'm not sure what you've been told, but Mrs. Davidson is dead, and she had a wound in her neck. There'll be an autopsy, but we're assuming that a knife we found nearby was the cause of her death."

"My lord!" Dr. Granger collapsed into the nearest chair, which happened to be the one Manziuk had been using. "She bled to death?"

"Yes."

He took a deep breath. "You'll have to forgive me. I realize this sort of thing must be common for you, but it doesn't happen here."

Manziuk sat down on the edge of the wing chair. "Dr. Granger, I need to know if you were on this floor earlier today?"

"Yes, I was, but I didn't see Ingrid. I spent about twenty minutes with Kenneth Harper and then I left."

"Do you know what time that would have been?"

The doctor took a cellphone from his pocket and checked it. "I came up at a 1:45 and left at 2:05. I had another appointment on the fourth floor at 2:15." He held out the phone. "You can see for yourself if you want."

"That's okay. Did you see anyone other than Mr. Harper while you were here?"

"No." He frowned. "Wait, I take that back. On my way to Kenneth's condo I saw Mrs. Rossi's husband. He was at the other end of the hallway near their condo. On my way out I saw no one. Not that I was looking around at all. I was in a hurry."

"Do you always make house calls?"

"No. We have offices on the main floor. Most of the time people come to us. But a patient on the fourth floor has pneumonia, and I preferred to go to her room rather than endanger her by making her get out of bed and come down. Mr. Harper contacted me this morning, and I didn't really have an appointment slot available, so I cut short my lunch and popped in here on my way to the fourth floor."

Manziuk looked at the map Audra had given him. "I see that his condo is very close to the elevator, so you were only in the hallway a short time."

"Yes. And I was in a hurry both coming and going. I only noticed Mr.—er, Catarina's husband— because he was whistling."

Manziuk shuffled the papers. "Mr. Davidson told us you thought his wife might have dementia or Alzheimer's."

Dr. Granger sat up straighter. "Those were two of the possibilities. There were others. That's why we perform tests."

"What sort of tests?"

"I wanted to find out how aware she was of her surroundings and how good her short-term memory was. But we were also doing blood tests to make sure there were no vitamin deficiencies or thyroid or anemia issues. And I was going to make sure she wasn't taking over-the-counter medicines that might be interfering with the medications I'd given her. I planned to do a pain test, too. I've seen pain affect people in ways you'd never expect."

"Without having done the tests, what would your gut instinct say was the problem?"

Dr. Granger made a face. "I try never to go by intuition because it's very easy to make mistakes that way. But if you're asking me what the odds were, then I'd have to say it was likely multi-infarct dementia, which is essentially caused by tiny strokes in the brain. We'd have done an MRI and a CT scan to look for that. A lot of the symptoms I've been told about seemed to fit."

"And if she had that, could she have continued to live here?"

Dr. Granger licked his lips, then shook his head. "Not for much longer, I'm afraid. The facility wasn't designed for that level of care."

"Where would she have gone?"

"I suppose they might have rented an apartment nearby and hired round-the-clock nursing for her. Or she could have lived with one of her children. But a nursing home makes the most sense, and that's what I'd have recommended. I could have gotten her into one. Money was no problem."

"You need *money* to get into a nursing home?" Ryan sounded incredulous.

Manziuk thought Dr. Granger's face registered surprise, as if he hadn't noticed she was in the room. "Most nursing homes have subsidized beds for people who don't have the money."

"Do you get better care if you have money?"

"There might be fewer staff in subsidized homes, but I'd hope the actual care is the same." Dr. Granger looked appraisingly at Manziuk. "Are you done asking questions, Inspector? I have hospital rounds."

"Just one more. What health issues did Mrs. Davidson have?"

"She was overweight, diabetic, and had high blood pressure. She also had a hip that needed to be replaced."

"All right. Thank you for your time."

Dr. Granger leaned forward. "Now I have a question for you. Who is doing the autopsy?"

Manziuk looked up in surprise. "Dr. Weaver."

"Would you have any objection to my observing?"

"No. Any reason in particular?"

"I guess just curiosity. About the dementia. I'd like to have a look at her brain."

"You can inform Dr. Weaver that you have my okay in case he needs it."

"Thank you. I'll check with him."

Manziuk walked out with Dr. Granger and told the police officer who had brought him up that he could leave.

"What did you make of him?" Manziuk asked Ryan when he returned to the office.

"Hard to say. He seemed a bit conflicted. Blustery in the beginning, shocked, kind of sad, and then sort of clinical at the end. Wanting to go to the autopsy."

Manziuk nodded. "So are we ready for Mrs. Carlysle?"

"As soon as I finish this cookie."

Manziuk raised his eyebrows. "I thought you didn't eat sugar."

"I thought I'd try one."

"Good, huh?"

Her mouth full, she mumbled, "Very."

Manziuk looked at the tray Olive had brought earlier. He picked up a meringue and bit into it. He shut his eyes. "Oh, yeah."

While he had his mouth full, Ryan said, "Can I ask the questions this time?"

Manziuk's eyes opened wide. He looked at her for a few seconds, then took a deep breath. "How about we try something new?"

"If you're going to tell me to just act like a secretary, I'm not going to be happy."

"No, I have something else in mind. Let's move things around a bit so that we're in more of a triangle and people don't have to turn their heads to see you."

EIGHT

When she'd noticed her in the dining room, Ryan had guessed Elizabeth Carlysle's age at forty-five, fifty at most. Seeing her up close, she revised her estimate. Elizabeth's long black bangs contrasted a little too much with her ivory skin to be natural. The skin on her neck looked a bit stretched, and there were numerous tiny wrinkles around her eyes and mouth. Late fifties, even sixties, maybe, but still not old enough to fit in with the rest of the residents.

Elizabeth crossed her shapely legs in the short black skirt and dark nylons, ending in red very high heels.

Ryan smiled. *You'll never catch me wearing heels that high.* She leaned forward. "Mrs. Carlysle, we just have a few questions. What was your relationship with Mrs. Davidson?"

"Relationship?" Elizabeth rolled the word on her tongue. "I don't think we had one. To be honest, I don't think we've *ever* had one."

"What do you mean by 'ever'?"

"I don't know if you're aware, but my husband Norm, Ben Davidson, Frank Klassen, and Frank's wife Violet all knew each other since elementary school. They also went to the same university, where Ben met Ingrid. Ben married Ingrid, Frank married Violet, and Norm married a girl he met at the university. After she died, Norm met and married me. So I was never really part of their little group, and to be perfectly honest I never fit in."

"Why was that?"

Elizabeth shrugged. "Violet's life revolved around Frank and their daughter, and Ingrid's life revolved around Ben and their children. Norm and I didn't have children, and we don't live in each other's pockets. My life revolved around my career. So, although we were polite to each other, I didn't have much in common with either Violet or Ingrid. In fact I encouraged Norm to see Ben and Frank on his own time and not involve us in couples' activities."

Manziuk spoke for the first time. "How has it been living in such close quarters?"

Elizabeth flashed him a smile. "To be quite honest, it's been hell."

"I realize that appearances can be deceiving, in particular with women, but you seem, if I may say, younger than the others."

Ryan watched in awe as Elizabeth batted her eyes at Manziuk. She'd always wondered what that expression meant, and now she knew. A lot of rapid fluttering of the eyelids, and simpering.

"Well, I actually *am* younger in years." Ryan catalogued the older woman's smile as coy. She was actually flirting with Manziuk. "But the real problem is that I *feel* so much younger than the rest of them."

Ryan interrupted. "Have you thought of moving out?"

Elizabeth lost her smile as she turned toward Ryan. "Yes, but Norm loves it here, so I've been making the best of it." She looked back at Manziuk. "I still perform and teach, so I do get out."

"And what is it that you do?"

She raised her eyebrows. "Thanks for the ego boost. I sing. And I give voice lessons to advanced students."

Manziuk slapped his knee. "Of course! I knew I ought to recognize your name! My older son, Conrad, has several of your albums. He's very much into jazz."

She tipped her head in acknowledgement.

Ryan waited a second. "Getting back to Ingrid, did you see much of her here?"

Elizabeth shrugged. "At meals, of course. Other than that, not really. I might see her in the distance, but I never went out of my way to talk to her, and she more or less ignored me. Especially in the last while. To be honest, I think she was a bit gaga."

"Gaga?"

"Oh, you know, losing it. I may not have had much in common with her, but she used to be a very outgoing happy sort of person.

She made jokes, even if I didn't get most of them. I've seen none of that for a long time. Just a tired old woman."

"Do you have any idea who might have wanted to end her life?"

Elizabeth jerked. "You mean like a mercy killing? The only person who'd do that is Ben." She lowered her voice. "Violet could have done it, but she isn't here any more, is she?"

"Did you go into the common room this afternoon, or see anyone else going in?"

She shook her head. "I rarely go there. And I wouldn't have noticed anyone else. I was busy in our condo most of the day." She stopped. "No, wait a minute. I'm forgetting. I went to the recording studio for a while after lunch to practise. I was there when the call came over the intercom for everyone to go to the dining room for tea and an announcement."

"What time did you go into the studio?"

"I don't know. I was there for maybe half an hour—maybe a bit longer."

Manziuk said, "Anything else you can tell us that might help our investigation?"

She smiled at him. "I'm afraid not. But I do hope you find whoever did this. I won't be able to sleep until you do."

After Elizabeth left, Audra came into the office. "Ben's son is here, and he'd like to speak with you."

"Yes, certainly."

Bruce Davidson was taller than his father but otherwise every inch the image of what his father must have looked like thirty or so years before—right down to the brown glasses. "Thanks for seeing me. I must admit to being stunned by what I've heard. Dad said Mom was stabbed to death while sitting in her chair in the common room. Is that really true?"

Manziuk indicated the wing chair, and both men sat. "We can't be certain until we have the autopsy results, but that's how it looks."

"This is just bizarre."

"I think everyone here has a similar feeling."

"Do you have a suspect?"

"We're currently gathering evidence. But no, there's no obvious suspect at this point. Do you have any suspicions yourself?"

Bruce shook his head. "I can't imagine anyone here doing this."

"Well, if you think of anything at all, please let us know."

"I'd like to see my mother's body, and I want to get my Dad away from this. Is that acceptable?"

"Certainly. An officer will go with you if your dad needs to get anything from his condo. As for your mother, her body has been taken to the Forensic Services and Coroner's Complex. Detective Constable Ryan will give you the address. Dr. Weaver is the coroner. I can give you a note on one of my cards that should get you in."

While Manziuk was writing on his card, Ryan jumped in. "Mr. Davidson, who benefits from your mother's death?"

He looked at her in surprise. "I take it you mean financially? No one, really. Dad and Mom had their wills drawn up years ago, and most of their money was put in trust funds for their grandchildren. As for the business, Dad, Mom, and each of their children—five of us—is a partner in the family business. We all have equal shares. Mom's share will be split among those remaining. The same when Dad goes. Each grandchild will become a shareholder at the age of thirty-five. The only things Mom might have had of her own would be personal mementos that have only sentimental value."

"No one in your family is in need of the extra money from your mother's share?"

"No, I can assure you on that. We're a very close family, and if one of us had a need, they'd only have to say so."

"What about enemies, either here or outside?"

"None that I'm aware of. She was always well-liked, and she was loved by her children and grandchildren. I know she'd been going downhill recently, but I don't think she was a problem for anyone except maybe Dad, and he would never have harmed her. We'd actually been urging Dad to get her into a nursing home so he didn't have to do so much, but he told us in no uncertain terms that after all she did for him over the years, he owed it to her to look after her himself."

"What about the idea of a mercy killing?"

Bruce raised an eyebrow. "Stabbing her in the neck? I really don't think that qualifies as merciful."

Moments after Bruce had gone out, Audra stepped inside again. "Please excuse me. I don't like to bother you, but Scarlett wonders what she should do about dinner. Several of our residents have medicines they need to take with food, and they're already pretty upset without being hungry, too. Would it be possible for us to make them something light, or should we plan to bring in food?"

Manziuk sighed. "I understand. But I'd rather not have the kitchen used."

"Okay. We occasionally order food from one of the restaurants on the lower levels."

"Why don't you do that tonight? We can let the officer at the front desk know to let the delivery person bring up whatever you order."

She smiled in relief. "Certainly. Do you care when we have it?"

"No, just keep everyone together in the dining room until we've finished the interviews. If anyone needs to get medicine, make sure they're accompanied by one of the police officers."

"Thank you so much!"

Ryan stood up. "I'll come with you and let the officers know what's going on."

"Can I order for you and the other officers guarding us?"

Ryan looked hopefully at Manziuk, and he nodded.

As the two women left, Audra asked Ryan, "Do you prefer fried chicken, Chinese, Indian, Thai, or pizza?" And Manziuk thought, *This should be good; Ryan will tell her to order everyone a grilled chicken salad.*

The man entering the office would have been at least six-foot-two if he hadn't been so hunched over. His hair was grey, his cheeks ruddy, and he was getting jowls. He was forty or more pounds overweight. "I'm Norm Carlysle. I asked to be next. I was getting antsy sitting in that room staring at the others." His voice was deep and husky, perhaps a bit hoarse.

Manziuk thought he looked almost old enough to be Elizabeth's father. And while his wife had looked ready for a business luncheon in an expensive restaurant, in his faded and stained blue jeans and a Toronto Maple Leafs T-shirt that had seen far better days, Norm looked more like a homeless man.

"I completely understand. Please sit down."

"Not sure I can help you much."

"Can you tell us where you were after lunch?"

"Sure. I went straight to my studio in our condo. When I realized it was getting close to tea time, I cleaned up. Liz wasn't around, so I wandered out. I saw Mary in the common room and sat talking to her for a bit. All of a sudden Mary got a funny look on her face. I was going to ask her what was wrong, but Lyle came in just then, and she asked him to check on Ingrid, who was in a chair a little ways from us. Lyle walked over, and then he got this awful look on his face. Seemed about to be sick. He said she was dead." Norm shook his head. "Terrible thing! I've known Ingrid for years and years. And we just lost Violet not long ago. Shocking to lose both of them in such a short time."

Ryan said, "Your wife told us that you've known Ben for a long time? Ingrid, too?"

Norm sat back. "Ingrid was a year older than us. Ben met her during university, and they became an item. Got married right after he graduated."

Manziuk asked, "What did Ingrid study in university?"

"She never graduated. Took some general courses but wasn't really into that sort of thing. She worked as a waitress in a coffee shop near the university. She enjoyed that. More of a people person than a student. She was into sports, too. Played baseball and skied and other things. I think she did some acting, too, or maybe it was modelling, but I don't think she was all that serious about it."

"Was she happy with Ben? Did she ever stray?" Ryan asked.

Norm laughed. "Not Ingrid. Her family was all she cared about. And she never wanted the limelight. She was perfectly happy to let Ben have that."

"Have you noticed a difference in her since you moved in here?"

His face saddened. "Well, not in the beginning, but the last year or so, I'd have to say that's the case. I said to Liz the other day that Ingrid had completely lost her sense of humour. She used to be always laughing."

"Did she have any enemies here? Anyone who didn't like her?"

He frowned. "Not *enemies*. I expect there are a few people who didn't like her that much. Liz would be one of them. To be honest, I didn't spend any more time around Ingrid than I had to. I didn't like to say anything to Ben, but she seemed to be losing ground fast."

"You didn't say anything to Ben because you thought he hadn't realized?"

"Oh, he'd have realized all right. But if he didn't say anything, it was because he chose not to. I didn't want to say or do anything that might force his hand. And she wasn't bothering me. Not really. I didn't sit beside her for meals."

Manziuk noticed Norm's right hand shaking, a tremor, barely noticeable. Without looking down, Norm put his left hand over his right one and held it. The shaking stopped.

"After lunch today, you went to your condo?"

"Yes. There's a painting I wanted to finish by tomorrow, so I was anxious to get right back to it. Liz had to practically drag me away to get me to lunch in the first place."

"After lunch your wife went back to your condo with you?"

"Yes, I'm quite sure she did. But I went straight into my studio to paint, so I didn't notice her after that. All I know is that she wasn't there when I came out of my studio, so I went looking for her. She told me afterwards that she was in the recording studio."

"Is there anything you can think of that might help us figure out who did this to Ingrid?"

He shook his head. "I wish there was." He looked at the wall behind Ryan, as if seeing something else. "That man Ken. He's been here just about a month, and two women are dead. Maybe he's a—what is it you call them?"

"Serial killer?" suggested Ryan.

"Yes, that's it. Or that young guy Catarina had the gall to marry a few weeks ago. His moniker is Nikola, if you can believe it. No one knows anything about him." Norm seemed lost in thought for a second. Then he became animated again. "Or who knows, maybe Hilary got tired of Ingrid always giving her black looks. Although I probably shouldn't say 'black looks.' I expect that isn't PC these days." He shot a look at Ryan and made a sound that might have been a laugh. "I do try to say the right things, but habit is strong."

"Do you mean Ingrid was looking at Hilary in a nasty way?" Ryan asked.

Good girl! Manziuk had been certain she'd get sidetracked by Norm's comment; instead, she'd managed to stay focused on the interview.

"Yes, nasty is good. But she might not have meant it, you know. Might not have realized how it looked. And that's not to say Hilary might not have looked at Ingrid the same way. I don't think they got along."

"Hilary is another resident?"

"Yes, she's pretty new, too. Been here, oh, not quite a year. Nobody knows much about her, and what we do know—well, she doesn't really fit in. The people here are serious artists."

"Hilary isn't a serious artist?"

Norm shook his head. "She's only here because of her husband, Grant Brooks. But now that he's gone, she has no business being here, and the board wants her out. She'd never have gotten in here on her own." Norm's face was red, and he was trembling. "My goodness, she was an exotic dancer!"

After a short silence during which Manziuk tried to find the right words, he settled for "Anything else you can tell us?"

"I will say this place has been depressing for the last couple of weeks—well, I guess since Violet died. Liz doesn't much like it here at the best of times. I hope once we get past all this we can get back to the way it was before."

Manziuk stood. "All right, Mr. Carlysle. Thank you for your time. Do you need help getting up? These chairs are kind of low."

"Maybe just an arm."

Manziuk moved over to help him. Norm grabbed Manziuk's arm and pulled himself up. "The old joints aren't quite what they used to be." He laughed. "You don't really notice you're getting old, but it happens all the same. One day you suddenly look in the mirror and you say to yourself, 'Who on earth's that old codger looking at me?'"

Norm had barely left the room when Ryan laughed. "The bit about an exotic dancer? Did he mean what I think he meant?"

Manziuk grinned. "If he did, I can see where she might not fit in here."

"I wonder which one it is?"

"I'm guessing the one that asked to go to her room for a shawl. The one with the dark red hair and the bright red blouse."

"That would be my guess, too."

A loud rap indicated the next person. Before Manziuk could get up, the woman in red stepped into the room, her blouse now partially covered by a long black shawl embroidered with red and yellow flowers. Pausing in the doorway, she announced, "I am here!"

Ryan whispered, "This should be interesting."

Manziuk jumped up and escorted the woman to the wing chair and helped her arrange her shawl until she was satisfied.

"Now I am ready." She sat up straight. "Detectives Manziuk and Ryan, how may I help you?"

Manziuk said, "And you are—"

"Oh, yes, of course. How foolish of me. I am Catarina Rossi." She bowed her head slightly. "Yes, it is true. *The* Catarina Rossi. When I am not travelling, this—" she gestured with one arm— "is where I have chosen to spend my retirement years."

Ryan shot a look at Manziuk and stifled a smile at the utter confusion on his face. Fortunately she'd quickly googled the name. "Have you retired from acting, Ms. Rossi?" She hoped she'd kept the smugness she felt out of her voice.

Catarina smiled at Ryan as a queen would smile at an ignorant but devoted subject. "Not completely, my dear. My fans wouldn't allow that. Now and then I take on a small part that interests me. But my days of spending months on a Broadway stage, and working eighteen hours a day—those days are gone."

"I'm surprised that you're living here. I thought you were settled in the US. California, wasn't it?"

Catarina nodded. "I had a *very* beautiful house in Santa Monica. But it is so much effort to maintain a house and all the staff. And I found we rarely used it. I still have my condo in New York and my beach house in Florida, but I rarely use them either. My children mostly use them for vacations. And now my grandchildren!" She threw them each a radiant smile. "Do you know I recently met my first great-grandchild? Time, it has flown."

"You're a Canadian citizen?" Manziuk asked.

"Of course. I was born in Italy and have lived mostly in the United States, but I was raised right here in Toronto, and I felt the need to connect with my roots. I also wanted a place where I could be myself and not have to worry about fans bothering me, a place where I could come and go as I please.

"When my friend Ben Davidson told me about Serenity Suites, it suited me to come here. But I also have a small villa in Italy. And if I decide to fly there, I simply have to say 'I am going.' And if I want to come back, then I come. And if some of my family wants to visit me, we have a guest suite they can use, or there are plenty of hotels in the area. And for the most part it has been good. Like a family, in some ways. But not *too* much like one." She laughed.

Ryan had been watching Manziuk, who was clearly looking for an opening. When Catarina paused for a breath, he saw his chance. "Mrs. Rossi, where did you go after lunch today?"

"After lunch? Why, I went to my condo. I have a routine, you see. After lunch I lie down for one hour. Then I read until tea time. That is my siesta time."

"Did anyone see you during this time?"

"Nikola came back with me, and he was playing his guitar in the sitting room, I believe."

Ryan was looking at her copy of the list of residents Audra had brought them. "Nikola Vincent?"

"Yes."

"He's your husband?"

"We were married on July 20th."

"I see."

Manziuk smiled. "You'll have to forgive us. We find it difficult to keep everyone straight. I take it you knew Ingrid Davidson?"

She shrugged her shoulder. "Knew her, of course. I have lived here for three years, and she was already here when I moved in. But I have to confess I never got to know her well. Now, her husband, Ben—him, I like. He is such a wonderful conversationalist. He knows everything and everyone! But Ingrid had very little conversation. Once we had talked about all of her children and all of my children and shared photos, there was little left to say."

Catarina leaned forward as if to share a secret. "I hate to say this, and you must not repeat it, but I have no idea how Ben stayed with her all these years. You could talk about almost anything with him, and he'd be right there with you, but she was like a big stone he had to drag around. Yet he seemed devoted to her. Most impressive."

She leaned back in her chair and laughed again. "Here I am rattling on. What did you want to know? I'm afraid I know nothing that might help you. I believe there was some kind of accident, and whoever did it is afraid to confess. Likely one of the staff."

"Have you ever seen one of the staff in the common room with a knife?" Ryan asked.

Catarina looked puzzled, then burst out laughing. "I see what you mean. No. A hammer, perhaps. A screwdriver. But no knives." She frowned. "But you cannot believe someone did this on purpose! Where did you say the knife was found?"

"On the floor next to her," Ryan intoned, "covered in blood."

Catarina grimaced. "How dreadful! I cannot imagine anyone doing that on purpose. Anyone here, I mean. Out there—well, anything can happen."

Manziuk spoke. "Sometimes we don't know people as well as we think we do."

"Yes, that is true. But we *are* talking about Ingrid, are we not? She was—she was an unimaginative, not-very-likeable, dumpy old woman. Who would want to murder her? It makes no sense!"

After Manziuk had escorted Catarina out, he said to Ryan, "Not our exotic dancer."

Ryan shook her head.

"Nice play. She'd have been quite dismayed if neither of us had known who she was."

"Google is our friend."

"Apparently."

"There's all kinds of stuff on her. Apparently she's very well known in the theatrical world. And very rich."

"So it would seem."

There was a pause as Manziuk checked their list of residents and staff.

"So is it working?" Ryan asked.

He looked up. "Is what working?"

"Me being the bad cop?"

"I think so. Don't you?"

"Yeah." She grinned. "I kind of like it."

A soft rap signalled the next interviewee. Manziuk opened the door to a small, white-haired woman. She was just over five feet tall, thin, with slightly bent shoulders. She was wearing a white and grey striped dress with a pink sweater. Silver-rimmed glasses perched on her nose. "Audra told me just to walk in, but of course I couldn't do that."

"And you are?" Manziuk asked.

"Mary Simmons."

"Please come in. Is it Ms. or Mrs.?"

"Oh, I've never married. Not that I want anyone to feel sorry for me. It just didn't happen, that's all. I have no idea if I'd have liked being married or not. I think perhaps not. So much nicer not to have to always be worrying about what the other person wants, don't you think?"

"Yes," Ryan said. "I quite agree."

Mary looked past Manziuk. "Oh, my dear, I didn't notice you over there. Of course those who *are* married, at least the ones who *stay* married, seem to like it. Most of them."

"Please sit down, Ms. Simmons." Manziuk waited until she was comfortable and then took his own seat. "We're trying to get an idea of what happened here today and what Mrs. Davidson was like as a person."

"I have no idea who the perp is. I've been racking my brain the whole time we were in the dining room. I sensed Ingrid was going to die soon but not like that."

Manziuk raised his eyebrows. "You sensed she was about to die?"

"Well, she just seemed so listless. And when she nodded off in the common room, which she did several times a day, her breathing was very shallow. It seemed to me that one day she'd fall asleep and not wake up."

"Were other people concerned about this?"

Mary smiled. "No, only me. But then, I've known her most of my life, and I could see she'd gone sadly downhill. Violet and I often spoke about it. I'm not sure the men noticed, although of course Ben must have. Well, he'd have to, wouldn't he?" She looked from Manziuk to Ryan. "That's why, when Violet, and not Ingrid, died in her sleep, it was so hard to accept."

Manziuk leaned forward. "We've had several people mention Violet's death. Had you known her a long time?"

"Oh, my, yes. Since we were toddlers really. Our parents' houses were only a block apart."

"Was there any reason to think Violet's death wasn't natural?"

Mary pursed her lips and shook her head. "No—oo."

"You seem uncertain."

"Well, it was just so completely unexpected." She looked from Manziuk to Ryan and back to Manziuk. "You see, detectives, I watch a lot of crime shows on television and read mysteries. Sometimes I think I should have been a mystery writer instead of a singer. But then, I did love entertaining the children."

Manziuk frowned. "You sang for children?"

"Oh, yes. I made many records, not under my real name, so you wouldn't recognize it. I went by the name of Milly Dean."

"Really?" Manziuk smiled. "I have two sons and a daughter, and when they were little they absolutely loved your music! And the TV show, too."

Mary beamed. "Oh, how nice to hear. Yes, my records were very successful. You know, they wanted me to go on TV as myself, but I just couldn't. I was terrified. I said, 'Figure out a way for me to sing and talk but not have to be in front of the camera.' So they did! They used puppets and cartoons, and no one ever saw me. It was perfect. Ben was instrumental in that, you know. He was my executive producer."

"I didn't realize that."

"Oh, yes, we go way, way back. I knew him from when we started school. Frank and Norm, too. We were all dreamers back then. And we were fortunate in that most of our dreams came true. Of course Frank didn't know then that he wanted to be a writer. He wanted to be a teacher, and he became one. But later he began to write, and it worked out beautifully. And Ben didn't dream of being a talk-show host and a producer; he wanted to be a comedian. Only he was never good at doing stand-up, so he went into broadcasting. But when he interviewed people, it always came out sort of funny. That's why they got the idea of him doing a talk show, and it was perfect for him."

"Yes, I used to listen to his talk show."

"*Used to*. Everything's changed."

There was a moment of silence, broken by Ryan's voice. "You were talking about Violet's death."

"Oh, yes, and then I got sidetracked. I believe I had started to say that I'm an avid mystery reader, so sometimes I might see things that aren't really there. Lyle teases me about being like the boy who cried 'Wolf!' So I don't want you to give any more weight to my opinions than you think they merit, but honestly, I just can't believe Violet died the way they say! Just because you're old doesn't mean you should up and die with no warning, and everyone should just accept it and act as if nothing untoward has happened. There ought to have been an autopsy."

"Were the police involved at all?"

"From what Audra said, there were a few of them here, and I believe the coroner came, but he more or less just talked to Dr. Granger, and that was it. I don't know what Dr. Granger told him, but I expect it was just the usual 'old age' routine. I don't know what Frank thought because he didn't say anything, but Norm and I both thought there should have been more of an investigation. I think Audra did, too, but she'd never say it to me."

"You and Violet were close?"

"Neither of us had a sister, so we became each other's sister."

"And as far as you know, she had no reason to think she might be dying?"

"Oh, she knew she was dying. But not that way."

"I'm not sure what you mean."

"Hardly anyone knew it, but she'd been diagnosed with pancreatic cancer. Dr. Granger knew, of course, but she swore him to secrecy. And I assume Frank knew. I don't know when Trish found out. Of course Dr. Granger and Audra knew, and I expect Derrick and likely some other medical people. Anyway they'd told her she was good for six months to a year, but she was getting all her affairs in order just in case it was quicker. But nothing she said led me to think she had any fear of dying any other way." Mary licked her lips. "Maybe it was for the best for her to go quickly, but it just didn't feel right to me."

Manziuk asked, "Why do you think she didn't want people to know?"

"She never liked people fussing over her. She just wanted to be left alone and live each day as usual. Of course, eventually when it got worse, they'd find out. But she wanted to delay that time."

"What about getting chemo or having surgery?"

"She said she had no intention of being a guinea pig just to have a few more weeks or months. Not at her age."

Nine

Manziuk cleared his throat. "Getting back to Ingrid—Mrs. Davidson. I understand that you were in the common room on the day of her death?"

"I was sitting about two dozen feet away from her, talking to Norm and Lyle."

"Which of you was in the room first?"

"Ingrid. She was there earlier when I looked into the room, and she was still there the second time when I came in and sat down."

"Do you have any idea what time it was when you first looked into the room but didn't stay?"

Mary thought a moment. "Probably just after two o'clock. I remember thinking it was just under an hour until tea and that I'd have plenty of time to do the Sudoku puzzle in the newspaper. Of course I'd brought a book along, too, in case the puzzle was too easy, but I decided to take another turn around the hallway before I settled down."

"Could you tell if Ingrid was sleeping or awake?"

"I'm pretty sure she was awake." She concentrated for a few seconds. "Yes, she was! She was working on a baby blanket. It was pink and white, and when I looked in she was holding it up. Likely seeing if she'd missed a stitch, poor thing."

"Was anyone else in the room?"

"I can't be one hundred percent certain, but I didn't see anyone."

"But you didn't actually go into the room?"

"No, I wanted to walk a bit more."

"Earlier, right after lunch, where did you go?"

"I went to my condo, as usual. I like to have a little rest after lunch. I don't necessarily sleep, but I lie down and read for a bit. I was there for maybe half an hour. I think I might have dropped off."

"So that would be about 1:30?"

"Yes. Then I puttered around a bit. I organized the top of my dresser. Then I put away a stack of books I've read recently. My shelves are full, so every time I get a new book something else has to go. I chose a few to pass on. Then I decided to go for a little walk and picked up my book and left."

"Did you see anyone while you were walking?"

"Let me think." She touched her mouth with one finger as she looked down at her lap for a moment. "Oh, yes! I saw Tess. Wednesday afternoon is her day for doing Norm and Elizabeth's laundry, so I assumed she was coming from their place. She passed me and said hi, but she didn't stop."

"Okay. What next?"

"I walked down to the end of the hallway and turned left. I looked in at the common room and only saw Ingrid, so I decided to walk a little bit further. The way our floor is laid out, it's in a big rectangle. I often walk around the rectangle two or three times, just to get some exercise."

"So you looked in the common room and saw Ingrid there knitting, but you didn't go in right away.

"Yes. Except she was crocheting. She liked doing that more than knitting."

"All right. So where did you go next?"

"I went to the end of the hallway past Audra and Derrick's office. Everything was quiet except at the laundry. Tess was there, so I stopped and chatted with her for a few minutes."

"Okay."

She frowned. "Then what? Oh, yes, I know. The door to the exercise room was shut and locked. I know because I tried it. The games room door was open, and I heard two people talking as I walked past. I just peeked in quickly, and it was Nikola and Derrick. They were talking about some kind of shot you could make, so I didn't disturb them. I don't know anything about pool or billiards or whatever you call it now. In my day ladies didn't go into a pool room."

"So you kept walking?"

"Well, just then I saw Trish coming toward me from down the hallway. As she came close, I could see she was crying. I don't think she even saw me until I said her name."

Mary paused, so Ryan prompted her. "What happened next?"

"Well, she ended up walking back to my place with me and coming in for a few minutes. She'd been talking to Frank, and he'd been rude to her. I told her she should be used to that by now. Frank's rude to everyone. Has been for years." She shook her head. "He used to be much better at hiding it, but lately he just doesn't seem to care what anyone thinks of him."

"Did she stay in your condo long?"

"No. It was actually kind of funny. I told her that her father was nothing more nor less than a spoiled brat, and I couldn't believe I'd once fancied myself in love with him. She got a funny look on her face, and then she laughed and said, 'I just wish Mom hadn't done such a good PR job!' When Trish left, I watched her walk to her suite, and then I headed down the short way to the common room. Oh, I stepped inside the kitchen to see if I could find out what Scarlett was making for tea."

"Did you talk to Scarlett?"

"Just for a second. She was busy. And Olive was there, too."

"Where did you go next?

"I went to the common room to do the Sudoku. Ingrid appeared to be sleeping, so I found a chair near the door and worked on the puzzle. And then Norm came in and said he was looking for Elizabeth. I expect he knew perfectly well she was in the recording studio, but he just needed something to say. He knew better than to interrupt her." Mary grinned. "She's as bad as Frank, only sarcastic instead of rude."

"What happened next?"

"After a little while, Lyle came in. About that time I realized something was wrong with Ingrid, so I asked Lyle to check on her." She shook her head. "How ironic that when she actually was dead, I thought she was sleeping. It just goes to show you can never be sure of anything."

"What time would it have been when you went into the room and sat down?"

"It was 2:28. I looked at my watch to see how much time I had before tea."

"Tea is at 3:00?"

"Always."

"And how long were you there before the others came in?"

"Before Norm, maybe five minutes. Lyle another five or so."

"You're sure no one else was in the room when you went in?"

"I didn't see anyone."

"And no one else came in while you were there?"

"No."

"Not even someone who would have been, shall we say, part of the background? A person cleaning, for instance."

"No, I'd have noticed. The puzzle was pretty easy so I wasn't terribly distracted by it."

"All right. Thank you very much for your help."

"Thank *you* for taking the time to talk with each of us and listening to what we think."

Taken aback, Manziuk stared at her, trying to recall if anyone else had ever thanked him for carrying out a routine interview.

"Ms. Simmons," Ryan said, "please remember this isn't a mystery novel."

Mary smiled as she stood up. "You mean don't fancy myself as Miss Marple or Miss Silver or one of those other old-lady sleuths. No, dear, I won't. I like my neck too much to put it at risk." She paused and looked flustered. "Oh, dear, I shouldn't have said that. I'd forgotten what happened to Ingrid."

Manziuk said, "If you remember anything else, even if you don't think it's important, let us know. This is my card."

"I shall, detectives." Nodding to both of them, she left the room.

As soon as the door closed, Ryan said, "So Ingrid died between 2:00, when Mary first saw her in the common room, and 2:30, when Mary came back to it."

Manziuk shrugged. "Assuming she's telling the truth."

"Do you think she was lying?"

"Nearly everybody lies about something."

"Excuse me. Audra thought you'd want this here." Olive was carrying a large tray.

Manziuk was happy to see that Thai had won—lemon grass coconut milk soup, green mango salad, pad thai, red curry beef, ginger chicken, and mixed greens, with sticky rice. There were also two pots of green tea, and a small cooler held two bowls of mango sherbet. "Not bad."

"If you skipped the rice and the sauces, it would be better."

"Well, you skip away. I'm going to eat every bit of it."

"Murder makes you hungry, does it?"

The next person to come in was an elderly man on a motorized scooter. Realizing it was the man who had looked away when he was addressing the residents, Manziuk stood and went toward him. "Thank you for coming."

The man nodded and set the brakes.

"Are you comfortable, or do you want to move to a chair?"

"Let's get this over with. I have important things I should be doing today."

Manziuk went back and sat in his chair. "Your name is?"

"Frank Klassen."

"Well, Mr. Klassen, I'm not sure how to put this, but I understand that your wife, Violet, passed away recently."

Frank frowned. "She did, but that's got nothing to do with this."

"I understand. I just wanted to say I'm sorry for your loss."

"Never mind the small talk. What do you want from me? I don't know anything about Ingrid's death."

Ryan took over. "Mr. Klassen, were you in the common room at all today?"

Frank's eyes narrowed as he looked over at her. "No, I wasn't. I rarely go in there."

"Where did you go after lunch?"

"To the office I use—next door to this one."

"You spend a lot of time there?"

"From 9:00 until noon and from 1:00 until 6:00 every day, six days a week."

Manziuk asked, "You're a writer?"

Frank took his time turning back to face Manziuk. "I'm working on my twenty-ninth book."

"I'm sorry. I ought to recognize your name, but unfortunately, this job doesn't leave me a lot of time for reading."

Frank shrugged. "Not everyone reads the kind of books I write. As a policeman, you probably see enough ugliness."

"Your books are—"

"The category is thriller."

"I wish I had more time to read. I enjoy a good mystery. I've managed to read quite a few of Dick Francis's books."

Frank nodded. "Francis was good, I'll grant you that. A few of his books are great. I prefer a little more action and less introspection myself."

"You like to keep your reader on the edge of his seat?"

"I do. The biggest compliment you can give me is that you didn't get any sleep."

"Because of reading the book, or the fear it invokes?"

Frank chuckled. "Either one is fine with me."

"I'll have to look for one of your books next chance I get. Were you writing today as usual?"

"I was. I had breakfast and then wrote until noon. I went to the dining room for lunch and was back at work by 1:00. When Audra asked us all to go to the dining room, I was very reluctant to leave my work, but since it was almost tea time I did as asked. Of course I stopped to save my book to my flash drive before I left. I never go anywhere without my current book." He held up a chain that hung around his neck and showed them the small blue flash drive on the end of it.

"Did you see or hear anyone while you were writing after lunch?"

Frank shook his head. "I keep the door shut and my music on."

Ryan pushed. "So you saw no one at all?"

Frank seemed about to take offence at the question but paused. "No, I'm wrong. I did see someone. My daughter had the nerve to walk into my office a little after lunch. Don't ask me what time it was. I informed her that the only reason to interrupt me is if the building is on fire or someone died next door." He looked momentarily disconcerted. "Not expecting either to actually happen, of course."

Manziuk asked, "Were you surprised by Mrs. Davidson's death?"

"Naturally."

"Do you have any suspicions as to what might have happened?"

"As I understand it, she was stabbed. That seems ridiculous to me but, if it's true, I'd say that one of the staff thought they were doing her a kindness. That, or someone had a grudge against her. I'd look for someone with a short temper."

Ryan took over again. "Mr. Klassen, to get back to your wife—"

Frank turned to glare at her, a flush creeping up his face. "My wife died from natural causes. That has *nothing* whatsoever to do with what happened to Ingrid!"

"So you have no suspicions that your wife's death might not have been natural?"

"I do not, and anyone who says otherwise is wrong."

"You understand that because of the suspicious death today and the fact that your wife died quite recently, we need to ask these questions?"

"No, I don't. Violet's death has absolutely nothing to do with Ingrid's. And if you start trying to connect dots and sniff down rabbit trails, I'll be calling my friends at City Hall. My wife is at peace, and that's my only concern. I won't have her brought into this or have my daughter upset."

Ryan raised her eyebrows. "Mr. Klassen, *you* may be satisfied there's no connection, but *we* need to be satisfied, too."

"Well, you can take it from me that if I thought there was anything suspicious about my wife's death, I'd say so. Especially in light of Ingrid's. Now, do you have any other questions about Ingrid's death? If not, I assume I can get back to work in my office?"

Manziuk stood up. "I'm sorry. We have to finish searching the area first."

"Don't let me keep you." Frank turned his scooter and went to the door, where he hit the automatic open button and exited.

The next arrival was the woman Manziuk had noticed earlier. While the other residents were Caucasian, her skin was like dark chocolate. Long curly black hair held back by a black band framed her head like a halo. She wore a flowing navy, purple, and fuchsia blouse with a bright fuchsia necklace and earrings, purple pants, and low-heeled purple slippers. She moved slowly with the aid of a carved wooden cane with a silver knob.

"Good afternoon. Where do you want me? In this chair?" Her voice was low and soft and had a hint of what Manziuk thought was a British accent.

Manziuk stood as she took her seat. "Now, how may I help you?"

"Your name is?"

"Hilary Brooks."

"And you've been a resident here for how long?"

"My husband and I moved in just over eleven months ago. Unfortunately he died in May."

"I'm sorry."

She inclined her head. "I have adjusted."

"How do you like living here?"

Hilary looked over at Ryan. "I see your assistant is a woman of colour."

"His partner," Ryan corrected.

"Ah, I see." Hilary smiled. "I'm afraid I didn't catch your name."

"Detective Constable Ryan."

"Well, what I was going to say was that *you* can probably guess how I find living here."

A slight smile touched the corners of Ryan's mouth. She nodded.

Hilary looked back at Manziuk. "In one word, Detective, 'awkward.' But on the other hand, I've been in many situations during my lifetime that were a lot worse than awkward."

"Did your husband also find it awkward?"

"Grant was white, Inspector. So while he was sympathetic to my problem, he only knew peripherally how I felt."

She leaned forward. "I'll let you in on a little secret. Grant knew Ben quite well, but only through business. Grant was a financier who was involved in producing an assortment of things, from movies to television to live shows. Some years before Grant and I were married, Ben told him about this place, and Grant put his name on the list. When an opening came up last summer, he got it. But they knew nothing about me."

"Why was that?"

"Grant and I met in Montreal, where I was living. We married not long after meeting each other and, aside from a few trips back here, he stayed there with me. So, when the time came for us to move into Serenity Suites, I was the little surprise Grant brought with him. As you might guess, not everyone was happy. Grant was willing to move out, but I wanted to stay. And since the contract had already been signed, they couldn't get rid of us without being served with a lawsuit citing racial discrimination."

"I'd have thought people involved in the arts would be more liberal-minded." Manziuk said.

She smiled. "Only about things that matter to them."

"So you've chosen to stay here even though it's uncomfortable?"

"No one is outwardly hateful, and the staff is actually wonderful. So I stay. Besides, I have a dislike of being told what I can and cannot do." She shook her head. "They won't make me leave."

"They've tried?"

"They're trying right now. The administrator, Ms. Arlington, has told me I have to leave. But I won't let them win."

Ryan said, "Mrs. Brooks—"

"Hilary is fine."

"Hilary, how well did you know Ingrid Davidson?"

Hilary turned slightly to face Ryan. "Not well at all. She made no attempt to be friendly. I felt sorry for her, which I'm sure she wouldn't have appreciated."

"Why did you feel sorry for her?"

"Because it was very clear that she was losing her wits. To be honest, I felt even sorrier for Ben. The poor man tried to pretend everything was okay, but it clearly wasn't."

"Have you any idea who might have wanted her dead?"

"No."

"Nothing you observed?"

"Nothing. And I find it impossible to believe it was intentional. She was an old woman who was getting older and more senile by the moment. Why would anyone deliberately kill her?"

"Well, a knife somehow got into her neck, causing her to bleed to death."

Hilary looked thoughtful. "Is that how it was done? I'd heard something about a knife, but not where. That sounds—almost personal. Not like a quick and easy pill that makes you sleepy and then you never wake up. A knife, used up close like that, sounds more as if someone hated her."

"Where did you go after lunch?"

"To my place."

"You went directly there?"

"Yes."

"And when did you leave?"

"When Audra asked everyone to come to the dining room."

"And during that time, did you see anyone?"

"Just Audra."

"You mean she came to your condo to ask you to go to the dining room?"

"No, earlier. She came to visit me for a few minutes. You may find this strange, but Audra and I have become friends. All of the staff are kind to me, but especially Audra."

"So she came to your condo after lunch today?"

"Not right after. Maybe twenty minutes after I got there. Something like that."

"What were you and Audra talking about?"

"A few things. My frustrations with Ms. Arlington and the board; Audra's ex-husband, who is a total jerk; how she might get custody of her sons." Hilary leaned forward. "I say that much because I have no doubt she will tell you; the specific things she's told me, they're not mine to share but hers."

"How long was she with you?"

"I'd say half an hour, maybe a few minutes less."

"What did you do after she left?"

"I danced for a while. Then we got the call to go to the dining room."

Manziuk broke in. "You danced? Someone told us that one of the residents here was a dancer."

"Yes, that would be me. I dance now only for my own enjoyment, but I've been a dancer since I was four years old."

"What kind of dancing?" Ryan asked.

Hilary laughed. "What were you told? No, don't say it. All my life, I have been a ballet dancer at odds with a world that had—still has—little use for black ballet dancers. When I was going to get thrown out of my room for not paying the rent or when I needed to eat, I did whatever kind of dancing I could get."

"You must have had a great deal of determination," Manziuk said.

"My father called it mule-headedness."

"And how successful were you?" Ryan asked.

"I became a *prima ballerina* for several ballet companies, if that's what you mean. And later a choreographer. I never could get into the best companies, but the ones I was part of were mostly good, with dancers who were committed to their craft. It was never easy. Many times I wondered if it was worth it. But of course, when we begin, we only have our dreams. If we could see the sacrifices and struggles ahead, how many of us would set foot on the path to reach those dreams?"

The next resident was an older man of medium height with a full head of wavy steel-grey hair, twinkling hazel eyes, and a warm smile. His voice, too, was warm and inviting. He held out his hand to Manziuk. "Lyle Oakley. Pleased to meet you."

"Thank you for coming, Mr. Oakley. Just a few questions."

"No problem. Glad to do what I can for poor Ingrid. Not that anything we can do now will help her, though, will it?"

When all three were seated, Manziuk asked, "Did you know Mrs. Davidson well?"

"I did." He laughed. "Well, 'knew' in the conversational sense, not the biblical one."

Manziuk smiled. "Have you lived here long?"

"Oh, yes, I came in when it opened. Ben and I go way back. As soon as he told me about this place, I knew it was for me. And I was right."

"You like living here?"

"For someone like me, it's absolutely perfect. I don't cook, and I don't want some housekeeper hanging over me thinking she has to take care of me. Plus I hate having to hire help and keep them happy and whatnot. Here, I buy my condo and pay annual fees, and everything else is taken care of for me."

"What was your occupation?"

Lyle chuckled. "Wondering how I pay the bills? I'm an actor. Still working actually, although not that much. Not a lot of call for old men, but some. I was actually out filming a commercial this morning. Had to be there at 7:00, and I was back at noon. Easy work, and it pays well enough. I do the odd play if it suits. Occasional walk-ons in movies. My agent finds me enough to do to make it worthwhile to keep me as a client." He leaned forward. "If you feel bad that you don't know my name, you shouldn't. I was never the star type. I always preferred to be one of the ensemble."

"And how do you get on here?"

"Oh, fine. I enjoy most of the other residents. Being artists of some sort, they're interesting you know. It's true that one on one, some of them can get tedious, but as a group they're very entertaining."

"And how did Ingrid fit in?"

Lyle grinned. "She didn't. But she was used to that."

"Can you explain what you mean?"

He repositioned himself in the chair to make himself more comfortable. "Well, Ingrid wasn't an artist, you know. Ben was a big star—one of the few truly big Canadian celebrities, but Ingrid couldn't have cared less about all that. She just stayed home and looked after her family and did all the things any suburban wife might do in those days. A bit *Leave It to Beaver*. She never wanted a career or to be in the limelight. But she thought the world of Ben. Would have done anything for him. So she put up with all the things involved with living in his world, none of which would have been her choice."

"And you know this because?"

"Oh, she told me. Over the last five years we'd had any number of conversations. She told me all about her family, and what her life was like. And Mary and Violet both told me things, too. Of course they knew her way back when."

Manziuk thought for a moment. "Mr. Oakley, you said you'd talked to Ingrid a lot over the past five years. Did you sense that Ingrid was perhaps not all she had once been?"

He nodded. "Oh, yes. Lately she'd been going downhill fast. She was nothing like her younger self. But we all get old, don't we?"

Ryan leaned forward. "Do you have any idea as to who might have disliked her enough to stab her?"

Lyle turned toward her. "Well, I know it wasn't me. Other than that, no idea whatsoever." He paused for a moment, and his expression sobered. "No, that's not true. Ben didn't do it either. In all the years I've known Ben, he's never once strayed. You just had to see him look at Ingrid to know he was totally besotted. He'd never have caused her even a second's pain."

Manziuk said, "Where did you go after lunch today?"

"I went into the common room and finished the newspapers I'd been reading earlier this morning."

"How long were you there?"

"Fifteen or twenty minutes. No one else came around, so I wandered over to the billiards room. No one was there, so I went and knocked on Kenneth's door. Figuratively speaking, that is. We have an intercom system. No doorbells. Anyway, he said he'd come out to play in half an hour, so I went back to my condo for a while. Then I met him in the billiards room sometime after 2:00—around a quarter after, and we had a couple of games. And after that Kenneth went back to his place, and I went to the common room, where Mary and Norm were sitting talking, and Ingrid was presumably sleeping. Mary said she had a feeling something was wrong with Ingrid. Which Mary had said I don't know how many times before. But I let her persuade me to check, and then of course I saw the blood and I knew Ingrid really was dead this time. I sent Mary to get help."

"What did you do after you sent Mary for help?"

"I waited for the others to come. Guarding her, I guess. Not that anyone else was around. Just Norm, and he was pretty cut up."

"Who came into the room first?"

"Mary brought Audra, and she went over to Ingrid. She never said a word, just put her hand on Ingrid's neck. Not the side where the cut was—the other side. I assume she was looking for a pulse. Then she stood back. I thought she was going to be sick.

"Mary was standing in the doorway jabbering about how she knew it was going to happen one of these days. I told her to shush. And Norm got up and went over to her and put his arms around her, and they both started crying. Then Audra called the police. She asked me to stay where I was and keep everyone away until the police arrived, and then she took Mary and Norm to the dining room."

"You have an excellent memory."

"I've always had my lines memorized straight off. My one little talent."

"How long was it before the police arrived?"

"Not long at all. Maybe five minutes. Olive brought a young policewoman into the room and left her with me while she went back to the elevator to watch for more of them."

"So more police officers arrived?"

"Yes, they just kept trailing in, and I told my story a few times, and then they finally sent me to the dining room. Scarlett had the tea ready, and I felt guilty taking it, but I needed a drink by then. Everyone else was there, and they all had questions, of course, but there was a police officer in the room, and he asked us not to discuss the death. Which I appreciated. By that time I was feeling pretty ill."

He shook his head. "I keep expecting to wake up and discover this has all been a bad dream. It makes no sense. Why on earth would anyone want to stab poor Ingrid?"

In contrast to Lyle Oakley, the next man seemed reluctant to enter the room. Of about average height, he was thin, with sparse white hair, a goatee, and sad eyes. The navy dress pants, pale blue striped shirt, and light grey cardigan made Manziuk wonder if he was a retired professor.

"Kenneth Harper." The man held out his hand. Manziuk stood to shake it, and then Kenneth moved toward Ryan and shook her hand as well. He pointed to the wing chair. "I assume you want me to sit here?"

He sat and crossed his right leg over his left knee. "I don't think I can help you much, but I'll do my best."

Manziuk said, "Mr. Harper, I believe you've only lived here a short time?"

"That's right. I moved in on July 1st. So not two months."

"You knew some of the other residents before?"

"I knew Ben. I was a guest on his show a number of times. We sort of hit it off and became friends. I'd also met Grant Brooks, Hilary's husband. He was one of the financial backers for a couple of my concert tours."

"Concerts? You're a musician?"

"A singer."

"I see. So you knew Ingrid Davidson?"

Kenneth smiled deprecatingly. "I'd met her, of course. But I'm not married myself, and a spare man is often a fifth wheel at social occasions. I usually met Ben for coffee or drinks, and we occasionally went golfing."

"Did you notice any difference in either Ben or Ingrid when you moved in here?"

Kenneth looked down. "Well, we've all gotten older, haven't we? But I guess I'd say Ingrid hadn't aged very well. She seemed pretty fragile. I can't say I'm surprised by her death, although what I hear about her being stabbed is certainly difficult to believe."

"Mr. Harper," Ryan said, "can you tell us your movements after lunch?"

He turned a bit to look at her. "Certainly. I went to my condo. After a while Lyle invited me to have a game of billiards. We made an appointment to meet at 2:15 or thereabouts. Dr. Granger came to see me at 1:45 as we had arranged previously. He left shortly after 2:00 for another appointment. Then I went to the billiards room to meet Lyle. We were there for a good half hour, and then I went back to my condo and was there until Audra asked us all to go to the dining room."

Manziuk asked, "What were you doing in your room after lunch?"

"Writing a letter to my children. I'm afraid I find writing to them very stressful."

"Your children? You indicated that you weren't married."

"My wife died a long time ago." He looked down. "I'm afraid I was—I was unable to handle things, and I let my sister-in-law raise my children. Something I've lived to regret." He looked up. "Anyway, we don't communicate very much, but now and then I send them a note, or they send me one."

"That sounds like a difficult situation."

"Especially since my wife's sister never liked me and encouraged me to stay away. However, the irony was that after the dust cleared, I discovered that my voice—my singing voice that is—was far better than I'd ever imagined, and I ended up carving a nice career for myself."

"All things work together for good," Ryan mumbled.

Kenneth turned toward her and said sharply, "What did you just say?"

"Oh, just something my Gram often says. I've always taken it to mean that things have a way of working out even if we can't see it at the time."

Kenneth frowned. "That's one way to look at it."

"Do you have any suspicions as to who might have killed Ingrid?"

"None whatsoever. If it had been a mercy killing—an overdose of sleeping pills, perhaps—I might believe Ben could have done it, but I can't imagine his stabbing her."

Ten

When Kenneth was gone, Ryan exclaimed, "Wow! He kind of snapped at me."

Manziuk thought about this. "Interesting reaction."

"I thought he was going to attack me there for a second."

"I have a feeling there's more to his story than he gave us."

Ryan tilted her head to one side. "I can't see that it has anything to do with Ingrid's death though."

"Nor can I."

"I think that was the last of the residents." Ryan checked her list. "No, wait. There's one more. Mrs. Rossi's new husband."

"That should be interesting."

The office door opened to admit a slim man in moccasins, ripped jeans, and a black T-shirt. His long dark hair was tied back at the neck, and he had a fairly full beard. Manziuk guessed his age as mid-thirties. The young man was smiling. "You're having a long day. How on earth do you keep us all straight?"

Manziuk looked at the list Audra had given them. "Mr. Vincent?"

"Nikola, please."

"All right, Nikola. We just have a few questions for you."

He sat down in the empty chair. "Fire away."

"Mr. Vincent, are you retired?"

Nikola laughed. "I know what you're thinking, and you're absolutely right. Catarina is eighty-one years old, and I'm forty-two. Anyway, no, I'm not retired. I play guitar. In other words, I'm a musician."

"Thank you for clarifying that. What we need to know is your whereabouts after lunch today."

"Catarina always has a nap after lunch, so I was in our sitting room, playing my guitar softly so as not to disturb her. She may or may not have heard me. Gulab was there, too, cleaning.

"After a while I went to the billiards room. No one was there, but I hung around for a while practising trick shots. Then I went back to our place. I was there playing my guitar until the call to go to the dining room."

"While you were in the billiards room, did you see anyone?"

Nikola thought for a second. "Derrick looked in for a few minutes."

"Derrick?"

"He's one of the staff."

"I understood he was away today."

"Just for the afternoon. He was on his way out when he popped in to talk to me."

"What time might that have been?"

"I remember Derrick saying it was after 2:00 and he needed to get a move on or he'd be late."

"Did you see anyone on your way back to your condo?"

"I stopped in at Audra's office for a few minutes. I had a question I wanted to ask her."

"And was she there?"

"Yes, she was working at her desk."

"And you were there for how long?"

"Five minutes at most."

"Thank you. Tell me, did you know Ingrid well at all?"

"I can't say I know anyone here well. We don't have that much in common. I mean, I see these people at meals, and I'll play some pool with one of them now and then, and I've sat in on a few card games, but that's about it. Cat and I go out quite a bit. To the theatre or shopping and so forth."

Ryan sat forward. "What kind of card games?"

Nikola grinned at her. "Mostly poker. You'd be surprised at how willing a few of these old geezers are to take your last penny."

"Which old geezers?"

"Frank and Lyle in particular. Norm plays, but he isn't that good or that invested in it. Ben will play occasionally, but he just isn't into it. Frank, on the other hand, really hates losing. And Lyle gets a kick out of bluffing you. They're both pretty good."

"Any of the women?"

"Well, Cat doesn't mind taking a hand now and then, but she isn't much of a gambler. She just likes to be with people who talk about things that interest her, which most of the women here don't. Liz has played a few times, but she gets too uptight and she hates losing, so…"

The door opened slowly. "Come right in," Manziuk invited.

The door opened wide to admit a tall blonde woman who looked to be about forty. She was wearing khaki capris, a green T-shirt, and tan sandals. Her gold hoop earrings glinted as she smiled. "Hello. I was afraid you might be saying something confidential." She held out her hand to Manziuk and then Ryan. "I'm Trish Klassen-Wallace. Patricia really, but I prefer Trish."

"Please have a seat." Manziuk gestured toward the wing chair. "Sorry to have kept you waiting so long. I thought we should meet with the older people first."

"Certainly." She sat very straight in the chair.

"I understand you've been staying here for a couple of weeks?"

"Yes, I came immediately after my mother died, and I looked after the funeral and then had to go through Mom's personal things and decide what to do with them. It's all taken longer than I expected, which I ought to have anticipated. So many decisions to make, and many of them complicated."

"Ms.—or do you prefer Mrs.?"

"Please, just call me Trish. Everyone does."

"Trish, because your mother died only a short time ago, and because she and Mrs. Davidson had apparently known each other for a long time, I've wondered a little about the nature of your mother's death and whether there might be a connection. I've been assured by your father and others that your mother's death was natural and that there's no reason to link them in any way, but I've also had a couple of people say her death was unexpected. What do you think?"

Trish sat back and brought her palms together up in front of her chest. "Oh, wow! That's certainly not what I was expecting you to ask." She put her hands down and held them between her knees. "First, let me say that this has been a rather unsettling two weeks. Mom's death was *very* unexpected for me. She was—she was the kind of person you—you just assume will always be there. And then she phoned me out of the blue to tell me she had inoperable cancer. The very next day my dad called to tell me that she was dead. I'd expected her to live into her late nineties, as her parents and other relatives have done. And now Ingrid—murdered! So you can see why this has all been overwhelming." She took a deep breath. "My understanding is that my mother died of natural causes. Are you implying that that wasn't the case?"

"I'm not implying anything. Simply asking if you have any questions or concerns about your mother's death."

"You're asking me if, since Ingrid was apparently murdered, Mom could have been, too. But Mom died in her sleep. There was no sign of—what do you call it—foul play?"

"Apparently not. However, without an autopsy we can't be positive."

Trish stared at her hands for a long moment, then looked up. "If nothing had happened with Ingrid, we wouldn't be having this conversation."

"That's true."

She brought her left arm up and rested her chin on her hand while looking up at the ceiling. Then she shut her eyes for a second before looking at Manziuk. "I really don't know what to say. I mean, it was all such a complete shock. When Mom told me she had pancreatic cancer, she said she'd have at least six more months. And before I'd even had a chance to process that, she was gone. But that isn't what bothers me the most. It was—her death was—almost—I guess the words I want to say are 'too easy.' I mean, you know what the word 'cancer' means to people. I was up all night after her call, and all I could think of was that there would be a lot of pain, and that she'd suffer. And then—boom! It was over, and there was no pain and no suffering.

"When we wrote her obituary, we used that phrase you sometimes see—'peacefully in her sleep.' And while one part of me is totally happy that she didn't have pain or suffer, another part of me finds it incredible that it could be so—so easy."

Ryan asked, "Do you think your mother was the kind of person who might have decided to end her life to avoid the pain, or perhaps to make it easier for you and your dad?"

Trish leaned back and took a deep breath. "That's such a difficult question. I mean, how can you ever know what's going on in another person's head? When I got here I discovered that in the last month, Mom had not only made me executor of her will but she'd also given me an unconditional power of attorney. And she'd somehow convinced Dad to do the same!" She shook her head. "How she got him to agree to that, I'll never know!

"But, as for ending her life, my gut feeling is no. My mother was a fighter. Not only that, but she believed it was wrong to take your own life. Or someone else's, for that matter. Her background was Mennonite. She didn't believe in fighting or going to war. And she was very much opposed to euthanasia."

"How do you know this? Did she tell you?"

"Well, her feelings on fighting and suicide I've known all my life, because she was never reluctant to give her opinion on things, whether it involved someone we knew or a story in the news. But I can be quite certain about the euthanasia because in one of his books, oh, maybe five or six years ago, Dad had a character who killed a friend who was dying and in pain. Mom and Dad got into quite a bit of a discussion about that. An argument, really. Mom was quite put out that Dad seemed to be condoning it in his book." Trish shook her head. "I can't believe she'd even consider killing herself, no matter how much pain she was in."

Manziuk said gently, "Could your dad—?"

She shrugged. "Maybe, if he saw her in a lot of pain, he might consider it. But it would be much more in character for him to demand that the doctors do something. But the thing is, she *wasn't* in a lot of pain. Not yet. And she'd apparently just told him about the cancer a day or two before she told me, so he hadn't had time to think about it either." She sighed. "Inspector, could you still tell? I mean, if Mom was murdered, could you find proof? She's already been buried."

"If it was murder, it's possible we could find something that would tell us. It's also possible it would be indeterminate, in which case we'd be no further ahead."

"You'd need to dig her up, wouldn't you? Dad would never agree."

"I'm sure he wouldn't. Of course we could always get a judge to give us an exhumation order if we felt it was necessary."

"And *do* you think it's necessary, Inspector?"

"I don't know at this point. It might simply be an odd coincidence. I just felt the need to ask you what your impression was."

"This has all been such a shock. And Ingrid's death, because of the nature of it, even more of a shock than Mom's. I guess I'd like to think about it some more."

"Certainly. Now, you knew Ingrid Davidson quite well?"

"My parents and the Davidsons have been close friends for all of my life. Their children were all a fair bit older than me, but I certainly know them." She frowned. "But…"

After a moment's silence, he prompted her. "But?"

"Well, being perfectly honest, Dad and Ben have always been really close, but I don't think Mom and Ingrid would have been friends if it were just them, if you know what I mean."

"So they were friendly but not friends?"

"Not *best* friends, for sure. Mom's best friend was Mary Simmons. Ingrid was, well, a friend of both of them, but only because of Ben and Dad's friendship.

"Ingrid was focused on her kids and her home. Mom was forty when I was born, and I'm the only one. Before me she had a number of miscarriages and had actually given up. And Mary never married. Mary had her career, and later on Mom had her cookbooks. Ingrid just focused on her kids. So they really had very little in common with her, but they were still friends, and the group of them often spent holidays together. Norm and Elizabeth, too, sometimes."

Ryan sat forward. "You can't think of a reason why someone would want to kill both your mother and Ingrid?"

Trish shook her head, "When you put it like that, the idea is ridiculous."

"All right, what about Ingrid? Why would someone want to kill her?"

"Have you considered that someone here might have done it while—I guess the word I want is *hallucinating*? But perhaps not that exactly. What I mean is, don't elderly people who have dementia sometimes get confused? You know, be talking to you one minute, and the next think you're a sister who died twenty years ago? Could someone have been confused and thought they were—oh, I don't know—this sounds crazy, but—carving a turkey, maybe? Or not realize the knife is a knife and think they're combing her hair? Couldn't it be something like that?"

Manziuk smiled. "At this point, I suppose that theory is as valid as anything else."

"What will you do next?"

"Finish talking to everyone, go over what we've learned, see if anything was found during the search, do some follow-up, and come up with some kind of a working theory as to what might have happened. I assume if we think of something else we can call you?"

Ryan spoke again, "For the record, where were you this afternoon, from lunch on?"

"I left the dining room with the others. It was about 1:00. I walked with Dad to his office. I'd been trying to persuade him to come out with me for the afternoon and get some sunshine, but he said no. He has a routine for writing and insists on sticking to it. So I went back to my room—the guest suite—and did some packing.

"I thought maybe Dad would go out with Mary and me for the evening. I was planning on going home tomorrow and taking the rest of Mom's things with me—the ones I haven't gone through yet."

Manziuk handed her his card. "You'll let us know if you find anything that might even remotely be connected with Ingrid's murder,"

"I will."

Ryan asked, "So were you packing all afternoon?"

She blushed. "No. There was something I wanted to ask my dad about, so I went to his office. He was, shall we say, less than thrilled to see me? He told me to go away and stop bothering him. He actually swore at me. I know his writing is important to him, but I guess I never realized what he's like when he's in the middle of a book." She looked down at her hands clasped together on her lap. "So I left. I was ultra careful not to slam his door on my way out, although that's exactly what I wanted to do."

"Where did you go after that?"

"I started back to my room. I—I was crying. It's hard to explain. I was feeling sorry for myself. I'd come here to help my dad, and he didn't seem to appreciate it at all." She looked up. "I guess you'd say I was always a 'daddy's girl.' But after being around him the last couple of weeks, I've begun to think Mom was a saint to put up with him all those years."

Manziuk asked, "Could he be getting a bit more difficult?"

"I certainly hope so. At least I don't remember him being so abrupt before. It's also possible Mom's death has affected him more than he's willing to admit."

"Did you see anyone on your way to your room?"

"Just Mary."

"Where was this?"

"In the hallway before I got to the guest suite. I ended up going to her condo for a few minutes. I tried to make a joke out of interrupting my dad and his reaction and ended up more or less crying on her shoulder."

"How long were you there?"

"Just a few minutes. Mary basically told me, 'That's Frank. Always doing what he wants and never thinking of anyone but himself.' And I had this blinding revelation that she was right, and I needed to get by myself and think about how much I had misjudged both of my parents all these years. So I went back to my suite to think and finish packing. I planned to leave right after breakfast tomorrow."

"Can you hold off on that? We may need to talk to you again."

Moments after Trish left, Ford poked his head in the door. "Got a minute?"

Manziuk looked at Ryan. "Can you ask Audra to hold back the next person?"

Ryan jumped up. "Sure, but wait until I get back to talk."

"Of course." Ford winked at Manziuk. "We'll discuss the weather. Or maybe the chances of that local baseball team, what's it called again?"

Ryan hit him as she walked past.

Ford strode around the desk and dropped into Ryan's empty chair. "She *is* still dating that pitcher, isn't she? Santana?"

"She says they're just good friends."

"Yeah, right." Ford positioned Ryan's chair so he could put his feet up on the desk, and put his hands behind his neck.

Ryan came back. "Okay, what have I missed?"

Ford grinned. "I just solved it, so you can pack up and go home."

"Works for me." She went to the wing chair and sat on the edge, looking at Ford expectantly. "So what have you found?"

Ford raised his brows. "I see things have levelled out here. Or maybe swung in a new direction. Does she give the orders now?"

Ryan bit her lip. "Please."

Ford laughed. "Okay, since you said 'please.' We did a cursory check of the room where the body was found and the hallways near it, and we've done a quick search of all the condos and the guest suite. We still have to check the staff living areas, the office, the kitchen and staff lounge, something called a theatre, an exercise room, a games room, the row of rooms this office is in, a laundry and a couple of storage rooms, and so forth. And the dining room. But if you want the residents back in their own places, they can go. Not the condo belonging to the woman who was murdered, of course. It's getting a much more thorough search."

Manziuk said, "As it happens, we've talked to all the residents so this works out well. We'll keep the staff in the dining room for now. I assume you'll do their living areas next?"

"Right."

"Do you have an overall impression of the place?"

"Seems well run. Calm. Comfortable. Restful, but not boring. I wouldn't mind coming here when I retire. Or tomorrow. First class everything from the carpets to the light fixtures." He thought a bit. "I'm no expert, but there's some expensive stuff around. Clothes. Jewellery. Paintings. Knickknacks. Souvenirs. And so forth." He grinned. "The people who pay to live here are probably a little ditsy, but, hey, they say creatives are like that."

"And did you learn anything, no matter how unrelated, that might be of interest?"

"Well, if someone here wanted a weapon, they'd have no shortage of possibilities. Lots of kitchen knives, a couple of paper knives, and an array of medicines that could cause anything from an overdose to instant death. Seriously, you asked me to watch out for possible poisons. The Carlysles have a studio with paints and paint thinners and things like that. And pretty well every one of the condos has something or another. Various types of pain pills, heart pills, sleeping pills, and a host of others—you name it, someone probably has it. I'll give you a list of them. Some in locked medicine cabinets, but most in unlocked ones, in drawers, in refrigerators, on top of dressers, or sitting out in the open on counters or tables."

"I guess that was to be expected."

He snapped his fingers. "Oh, and one other thing. About the other lady who died—Violet Klassen. Her daughter has a bunch of big plastic tubs of assorted papers and letters and journals in the guest suite. I gave them a cursory glance. A lot of them seem to be old recipes, many of them written out by hand. But she also wrote other stuff. More along the lines of journals. Her impressions and so forth. Might be worth looking for something in her most recent ones, assuming she was still writing them during her last few weeks."

"We'll mention it to her daughter," Manziuk said.

Ryan interrupted. "Didn't you find anything pertinent to the case?"

Ford laughed. "Patience, child."

Before she could protest, he waved his hand in the air. "How about a fancy leather sheath for a knife? And it's empty."

Ryan leaned toward him. "Where was it?"

"In the very last condo we checked. The owner is listed as Kenneth Harper."

Manziuk frowned. "Harper? Where was it?"

Ford swung his feet to the ground and sat up. He pulled a camera out of his jacket pocket and played with it for a moment. "Right here."

Manziuk and Ryan moved over to the desk so they could see the digital photograph.

"What you're seeing is the top of the desk in his study. The desk is pretty well covered with a laptop, books, papers, and so forth. The sheath was right here—" he pointed to a spot on the picture "—under this pile of papers and whatnot."

Ryan said, "We need to talk to him again. Find out if the knife belonged to him."

Ford grinned. "We found another couple of interesting things there. In the last week or two he's been doing a search on his computer for 'lethal stab wounds.' And there were some interesting letters on his desk, presumably waiting to be mailed. We're checking them for prints."

"May we see the sheath?"

Ford laughed. "Wow! '*May* we'! She's a fast learner."

Ryan put her hands on her hips. "Now."

Ford sat back, put his feet up again, and waited while Manziuk and Ryan returned to their chairs. "Sheath should be coming shortly. It's being checked for prints."

After Ford left, Manziuk and Ryan went to the dining room and spoke briefly to Audra and the two officers guarding the room. Then Manziuk addressed everyone. "I know it's been a very difficult day for all of you. I very much appreciate your patience while we've been talking to everyone and checking your rooms to make sure there's nothing and no one suspicious here."

"Do you know what time it is?" Frank shouted. "You've kept us prisoner in this room for hours. I need to lie down."

"It's 9:30, Mr. Klassen. And I came to let you know that our people have searched all of the residents' condos, so we're letting you return to your own areas. Please understand you can *only* go to your condos and not to any of the other rooms. We'll be continuing the search overnight, and hopefully you'll be able to use the other rooms in the morning. Except for the common room, of course. It may be off limits for a bit longer."

He looked over at the staff, still sitting at the back of the room. "We're going through the staff living quarters now, and we'll be interviewing you next. I realize some of you live off-site, so we'll talk to you first and then make sure you get home safely." He looked around at all the tired people. "Are there any questions?"

Lyle spoke. "How safe are we here?"

"Right now, we don't know who attacked Mrs. Davidson, or why. I'd naturally advise you to lock your doors."

"Our locks are voice-commanded. Some of the staff can unlock our doors with a voice code. Not implying anything, but that does mean none of us is completely secure."

"Can't you leave people here to guard us?" Frank asked. "We pay enough taxes. If not, perhaps we should hire some security guards."

"There will be people from our forensic team here all night. We can also station a police officer at each corner of the hallways, where they can see the doors to all of the condos. That way, anyone who comes into the hallway will be seen. That should keep you safe for tonight."

Audra asked, "If one of the residents should need help during the night, can they call Derrick or me as usual?"

"Yes, but one of our officers would accompany you."

"Do you honestly expect us to believe Ingrid's death was premeditated murder?" Frank's tone indicated his obvious skepticism. "Most murders are committed for gain or out of passion. How would either of those things fit with Ingrid?"

Ryan stepped forward and spoke before Manziuk had a chance. "We hope that this will turn out to be a terrible accident of some sort, but we can't assume that. For everyone's safety, we can't rule anything out."

Norm raised his hand. "Are you leaving after you've interviewed the staff? Will you be back?"

Manziuk answered. "We're going to finish interviewing the staff tonight, and we'll be back early tomorrow morning. I promise you we'll do everything in our power to determine what happened as quickly as we possibly can."

"And meanwhile we get to stay here and wonder which one of us is a cold-blooded murderer."

Manziuk looked at Norm, but then let his eyes travel around the room as he spoke. "Please remember, if you find anything out of the ordinary when you return to your condo—no matter how trivial—or if you remember something that might be pertinent, even if it's the middle of the night, please bring it to the attention of one of our officers. Even if it turns out to be nothing, it's safer for us to follow up than for you to keep it to yourself or, worse, play amateur detective."

Catarina looked at Nikola. "Well, you can't say that life here is boring now, can you?"

Ryan looked at her watch as the first of the daily staff came into the interview room—9:50. It had been a long day for everyone. The good news was that they were almost finished with the initial interviews.

Tess Cooper, the laundry lady, had caramel-coloured skin and long wavy hair held back with a band. Ryan guessed her age at early thirties. She explained that she came in from 9:00 to 4:00 each weekday.

Tess had seen both of the Carlysles in their condo at about 1:30 when she went to pick up a clothes hamper. She'd seen Ingrid going down the hallway past the games room. She assumed Ingrid was going to the common room and had become confused and missed the turn. She tried to get her to turn back and go the shorter way, but Ingrid ignored her.

Around 2:00 Derrick had brought in some towels to be washed. Just after that Tess took some of the Carlysles' clean laundry back and heard Norm talking to himself in his studio, but she neither heard nor saw Elizabeth. When she left she saw Trish turning into the hallway outside her dad's office.

A little later Mary peeked into the laundry room for a few minutes to say hello, and Olive brought some towels and dishcloths from the kitchen.

The next staff member was the maid, Gulab Brampton. She looked about forty, spoke with a strong East Indian accent, wore jeans, white tennis shoes, and an over-sized T-shirt with a Toronto Raptors logo. She said she'd been cleaning the Rossi condo from about 12:15 until Audra called for everyone to come to the dining room just before 3:00.

Catarina Rossi had come back after lunch and gone into her bedroom to lie down. Mr. Vincent had come in with her and sat around playing his guitar in the living room. He went out at about 1:30 and came back long before Audra asked everyone to go to the dining room.

Jared Wright, the building maintenance supervisor, was next. He'd been out with friends and had just returned. The police officer in the lobby had escorted him straight up.

He said he'd been up to the twentieth floor twice that day because of a dripping tap in the master bathroom in Lyle Oakley's condo. He came at 12:30 to check on the make and model of the tap before going shopping, and at 2:30 to install the new tap. He didn't see anyone either time.

As Jared left the room, Ford stepped in. "Here you go. The sheath, a couple of photos of the knife, and three letters you might find interesting."

"No partridge in a pear tree," Ryan asked.

Ford grinned.

Manziuk picked up the sheath in its plastic bag. "Would the knife fit?"

"Like a glove."

"And the letters?"

"On Harper's desk. They weren't sealed, so we had a peek."

"Okay, thanks."

Manziuk and Ryan took a few minutes to read the letters. Then Manziuk turned to Ryan. "Can you tell Audra I want to see the cook next?"

"You don't want to talk to Mr. Harper first?"

"No, first I want to make sure the knife isn't one of hers."

"Okay, but I have a suggestion."

"What's that?"

"Let me be lead questioning the live-in staff."

"Why?"

"Isn't it obvious?"

He thought for a moment. "You might have a point. It's late, and they're tired, and they'll probably be more comfortable talking to you. Okay, we'll give it a try."

"Of course you'll have to take notes."

Manziuk rolled his eyes.

Manziuk had just seated himself behind the desk and was eyeing the keyboard with disdain when the door opened to a large woman with dark brown skin and curly golden hair. She was dressed in a uniform of white top and black pants.

"I'm Scarlett." She collapsed into the empty seat. "I just can't believe what's happening here. Losing two of our ladies so close together. And Mr. Grant not long ago. You know, those are the first people we've lost in this building in the five years I've been here. A few moved out because they needed more care, but that's different from just up and dying on us, like Mr. Grant and Ms. Violet did. And now Mrs. Davidson!"

Ryan asked, "Is it Mrs. or Ms. Walker?"

"Just Scarlett is fine. I was married a long, long time ago, but I went back to my maiden name after I got shed of that sorry excuse for a man, and I was never tempted to get hitched again. But Ms. just doesn't seem right, and Mrs. Walker sounds like my mother."

"All right. Scarlett, how long have you been on staff here?"

"Since it opened. Over five years now."

"And you said the three deaths in the past few months are the only ones during that time?"

Scarlett's head bobbed up and down. "The only ones on our floor anyway. Most people get sick first and then die slowly. Or maybe they get in a car accident or something like that. But we've only had a couple who got sick enough to need to move to the hospital or a nursing home. Nobody died here before Mr. Grant had his heart attack. And then poor Ms. Violet dropping to sleep the way she did and not waking up. And now—well, you know 'bout that."

"What can you tell us about Mrs. Klassen's death?"

"Ms. Violet? It was a shock to all of us is what I can tell you. I thought I was going to have a heart attack myself when I heard." Scarlett leaned forward. "Did they tell you we were writing a book together? Course she did all the actual writing. I quit school in grade eight and never went back, so writing a book is way beyond me. But how it worked is that Ms. Violet gave me a bunch of old recipes, and I changed them up to make them healthier and more in line with what's available today. And then she used some of my own recipes, too. Ones I've made up. I cooked and measured, and we tasted and tested everything, and she wrote it all up. So the book is a mixture of her recipes and mine, all suited to seniors, and both of our names are on the cover." A sad look crossed her face. "I don't know what will happen now. Ms. Trish says it'll be okay, but if Mr. Klassen has his way, the book will never be published."

Ryan frowned. "Why is that?"

"He's never been a fan of her books. He couldn't care less if it gets finished."

"Do you know why that is?"

Scarlett looked away. "Best not to say any more. Anyway that's got nothing to do with what happened today with Mrs. Davidson, does it?"

"We like to know what's going on in the place where any suspicious death happens."

After making sure that Scarlett wasn't looking at him, Manziuk rolled his eyes very slightly.

"Well, all I'll say is that Mr. Klassen didn't like his wife getting friendly with the staff."

Ryan leaned toward her. "Did she tell you that?"

"She didn't need to. Been that way for the whole five years. He likes everyone keeping their place, and her writing a book with the cook didn't set easy with him. Not one bit."

"That didn't stop her?"

"I think it almost stopped her, but— I don't know what happened, and that's the truth. One day early on when we were still talking about possibilities, maybe a year or so ago, she came into the kitchen looking like she'd seen a ghost. I made her sit down and got her some tea with just a nip of brandy, and after a few minutes she said to me, 'Scarlett, I've just realized something I should have known a long time ago. I won't say any more, but I want you to please try to ignore Frank.' And she says, 'No matter what he says, we're doing this book.' And then she said, 'It's my little bit toward righting a great wrong.' That's all she ever said. But from then on she just ignored anything Mr. Klassen said to the contrary, and we kept going on it."

"And you have no idea what she was referring to?"

Scarlett shook her head vigorously. "She never said anything else about it, and I never asked."

"When Mrs. Klassen died, you said you were shocked?"

"Well, wouldn't you be? One minute you're in the kitchen laughing and talking about doing some book signings together, with her telling me I'm going even if she has to get Derrick to pick me up and put me in the car, my hat and all. And just a few hours later she's lying on her bed like a rag doll that a child's thrown away!"

"So you saw her earlier in the day?"

"Of course I did. Just before lunch. She was going to talk to the publisher later in the day and find out when the launch was going to be. She insisted I had to be at the launch, and I said I can't leave my job. And she said that Serenity Suites could afford to hire a caterer for a few days if they had to. And then I needed to get lunch on the table, so she went off. At lunch she was fine. On her way out she popped into the kitchen and said, 'We'll need to get you a new outfit, too!' and popped out again. And then she didn't show up for tea at three o'clock—" Scarlett took a tissue from her pocket and dabbed at her eyes.

Ryan looked at Manziuk. "Let's move to today. Where were you between 1:00 and 3:00 this afternoon?"

"I was in the kitchen cleaning up after lunch until maybe 1:30. Olive was helping. Then I went to my room for a short rest. At around 2:00 I went back to the kitchen to get tea ready. I was there until Audra came to tell me about Mrs. Davidson. Then I was in the dining room with everyone else. Well, first, Olive and I brought the tea in. It was all ready. It seemed wrong in a way, but I think it helped them a bit. Kept the blood sugar up, if nothing else."

"Was Olive with you the whole time you were in the kitchen?"

"Well, she was going back and forth to set the table in the dining room for part of the time."

"She wasn't gone for an extended period of time?"

"No."

"Did anyone else come into the kitchen between lunch and tea time?"

"I close the door when I'm out, but I don't lock it. So someone could have come in during the half hour I was out. Olive went to her room at the same time as me for a little break. Afterwards, while I was getting tea ready, it was just Olive and me. Well, Mary came in for a moment, and Audra came in at least once, but don't ask me when. I was focused on getting things ready."

Manziuk pushed his chair back and came around the desk to show her the photograph of the knife. "Do you recognize this?"

Scarlett put her hand to her throat. "Is that—is it the one?"

"Yes."

She studied the photos for a long minute. "No." Relief was evident in both her voice and the way she relaxed. "I *don't* recognize it. It's most definitely not one of mine."

Manziuk took back the photos. "Do you have any idea why someone would want to kill Ingrid Davidson?"

She shook her head. "Poor old lady. No, I have no idea at all."

"There's no one you suspect?"

"I just can't see anyone here doing that. But I also can't see how someone who wasn't from this floor could do it without being seen."

Manziuk looked at her with a bit more interest. "Good point."

Ryan said, "Well, let us know if you think of anything at all that might help us."

"And thank you for the meringues," Manziuk said. "They were very good."

"The recipe is in the new cookbook. If it gets published, I'll give you each a copy."

Eleven

The tall young man with light chocolate skin and a muscular appearance stood at the door. "Hi, I'm Derrick James."

Ryan shook his hand. "Please come in and have a seat. I understand you were out earlier today?"

Derrick sat on the edge of the chair and leaned forward. "Yeah, I went out around 2:00 and got back a few minutes after 5:00."

"How long have you worked here?"

"Just over three years."

"And your role is?"

He smiled. "Part assistant manager, part jack of all trades. I'm a registered nurse, but I'm also a physiotherapist and a qualified personal trainer. They were looking for someone to keep the residents active and fit, but who could help out medically if needed. Plus, the other live-in staff are female, and they wanted at least one male."

"How do you like working here?"

"I love it. Nice people, regular hours, great food, good pay."

"Are you from around here?"

"The Greater Toronto Area, yes. My family's in Oshawa."

"How well did you know Ingrid Davidson?"

"Fairly well. She had some problems I'd been helping her with. Her hip and her leg. I worked with her on an almost-daily basis. Mostly doing massage and heat."

"What was your opinion of her?"

He shrugged. "She was a nice lady. Proud of Ben, and proud of her kids and their families. I think she'd had a good life. But—" He looked down. "Well, she wasn't in very good shape. She had a lot of pain in her hip and her leg. And she was getting less and less able to remember things or to carry on a conversation. The last few months she'd become a shell of herself. I figured any day I'd hear they were moving her to a nursing home." He looked up. "I hate what happens to so many people when they get old."

Manziuk spoke from behind the desk. "When you got back today and learned that Ingrid had been murdered, what did you think?"

Derrick turned slightly to see him better. "I couldn't believe it."

Ryan said, "You said you left at about two. Where were you between 1:00 and 2:00?"

"After lunch? Well, I had a few things to do before I went out. I put away the equipment in the workout room, covered the hot tub, checked the steam room, and locked up."

"Why would you lock it?"

"Safety. It's usually unlocked, but I tend to lock it when I'm off-site. Audra can open it if someone wants in."

"All right. What then?"

"I took the towels to the laundry. I think that's all."

"Who did you see during that time?"

He thought a moment. "Well, no one comes to the exercise room right after lunch, so I was alone there. I saw Tess when I dropped off the towels. I went to my room just before 2:00 to change. On my way out I stopped to let Audra know I was going, and I took the long way to the elevator because I wanted to double-check that I'd locked the exercise room door. I heard someone in the billiards room so I looked in. Nikola was there, and I stopped to talk to him for a couple of minutes. I checked the time, and it was 2:05. I left a couple of minutes later."

"You didn't see anyone else in the hallways?"

He shook his head.

Manziuk said, "How well did you know Violet Klassen?"

Derrick looked over at Manziuk in surprise. "Violet? Well, she didn't come to my area much, but of course I knew her. I'd see her in the kitchen sometimes working on the cookbook with Scarlett. And of course I saw her around the place."

"How did you feel about her death?"

"That's a strange question. I felt bad, of course. And surprised. I know they'd recently found cancer, but she sure didn't seem sick to me." He looked from Manziuk to Ryan. "Why? You think there's a connection? But Violet's death was natural. And Ingrid's sure wasn't."

Manziuk continued. "When there are two deaths in the same place, so close in time, of two women who were friends, it's natural to wonder if there might be a link. But we have no reason to believe there was one."

Ryan chimed in. "So, if there was anything at all unusual about Violet's death, we need to know. Anything that might be worth checking."

Derrick pursed his lips. "Well, maybe there is one thing." He stood up. "Okay, so here's the thing. I'm taking a class at the University of Toronto. I leave around 2:00 every Wednesday, and I come back between 4:30 and 5:00. Got it?"

Ryan nodded.

"Okay, so the day Violet died was also a Wednesday. Two weeks ago today. I came back, and there were police here. So, if you're looking for coincidences, there's one for you."

"What do you remember about that day?"

He shrugged. "After lunch I did my usual stuff, same as today." He frowned in concentration. "Wait, there was one other thing. Just before I left, I remembered to pick up the step stool from outside Violet and Frank's condo and—"

"Step stool?"

"Scarlett has a nice one in the kitchen. It gets borrowed now and then when someone needs to get something from a top shelf. Violet asked me during lunch that day if I'd take it to her room and leave it at the door. Then she left me a message to pick it up at about, oh, maybe 1:45. I was busy at the time, and there was no rush. But on my way out, I remembered it and took it back to the kitchen."

"Did you see Violet when you picked it up?"

"No, she'd set it outside her door, where I'd left it in the first place."

"Did she tell you *why* she needed it?" Manziuk asked.

Derrick thought for a moment but shook his head. "She just said she needed something from a cupboard. I assumed she meant something from one of the top shelves. She was pretty short, so she had trouble reaching the higher shelves. I offered to help her get whatever it was, but she said she could do it. So I took the stool over just before they started leaving the dining room, which would have been shortly after 1:00. So, assuming she went straight back to her place after lunch, she'd have had close to forty-five minutes to do whatever she was doing."

Ryan thanked him. "We'll check into it."

Manziuk said, "Getting back to today, do you have any thoughts as to who might have disliked Mrs. Davidson? Did she have any enemies? Anyone who seemed to be overly bothered by her?"

"No, I don't think so. Not enemies, for sure. She could be kind of grumpy, but only in the last while. Before, she'd mostly talk about her family and what she was making for them. She did a lot of crocheting. Inoffensive, I guess you'd say. As for being bothered by her, Mrs. Davidson was someone you could easily ignore."

Ryan said, "What about Mrs. Klassen? Did she have enemies?"

"I don't think so. Mentally she was sharp, and she sometimes could be kind of blunt. But she didn't go out of her way to annoy people. *Mr.* Klassen is far more annoying."

Manziuk asked, "Are there any people here who don't seem to get along with any of the others?"

Derrick looked down. "Well, there are some who don't like Mrs. Brooks—" he looked straight at Ryan "—mostly because of the colour of her skin."

"You're sure that's the only reason?" Ryan asked.

He thought for second. "Maybe it's a bit more than that. I don't think they want to see her as one of them. Their equal. Partly because of her skin colour, but partly because the rumour is she was an exotic dancer for a time so, in their minds, she's not in their class."

"I see."

"The staff see the looks they give her behind her back and the way they stop talking when she comes near, or how they kind of ignore her even when she's right there with them."

"Everyone?" Manziuk asked.

"No, not everyone. But most of them."

"Frank Klassen?"

"Definitely. And the Carlysles, Ingrid, Mary, Mrs. Rossi, I guess Mrs. Klassen, and I think the new person, Mr. Harper, too." Derrick thought for a moment before adding, "I guess you'd need to include the Kanes and the Gerbrandts, too, even though they aren't here right now."

Manziuk was looking at the list Audra had given them. "The only residents you've left out are Mr. Davidson, Mr. Oakley, and Mr. Vincent."

"Mr. Davidson treats everyone well. Staff or resident, it's all the same to him. With Mr. Oakley, it's maybe a bit different. It's as if he wants people to like him, so he goes out of his way to treat everyone the same. And Mr. Vincent doesn't mingle much, but I'd say he treats everyone about the same. Much like Mr. Davidson." He frowned. "I don't mean that no one ever speaks to Mrs. Brooks. I just mean they don't treat her as a friend or as one of them. They're polite, but no more."

"Olive Yeung." The petite Asian woman, who wore a blue and white checked smock and jeans, looked terrified, and spoke so quietly she might have been whispering.

Ryan said, "Please sit down, Olive. We just have a few questions."

Olive sat and looked from Ryan to Manziuk and back.

"Olive, how long have you worked here?"

"Getting close to three months."

"I'm sorry. I'm having difficulty hearing you. Could you speak a little louder, please?"

"Three months."

"Thank you. How do you like it here?"

"Good," she whispered. Then, apparently feeling a wave of enthusiasm, she started to speak louder with more animation. "The people here are old, but they're interesting. Before, I worked as a chambermaid for a hotel, and I like this a lot better. And the staff here are great to work with."

"Did you know Mrs. Davidson very well?"

"Not really. She didn't talk much. And I don't think she ever asked me to do anything for her. Maybe pick up her wool if she dropped it. But not much. Not like Mrs. Rossi or Mr. Carlysle. They're always losing things and getting me to help find them." She smiled. "Mrs. Klassen asked for help sometimes, too. I liked her. She had a dry sense of humour. At least that's what Derrick called it. You didn't always know when she was joking."

"I understand you helped Scarlett after lunch and before tea?"

"Yes, I helped her clean up after lunch and then I set the table for tea and helped with a few other things around the kitchen. She's promised to teach me to cook, so I'm happy about that. Cooks make better money."

"You were in the kitchen from lunch until what time?"

"I was back and forth between the kitchen and the dining room until 1:30. Except when I took some towels to the laundry room and talked to Tess for a few minutes."

"What did you do when you left the kitchen?"

"Scarlett and I both went to our rooms at about 1:30 for a break. Then at 2:00, I went back to the kitchen."

"Was Scarlett in the kitchen when you got back at 2:00?"

"No, but Audra was coming out of the kitchen with a cup of tea. Scarlett came in a few seconds later. And after that it was just her and me until Audra came and told us what had happened to Ingrid."

"Did you see anyone other than Scarlett during the time you were in the kitchen? Did anyone come into the kitchen?"

Olive blinked. "Uh, Mary popped in for a little while. I'm not sure when."

After Olive left, Audra came in. "That's all of us. Is there anything else I can do?"

Manziuk indicated the wing chair. "Perhaps you can answer a few questions that have come up."

"I'll do my best." She sat down with her hands folded on her lap.

Manziuk got up and sat on the edge of the desk, facing her. "First, I'd like to know how surprised you were by Violet Klassen's death."

"Violet?" She sank back further into the chair. "I was *very* surprised by her death. We all were. I knew about the cancer, of course. Not everyone did. But my understanding was that the doctors had told her she'd still be here for Christmas. And usually cancer doesn't kill you in your sleep that way. So we—Derrick and I—were quite surprised."

"And bothered?"

"Well, some of those who watch crime shows wondered why there wasn't an autopsy. Mary Simmons has said that to me several times. She thought it felt wrong somehow—as if no one cared enough to find out what had happened."

"Did you say anything to Frank Klassen or his daughter?"

"I asked Mr. Klassen if he wasn't curious, and he said he was just glad she hadn't suffered."

"Did it occur to you that perhaps Mrs. Klassen decided to end her own life and Mr. Klassen wanted to keep that from being discovered?"

She nodded. "I've thought of it, and I've overheard a couple of people saying something of the sort to each other. But I don't believe it. Not with the book coming out. And even if I thought she was capable of doing something like that, I can't see her doing it without talking to her daughter first to say goodbye. She adored her daughter. At the very least, she'd have left her a letter or some kind of note. And as far as I know, she didn't. Trish said her mother had phoned her the day before to tell her about the cancer but that she didn't seem overly upset and was talking about things she needed to do."

"Could someone else—Mr. Klassen perhaps—have found a note and hidden it or thrown it away?"

Audra bit her lower lip. "I'm the one who found Violet, and I didn't see anything like a note. I suppose it could have been hidden in a place where only Mr. Klassen would find it, or she might even have mailed it to her daughter, but neither of them has said anything."

"So you'd have liked an autopsy?"

"I can't help but wonder what happened. Not that my curiosity is any reason for them to do one. But Dr. Granger and the coroner decided it was natural causes, and that was that."

"The coroner was here?"

"Yes. I called 911, so the police came, and firemen, and paramedics, too. Naomi—Ms. Arlington—was very upset with me. So was Dr. Granger."

"Do you know which coroner?"

"I don't recall his name, but he was here today. With the red hair."

"Ah, good. Dr. Weaver. So he agreed with your doctor that it was natural causes?"

Audra shrugged. "I guess."

"All right. Thanks."

Ryan spoke now. "What about Mrs. Davidson's death? How does that strike you?"

"I just feel so sad, and so angry. She didn't deserve that." Tears came to Audra's eyes, and she leaned forward, burying her face in her hands and sobbing. "I'm sorry. I've had to ignore what happened and look after everyone and—and stay calm. I'm sorry."

"Take your time." Ryan grabbed a box of tissues from the desk and held it out.

Audra took a handful and wiped her eyes. "Okay, I'm all right. Sorry."

Manziuk asked, "Ms. Limson, who was here when Grant Brooks had his heart attack?"

She gave him a strange look. "I was."

"And what happened?"

"Grant and Hilary had tickets to a concert. Grant had the heart attack while they were on the way down in the elevator. When the doors opened at ground level, Hilary yelled for help, and the security guard got Grant out of the elevator while the receptionist called 911 and then called for some of the medical people on duty. Everything possible was done, and he was sent to hospital in an ambulance, but the doctors who examined him at the ER said he was likely dead before he even hit the ground."

"Thank you for that information. Speaking of the other people, how well do you know Mr. Harper?"

"Kenneth? Less than the others, of course. He's only been here a short time, but he seems like a nice man, if very sad. Did you know he used to be a minister? He told me one day— You won't repeat what I say, will you?"

"Everything you tell us is confidential unless it has a direct bearing on a crime."

She shook her head. "No, no, there was no crime. Well, not in the way *we* think of crime."

"Now you've made me very curious."

"He told me that he was a minister, and he and his wife had a young family, and they were very happy. But his wife got breast cancer. She had a mastectomy, and the doctors thought they got all the cancer, but they were wrong, and she died. When she died, Kenneth said he told God he hated him, and he tried to hang himself. Only, his children found him and cut him down." She shook her head. "I don't think he's ever forgiven himself. And he barely has any relationship with his children. But if you're thinking he might have killed Ingrid, I can't imagine any reason for him to take the life of another man's wife, can you?"

Ryan asked, "Is there *anyone* here you think would be capable of taking someone's life?"

Audra smiled. "If I try very hard, and only in an abstract way, Catarina perhaps—if she thought it was for the best. Or Nikola, who must be somewhat cold-blooded. None of us knows why he married her but it must have been for her money. Maybe Elizabeth, if it would benefit her. Frank, but it would have to be for a life-or-death matter that directly affected him in some way. Mary, Lyle, Ben, Norm, Hilary… no."

Ryan raised her eyebrows. "Not Hilary?"

"Well, maybe. But I think only in self-defense, if then."

"So you don't think any of them would have done it out of compassion, to end Ingrid's suffering?"

"To be honest, I don't think anyone cared about her that much, other than Ben. And I'm positive he couldn't have done it."

"Could he have asked someone else to do it?"

She shook her head.

Manziuk spoke."What about the staff? Which of them could murder someone, not necessarily Ingrid?"

"I feel so weird saying this."

"But you know the people, and we don't."

"Well, maybe Scarlett, if she thought her life or that of someone she cared for was in danger. Olive—I don't know her well, but I think she'd be far too timid. Derrick looks like a macho guy, but he'd rather die himself than hurt someone else. Tess and Gulab, I don't know, maybe if someone was threatening their family." She paused. "Which leaves me."

Manziuk smiled. "It does."

"There are times I really wish I *could* murder someone, Inspector. But it would be my ex-husband I'd stick a knife in, not Ingrid."

"You're divorced?"

"Yes." She bit her bottom lip. "I expect you'll do background checks, so I may as well tell you. My ex-husband is a lawyer who knew how to make me look like a total idiot in court. I was a stay-at-home mom. After he told me he wanted a divorce, he offered to keep the boys while I got my new life started. Like a fool I believed him. He knew that if I left the boys with him, he'd gain the upper hand because it would look as if I was the one who'd moved out and abandoned them. And sure enough he ended up with custody of our sons. Not that he actually wanted them—he just wanted to 'win.' And win he did. He got to keep his girlfriend, our house, his car, and our boys. He even got the dog."

"That sounds very difficult. How long ago did it happen?"

"Over three years ago. The boys are twelve and ten now. I see them every other weekend for a few hours. He isn't an ogre, and maybe in some ways the boys are better off with him, but I miss them so much. And I miss being their mother."

"After the divorce, you got the job here?"

"I got it shortly after we separated." She bit her lip. "I was fortunate enough to know someone on staff here on another floor, and she recommended me for this job that had just come open. It was perfect. Anyway, that's all water under the bridge."

"Your boys live in Toronto?"

"Yes. I take the subway to see them on Saturdays. We usually go out some place. And in the summer I get them for two weeks, so I take them to a cottage. And they call me when they can." Tears came to her eyes and she wiped them away. "I've managed."

"Okay, getting back to the residents who live here. I know who Ben is, and I recognized Elizabeth and Mary and Catarina after they told me who they were, so I have a place to start. Lyle Oakley gave us a lot of information. But can you give us any background on some of the others?"

"I'll try. Who would you like to start with?"

"What about Norm? I understand he paints. Is he good, or is he here because of his wife?"

Audra smiled. "Norm's paintings sell for tens of thousands of dollars. Some of them are just stunning. Norm may come across like a sort of bumbler, but when it comes to his art, he's the real deal."

"Kenneth Harper?"

"He's a tenor who has sung all over the world. Mostly in operas. Even though he's getting older, he's still very much in demand, and he's able to pick and choose what he does."

"What about Hilary Brooks? She told us that 'they' want her out of here. Is that true?"

"Ms. Arlington could give you more information than me, but I believe there's a lot of truth in that. They're saying it was Grant who bought the condo, and he was the one who was approved to live here, and she can't stay without him."

"And is that normal?"

"It's one of the problems no one thought of ahead of time. When a couple comes in, and only one of the people meets the requirements and then that person dies or has to go into a nursing home, there's a great deal of difficulty. It would be the same if it were Ben who had died and Ingrid who was left. According to the rules, she couldn't stay here."

"But I thought Mrs. Brooks was a dancer?"

"Yes, and she considers herself more than qualified to be here. But unfortunately the board doesn't agree. Hilary believes it's because she's black, which of course would be actionable."

Ryan chimed in. "Why stay in a place where she isn't wanted?"

Audra looked at her. "Perhaps because she's spent most of her life fighting to make a place for herself and she's tired."

"What about Nikola?"

"There you have me. I don't even know where Catarina met him. In mid-July she went away for a short holiday, and she came back wearing a wedding ring. Nikola followed with his suitcases. All I know is that he brought several guitars with him, he comes and goes a lot but doesn't appear to have a job, and Catarina seems very happy."

"All right. We'll do some checking." Manziuk made a few notes.

Ryan continued. "We've been asking everyone where they were today during the time between the end of lunch and Mrs. Davidson's body being found."

"Of course. After lunch I hung around talking to people until everyone was out of the dining room. Then I went to the kitchen and out through the staff lounge to my suite. I was there for a few minutes, and then I went to the staff office. At around 1:30 I went to Hilary's condo and stayed there about half an hour. We were talking about this whole board situation. Then I came back to my office and was there until Mary came to ask me to come to the common room."

"Did you see anyone other than Mrs. Brooks during that time?"

"Let me think. I went into the kitchen to make some tea before I went to my office. Olive came in just before I left."

"Which door did she use?"

"The same one as me, the back one closest to our suites. Oh, and Nikola dropped into my office for a few minutes. That would have been maybe ten or fifteen minutes after I got there. He asked a question and I answered it and he left." Audra looked at Ryan. "That's all."

Ryan glanced at Manziuk, who shook his head. "I think that's all for now. We'll contact you if we need anything else."

"Let me give you my cellphone number then."

"And I'll give you mine. Contact us if you think of anything else—anything at all."

After Audra left, Ryan said, "She was perfectly honest up until that last question. I wonder what the question was that Nikola asked her."

"I assume it had nothing to do with Ingrid's murder, but something about it definitely got her heart rate up."

"Yeah." Ryan stood up and put her hands on the back of her hips and stretched. "Oh, man! This feels like one of those horrible math problems with two trains leaving from different stations and you have to figure out where they'll collide. Only it's more like six trains. So—" she looked at Manziuk "—what's next?"

"I think we need to ask Kenneth Harper where his knife is."

Ryan made a face. "His answer should be interesting."

"Ford also said Kenneth had been searching for 'lethal stab wounds' on his computer."

"But what could his motive have been?"

Manziuk shook his head. "Nothing obvious. There's also what Audra said about his being devastated when his wife died. Maybe he's loony and in some crazy way thought he was making up for the past or something."

"There could be a connection we know nothing about, of course." Ryan looked at her watch. "It's well after 11:00. Should I have Audra get him?"

Manziuk picked up the photo of the knife, the sheath, and the letters. "No, let's go and talk to him on his territory."

Kenneth was still dressed, although he'd undone the top two buttons on his shirt, when he opened the door to his condo and stared in surprise. "Inspector?"

"We need to talk to you about something," Manziuk replied. "I realize it's very late, but may we come in?"

"Yes, of course." He stood aside to let them in and led the way to his sitting room.

"We need to ask you about this." Manziuk held up the small plastic bag with the knife sheath. "Do you recognize it?"

Kenneth stepped forward to peer at it more closely. "Why, that looks like—"

"Is it yours?"

"I—I— Let me see." He started to leave the room, then turned back. "Come with me if you want."

They followed him down a short hallway to a room that was obviously used as a study. The desk was piled high with stacks of papers, books, and sheet music.

Kenneth began sorting through the piles. "It was right here. I know it was. I saw it just yesterday. No, maybe it was the day before. Not long ago."

They watched him go through the piles, tossing papers and books around.

At last he gave up. "I have one that looks just like that. It was here a day or so ago."

"This one was found here."

Kenneth whirled to stare at Manziuk. "Then I don't understand. Why didn't you say so?"

"When you saw it last, was there anything in it?"

Kenneth blanched. His eyes grew large. "No, you're not—! Oh, no. Not *my* knife!"

Ryan stepped forward. "Can you describe your knife for us?"

"I can do better than that. I have a picture." He began searching through the piles again. "It's a Japanese *tanto* knife. They date back to the tenth century. Samurai carried them. They also had a sword, called a *katana*, which people usually associate with them. But the small *tanto* was their last line of defense. It's what they used to commit *hara-kiri* if they failed. This one was made before the Second World War, when a lot of people in Japan started wearing them for protection. It was given to me as a gift when I sang in Japan about five years ago. Ah, there it is!" He pounced on a small photo album and quickly found a photo and held it up for them to see.

"That looks like the one that was found beside Ingrid." Ryan held out the picture of the knife that Ford had given them.

Kenneth fell back onto his desk chair. "I—I don't know what to say. I—I feel so mortified."

"Is this where you normally keep the knife? In a pile of papers?"

Kenneth's cheeks turned red. "No, of course not. I keep it in a locked cabinet. I'll show you."

They followed him back to the sitting room to a glass display cabinet filled with the mementos of his many years of performing: a few awards, concert programs, photos of Kenneth with various people, some famous and easily recognizable, and various artifacts, presumably from his travels. He pointed out a few of them. "That compass is from Egypt; the fan from China; the marionette from Czechoslovakia; the blowpipe from Brazil." He pointed to an area that was empty. "That's where the knife was kept."

"When and why did you take it out?" Manziuk asked.

"I took it out on Sunday. In the morning. I was thinking about something and wanted to look at the knife more closely."

"And you didn't put it back?"

"No, I decided it would be the best thing for my purpose."

"And what was that?"

He looked away. "I'm embarrassed to tell you."

"I assume it wasn't to murder Ingrid?"

"No, of course not. I barely knew the woman. I doubt if I've exchanged more than six words with her since I moved in."

"Then?"

"Is this confidential? I mean, you won't need to tell anyone?"

"The only reason we'd have to say anything is if it pertains to the murder."

"All right. I'm not ashamed to admit it. I was checking the knife to see if it was sharp enough to use to commit suicide. I wanted to make sure it was a real knife, not just a ceremonial imitation."

"And how did you decide?"

He smiled. "I tested it on a potato I pilfered from the kitchen."

"And after you tested it, you left it on your desk?"

"I planned to use it tonight, after I'd had a last day of Scarlett's great food. Sort of my last meals. But that's out of the question now." He gave them a wry smile. "I've had the strangest experience. When I first heard that Ingrid had been murdered, my instinctive reaction was to become very angry. No matter how senile Ingrid was becoming, no one—no one—had the right to deprive her of any of her time on this earth. And it immediately struck me that I had no right to take my own life either. I can't explain how surreal it was for me to have that thought and to know in my heart it was true. Besides, I have to stick around and find out who the guilty party is."

"May I ask why you had decided to take your own life?"

"Because I felt I had no reason to continue living." A smile touched his lips. "Other than Scarlett's cooking, of course."

"And you no longer feel that way?"

"No, I don't, though I can't explain why."

"Getting back to the knife," Ryan interjected. "Did you put it back in the sheath?"

"Oh, yes. The knife was in the sheath on my desk when I saw it last, either yesterday or the day before. I can't be sure. I've been busy doing a number of things in preparation. I didn't want to leave a mess of any sort." Looking at his desk he smiled. "Well, other than this kind of mess. I'm afraid I'm not good at keeping things organized."

"Let's focus on the knife. Who knew you had it?"

"Hmm. That will take some thinking. Perhaps we ought to sit down. I just boiled the kettle to make a cup of chamomile tea before going to bed. Would you like some?"

They waited while Kenneth bustled about in the kitchen, returning with three cups of tea and a plate of cookies.

He sat down and took several bites from a cookie and a few sips of his tea before saying, "Now, who knew about my knife? Well, the staff did. I think they've all been in here at some point. The woman who cleans and the one who does the laundry are here the most. As for the other residents, I'd say pretty well all of them have been in here at some point, and of course the knife was in the display case, so they'd have seen it. Now that I think about it, I recall explaining it to several people.

"I don't think Ingrid was ever in. But most of the others. And they may well have mentioned the knife to those who didn't come, too. It *is* rather unique. Which makes me wonder. I will get it back, won't I?"

"Not immediately."

"That's what I feared."

Manziuk raised his eyebrows. "I thought you said you wouldn't use it now?"

"Oh, I won't. I can assure you of that. But I don't want to lose it. It's actually quite valuable."

"I can't see that anyone would plan to use a knife that's kept in a locked storage cabinet. Or was the key easy to find?"

"I kept it in my wallet. And my wallet is usually in my pocket. There's a spare in my safety deposit box at the bank."

Ryan said, "Maybe someone saw it on the desk?"

Manziuk nodded. "Was anyone in here during the last few days?"

"In other words, since Sunday, when I took the knife out." Kenneth thought for a minute. "Lyle was here yesterday for a short time, but I don't recall that we went to the study. Derrick came to talk to me about something I'd asked him. Dr. Granger was here just after lunch today, and we did go in my study, but I think I'd have noticed him pulling the knife out of the sheath and putting it into his pocket."

He looked at his wall, frowning, for a long minute. "Ben and Frank were here on Monday evening for a short time. I don't think we moved out of the sitting room though. I think that's—no wait! Mary came in on Monday afternoon for a short while. Well, longer than I liked. She can get talking. I recall she wanted something from me." He snapped his fingers. "Yes, I remember. She's a mystery fan, and last week I happened to mention a book I have. She came to ask me if she could borrow it. And of course it was in the study, so we went there and I found it. She might easily have seen the knife. Or taken it while my back was turned."

Ryan had been writing the names down. "Mary on Monday afternoon, Ben and Frank Monday evening, Lyle and Derrick on Tuesday, and Dr. Granger today. Anyone else?"

"I'll have to think. May I talk to you later if anything else comes to mind?"

Ryan handed him her business card with her cellphone number and email address. "But why take it without the sheath?" She frowned. "I can't see anyone just putting it in a pocket. Not with that sharp blade."

"When you're out, is your door always locked?" Manziuk asked.

"It locks automatically. Because it's voice activated, I don't have to worry about having a key."

"Wait a minute. What about the people who come in to clean?"

Kenneth brightened for an instant, then shook his head. "No good. I was working in my study the whole time Gulab was here on Monday. I told her not to bother me, that the room could wait a week. And my laundry day is Friday, so Tess hasn't been in this week."

"Was that the only time the cleaning lady was here?"

"Well, she comes every morning to make my bed and tidy up, but I'm normally in my study with the door shut." He looked down. "I prefer it that way. I've never been good at chitchat."

"So she wasn't in your condo when you weren't in the study?"

"Not this week."

Manziuk sighed. "Okay."

"I'll let you know if I think of anything—or anyone—else."

"Speaking of which, we'll need you as a witness. I wouldn't want you to be unavailable."

"Oh, I'll be here, Inspector." He smiled. "Perhaps someday I'll tell you the whole story. You might find it amusing. So might whoever murdered Ingrid and unwittingly changed the direction of my life."

Ryan held up the letters in their plastic bag. "In case you should want to mail these, we have them. We'll return them if we don't need them as evidence."

"I see. But honestly, you can burn them if you want. I won't be sending them now."

"That reminds me," Manziuk said. "If you were planning to commit suicide tonight, why did you ask Dr. Granger to come here today?"

"I guess in a roundabout way I wanted a diagnosis. I wanted him to—to evaluate me—tell me if he thought I was behaving normally."

"And what did he say?"

"He said that some degree of depression is normal for everyone as they get older and their lives change, and that I was perfectly fine. He told me that the medicine I've been taking was the right dosage, and he suggested I take up a new hobby. You see, if I'd thought my depression was causing my suicidal feelings, I might have told him what I was planning to do so that he could do something to treat the depression. But since he said I was perfectly normal, I decided to go ahead with my plans."

Paul Manziuk turned off his car and sat in the garage for a several minutes. He was bone weary, and his brain was crammed with details—words and phrases, impressions, and suspicions. But he smiled.

"It was a good day, Woody. Would have been better if you'd been here, but Ryan didn't drive me nuts for once. I let her take lead on interviewing some people. Didn't stop her from interrupting me a number of times, but instead of getting mad I just interrupted her right back. And the crazy thing is, it worked! I hate to say it, but it's weird how often we think alike."

He opened his door and hauled himself out. "Woody, I guess my talking to you is weird, too, but I kind of like it."

Back at Serenity Suites, Mary lay huddled under her blankets with a box of tissues next to her. She was alternately crying and punching her pillow. Memories from the past were flooding her mind and overwhelming her. But those weren't the thoughts that made her cry.

Her tears were from the times in the common room when she'd looked over and wondered if Ingrid might be dead, and felt a little bit of a thrill at the idea. As if Ingrid's death would be a good thing. Had she really thought it would be exciting—even entertaining—for that to happen? Well, it had been anything but.

Most of the day had been pure torture. Trapped in the dining room with all those people, trying to make small talk, skirting around what had happened because the police officers were watching. Seeing Ben looking so old and bereft. Thinking what an old fool she'd been.

At 2:30 a dog-tired Jacquie Ryan was still lying in bed wide awake, her mind racing. She'd been foolish enough to check her personal email, and sure enough there'd been a note from Armando, pressing her to go with him to Hawaii. He wondered about two weeks instead of a month.

Armando was thirty-four. He'd told her that playing baseball was the only life he'd ever known. He had no intention of quitting, if he had a choice. He might not have many years left as a professional pitcher, but she knew he was hoping for at least five or six more even if he had to become a reliever. After that he wanted to stay involved in some way—maybe become a coach or go to the Dominican Republic, his homeland, to help teach kids there how to play baseball. So would he ever have a regular family life?

Was she the kind of person who could live in a relationship where she was alone a good deal of the time? Where she had to look after the house and kids while her husband was either away or distracted?

She sighed. She really, really didn't want to think about all this, but her mind kept churning new thoughts.

Most baseball players had little control over what team they played for. He could be traded tomorrow. What then? Would she be willing to leave Toronto and move to the United States? Could she get a job on a police force down there?

The first time she'd met Armando, she'd felt an immediate attraction to him. She'd fought it. Hard. After all the man was a suspect in a murder investigation! But the truth was she liked him way more than any man she'd known. And in the end she'd agreed to go out with him.

He was so very different from anyone she'd known. And the world he was comfortable in was light years away from her world.

Was it worth even *trying* to have a relationship? She had no more desire to go to Hawaii with him and his baseball buddies and their wives and girlfriends than she had to become a waitress at a fast-food restaurant.

She punched her pillow. She had to be at police headquarters in just a few hours, ready to start solving a case that was looking like the kind of puzzle she hated. Time to start counting sheep.

Part III

No man is an island, entire of itself;
every man is a piece of the continent,
a part of the main....
any man's death diminishes me,
because I am involved in mankind,
and therefore never send to know
for whom the bells tolls;
it tolls for thee.

—JOHN DONNE, *Meditation XVII*

TWELVE

When Paul walked into his kitchen at 6:45 on Thursday morning, Loretta handed him a large mug. Assuming it was coffee, he took a sip, then spit the liquid back into the cup. "What on earth is this?"

"Breakfast."

"Breakfast?"

"It's a smoothie. It's good for you."

He grimaced, then stared at the contents of the mug. "It's green. And it tastes kind of—I don't know—fuzzy."

"It has kale in it."

"Kale?"

"Curly green stuff. Like lettuce, only better."

"What else is in it?"

"Yogurt, a banana, blueberries, and matcha tea."

"That's breakfast?"

"I also boiled two eggs and sliced an orange for you. And you can have one piece of toast."

"Jam?"

"Honey, actually. And we need to talk about how you're going to make the right choices when you have to eat out."

"We do?"

"We do."

At five-foot-four and 120 pounds, Loretta was a foot shorter than her husband and half of his weight, but he sat down at the table and ate his breakfast without further comment. When he'd eaten the rest, he tried the smoothie again, then held up the mug and looked at it in surprise. "It actually tastes pretty good."

Loretta smiled. "Think green."

"So what am I supposed to eat for lunch?"

"Preferably a salad with protein. Grilled chicken, salmon, or another lean meat. Use olive oil with vinegar for a dressing. No cheese. Nuts are okay. Any vegetables and fruit are okay. Lettuce should be romaine or mixed greens, not iceberg. And no fries."

"Did you write it down?"

She handed him an index card.

"Ryan will laugh her head off. And she'll never let me forget."

"Oh, I don't think she'll laugh at you, but I *am* counting on her to remind you."

As was her custom, by seven Jacquie had already run for half an hour, lifted weights, showered, dressed in a pantsuit and blouse, run a comb through her short black hair, dabbed blush on her cheeks, and powdered her nose. As she left her room, she made sure her gun was firmly positioned at the back of her waist.

She greeted her grandmother, who was setting two bowls on the kitchen table. A slim woman of medium height, her grey hair was caught up in a hairnet, and her wine-coloured robe had seen better days. "Porridge is ready. Do you want strawberries on top?"

"That'd be great."

"I made green tea for you."

"Thanks."

Jacquie's Aunt Vida, a woman in her fifties, several inches shorter than Jacquie's five-foot-nine but about thirty pounds heavier, entered the room. She was dressed for work in a blue scrubs top enlivened with yellow and white flowers, blue jeans, and white slip-on nurse's shoes. Her black hair was cut short in a boyish style, and she already had her trademark red lipstick on. "I hope you put the coffee on, Ma."

"I always do, don't I?"

"Yes, you do." Vida gave her mother a hug. "And I for one appreciate it very much."

"You want porridge?"

"Ma, you ask me that every single time you make porridge, and every time I say no."

"Well, one of these days you might change your mind."

"That ain't happening." Vida plucked two pieces of bread from the toaster and smothered them in peanut butter and strawberry jam before sitting at the table and grabbing the large mug of coffee her mother had placed at her usual spot. "Ahhhh. Just what I needed."

Jacquie hid her smile by leaning over and pretending to fix the hem of her right pant leg. It was like living in their own version of *Groundhog Day*. Every morning was almost identical to the one before. And right now that was okay with her.

"You were home late, Jacquie," Vida said archly. "Out on the town with your friend Armando?"

"On a case. And I'll probably be pretty busy the next few days."

"Oh, what is it?"

Jacquie hesitated. "I guess you'll hear about it soon enough. An elderly woman was stabbed yesterday. That's all I can say."

"How elderly?" asked Gram.

"Around eighty."

Gram shook her head in disgust. "Mugged?"

"No, actually she was sitting in a chair in a seniors' home."

Gram eyes grew as big as saucers. "Well, I never."

Vida set down her coffee. "You've got to be kidding!"

"Wish I was."

"Someone stabbed an eighty-year-old woman? Was she killed?"

"Yes."

"Oh, my, what's the world coming to? Do you know who did it?"

"Not yet. It's our job to find out." Jacquie got up from the table. "And I need to get going. Unless we get a big break, I'll likely be home late again tonight."

Jacquie's mother, Noelle, walked into the kitchen. "Why are you going to be late?" Noelle, too, was dressed for work, in an abstract white, red, and black dress, a short grey cardigan, dangling silver earrings, and three-inch red high heels. Her mid-length hair hung forward on one side and was tucked behind her ear on the other.

Jacquie quickly set her dishes in the dishwasher. "Hi, Mom. I'm on a case. They'll tell you."

Noelle put her hands on her hips. "Jacqueline Ryan, I'm your mother. *You* tell me."

"Let her go, Noelle," Vida said. "She's got things to do. *Important* things."

"Well, I have important things to do, too! Like looking after my children. What case, Jacquie?"

"Elderly woman murdered, possibly by someone who lived with her." Jacquie grabbed the lunch bag and water bottles her grandmother had prepared and headed for the front hall, where she thrust her feet into comfortable black loafers and grabbed her black shoulder bag before sailing out the front door.

Noelle stared after her. "And what exactly was that supposed to mean?"

"Get the newspaper from the front door," Vida said. "I bet it'll have the details."

Their mother said, "Better to get your laptop, Noelle. You can google it."

By 7:30, Ryan and Manziuk were in Manziuk's office making a list of what they knew and questions that needed answers.

Time of death:

- Mary saw Ingrid in the common room, presumably alive, at just after 2:00.
- Mary entered the common room again at roughly 2:30 and stayed there. She thought Ingrid was asleep at first, but then thought something was wrong.
- Lyle found Ingrid dead at around at roughly 2:45.
- Her skin felt cool and clammy.
- Time of death was likely between 2:00 and 2:30.

Residents who had been in Kenneth's condo recently:

- **Ben Davidson** – Husband is usually the likeliest person, but he seemed genuinely distraught. Hard to imagine him stabbing his wife as a mercy killing. No one saw him. He said he was watching TV in his condo.

- **Mary Simmons** – A long-time friend of both Ingrid and Violet. Mercy killing might be a realistic motive. She admitted to being alone in the room with Ingrid at 2:00 and then again at 2:30. She had several times suggested to others that Ingrid might be dead. She was a huge mystery fan. She might be the most likely suspect.
- **Kenneth Harper** – Owned the knife. If he'd done it, would he be foolish enough to leave the sheath lying around for them to find? Did he know Ingrid well? Not as far as anyone knew. He'd have passed the common room on his way to the billiards room.
- **Frank Klassen** – If Violet was also murdered, he's at the top of the list. As a thriller writer, he'd likely know where to position the knife for most effect. But he was in his office, and he uses a motorized scooter, so it would have been difficult for him to get there and back without being seen. He'd have had to pass the kitchen, where Scarlett and Olive were working, without being noticed. As to motive, it was difficult to picture him performing a mercy killing. Maybe with his own wife, but according to his daughter he'd only learned about her cancer a few days before Violet died. That made it unlikely.
- **Lyle Oakley** – Alone from 2:00 until 2:15 when he met Kenneth in the billiards room. No apparent motive.

Residents who could have a motive but hadn't been in Kenneth's condo recently:

- **Norm Carlysle** – Had known Violet and Ingrid for many years. Possible mercy killing. Alone in his condo. Unlikely.
- **Elizabeth Carlysle** – In the recording studio right across the hallway. Could have easily slipped in and out. No apparent motive.
- **Hilary Brooks** – Her condo is quite close. Alone after Audra left. No apparent motive.
- **Trish Klassen-Wallace** – No apparent motive. Was at her father's office a little after 2:00. Might have gone to the

common room before or after. Not here when her mother died.

- **Nikola Vincent** – No apparent motive. Was in the hallway coming from the billiards room during the crucial half hour. Could have slipped in.
- **Catarina Rossi** – Difficult to imagine a motive, but might be capable of stabbing someone. However, Gulab was with her in the condo. Nikola was there for most of that time.

Staff who might have had an opportunity:

- Any of them might have entered the common room and not been noticed. Did all staff have the ability to enter residents' condos by voice override? None of the staff had an apparent motive other than possibly mercy killing.
- **Dr. Granger** – Was close to the common room when he went down in the elevator a little past 2:00. Might have been more motivated to help Ben than some of the others.
- **Derrick James** – Could have killed her on his way out at 2:00.
- **Audra Limson** – Had easy access from her office; tends to be all over the place. Would have passed the common room coming from Hilary's condo.
- **Scarlett Walker** – Was in the kitchen a short distance away.
- **Olive Yeung** – Same as Scarlett. She could have slipped out without Scarlett noticing.
- **Naomi Arlington** – Apparently not on this floor in the afternoon.
- **Tess Cooper** – In the laundry room, then to the Carlysle condo. Might have been able to go to the common room without being seen, but doubtful.
- **Gulab Brampton** – Cleaning in the Rossi condo.
- **Jared Wright** – Only there briefly near 2:30, but can't rule him out.

Questions:

- Were there fingerprints on the knife?
- Was the murder premeditated? Seemed to be, since Kenneth's knife was used. Someone had to sneak it out of his office.
- Was the timing premeditated? Maybe, but maybe not. Ingrid was often in the common room.
- Could killer have kept the knife on him or her waiting for the right opportunity? Hidden in a purse or a large pocket, sitting inside a newspaper or a magazine, maybe even tucked into a waistband or carried inside a towel?
- What was the motive? Obvious one is mercy killing. If so, the method is certainly not typical. Other possible motives: An older person with dementia who was irrational. Revenge killing from the past.
- Latter motive seems implausible given the location and the woman involved.
- Need a thorough check on Ingrid's background.
- Ben Davidson was very well-known. He might have made enemies on his talk show. Seems unlikely.
- Was Violet Klassen's death natural? If not, there might be a connection. Who knew she had cancer, and when did they find out? Trish learned the Tuesday before she died. Frank the previous Monday or Sunday, at least according to Trish. Dr. Granger, Audra, Derrick, and Mary also knew.
- What about Grant Brook's death? It was also unexpected.

"We need these questions answered ASAP," Manziuk said. "Have everyone on the team who isn't at Serenity Suites meet here at 9:00."

Audra stepped out of her living quarters and glanced at the nearest corner, where a police officer had been sitting the night before.

A different officer was there now. He looked bored. Just past him Nikola was stepping out of his and Catarina's condo.

"Good morning." Nikola took several steps toward her.

"I hope so." She turned her face away so he wouldn't see her eyes, which she was sure were still red and swollen

He came closer. "What's wrong? Has someone else been hurt?"

Without looking at him, Audra shook her head.

"What then? You seem upset. Have you heard something more from the police?"

She finally looked at him. "No. Nothing. I'm fine. Really."

He frowned. "You look like you've been crying. That Arlington witch isn't blaming you for this, is she?"

"No. I'm fine, really. I—I have allergies."

He looked down the hall. "There's no one here except us. You can tell me the truth."

"No, it's—it's personal. Nothing you need to worry about."

"But I *choose* to worry about it. Tell me."

"I—I—there's so much happening. Ingrid!"

"I didn't realize you were that close to Ingrid."

"Well, not exactly." She looked down. "I'm sure Ben and Mary are very distressed. And I care about them. And maybe I feel as if I ought to care more about Ingrid."

"Do you want to talk about it?"

She raised her eyebrows. "You're a therapist now?"

Nikola smiled. "No, I'm an objective listener. Someone who neither reports to you nor depends on you."

She shook her head. "You're Catarina's husband. And even though you might not *need* to be here, you *do* live here. That makes you a resident."

"True."

"Please excuse me. I have a lot to do this morning."

He stepped back. "Very well. However, I suggest you go back to your room first and wash your face with cold water and put on more make-up to hide the redness. Or, if you find that too difficult, practise the allergies lie so it sounds more truthful."

After a sleepless night Kenneth stood on his balcony, hands on the railing, eyes fixed on the tops of the trees in the Don Valley. A beautiful scene, but he wasn't even aware of it.

"Well, God, as you know, when I made my plans Sunday morning, I said, 'If I'm wrong and you're really there, please stop me.' I was only half-serious, of course. I had no expectation that anything would stop me. But of course I was stopped, and in the strangest way possible. By having a murderer take my knife and use it on his victim."

He took a deep breath. "If you're the one who stopped me, then it means I've been wrong all these years. But I guess you know that. And I guess you know I never really stopped believing you exist. I've just been angry. I couldn't believe you'd let something so terrible happen to us. Miriam was the best thing that ever happened to me. That's so clichéd, but *you* know what I mean."

His eyes filling with tears, he bowed his head. "But it wasn't about her, was it? It was about me. Me not wanting to deal with my loss. Me not wanting the responsibility of my children. Me not wanting my perfect world to change in any way. I blamed you when I was at fault. It was easier to pretend I'd lost my faith than it was to let everyone know how bloody selfish and self-centred I was.

"Yes, I missed Miriam but, more important, I missed how she looked after everything so I could just live in my little ivory tower studying theology and writing my oh-so-important sermons and ignoring the world I lived in. Ignoring my children. What a fool I was!"

He shook his head. "It would be so easy to throw myself over this railing."

Derrick was in the staff lounge with Audra when one of the officers guarding the hallways entered to say Lyle Oakley had asked for him.

Lyle apologized to him. "Sorry about that. I came out of my room, and right away a policeman was there, asking me what I wanted. I felt like a six-year-old who'd been naughty, so I stupidly said I needed your help. He told me to come back inside and he'd get you. So here we are."

Derrick laughed. "Yeah, it's kind of weird having them watch our every move. I actually wasn't sure what to do this morning. Audra and I were allowed to go to the staff lounge and the kitchen, but not to our office or the exercise room, where we normally go. So your call actually gave me something to do. And since I'm here, is there anything I *can* do?"

Lyle shrugged. "I mostly wanted a newspaper. I'd normally be reading it in the common room right now, but with all the restrictions, I can't go there. I don't know where they'd have put the papers."

"I can find out."

"Oh, don't bother. I can turn on the telly if I need the news. Or my computer, I guess. Do you want to sit down a minute?"

They found chairs in the cluttered living room. Lyle leaned toward the younger man, his face anxious. "How long do you think we're going to be kept prisoner here?"

"I think they'll probably finish searching the rest of the rooms sometime today."

Lyle frowned. "Yes, but what if they don't find anything? What if we have to go on like one of those mystery novels Mary reads, waiting for the next one to be knocked off? Just a few days ago she was telling me about that book of Agatha Christie's that was made into a movie—*Then There Were None*—where everyone on this island is killed, one by one." Lyle licked his lips. "I figure this life is all we get, so I want to squeeze out every hour of time I can get."

Derrick smiled. "I'm not so sure this life is all we get, but I don't want anyone's time shortened by murder."

"What will happen to us if the police can't solve this? That's what I want to know."

Derrick sat back. "I think we need to see what the police discover first. Who knows? They may solve it today. And if not—if they're really stumped—I suppose you'd be justified in moving out."

Lyle looked horrified. "I don't want to move. This is my home!"

"Then we'd better pray that the police find out who did this quickly."

"I've never been a praying man, but I might start over this."

Derrick smiled.

Lyle cocked his head on one side. "Who do *you* think did it?"

Derrick shook his head. "I have no idea."

"No suspicions?"

"Not really. I have trouble believing it even happened."

"All those times Mary said she thought Ingrid was dead, and she wasn't. And then this." Lyle's eyes bored anxiously into Derrick's. "I've started wondering if it was Mary. Maybe she wanted it to be true so badly she did it."

"Really?"

Lyle nodded. "Mary was alone in the room with her. And she reads those mystery novels, one after the other. She'd know how to do it. I'd bet you hundred to one odds it was Mary."

Audra's voice on the intercom ended this discussion. "Breakfast will be served in the dining room at 8:30 as usual. Come as soon as you're able. Let me know if you need help with anything."

Derrick turned toward Lyle. "Well, I guess we're free to go out now. And look, if you have reason to suspect Mary, you should tell the police. I can't see her doing it, but who knows? And they did say to tell them anything we might know, no matter how small."

Lyle nodded. "I don't like to get her in trouble, but I'll be honest. Right now, I wouldn't want to be alone in a room with her."

Frank drove his scooter into the dining room and looked at the four tables.

Elizabeth and Norm were in their usual seats, but he didn't want to sit anywhere near them this morning. They'd just want to talk about Ingrid and Ben. Nor was he going to sit anywhere near that Hilary woman, or the annoying Catarina and her husband. What had Elizabeth called him? A toy boy?

Lyle was sitting alone in his usual spot at the far end. Sighing, Frank moved toward his table, the least of the evils this morning. He slowly got off his scooter, waiting for Olive to rush over and give him her arm to help him into his chair, then move his scooter out of the way.

Lyle smiled shyly at him, but was sensible enough not to speak. Good. Frank didn't want to talk to anyone; just get on with his life. And he knew his rights. If the police wouldn't let him in his office after breakfast, he'd be on the phone to the mayor before they knew what was coming. Ever since Violet's death, he'd hardly been able to get any writing done, and it was high time he got back into his rhythm. It was bad enough he'd lose another day for Ingrid's funeral, but that was unavoidable.

Olive set a plate in front of him. Good. A sensible breakfast of bacon and eggs and toast. He preferred white bread to the whole grain Violet had insisted he eat, but he could overlook that as long as he got his bacon.

Lyle was already busy stuffing in his eggs, which looked done to perfection, runny but not too runny. Frank relaxed. He didn't even look up when Kenneth took the chair on his right and spoke quietly to Lyle. But he almost jumped when a voice said in his ear, "How are you this morning, Dad?" He looked up to see Trish sliding into the empty spot next to him.

"Fine. Just want to eat and get to work. Oh, before you leave, tell the cook I want my toast with white bread from now on."

"Okay. But I might not be going home today after all. The police told me they might want to talk to me again."

Frank paused with his fork in the air. "What do they need to talk to *you* about?"

"I'm not sure. I expect they're looking at every possibility."

"Well, tell them to go jump in the lake." He put a forkful of egg in his mouth and felt a surge of pleasure. *Perfect!* "I told you to go home a week ago."

"You know I had too much to do here."

"Well, tell them you don't know anything."

"That's easy. I *don't* know anything!" She buttered her toast. "Anyway don't worry about it. I'm sure it's nothing. I just wondered if they might have more questions about Mom."

He frowned. "Why should it have anything to do with her?"

"They asked me about her death. If I had any concerns."

"She had cancer. She died of natural causes. Her doctor and the coroner both said so."

"But, Dad, what if Mom's death wasn't natural?"

Frank glared at his daughter. "What are you talking about? The doctor and the coroner were perfectly satisfied that her death was from natural causes. If the police say anything about it, tell them to mind their own business. And you go home today as you planned.

It's bad enough that Ingrid died in such a demeaning way; I won't let the police drag your mother into this mess."

Mary had awakened shortly before 8:00 that morning feeling tired and old. She didn't actually need a walker, but it came in handy when she did her laps through the hallways or went shopping. While she had to admit she moved faster and with more ease when she had something to push, she mostly liked it because the wire basket was handy for carrying books or shopping bags, and the walker itself became a seat when she needed to rest for a few minutes.

This morning she felt so little energy that she didn't think twice about using the walker just to go to the dining room. Mary immediately saw that the table where she normally sat with Lyle and Kenneth was full. She looked around in consternation, and finally took a chair at the table with Norm and Elizabeth. "I see Frank moved over there next to Trish."

"Actually," Norm said, "Frank sat there first. Apparently he didn't want to sit with us today."

"Perhaps he suspects us of doing away with Ingrid," Elizabeth said. "Personally I suspect him." She shivered. "I do hope the police solve this quickly. I don't want to live in a fishbowl much longer. I'm surprised they let me out to teach my class last night."

"I'm sure they don't suspect you. They'll likely tell us today who did it."

Mary made a face. "I doubt it."

Elizabeth frowned. "You don't think they can solve it?"

"I hate to think it, but I expect they'll do the minimum and then get busy with other things."

"Why do you think that?" Norm asked.

Mary pursed her lips before answering. "Because it isn't such a big deal when someone our age dies. They think we've had our shot at it, I guess."

Norm slowly nodded his head. "I guess that could be true. It's much worse when a young person dies. And a total waste to see a child's life cut off."

"Huh!" Elizabeth said. "That depends on the child. People always talk about the innocence of children. But if you've been around children much, you know what vicious and nasty little things they can be. Even toddlers can deliberately set out to make other children cry, and while it might appear to be accidental, I've seen the looks in some of their eyes. Delight, satisfaction, even a sense of power."

Norm shook his head. "That's a pessimistic way to think."

"I wasn't talking about children," Mary said. "I was talking about people's attitude toward us."

Norm looked puzzled. "Old people, you mean?"

Elizabeth glared at him. "Don't go calling *me* old!"

Norm smiled. "You're seventy-two. What should I call you?"

"Call me irresponsible..." Elizabeth began singing the old Frank Sinatra hit, then stopped. "You're only as old as you feel, and I don't feel old. They say sixty is the new forty, so that makes seventy the new fifty." Her tone changed. "But if I stay around these people much longer, I may *start* feeling old. Moving here was a mistake."

"I like it here," Norm countered.

Elizabeth shot him an annoyed look.

"Agatha Christie understood," Mary said. "She believed most people cling to life no matter what their age."

Elizabeth glared at her. "And what's wrong with that?"

"I never said anything was wrong with it. Why shouldn't you get every second you can? No one has the right to take what isn't theirs. Especially someone's life. You can't get all sorry later on and give a life back the way you could a stolen car."

Norm stared at her. "So you're saying the police won't care enough to solve this? But that's just wrong."

Mary shrugged and took a bite of her toast.

Nikola realized just how hungry he was *and* how quickly he'd become used to Scarlett's excellent cooking. It was only bacon and eggs, but he was positive it was the best bacon and eggs he'd ever had.

Beside him Catarina took a dainty bite and then looked around. "It is unfortunate the Gerbrandts and the Kanes are away. They are missing all the excitement."

Nikola made a face. "Only *you* would feel sorry for someone who's missed out being suspected of murder."

"I like to experience things, and as much as it surprises me to realize this, being part of a murder investigation is something I have not experienced before."

Nikola laughed. "I'm sure being accused of murder would be even more exciting."

Catarina thought about this. "I do not anticipate being accused, but if I were to be, I should take full advantage of the opportunity to discover how it feels. However, I daresay it is enough to be part of the investigation. Going to jail would no doubt be uncomfortable."

"Yes, I'm sure it would. Although perhaps not as bad here in Canada as in some parts of the world."

Catarina used her linen napkin to wipe a small amount of egg from her lips. "Well, I for one am anticipating a very interesting day, and I plan to enjoy myself."

"That makes one of us."

Hilary sat alone at the final table. Phillip and Joyce Kane would normally have been sitting with her, speaking quietly to each other and barely acknowledging her presence. They'd talked happily enough to Grant when he was alive, but since his death they seemed to think they could carry on as if it were only the two of them at the table.

She didn't actually mind not having to talk to anyone during meals, particularly breakfast as she'd never been a morning person. But it was stressful with them sitting across the table from her, knowing they were as aware of her as she was of them, feeling that if she said anything to them, it could cause a scene.

Perhaps, before they came back from their holiday, she should ask Audra if they could put another table in the room—maybe a smaller one—so that she could sit by herself without the added strain of being pointedly ignored.

Audra came in from the kitchen and stopped next to her chair. "Is everything okay?" she asked softly.

Hilary smiled at her. "Yes, lovely. The coffee is particularly good this morning."

"Did you sleep?"

"I have to confess that I did. Probably due to the relief of getting back to my own place after the long confinement in this room."

"I expect the detectives will be here soon. I gathered that they may have more questions for us."

"I expect that's normal. After talking to all of us and doing a search of our rooms, I'm sure they have all kinds of questions. Must be a bit like solving a particularly difficult jigsaw puzzle, wondering where each piece fits." She tilted her head to one side. "It might be interesting actually. For people who like solving puzzles." She laughed. "Not me, I'm afraid."

"Nor me. Don't hesitate to let me know if you need anything."

Hilary watched Audra move from table to table, satisfying herself that everyone was okay. *No, come hell or high water, I'm not going to let them force me out of here.*

Thirteen

At 9:00, Manziuk and Ryan met with other members of the homicide team at police headquarters. Ryan went over what they knew, which wasn't much. They had the knife, so, provided the autopsy results didn't bring them something out of left field, the cause of death was clear. That was about it.

The only fingerprints on the knife were from Kenneth Harper's left hand. Not only were they smudged, but they also showed he'd held the knife sideways, so no way he could have shoved it into someone. The only prints on the sheath were also Kenneth's.

There was no obvious suspect. There was no obvious motive. As for opportunity, it was hazy. No witnesses had seen anyone going into or coming out of the common room prior to Mary's arrival.

The bottom line was that it appeared that someone on the floor had to be responsible. But there was still a great deal of work to do. Manziuk gave out the assignments.

- Check into the ownership of Serenity Suites.
- Find out if there had been any lawsuits, threats, staff firings, or anything unusual related to the building.
- Look into the pasts of the residents of the twentieth floor, especially Mary Simmons, Violet and Frank Klassen, Ben and Ingrid Davidson, Kenneth Harper, and Hilary Brooks.
- Check the backgrounds of all staff members on the twentieth floor, both live-in and daily. And any other staff who were on the premises that day.

- Follow up on the earlier deaths of Grant Brooks and Violet Klassen.
- Dr. Weaver would autopsy Ingrid Davidson at 3:00.

Back in his office, Manziuk called the police officer who had responded to the 911 call about Violet Klassen.

When he ended the call, Ryan looked up. "Anything?"

"He's going to send me a copy of his report as well as his notes. He had a gut feeling that her doctor wasn't saying everything he was thinking, but he had nothing to substantiate it. There were no indications that her death wasn't natural. The place looked like she got the best of care, and the woman was seventy-eight years old. Plus her doctor said she'd had a diagnosis of inoperable cancer."

"Sounds like there were grounds for wondering about suicide, but no one wanted to rock the boat."

"That would be my guess, too."

"Are we going to do anything about it?"

"I'll wait until I see the report. And I want to talk to the daughter again."

"You're thinking of requesting an autopsy?"

"I'm considering it."

"Does her family have to agree?"

"Not if I can show just cause and get a court order. But I was thinking of asking the daughter for her permission first. She said she's the executor of her mother's will and she has power of attorney from her dad, so we might not have to involve him."

"What about Grant Brooks?"

"We need to find out who signed his death certificate."

"What do you bet it was Dr. Granger?"

"We'll see."

"So right now we have exactly nothing."

"Pretty well."

Ryan took a deep breath and expelled it. "Seldon isn't going to like that. Neither is Benson. He's going to have every reporter in town after him."

"I expect this is going to be a very long day."

"Maybe I'd better cancel my appointment for the spa."

After attending Manziuk and Ryan's briefing and checking in with Superintendent Seldon, Special Constable Sam Benson prepared for his next challenge.

With his Nordic good looks, imposing height, quick wit, and ability to put anyone at ease, Benson hadn't been on the force long before he'd been earmarked as a natural for public affairs. Now in his mid-thirties, he gave seminars to police groups around the country on how to deal with the public.

At 10:30 he was meeting the administrator of Serenity Suites. Ms. Arlington had apparently called somebody high up early that morning with a long list of complaints about the way the police were handling the case. From the moment the case had begun the previous afternoon, it had been Benson's job to run interference between the police and the press, all the while urging Manziuk and his homicide team to make everyone's life easier by solving the crime within the next five minutes. His job had just expanded to include soothing Ms. Arlington. From what Seldon had told him, the woman had her panties in a twist. However, Benson was confident that a little tact and charm on his part would calm her down and convince her to stay out of the way of the investigation.

He took no pride in this assumption. In moments of extreme honesty, which happened only rarely and after several drinks, he'd admit to a few close friends that he really didn't know why women, especially those who'd chosen a career over a family, had virtually zero resistance when it came to dealing with him. He'd been told that those under sixty had fantasies about him as their perfect mate; those over sixty saw him as the ideal son. Whatever the reason, he was secure in his belief that Ms. Arlington would fall in line.

He checked his teeth in the car mirror. Then, certain that his smile was ready, he started his car.

A few residents were still in the dining room; the rest had returned to their condos. Scarlett and Olive were busy cleaning up breakfast and getting lunch preparations under way. Derrick was reading in the staff lounge.

For the past half hour, Audra had been hovering in the hallway outside the door to the kitchen, her ear awaiting the soft whooshing sound the elevator made. Finally, she heard the sound. A moment later, Manziuk and Ryan came into sight at the end of the hallway. *This is it*. Hurrying into the kitchen, she announced, "They're here."

Manziuk asked Ryan to get the master key from the Ident team so they could get into the office they'd used the day before. He then entered the kitchen to find all four live-in staff waiting for him in apprehension. Olive, who had just come in from the dining room, had paused in mid-stride. The others stood in a semicircle like a trio of ice sculptures.

"Good morning. Is everything okay here? All the residents up?"

"Yes," Audra said, "everyone seems fine. They're wondering how long it will be before they can use the other rooms. Frank in particular would like to be able to write in his office. He goes there every morning as soon as he's finished his breakfast."

"That would be the room next to the one we're using?"

"Yes."

"I'll find out if it's been searched yet. But since Mr. Klassen is free to use his condo, I'm not sure I see the urgency."

"He's never liked working in his condo."

"Well, I'll talk to Ford and let you know what he says about the rest of the rooms."

"Thank you."

"I'll leave the police officers at the corners of the floor until we've completed the search."

"Very well."

"Would you like some breakfast?" Scarlett offered.

Manziuk smiled. "No, thanks. I wouldn't object to some coffee."

"And Detective Ryan?"

"She'd prefer tea."

"Olive will bring it shortly."

"Thank you."

Audra said, "Inspector, I have some time off later this morning and after 3:00 this afternoon. If you need anything, Derrick will be here to assist you. If you need me, you have my cellphone number."

"Thanks for letting me know. We should be fine."

Manziuk walked across the hall to the office. The door was open, and Ryan was setting up. He was barely inside when Olive arrived with cups, a thermos for each of them, and two beautifully arranged plates of fruit, each accented with two small blueberry scones.

"Oh my," Ryan said.

Manziuk nodded. "I could really get used to this."

"I hate to say it, but so could I. At least most of it's healthy."

Manziuk popped a grape into his mouth. "Okay, who did we want to talk to first?"

Ryan settled into her chair and opened her laptop. "I arranged for Dr. Granger to come here at 11:00. Hopefully, he'll be on time."

"I'd like to talk to Ford sooner rather than later."

"He isn't in yet. Kelly said Ford went home to shower and change. She'll have him come here the moment he gets back." She paused to check her notes. "We wanted to talk to Frank's daughter again. Should I get her?"

"Let's pay her a visit."

Trish Klassen-Wallace opened the guest suite door. "Oh, good morning. I take it you have more questions?"

"We do. May we come inside?"

"Certainly. The sitting room is filled with Mom's bins and files, but we could sit at the dining room table."

"We're wondering whether it would be worthwhile to exhume your mother's body and do an autopsy."

"That's what I thought you were going to say." Trish rested her elbows on the table, propped her chin in her hands, and sighed. "Inspector, I broached the topic with my dad at breakfast this morning, and he became quite angry and insisted that there's no connection."

"I expected him to be upset."

"But you still want to go ahead?"

"Not immediately. But I want to be able to do it if we feel the need. And since you were planning to go home today, I thought I should talk to you about it."

"She seems to have died from natural causes, so what would you be looking for? Sleeping pills? Poison?"

"Yes, something like that. Perhaps a needle mark."

She frowned. "Would those things still be there for you to find?"

"It depends. Some things dissipate very quickly, but not all. And since she's only been interred for a couple of weeks, there's a chance that we could find something—assuming there's something to find."

"I see."

"Which brings us back to our reason for considering this. Even though the death certificate was signed immediately and not questioned at the time, her death appears to have been unexpected. Several staff members and residents have said it. Her doctor said it yesterday, albeit reluctantly. You said it—"

"And my dad?"

"Your dad is adamant that her death was of natural causes. He threatened to call his friends at City Hall if we suggested otherwise."

"So you're asking me as executor of my mother's will to give you permission to exhume her body, knowing my dad is going to be very angry with both you and me?"

"Yes."

She bit her lower lip. "Can I think about this? I mean, I guess I need a reason beyond just curiosity. If it would help find out who killed Ingrid, I'd do it in a heartbeat. But will it?"

Manziuk shook his head. "I don't know. But if we did find something, it would drastically change our focus in terms of a motive."

"If you had any kind of proof that someone might have wanted to kill both of them, I'd do it. But it's so hard to agree without a strong reason. And I don't know what Dad would do. When he gets angry, he can be very resourceful."

"If we have to, I can go to a judge and do it that way."

"That might be better. At least then he wouldn't blame me. But you'd have to have a solid reason, right? Not—what do they call it on those police shows I watch—a fishing expedition?"

Manziuk smiled and nodded.

"Well, I'd appreciate it if you'll try to find one."

Ryan said, "You were planning to take your mother's papers home with you?"

"Yes. I still need to go through everything in the sitting room."

Ryan glanced at Manziuk. "I know this is a long shot, but what if we got a couple of members of the forensic team to help you go through them? Just in case there's something here that gives us the reason we need. Could you stay another day?"

Tricia nodded. "Yes, of course. That makes sense. I have a feeling your people will likely be bored to tears, but if it will help in any way, even to close that door, then I'm game."

Manziuk nodded. "I think that's a very good idea."

"All right," Ryan said. "Is it okay if they work with you here?"

"Yes, of course. I can move things around a bit and expand this table. There should be lots of room for three of us."

Ford was sitting in their office when they returned, his feet on the desk. "So you *are* here. I was beginning to think Kelly was hallucinating due to lack of sleep." He shook his head. "The older I get, the less I care for these all-nighters."

Manziuk took his seat. "How's it going?"

"We're just about to pack up our gear. You can release the rest of the rooms whenever you want."

"They'll be happy to hear that. Did you find anything that's going to help us?"

"Not really. More information, but probably nothing that's going to help you find a murderer. Not that we could see, anyway."

"So, having looked at every inch of this place, what's your overall impression?"

"Well, if I had the money and was near retirement age, I'd be putting myself on their waiting list. It's well maintained, doesn't seem at all institutional, and the food is terrific." Ford grinned. "And I'm not just going on hearsay—they've been feeding us the whole time we've been here, and we're all tempted to find more things to do so we can stay a few days longer!"

"So lots of positives?"

"The vibe we got was 'this is home.'"

"And no clues as to why a woman died in the common room?"

"Only the knife."

Manziuk sighed. "I was afraid of that."

Ryan asked, "What about the staff rooms?"

"There are four who live in, and they have small apartments they call suites. They're all in good shape and tidy." He grinned. "Well, all but one of them."

He looked down at his notebook. "As for personal things, Derrick James has books all over the place. Mostly textbooks on nursing and physiotherapy and related subjects. His current interest appears to be geriatric psychiatry. Seems to be taking a class in that area, and he has quite a few books out on his desk that he's reading or about to read. He also has a lot of music, mostly Christian worship and praise. At least four Bibles, in different translations. I saw somewhere—I think it was on a picture—that his dad is pastor of a large church here in the city, so that likely explains it.

"Audra Limson has two young sons, and she's not happy with their situation. Their dad has custody. Seems strange, given her background as a nurse and her position here. Aside from pictures of her kids and a few letters from lawyers and so forth, not much of a personal nature in her suite. One interesting thing though. She had three torn-up letters in the wastebasket next to her desk. None of them were finished, but the gist of them all was that she was resigning from her job here."

"That's definitely interesting," Manziuk said. "We'll need to ask her about that."

Ryan made a note. "She didn't give any indication she wasn't happy here."

"I have them if you want to see them," Ford continued, "but they didn't say much. Just that she was resigning her position, giving two weeks' notice, etc. etc. No reason was given."

"Okay, we'll follow up." Manziuk said. "Who's next?"

"Scarlett Walker has cookbooks lining her walls. Along with quilts. Kelly was quite impressed. Says they're all handmade and some are worth a lot of money. Her place was spotless. Everything organized to the max. The hangers in her closet are literally all the exact same distance apart as if she uses a ruler. Her drawers all have little dividers so every item has its own space.

"And then there's Olive Yeung, who is young and has a room that looks like that of most teens, clean but messy. She reads the kind fan magazines you see in drug stores and supermarkets. Seems to be interested in male actors and singers. She has six large bulletin boards, and she cuts out pictures of the guys she likes and pins them up. She also has a couple of partially-filled boxes of pictures, probably older ones she's replaced—they had pin marks in the corners. Aside from that, not much. Well, clothes. The inexpensive kind teenage girls buy. Lots of them. Camisoles and jeans and plaid shirts. Doubt if they get much wear around here since the staff seem to wear scrubs."

"Okay, so nothing that offers a motive or any indication of a personality problem."

"Nothing I could see. Of course Scarlett's neatness thing might be so over the top she considered Ingrid a blot on the place, or Derrick might be a fanatic who thinks he's God's angel of death, or Audra might be—"

Manziuk laughed and held up a hand. "Okay, we get it. Anything in the other rooms? Laundry area? Exercise room? Billiards room? Frank's office?"

"Nothing out of the ordinary. Laundry room is just what it says. Exercise room is state-of-the-art. Latest equipment, everything ship-shape. Same with the billiards room and the theatre. You'd barely know anyone uses them. They have a recording studio that is good enough to record an album in it, or so Kelly says. Her boyfriend is into music, and she was going, 'Oh, he'd love this!'

"Nothing out of place in the crafts room, the washrooms, or this room. As for the office next door, I'm told Mr. Klassen is working on a book. It looked that way. He had a lot of history books, some reference books on writing, some copies of his own books, a printer and some paper, some file folders, most of which were information about characters and plot ideas and letters from his publisher from what I could see."

Ryan asked, "Did you look at his computer?"

"Joey gave it a quick once-over. Nothing out of the ordinary. Found the new book he's writing. He's got maybe thirty thousand words done. The only thing that might be slightly unusual was a letter to his editor telling her the book was going well, but that he was going to need more time due to his wife's death. He sent that the week after his wife died."

Manziuk nodded. "That seems reasonable. It must be difficult to focus at this time."

"Not necessarily," Ryan said. "I mean, it could be a useful excuse. What was his original deadline for the book, and how far along was he when she died?"

Ford shrugged. "I can get Joey to take a look right now before we release the room."

"Yes," Manziuk said. "Do that. Also, you mentioned looking for a reason to stay longer. We actually have another job for two of your team. We need to go through all of Violet Klassen's papers."

Ford frowned. "Seriously? We had a quick look at them, but they didn't belong to the victim."

"No. But Violet was a close friend of hers, and she died only a couple of weeks ago herself. Apparently she kept journals for years, and I'm hoping she was an observant woman and that she wrote down something that will give us a clue."

"All right. Kelly will jump at that. I'll let her choose a partner and take charge of it."

"Good. The sooner the better. Trish will work with them since she knew her mother best."

Ryan asked, "When you did your search of the rooms, did you look for bloodstains?"

"We did, of course. And, no, we didn't see anything. Not in their hampers or in the drawers or closets. We particularly looked for anything that was damp from having been recently washed, but there was nothing."

Manziuk thanked Ford, who slowly got to his feet. "Right. I'll send you a written report of everything we found, but in all honesty, I don't think it's going to help you."

"We've got background checks going. Hopefully something will turn up there."

"When's the autopsy?"

"This afternoon, but I don't think it'll tell us anything new."

"Okay." He walked to the door and opened it. "Good hunting."

"I just thought of something," Ryan said. "You might want to ask Mrs. Klassen's daughter if she knows which of the bins were on the top shelf of the closet."

"Huh?" Ford frowned.

"She borrowed a step stool the morning of the day she died. Derrick James thought she might have wanted to get one of the bins on the top shelves."

When the secretary ushered him into the office of the administrator of Serenity Suites, and he caught his first glimpse of Naomi Arlington, Special Constable Sam Benson gulped. Okay, so not quite the vulnerable middle-aged woman he'd been expecting.

While he smiled and stepped forward to shake hands, his mind was rapidly creating a new line of attack. Or possibly defence.

Manziuk and Ryan had asked to speak with Mary Simmons next. She came in pushing a walker, which she set it to one side and then sat down on the wing chair. "Do you have a suspect?" she asked eagerly.

"Not yet," Ryan said.

Manziuk smiled. "I understand you like mysteries. Who are your favourite authors?"

"Oh, my, yes, I don't know what I'd do without my mysteries. Wither up and die from boredom likely. Agatha Christie, of course. Dorothy Sayers. Ngaio Marsh. Georgette Heyer. Most of the old ones. But lots of the newer ones, too. P. D. James, Louise Penny. Peter Robinson. Vicki Delany. Barbara Fradkin. Rick Blechta. Lou Allin. Anything with a good puzzle to solve."

"Do you read Frank's books?"

She made a face. "I read them. But only because he expects it. They're not my cup of tea. I don't like his opinions or his language."

"Can you be more specific?"

"He has unnecessary violence. Gutter language. A lot of the nasty kind of sex. I can lend you a book or a bunch of them if you want to see for yourself. I've read a lot of writers, including Stephen King and others in the thriller vein, but few of them are this nasty."

"Pornographic?"

She shook her head. "No, not that. More along the lines of serial killers and showing what they do, detail by detail. And almost daring the reader to protest."

"I wouldn't mind having a look at them. Constable Ryan can go with you to your condo and borrow a few. Maybe a couple of earlier ones and later ones, so I can compare?"

"Certainly." Her eyes narrowed. "But I don't think you invited me here to talk about Frank's books."

"You're right. Mary, we're interested in Violet's death. Not that we suspect foul play but simply because we need to be thorough. You knew Violet well. Did you notice anything different about her in the last few months?"

Mary sat back and blinked several times. "Violet? I don't—Well, let me think. She was working with Scarlett on the cookbook, of course. And she seemed to be enjoying that." She frowned. "You know, this past year she was actually more light-hearted than I can remember her being in a long time. I think she was really having fun working with Scarlett." She clicked her tongue. "Strange. That hadn't occurred to me until this very minute. Violet and Scarlett were like a couple of schoolgirls, really enjoying themselves. I actually heard her laugh out loud a few times. And she *never* did that. The most you ever got from her was a smile."

"I'm assuming you saw a change in her after she found out about the cancer. Is that true?"

"I don't actually know when she found out about the cancer, but I'd guess it was about the middle of July. I remember asking her one day if the book wasn't going well, and she looked at me in surprise and asked me why I'd said that. I said she seemed down in the dumps, and she frowned at me and said no, she was perfectly fine. I'd forgotten that."

"When did she tell you?"

"Let me think. I guess it was about a week or so before she died."

"Who else knew?"

"Dr. Granger, of course. And I think Audra and Derrick."

"Do you know when she told Frank?"

"Only that she hadn't told him when she told me. But she planned to tell him and then Trish before much longer."

"We asked your opinion of Frank's books. What about Frank himself?"

"Well, he's arrogant and chauvinistic, and he's gotten worse with age. I don't know how Violet stayed with him. I wouldn't have, I know that. But she saw him through rose-coloured glasses."

"Ms. Simmons," Ryan said, "was Violet capable of taking her own life?"

Mary shook her head forcefully. "Never in a million years."

"Even if she thought she was going to have a painful death?"

Mary was still shaking her head back and forth. "No."

Manziuk asked, "What if she wanted to avoid having people feel sorry for her? Since she seemed reluctant to have them know—"

"Never."

Ryan frowned. "Why are you so certain?"

"Violet was raised Mennonite. She was taught that suicide was wrong. I know that for a fact because we had a couple of friends who committed suicide. One of them was years and years ago, and one was more recent. You know how suicides used to be buried outside of the church grounds? I think Violet believed in that; by committing suicide they were somehow rejecting God because they didn't trust him to look after them. I heard her comments when someone famous died from suicide or a drug overdone, and she had no sympathy at all. She thought it was one of the worst things a person could do, almost as bad as murder. In effect, you were murdering yourself and taking the right to decide your lifespan away from God, where it belonged."

"You don't think her feelings might have changed when she was told she was going to die from cancer?"

"Not for one moment. Violet was one of the strongest people I've ever known. And she was harder on herself than anyone else."

"You said something earlier—that you weren't sure they'd investigated her death sufficiently. So do you believe she died of natural causes?"

Mary looked down for a moment as if searching for the right words. Then she looked Ryan in the eye. "If she didn't, then it was murder. Because it wasn't suicide."

"It could have been an accident."

Mary rolled her eyes. "As in she accidentally drank the cleaning fluid instead of her orange juice?"

"Something like that."

"If she ingested a poison, it wasn't an accident."

Manziuk asked, "So can you think of any reason why someone would murder her?"

Mary shrugged. "That's where I get stumped. But then, I can't imagine any reason why someone would stab Ingrid either."

"The two deaths are quite different."

"In some books I've read, the murderer just used whatever came to hand. If you think about it, it would have been difficult to stab Violet. She never sat around sleeping like Ingrid did. Be much easier to put something in her orange juice, or switch one of her vitamins for something else. And contrariwise, how could someone give Ingrid a poison when it was Audra who gave her the insulin injections and other meds? Maybe the murderer just used whatever worked best for each person."

"But we still have no motive for either death."

"I know. That's the problem."

"Well, you've certainly given us some things to think about."

"Is that all?"

"For now."

As Mary got up, she turned to Ryan. "You come and get those books any time. I'll be in my room for the next while except for lunch."

"Why don't I just come down with you now? Is that convenient?"

"Certainly. I have a nice bag I can put them in. You come along and we'll see what we can find." She turned to Manziuk. "Good morning, Inspector. We're counting on you to nail whoever did this."

FOURTEEN

Several minutes after 11:00, Dr. Granger strode into the office, stopped in front of Manziuk, and glared at him. "What's so urgent I had to make my elderly patients wait while I came up here?"

"Do sit down, Doctor."

Ryan came in behind the doctor, carrying a cloth bag stuffed with books. "We're sorry to inconvenience your patients, but I'm sure they're used to waiting."

Dr. Granger started and blinked, then glanced sideways at her.

"Please have a seat, and we'll try to do this quickly." Ryan set the bag of books on the desk and took her own chair.

Dr. Granger glared at her but looked around for the chair and sat on the edge, leaning forward as if only there for a second or two.

"Thank you for coming," Manziuk said. "We have some questions about Violet Klassen's death."

"*Violet's* death? But, my dear detectives, there is no similarity whatsoever between her death and Ingrid's!"

"Our question has to do with whether or not you had any suspicions that Violet's death might have been suicide? Any suspicions at all, be they ever so unlikely."

The doctor licked his lips and looked at the recorder sitting on the desk. "If I did have any suspicion, it was only a vague sense of unease. There was nothing to indicate that suicide was even a remote possibility. Nothing! My very fleeting—and I emphasize the word *fleeting*—thought was that at least this way she wouldn't suffer. But I had no reason to think that she had anything to do with her death.

It was more a sense that she was spared. And to be honest I can't begin to see her even considering suicide. And absolutely not without leaving a note for her family. She died from the cancer and old age."

"Old age is rather a vague cause, isn't it?"

Dr. Granger shook his head. "Not at all. It simply means that some part or parts of her body gave out. It could have been a heart attack, an aneurysm, a stroke, kidney failure, a blood clot... There are any number of possibilities."

"It didn't occur to you to ask for an autopsy?"

"An autopsy would have only caused more anguish for her family and would prove nothing. Even if she did commit suicide, what possible good would knowing it serve? Even worse, an autopsy might have been inconclusive so people would always wonder."

Ryan asked, "Have you had any other deaths in here that were perhaps not one hundred percent clear-cut?"

Dr. Granger smiled. "Serenity Suites is a retirement residence, not a nursing home. There are few deaths, and those are easily explained. Trust me, we don't have a serial killer doing away with our residents."

Manziuk said, "What about Grant Brooks?"

Dr. Granger relaxed in the chair and crossed his knees. "Mr. Brooks had a massive heart attack. Medical staff were there in seconds and did everything they could."

"Had you warned him he was at risk for a heart attack?"

"Not in so many words. But his cholesterol was somewhat high. He liked rich food and good wine and a cigar after each meal, and he hated exercise."

"So you have no doubt about his cause of death."

"None whatsoever. Neither did the heart specialist who signed the death certificate."

"What about Mrs. Klassen? Could she have had a heart attack?"

Dr. Granger shifted uncomfortably. "Anything is possible. Aside from the cancer, she was in good health as far as I could tell. She seemed to take good care of herself. You might say she was a bit of a health nut in terms of eating and so forth. She walked every day and even used free weights. But she was an elderly woman, and she had pancreatic cancer."

"The cancer wasn't treatable?"

"We could have operated. However, there was no guarantee we would get it all. We'd also have used chemo. But she said she'd prefer not to." He leaned forward. "Now, I don't mean it was an easy fix. It wasn't. And it's very likely anything we did would have only staved it off for a short while. Pancreatic cancer is one of the worst in terms of survival rate."

Ryan spoke. "Since Mrs. Davidson was murdered and since she and Violet were close friends for many years, do you *still* think an autopsy was unnecessary?"

He turned toward her and frowned. "You aren't seriously thinking about exhuming her body, are you?"

"I'm asking, in the light of recent events, if you think it might make sense to do so?"

"No, I don't."

Manziuk said, "Please give it some thought before you answer. Ignore the fact that the family might not like it, or that it might make you look bad if something is found, and think about what is the best thing to do. No, the *right* thing to do. Ingrid Davidson was viciously stabbed in the neck and left to bleed to death by someone who either lives or works on this floor. Hers might not be the last death."

Dr. Granger stared at his feet and licked his lips. "Violet died of natural causes."

Ryan paused in making notes. "You don't know that for certain."

"She looked very peaceful. Nothing was out of place."

Manziuk said, "So you're basing your assumption that her death was natural on the fact that to all appearances she looked as if she simply laid down for a nap and died in her sleep?"

"Well, yes."

"But if she'd taken a heavy dose of sleeping medicine, isn't that exactly how she'd look?"

"I suppose so. But you'd expect something to look unusual. An empty pill bottle maybe."

"Did you look for an empty bottle?"

"No, but there wasn't one."

Ryan said, "So there was no empty bottle sitting on the night table, perhaps with the lid off, calling out, 'This is not normal'?"

He didn't respond.

Manziuk shot a quelling glance at his partner. "Was there a search of any kind?"

"I don't believe so."

"Did anyone suggest there should be?"

"Audra might have."

"Who cleaned up her room?"

"I assume the maid who works on this floor. Audra may have helped."

After Dr. Granger left the office in a huff of impatience, Ryan looked at Manziuk. "Now what?"

"I'd like to check with Joey to see if he's found out anything more about Frank's book deadline. Maybe see his office for myself before we let him back in. I'd like to have a better picture of who he is. The bit about the deadline bothers me. He works in there every day, from breakfast to dinner. And everyone has said he didn't appear to be devastated over his wife's death. So why would he be so far behind in his word count that he had to tell the editor his book would be delayed?"

Frank's office was almost identical to the one they were using except for its large bookcase filled with books and papers all over the desk.

"Anything?" Manziuk asked.

Constable Joey Coxwell looked up from his work. "Check out these letters. Frank's deadline, which he agreed to nearly a year ago, is the end of September. And the expected length of the book is ninety thousand words."

"And he has thirty thousand written?"

"As far as I can tell."

"He's been coming to the office for the last year but not writing? That makes no sense. Is he sleeping? On the Internet? What?"

"I've been checking his trail. There are a few porn sites he visits almost daily, but not for huge amounts of time. More like he checks in to see what's new."

"Okay."

"Then there are a couple of other sites he visits under the alias Cowboy Max. One of them is a police site, and the other seems to be focused on how to identify and capture terrorists. He appears to spend a good deal of time conversing with people on both those sites. Mostly men, but some women. They talk about all kinds of things to do with policing, investigations, scientific findings, weapons, political unrest, and so forth. There are a lot of posts, and people get pretty heated. Quite a bit of discussion, really."

Ryan said, "From what Mary says, both sites would be in keeping with what he writes about in his books."

"He also spends some time on Facebook as himself, talking to fans and other writers."

"So how much time does all that take?" Manziuk asked.

"Two or three hours a day."

"So the rest of the time that he's in the office," Ryan said, "he's either reading the books on his shelves or trying to write but not getting much done?"

Manziuk nodded. "That's how it appears."

"Joey, can we see the new book?"

He opened a file and moved away so Manziuk could sit on the chair and read. Ryan stood at his shoulder.

"What do you think?" Joey asked after about ten minutes.

Manziuk made a face. "I need to have a look at the books we got from Mary, and I have no idea how a first draft ought to look, but it looks pretty rough to me."

"Maybe he's having difficulty," Ryan said. "Maybe his ideas have dried up."

"That's how it seems to me."

"And that might explain his grumpiness to everyone."

"Possibly," Manziuk smiled. "But I remember someone at a conference saying that people's natures don't change as they get older; they just lose their ability to disguise their true nature."

"That's good." She thought for a moment. "So Frank was having trouble writing. Is that what it comes down to?"

"It's possible."

"But what does that have to do with Ingrid's death?"

"Probably nothing. But I'm keeping an open mind about Violet's death."

"You think he could have killed Violet so she didn't find out he was no longer able to write?"

"I think he's a very proud man. If what we suspect is true, it must be killing him."

Alone at her table waiting for lunch, Hilary scanned the room. It was very quiet. Almost sombre. Catarina and Nikola sat conversing quietly at their table; Mary was sitting with Elizabeth and Norm, but none of them were talking; Frank and Kenneth were silently waiting for their food; Trish and Lyle carried on a low-voiced conversation. Audra stood in the doorway to the dining room watching.

As Olive and Scarlett started bringing in the food, the mood lightened somewhat. But all conversations stopped when Ben and his son Bruce walked into the room. Without hesitation, Bruce pulled out a chair next to Hilary and waited while Ben seated himself. Bruce took the chair across from Hilary. "Bruce Davidson," he said to her.

"Hilary Brooks."

Olive brought plates for Ben and Bruce.

"I'm not very hungry," Ben said to Hilary, "but Bruce insists I eat anyway."

"You'll feel worse if you don't," Hilary said. "I know that from experience."

Ben looked at her. "Yes, you *do* understand, don't you?"

"Very well."

Ben noticed his son looking at him quizzically. "Hilary's husband was Grant Brooks. You've met him."

"Oh, yes. Certainly."

"Grant died this spring from a sudden heart attack."

Bruce frowned. "No warning?"

Hilary shook her head. "None. We were on our way to dinner and the theatre. We got into the elevator to go down and about halfway there, Grant suddenly grabbed his chest and collapsed on the elevator floor. When we hit ground level, I called for help. People came right away, but it was no use."

"That must have been devastating."

"Yes. But not unlike what's happened to your mother, except that her death wasn't natural. They call heart attacks the silent killer. Your mother's killer was human."

"But at this point still silent. Unless the police know more than I think they do."

"Whatever the cause, when you lose someone you love, you're at first numb and then you're in desperate pain for quite a long while until, very gradually, you realize that you're still alive, and you must create a new path for yourself, but without forgetting the past."

Ben was nodding. "I did that once before. A long time ago, I lost someone who was very dear to me. I thought my world had ended. I literally went through the motions, alive and yet not really living. And then a couple of years later I met Ingrid, and gradually I learned to live once more." He sighed. "I'm not sure I want to do that again, not at my age."

Bruce said in a low voice, "Dad, I know how hard this is, and I hate to say it, but you know Mom wasn't going to get better. In some ways maybe it's better this way. Not that I'm even for one second condoning whoever did this. But it's spared her the agony of getting more and more lost in another world, and you the agony of having to watch."

Ben snorted. "Well, if someone did this thinking it was a kindness, I certainly don't feel any desire to thank them."

"Of course not. Nor do I. I'm just trying to make the best of a bad situation."

"I know."

"People should be allowed the time to grieve while the other person is still with them," Hilary said. "It's not only about the dying person. It's also about their family and friends. Whoever stabbed Ingrid also stabbed every member of her family and her friends and anyone who knew her. That's why this person must be caught and stopped."

Ben's lower lip trembled. "Hilary, I know Ingrid wasn't very kind to you. I'm sorry." He reached toward her and touched her shoulder.

Hilary reached up to pat Ben's hand. "No matter. She was already in another world when I came here. She barely knew I existed. So sad to have anyone's life come to that."

Since Ryan had to be at the autopsy at 3:00 and Manziuk wanted to get back to headquarters to brief Superintendent Seldon on the investigation, they decided to separate for a few interviews. But before they could start, there was a quick knock and the door opened wide enough for Benson to pop his head in. "Bad time?"

"No, it's a good time," Manziuk said. "How's it going?"

Benson came in. "I just spent an hour and a half with the administrator of Serenity Suites."

Ryan laughed. "Ms. Arlington? That long? Really?"

He slumped into the vacant chair. "She's quite concerned about the inevitable news stories having a negative impact on people on their waiting list for condos. And possibly even causing some people to move out. She needed assurance we won't bad-mouth Serenity Suites to the press. And wanted us to say nice things like 'This was clearly a one-time thing. Personal vendetta. Nothing to do with the building or its management. The police can assure people it won't happen again.' And so forth.

"She gave me a tour of the building, from the lowest floor of the parking garage to this floor, which is apparently the top. She did everything possible to assure me of the safety of each and every resident and staff member, while at the same time threatening me that if anything untoward—my word not hers—happened, it would be entirely our fault." He shook his head. "And she didn't stop talking for five seconds."

"Sounds like you may have met your match," Manziuk said.

"Ha, ha." He closed his eyes. "Seriously, I'm exhausted."

Neither of the others said anything. After a moment, he opened his eyes again and sat up. "So what have you got for me? Ms. Arlington is exhausting, but she does have a point. The last thing we need is for people to start thinking that residences for seniors aren't safe. And you know how many reporters would be like fish in a feeding frenzy if they thought there was even a germ of truth to that." He grimaced. "So is it a one-time thing? A personal vendetta? Do we have an avenging white-haired granny or grandpa on the loose? Or a renegade doctor or nurse?"

"We don't really know what we have at this point," Manziuk said. "All we can honestly say is that we're doing our best, but we won't be able to solve this in a few hours."

"Don't you have fingerprints or DNA you can check? Didn't the killer get splattered with blood? Surely there has to be some obvious marker that will lead you to the nasty old granny or grandpa."

Ryan rolled her eyes at Benson. "I assume you aren't serious."

"Just paraphrasing Ms. Arlington. She really can't understand what's taking so long. Figures you should have had it solved last night in time for the newspapers to print a story this morning about the arrest. She's really annoyed she has to field questions and concerns from the board, staff, and residents, not to mention the families of people currently living here and, more important, potential residents. She's apparently already had to remove a number of names from the waiting list. She doesn't feel we have any respect for her or her position, which is very precarious. We obviously don't appreciate that she might even be blamed for this if the company starts losing money."

Manziuk smiled. "Sounds like you had a fun ninety minutes."

"Was it really ninety minutes? It felt like an entire day." He shook his head. "And the worst part is, I gave her my card, so I'll likely hear a lot more from her in the future. Please, I'm begging you, solve this case quickly so I never have to go near her again!"

After Benson left, Ryan stayed to read Ford's report, while Manziuk went to the dining room and told the residents they could now use all the rooms except the common room. There was a general sigh of relief.

"Does this mean you've figured out who did it?" Lyle asked.

"I'm sorry. I can't talk about an ongoing investigation. But I can tell you we are working hard."

"Well, I'm sure that makes us all feel good," Elizabeth said.

When the residents had all filed out, Audra looked at Manziuk. "Are we all in danger?"

"I don't think so, but I would advise people to lock their doors and be cautious."

"But there won't be any police officers here tonight."

"No. Though perhaps you could ask Serenity Suites to provide a security guard."

"Maybe... Inspector, do you think you'll ever arrest someone for this?"

"I promise you I'll do my best."

"Thank you. Some of them think you won't bother because they're old."

"They're wrong."

"I hope so."

"Ms. Limson, do you have time for a quick question?"

"Yes, of course."

"Who cleaned Violet's room after her death?"

"Gulab."

"Did you give her any instructions?"

Audra looked at the floor. "I asked her to look for anything out of the ordinary."

"And did she find anything?"

"Just a wine bottle."

"Why was that out of the ordinary?"

"I'd never seen Violet drink anything stronger than tea or hot chocolate."

"How do you know it was hers? Might it have been Frank's?"

"As far as I know, Frank doesn't drink anything except an occasional brandy. And the bottle was on her side of the bed in a narrow space between the bed and the night table."

"And it wasn't normally there?"

"Gulab said she'd never seen it before. But she also said that Violet could have hidden it on the days she knew Gulab was cleaning the room. Unlike most of our people who let Gulab make their beds and tidy up each morning, Violet made their bed every day except for Thursday, when Gulab changed the sheets and cleaned their condo."

"Was the bottle empty?"

"No. It was a little less than half full."

"Did anyone drink any of the wine?"

"I did."

"And?"

"I just had a sip. It seemed fine. I'm not much of an expert, but it seemed like a very good wine."

"Red or white?"

"Red."

"What happened to the bottle?"

"I gave it to Scarlett. She uses wine in cooking, and I thought it was too good to throw out."

"Was it a brand that was bought for the bar in the common room?"

"No, I checked."

"Was there a wine glass?"

"Yes, on the night table beside the glass for her orange juice."

"Orange juice?"

"She had a routine of taking her vitamins with a glass of orange juice after lunch. Gulab was positive about that."

"Was the juice glass empty?"

"Yes, but there was a small residue, so we were able to tell what it was."

"Where did the juice come from?"

"A container she kept in their refrigerator."

"Was there more juice in the container?"

"No, it was empty, and she'd put it in the recycling bin."

"So no one tested the orange juice residue to make sure there wasn't something in it?"

She shook her head. "I suggested to Dr. Granger that a lab could test the little bit that was left, but he said that was ridiculous."

"Was there anything else? Anything at all."

"I don't think so. Gulab might remember more. That whole afternoon was like something from a nightmare. I still have trouble believing it really happened."

"Is Gulab in today?"

Audra looked at her watch. "She should be here now. When they left last night, I told her and Tess to take the morning off and come in around 1:00. Gulab should be cleaning Lyle's room today."

"I'd also like to talk to Mr. Klassen again. Would it be easier if I went to see him?"

Audra bit her lip. "Yes, I think so. Otherwise he'd have to get onto his scooter and then off again after. But I believe he was going to his office, and he won't like being interrupted. Do you want me to come with you?"

"That's okay. I'll take my chances."

She raised her eyebrows but said nothing more.

"Oh, I have one other question. Why are you planning to resign from this job?"

"How did you know?"

"The partially-written letters of resignation found in your wastebasket."

She put her hand to her throat. "Oh! I hadn't realized. I mean, I knew you were searching everywhere, but I didn't realize you'd find them."

"Do you have another job lined up?"

"No."

"I understood this job pays very well."

"My husband is sending the boys to a school north of Toronto. I need to move up there so I can see them on weekends."

"You can't drive up on weekends?"

"I don't have a car."

"Honestly? That's your reason?"

She hung her head. "I can't tell you."

"Why not?"

"It's very personal."

"If it has nothing to do with our investigation, I won't say a word to anyone."

"I—you see—I—I promise it has nothing to do with your investigation."

"Ms. Limson, just tell me."

She looked down. "I can't stay here when I'm attracted to one of the residents."

"Nikola Vincent?"

"How did you—?"

"He's the only one near your age."

She threw him a sad smile and whispered, "I have to leave."

"I understand."

Manziuk found Gulab Brampton vacuuming Lyle Oakley's sitting room. "Cleaning up Violet's room after her death?" She shut off the vacuum and put a hand to her throat. "Oh, yes. I remember it as if it was yesterday."

"What can you tell me?"

She sat on the edge of a chair. "It was very tidy, as usual. Nothing out of place except the blanket and pillow she'd placed on top of the comforter, the two glasses on her night table, and the bottle of wine next to the bed."

"She always napped on top of the bedcovers?"

"Always. She made the bed in the morning. And to not disturb it, she laid a blanket on top and just took her pillow out and put it back after. I know that because she'd told me what she did. The duvet was white, and she worried about getting it dirty."

"And the blanket was fine? Nothing on it?"

She frowned. "Do you mean blood?"

"Or anything spilled? The wine or the juice, for example."

"No, nothing."

"How full was the wine bottle?"

"It was about half full, maybe a little less."

"What happened to it?"

"When I was finished cleaning the room, I took it to Audra, along with the glasses."

"Why?"

"She'd asked me to look for anything out of the ordinary."

"Was there anything else you noticed—anything at all?"

She gave him a measured look. "I searched for a suicide note, but if there was one I couldn't find it."

He kept his surprise from showing. "Where did you look?"

"On the dresser, in the drawers, in her office, in the sitting room, in Frank's study. Any place I could think of."

"Had someone asked you to do that?"

"Audra did."

"And you found nothing?"

She shook her head.

"What about the vitamins she took after lunch?"

"She kept them in her night table in a small organizer case that held two weeks' worth. She filled it every other Saturday."

"And it was fine?"

"Looked perfectly normal. Each day's pills were there. Only four days' worth, including Wednesday's, were gone."

"Did she have sleeping pills?"

"No, I'd never seen any in their medicine cabinet, and I purposely looked for a pill container of any kind that day. I looked in the medicine cabinet, under the bed, in the drawers, even in the garbage and recycling bins."

"Did Audra ask you to look for that, too?"

"Yes. I'm not in trouble, am I? Or Audra?"

"No, neither of you is in trouble. It was the right thing to do." Manziuk sighed. "So you found nothing at all to indicate that Violet might have taken her own life?"

"No." Gulab's eyes welled up with tears. "And I don't think she would have. She wasn't the kind to leave a mess for others to fix. She wasn't chatty at all, and she liked everything done in a certain way, but she was a right nice lady. I miss her."

Ryan found Derrick, not Audra, in the staff office, typing on a computer. He smiled and leaned back in his chair. "Hello there. Can I help you?"

"I was looking for Audra. We have a question about medicines."

"She's taking a bit of a break. But I might be able to help you." He motioned to a chair kitty-corner to his desk. "Have a seat. What is it you want to know?"

"We noticed that the people on this floor—both residents and staff—keep medicines—prescriptions as well as over-the-counter products—in their own bathrooms. That seems unusual."

"Not really. This isn't a nursing home where the nurse brings the meds around with a cart. Nor is it a regular condominium where the residents may not even know who lives next door. It's somewhere in between. So the norm is that the people look after themselves. But since we're realistic, we know that as people get older they have more medical issues, so there are on-site staff with medical training to help as needed."

"So the nurses don't hand out medicines?"

"Not routinely, no. However, we do in certain circumstances. For example, if someone becomes ill or has an injury that doesn't require hospitalization and needs some help—in particular a single adult who lives alone—then we'll step in and give them the care they require. That might be doling out medicine, giving baths, changing bandages, or whatever's required."

"What about the Davidsons?"

"Ingrid has—had—diabetes and required insulin shots. She wasn't able to give them to herself, and while Ben was game to try he was horribly inept. Mostly he was terrified he was going to do something wrong and hurt her." Derrick sighed. "Plus she wasn't as cooperative as one would have hoped. So Audra and I gave her the insulin, and then somehow we ended up giving her all her meds."

He picked up a pen and tapped it on the desk. "To be honest, Audra and I were afraid she might mix them up or either forget to take them or take too many. Ben was quite relieved when we offered to look after them. They were kept in a locked medicine cabinet in their bathroom, and we just went in and got them and gave them to her at specific times."

"I thought the policy here is that if people need to be in a nursing home, they have to leave?"

"Right."

"So Ben had to have known it was only a matter of time until she'd have to leave?"

"I think everyone knew that."

Ryan thought for a moment. "Is there anyone else you give medicine to?"

"Not at this time, no."

"I believe you have other medicines in a locked cabinet in this room?"

"For emergency use only. Say someone has a heart attack, we want to be able to treat it right away. Or food poisoning. Even a migraine. Toothache. Just some basics, that's all."

"How easy would it be for someone other than you and Audra to get medicine out of this office?"

"The cabinet is locked, and Audra and I are the only ones with keys. Same with the door. It's locked when one of us isn't here, and we're the only ones who have voice recognition to get in."

"What about the other residents? Could they access someone else's medicines?"

"Well, maybe. The medicine cabinets in the bathrooms all have locks, but I'm guessing most people don't lock them. On the other hand, all condo front doors lock automatically when they're closed, and because they're voice activated, only the people who live inside that condo have access, plus Audra and me. Well, there's Jared, who has master keys to every floor. But Jared only comes up occasionally, and never without a reason. We also have a single master key for this floor that Audra and I could use in a pinch, but it's kept locked in a drawer in our office. You guys have been using it."

"So, except for you and Audra, only the resident who lives in the condo can get in?"

"Normally. Except that a few residents have added someone else to their intercom voice recognition. Say you have a son or daughter who visits a lot, you might give them voice access. Bruce Davidson, for example, likely has access to Ben's condo."

"Of course any visitor presumably could ask to use the bathroom and get medicine out of an unlocked cabinet."

"Well, all the condos have a second bathroom that visitors would normally use. The medicine cabinet is in the bathroom off the master bathroom." Derrick made a face. "Although now that I think about it, a lot of people keep their prescriptions in the kitchen right out in the open."

"Yes, that's where my Gram keeps hers."

"You have a grandmother here in the city?"

"I live in her house actually."

"Ah, that's so nice." He smiled. "My dad's parents live in BC, so I don't see them much. My mom's father lives here in the city, but her mother died when I was very small so I don't remember her."

"My grandfather died quite a while ago. And my other grandparents are in Jamaica. I've only seen them a few times."

"Did you come here from Jamaica?"

"When I was small. My mother was born here, but my father was Jamaican. Mom met him when she was visiting some of her family there, and they fell in love and got married within a couple of months. Then she applied to get him into Canada. It took a while. She stayed in Jamaica most of the time, and I was born there."

"Everybody has a story. And I love hearing them." Derrick tilted his head. "So do you live with your grandmother, or does she live with you?"

"I live with her." At the question in his eyes, she added, "I moved in with her the day I turned sixteen. My father died when I was small, and later on my mother married a total jerk. The first day I could legally leave, I was gone. A year or so later my mother left him and moved in with Gram, too. And then my uncle died, and my aunt and her daughter moved in temporarily." She sighed. "That was five years ago."

Derick's eyes widened. "You have five women from three generations living together?"

"More like four generations. My cousin's only a couple of years younger than me but she acts more like a teenager than an adult."

"Do you have to share rooms?"

"No, thank goodness. It's an old three-storey house with enough bedrooms, but not nearly enough bathrooms!"

"I'll bet."

She stood up. "Anyway, I need to get back."

"If you have any more questions, I'll either be here or in the exercise room. You can page me on the intercom, too. My number is 2002."

"All right."

He followed her to the door. "A pleasure meeting you." He held out his hand, which she hesitantly shook.

"Oh, one more question. Was Ingrid the only one who needed extra help?"

"Well, Frank manages pretty well most of the time, but he occasionally needs help getting on and off his scooter. Especially now that Violet's gone."

"So he can't walk at all?"

"He can walk a few steps as long as he has something—or someone—to hang onto. But sometimes at night he's tired or in pain so he'll ask for help. Usually that's me, but if I'm out it's Audra. She could ask one of the male staff from another floor to come up if necessary."

"What about Norm? I noticed his hands shaking. Was he just nervous, or is there something wrong with him?"

"He's been recently diagnosed with Parkinson's. It's a tragedy really. He's an artist so he needs to be in total control of his movements, and it's getting more and more difficult for him. But he and Elizabeth seem to be managing all right thus far."

"Speaking of Elizabeth, she seems to be, well, not exactly a happy person."

He laughed. "She has a kind of dry humour that can be taken wrong. But I do think she's frustrated. She's younger than anyone here—other than Nikola of course, but that's another story entirely. I think she'd like to be going out and doing more things, and Norm is happy to kind of vegetate."

"Thanks for the information. Now I have to get going. I have an autopsy to attend."

"Ingrid's?"

"Yes."

"Poor thing. Well, if you have any more questions, I'm here." He reached for his wallet. "Why don't I give you my card? I'm really praying you guys are able to find out who did this. If there's anything at all I can do to help, call me."

Manziuk knocked on the door of Frank's office, then went in.

Frank looked up from his computer. His scooter was parked near him. "What is this? I'm busy."

"I just have a few questions, Mr. Klassen. I thought it might be easier if I came to you. I hope you don't mind."

"It would be easiest if you just left me alone. I have work to do, and I don't know a blessed thing about that woman's death."

Manziuk sat down in the wing chair in front of the desk. "I'm sorry to bother you, but my questions actually aren't about Mrs. Davidson. It's about the book you're writing."

"What's my book got to do with anything?"

"I understand you have a deadline coming up soon?"

"That's right. What of it?"

"We found a letter from you to your publisher asking for an extension. And it seems that you're quite a bit behind in the writing. Yet you come in here every day. I assume this book isn't going well?"

"Even assuming it isn't, why exactly would that have anything to do with you?"

"We're following up anything out of the ordinary."

For the first time since they'd met Frank, he laughed. "Well, you're on the wrong track. This is nothing out of the ordinary. Or didn't you find all the other letters I've sent to my editor asking for extensions?"

"Other letters?"

"Other than the first book, which I'd finished before I sent it out, I've been late on every single book I've ever written."

"You have?"

"If you don't believe me, ask my publisher."

"But you only have thirty thousand words written, and your contract says it needs to be ninety thousand. And the deadline is very close."

"So?"

"So what do you do in here every day?"

"I think. I plan. I research. I write up charts. I throw out bad ideas and I test other ideas. Have you read any of my books?"

"Not yet."

"Well, read one. You'll find they're very intricate. I weave true events into a fictional plot line that has action, adventure, suspense, and a little sex. That takes a lot of planning. Did you look at my plans?"

"No, just the file with the book."

"Well, come here then."

Manziuk moved to Frank's side as he opened files. "My character descriptions. I have a bunch of areas I fill out for every character of any importance." He clicked, and another file opened. "My setting. I do all kinds of research on the location I use in each book." Another click. "Historical facts. Although the books are contemporary, every one deals with a slightly different area of history, so I have to do a lot of research on the people and events." Yet another click. "My plot line. Before I write a word, I write details on every scene and move them around until I'm satisfied. And the more books I write, the more I have to go back and cross-reference all my other books to make sure I haven't used the same names, characters, plots, or settings in other books. Just checking all that can take hours.

"When all that is complete, I write the first draft of the book, focusing on the action and dialogue. I write between five and ten thousand words a day at that point. Then I go over it and add all the description of the characters and the setting and so forth."

"I apologize. I had no idea how much planning was involved. So you're at the writing stage now?"

"The first draft stage. My planning always takes longer than I think it will. And that's why I always end up asking for an extension. And they always give it to me. However, due to Violet's death, and now Ingrid's, I've lost nearly three weeks of writing time. I could have written the entire first draft in that time."

"I see."

"Now, unless you have any other questions, I need to get back to work. When I write, I'm literally in another world, and every time I'm interrupted, even for a minor thing like overhearing a noise from another room, I'm sucked right out of that world, and it usually takes me an hour or even a day to get back. Which is why I choose to work here, where it's soundproof and there are no distractions." He glared at Manziuk. "Normally."

Fifteen

Manziuk was in the parking garage of Serenity Suites about to leave for police headquarters when his cellphone rang.

"We've found something!" Constable Kelly announced. "You might want to come and see this."

Thankful he wasn't halfway to headquarters, Manziuk headed back up to the suite where Kelly was helping Trish go through Violet's files and bins.

Trish was waiting in the hallway outside the door. "Inspector, I'm just flabbergasted." She threw up her hands. "You'll need to see it for yourself. We're in the dining room."

He followed her through the sitting room, where Constable Ari Bixby looked up from a pile of file folders and gave a slight wave, to the next room, where Kelly was seated at a computer on the dining table.

Trish sat down across from Kelly and motioned to Manziuk to a chair at the end of the table. "We found printouts of Mom and Dad's financial records, then we went into Mom's computer to double-check them. And they seem to be correct. You need to understand I've already seen the bank balance from their joint account, so I know how much money they have and where it is. But I've always believed that all of their money came from the sales of Dad's books. In fact, from the things Dad said, I've always believed that Mom's cookbooks cost him money." She paused and took a deep breath.

"And?"

"And I was wrong on both counts."

"Here." Kelly turned the monitor."You can see it clearly."

"What am I looking for?"

Trish pointed out the items they'd found. "Last year's royalties for Mom's cookbooks are on the second line, and the royalties for Dad's books are right below them on the third line."

"Hers are on the second line?"

"Yes."

"Hers are almost six times higher?"

"At least."

"We've gone through every year, and it's been like that from the year her first cookbook came out," Kelly said. "Not as much of a difference to start with, but it's increased every year."

"You can also see the payments that have gone into my parents' joint account each month—all of the money from his books and a portion of hers. The rest of her money was hers to play with."

Manziuk stared at her. "To what?"

Kelly opened a second file, and a bar graph appeared.

"What are these?"

"Violet's investments," Kelly said. "As you can see, each year the bar goes higher and higher. That's all money she made through investments."

Trish's voice rose with her excitement. "Apparently Mom had been investing in the stock market and doing really, really well. She also seemed to be getting quite a bit money from a numbered company. We're trying to figure out what it is. She must have had a lot of shares in it. I talked to her lawyer, and he knows nothing about it. I called her accountant, but he's off on some hiking expedition in the Australian outback."

Manziuk frowned. "You're certain this is your mother's doing?"

"This is the computer that was in her office. All of the papers and the bank books for two other accounts in *her* name only were in her filing cabinet. Earlier this week when I asked Dad if he needed any help with his banking, he told me my mother took care of all that. At the time I thought he was taking about day-to-day things like getting cash from the bank and paying bills, but now I think he literally meant everything."

"Do you think your dad knows about all this?"

Trish shook her head. "I really don't think so."

"Do you honestly think she could have kept it from him?"

Trish shrugged. "It's crazy, but I think it's entirely possible. Dad always told people the cookbooks cost him money. In his mind he was the famous writer, and she was the little housewife who wrote cookbooks to pass the time. I think she let him go on thinking that he paid for everything from his book sales to avoid bruising his ego."

Kelly held up a couple of folders. "We found contracts for all the books—hers and his. They're all in envelopes, and the envelopes for the contracts for Frank's books are all addressed to Violet. My guess is she was acting as his agent."

Trish continued. "It's kind of hazy because I was only about fourteen or so at the time, but when Dad first started selling his novels, I remember him complaining about having to deal with the contracts and other business stuff." She brought her hands up and rested her chin on them. "She must have just quietly taken over, at the same time letting everyone think he was the one who did everything." She shook her head. "I could just scream! Talk about an enabler! I'm just so angry with him and so exasperated with her!"

"Well, I'd say this adds to the need to exhume your mother's body," Manziuk stated.

Trish stared at him. "How?"

"For starters, this convinces me that she wouldn't have committed suicide without documenting what you'd need to do to look after your father. And it creates doubt as to whether we know what all was going on in her life. Your mother wasn't merely an elderly lady who was marking time until her death; she had a number of things going on, and there's a good deal of money involved."

"You're right. She'd never have left things in this much of a mess." She drummed her fingers on the table. "What it comes down to is whether I really want to know for sure if her death was natural or not. And the longer we wait, the harder it will be to tell if there was something other than natural causes." She pursed her lips. "All right. If you have the paper, I'll sign it."

When Trish had signed the form giving her approval for the autopsy, Manziuk asked, "Are you going to tell your father about any of this or wait until afterward?"

Trish bit her lip. "I don't like to deceive him." She shrugged. "But, surprise! I guess I take after my mother, who seems to have kept all kinds of things from both him and me. I'm not going to say anything about the money for now. As for the autopsy, if you don't find anything, perhaps he never needs to know."

Kelly said, "Should we keep going through the bins?"

"Definitely," Manziuk told her. "Given what you've found so far, there's a good chance you could find something else."

Audra was sitting in the office thinking about her priorities when Nikola walked in. "Yes? May I help you?"

"Actually I stopped by to see if there's anything I can do to help you." He turned a chair around and straddled it.

"Fine, thanks. Busy." She turned to her computer and began typing.

"So aren't you going to tell me about it?"

"About what?"

"Why you were so upset this morning when I saw you in the hallway."

She bit her bottom lip. "We had a murder yesterday. Isn't that enough?"

"I don't think Ingrid's murder made you look that sad."

She looked away. "I can't talk about it. Especially to *you*."

"Why *especially* not to me?"

"What would Catarina say?"

Nikola laughed. "Cat would say, 'Why are you just talking—why don't you do something to help her?'"

Taken by surprise, Audra blurted out, "Would she? But what—" before catching herself. "There's nothing you can do."

He shrugged. "Since I don't know what the problem is, I have no idea if I can help or not, do I?"

"There's nothing *anyone* can do."

"Now you've thoroughly confused me, you *have* to tell me. Otherwise I'm going to assume you're confessing to Ingrid's murder."

She tossed her head back. "Of course not. I'm worried about my sons. That's all."

He frowned. "What about your sons? Has something happened to one of them?"

"No, but they—they begged me to come and get them." Tears came into her eyes, and she wiped them away. "They hate their stepmother, and Giles is always busy. They don't understand that I can't—that it's not my choice—that the judge gave Giles custody and I have no say."

"When I saw you yesterday morning, is that why you'd been crying? You'd just spoken with them?"

She nodded. "Yes. And later on I spoke to Giles. He's sending both boys to a boarding school north of Toronto in September. They don't want to go, and there's nothing I can do. And it will be much harder for me to visit them there."

"How old are your sons?"

"Graham is ten, and Gavin is twelve."

"I see. Please tell me more. Why are they with your ex-husband?"

"He's a lawyer. He had an affair. Probably not for the first time. But this time the woman—a very young woman—got pregnant. Because she was his senior partner's daughter, he decided he had to marry her. So naturally he divorced me. And because he's a lawyer and knew all the legal loopholes and had friends and money, he got to keep the house, the car, and the boys, and all he had to give me was a thousand dollars a month until I marry. And I get the boys for one day every two weeks and two weeks in the summer." She began to sob. "My sons tell me Giles's wife hates having them in the house and wants Giles to send them to the boarding school." She covered her face with her hands. "I'm sorry."

"Nothing to be sorry about. We'll just have to come up with a plan for you to get custody of the boys. I suggest we start by getting a private detective to document how the boys are being treated by their father and stepmother. We'll need to give the judge indisputable proof that their father isn't doing a very good job and their stepmother wants nothing to do with them."

She smiled and shook her head. "You're being ridiculous. Hiring private detectives costs a lot of money. And anyway they couldn't find out what's going on inside the house."

"Well, there must be something we can do."

"We? There is no 'we.' And do you do realize that if Naomi knew I was talking to you about my personal problems, she'd fire me without a moment's hesitation."

"Really?" He made a face. "All right. I guess we have to talk about something else. Have you read any good books lately?"

She turned back to her computer. "I have work I need to do."

"Actually I have a serious question. And it's not about you. What's with Hilary?"

"What do you mean?"

"She sits alone at a table every meal and never talks to anyone except you. Why is she here if she doesn't want to associate with any of the other residents?"

Tears came back into Audra's eyes. "It's not her! It's them. They hate her."

Nikola frowned. "What do you mean they hate her?"

Audra looked away. "Forget I said that. Please."

"I don't understand. I thought it was her being standoffish. When I first came here, I'd say hello, and she'd just mumble something and never look me in the eye. So I stopped."

Audra sighed. "She's really very nice. What you call her standoffishness is a barrier she's put up because she knows she's not wanted here."

"She isn't?"

"I shouldn't be telling you this."

"Why not? I live here, and so does Catarina. Why does Hilary think she's not wanted?"

Audra looked away. "It's a long story."

"Well, just give me the bottom line."

"Okay, if you want the truth, I'll give it to you. Naomi told Hilary she's putting her condo up for sale next Monday and Hilary has to leave by September 30th or she'll have her moved out by force."

"Catarina has never mentioned this to me. Who else knows that Naomi is trying to get Hilary evicted?"

"Derrick. And the Residents Board of Serenity Suites. They're the ones who want her gone. I guess it's not fair to blame Naomi. She's only the board's tool. But she seems to enjoy her job too much for me."

"Who are the people on this board?"

"Each floor has a representative elected by the residents who live on that floor. The representative for the twentieth floor is Frank Klassen."

"And let me guess, Frank would be happy to see Hilary go?"

"Frank has been quite vocal about her not qualifying to be here."

"I see. Is there anyone else on this floor who might have some pull with the board? Someone who might not agree with Frank?"

"I don't know. Maybe Ben. He was a friend of Grant Brooks, Hilary's husband. It's because of Ben that Grant and Hilary bought their condo."

"So what if we talk to Ben about it? Ask his opinion?"

"I can't do that. I can't involve a resident in my concerns. Especially not Ben, not after what just happened to Ingrid."

"Has Hilary told anyone else about this? Any of the other residents I mean?"

Audra shook her head. "I don't think so. She has no friends here other than the staff."

Nikola sat thinking for a minute. "Okay. What if I talk to Hilary and bug her until she tells me, and then Cat and I talk to Ben? That way you're not involved and no one can get mad at you."

Audra stared at the top of her desk.

He leaned forward. "Look, do you want Hilary evicted?"

"No, of course I don't. It's totally unfair! She qualifies as much as any of them do."

"So why not let me try?"

"You've never shown any interest in the other residents before now."

He smiled. "Well, better late than never, yes?"

Reluctantly she agreed.

Needing to talk to someone, Kenneth asked Derrick to come to his condo. They went into the sitting room and took seats.

"Derrick, at lunch today I asked Lyle if there was anyone here who not only believed in God but seemed to genuinely care about others, and you were the one he thought of. I don't know you very well, so I hope you don't mind. *Do* you believe in God?"

Derrick smiled. "Absolutely."

"When I was your age, I believed in him, too."

Derrick became serious. "What changed your mind?"

"Things that happened. Terrible things that God either caused or allowed."

"I see."

"I used to believe God cared about us. Then I stopped believing. And now I just don't know."

"It sounds like you're talking about the eternal question of why God allows good people to suffer?"

"Yes, but so much more. Not merely 'good' people, which is a relative thing, but why does God allow 'his' people to suffer?"

"The Old Testament has many stories of God's people's suffering. Abel, Moses, Joseph—"

"But there's always the corollary that someone is to blame. Abel was murdered by Cain; Moses' predicament was caused first by the rulers of Egypt and then the stubbornness of the people he was leading; Joseph was treated badly by his brothers. And even if you go to the other side and say maybe Abel was a prick to live with, Moses had a hot temper, and Joseph was an arrogant jerk, we can always come back to the old argument that it was Adam and Eve who brought evil into the world, and God stood back and watched it happen and did nothing. And that's my key point. He did nothing to stop it. So, sure, blame it all on Adam and Eve or Satan or whoever, but if God doesn't cause the evil, he allows it to happen when he could easily stop it."

"Miracles also happen," Derrick said softly. "God often brings good out of evil, like Joseph's saving his family from starvation."

Kenneth's face tightened. "My wife was a wonderful person who didn't deserve to have that horrible disease, never mind die from it. My children didn't deserve to lose their mother. God could have stopped the cancer from entering her body. He could have let the doctors find it in time to stop it. He could have done something!"

"Losing her must have hurt so much."

Kenneth looked at the carpet. "Many years ago I had a friend who went to Africa to plant a church. While there his wife gave birth to a son, but two days later the baby died because of inadequate medical help. My friend lost his faith and resigned from his position. One day my friend's wife came to me and said, 'My husband blames God for our son's death. And now we're talking about getting a divorce.' And do you know what I said to her? I said, 'This is a test, and your husband is failing. You need to pray more. You need more faith. Just trust God, and everything will be okay.' And she went away, presumably to pray harder and to trust God. And her husband divorced her and became a gambler and a philanderer, and as far as I know he died still angry with God. What that poor woman suffered! And my glib response increased her suffering."

Derrick took a deep breath. "And later when your wife died, you turned *your* back on God?"

"I told him I hated him. But, as hard as I've tried, I've never been able to convince myself he doesn't exist." He laughed bitterly. "All these years while I've been pretending he doesn't exist, he's never been even arm's length away from me."

Derrick nodded.

"Do you want to know something funny? I might as well tell you since I've already told the police. I planned to stab myself after dinner last night. I was going to leave a message for you to come over at 10:00 last night so you'd find me. I didn't want Gulab to find me this morning when she came in to make my bed."

"Yes, much better that I find you than Gulab. That was sensible."

"Was it?" Kenneth looked down. "Anyway, I was all set to do it, but then someone stabbed Ingrid. And do you know what my first thought was when I heard she'd been stabbed? *No one has the right to take a life.* It was as if a light had gone on in my head. A blinding, neon red, flashing light. It hit me that *I* had no right to take *my* life either." He stood and started pacing in a circle around the room, then stopped in front of Derrick. "I told all that to the police, but what I didn't tell them, because they might have thought I was crazy, was that the moment I had that thought, I knew God was talking to me. And since then I've wanted to talk to somebody who would understand and who could help me figure out what to do next."

Derrick waited for a moment, but Kenneth had stopped talking. "So your problem now is that you have to decide whether to go on pretending he isn't there or just begin talking to him again?"

Kenneth sank onto the chesterfield and put his head in his hands. "I've completely messed up my life."

"No more than many other people have done."

"It's like scales have dropped from my eyes. Job lost everything—wife, children, servants, business, money—and never blamed God. I lost my wife and then I completely screwed up everything else and blamed God for it all."

"Well, it's not as if he doesn't already know. So why not confess to him what you've just told me? He's the God of second—third—fourth—fifth—millionth chances."

"Yes, but..."

Derrick moved closer and put his arm around the older man's shoulders.

Kenneth leaned against him. "Oh, God," Kenneth sobbed, "please forgive me. I have sinned against you and against my family and against my church and against myself."

Ryan walked into police headquarters a few minutes before 5:00 and headed to Manziuk's office.

"How did it go?" Manziuk asked her.

"Pretty good actually. I neither keeled over nor ran out. In fact, I kind of enjoyed it."

"Well, that makes one of us."

She threw him a quick smile. "You can give me all the autopsies if you like. It's actually kind of fascinating. I never thought about it before, but I might have liked being a doctor."

A smile touched the corners of his mouth. "I would be more than happy to let you handle that part of the job." He gestured to the empty chair in front of his desk. "Speaking of which, did Dr. Granger show up?"

Ryan sat down and pulled out a notepad. "He was there when I arrived. He and Dr. Weaver seemed to know each other. I couldn't always follow what they were saying, but I kept asking them to explain, and they eventually started talking English instead of what I assume was Latin."

"What did they find?"

She glanced at her notebook. "Cursory examination of her brain showed definite signs of shrinkage to the cortex and enlarged spaces in the folds of the brain. Both consistent with Alzheimer's disease. Probably quite advanced." She looked up. "They're sending her brain for further tests. Mr. Davidson gave permission."

She glanced back at her notebook. "The X-ray showed that her bones were brittle. Dr. Weaver said she would have needed a hip replacement, and Dr. Granger agreed. She also showed signs of a few injuries in earlier years—a broken tibia and a broken clavicle. And she'd had surgery on her right knee, probably many years ago. She'd had her appendix removed at some point since there's a scar on the right side of the lower abdominal area as well. And she'd given birth, likely to more than one child. She had needle marks, presumably from insulin injections for her diabetes."

"Nice but not relevant."

"There was a single stab wound to the right neck, beneath the ear. It was about three inches at the deepest part and an inch wide. It severed the external jugular vein, causing it to bleed out. Unconsciousness would have occurred very quickly, and it would have been fatal in a couple of minutes."

"I asked if she might have cried out, and Dr. Weaver said she could have gasped, but likely not made a loud call. And she'd have become unconscious very quickly."

"So not surprising no one heard anything."

"Dr. Weaver and Dr. Granger spent some time debating the angle of the knife to figure out how it was held. She was sitting, so whoever it was would presumably have been above her. So did the assailant bring the knife down from above, or did he come from beneath?" She grinned. "It was kind of like in the movie *Twelve Angry Men*, where they talked about how you hold a switchblade."

Manziuk smiled. "Love that movie! So what was the verdict in our case?"

"They decided the knife had been held parallel to the ground and carefully inserted into the neck, in other words, not at an angle at all but level. That makes it pretty well impossible to tell how tall the assailant was. He might even have been kneeling. As to whether the assailant was right- or left-handed, we looked at photos of the chair. Because it was in the centre of the room, the assailant might have come from either the front or the back. So there was no way to tell whether the right or left hand was used.

"I asked if the assailant would have had blood on him, and Dr. Weaver said if it had been the carotid artery that was cut, blood would have sprayed out, but not the jugular vein. There might have been some stains on the hand and forearm and the front of the shirt, but there might just as easily not be any."

"Ford said they found nothing in the residents' rooms with blood stains, and nothing that was damp from being washed."

"Yeah."

"Did he say how much force would have been needed?"

"Dr. Weaver said that, assuming it was the knife that had been found with the body, and he had no reason to think it wasn't, it wouldn't have been much harder than sticking a knife in a banana. He also said that whoever did it was either lucky or knew exactly where to put the knife. We agreed that nowadays almost everyone has checked their pulse by putting a finger to the neck in that area. So did the person aim for the carotid artery, which would have sprayed out, and hit the jugular instead? Or did the person know where the jugular vein was, and aim for it?"

"Right."

"So that's my report." She put her notebook down and looked at him. "Your turn. How was Seldon?"

"Anxious that we solve this."

"Duh!"

He updated her on his afternoon. "I got permission from Trish to exhume Violet's body. Seldon agreed. He wants this solved fast, so he's going to do his best to push the exhumation through quickly."

"Probably doesn't hurt that Ben's a friend of his."

"Probably not."

"Anything from Ford yet?"

"I was waiting for you to get back. He wants to see us."

Even though it was after 6:00 when Manziuk and Ryan walked into the situation room at police headquarters, they found several detectives busy on computers.

Ford hurried over. "We've got quite a bit done on the background checks. Who do you want first? Staff or residents?"

Manziuk said, "Let's go with staff."

Ford led them to a young woman at a nearby computer. "Brianna, let's hear what you've got."

She clicked on a few files, adjusted her red-framed glasses, and cleared her throat. "I put them in order of their position.

"Audra Limson. Age forty-four. Her parents came here from the Philippines. Her dad has a small grocery store, and her mother helps there. They raised six children, all of whom have post-secondary degrees. Audra is the second youngest. She's divorced. Ex-husband is a lawyer named Giles Limson. His father is Filipino, but his mother is of French ancestry from Quebec. They have two sons aged twelve and ten. Names Gavin and Graham.

"Prior to her marriage and until she had her second son, Audra worked as a hospital nurse. Her record is exemplary. She stayed home with her sons after the second one was born. A little over three years ago, she abandoned her family and went back to work as a nurse. Custody of their two sons was given to her husband. She got her current job three years ago. No arrests or convictions."

Ryan frowned. "Audra abandoned her family? That's hard to believe."

Manziuk nodded. "She certainly doesn't seem the type. Unless there's something else in her past that we haven't found yet. Should we follow up?"

It was Ryan's turn to nod. "We've been assuming she's telling us the truth. What if she's lying? She's all over the place there and can override any of the locks, so she could have easily taken the knife and stabbed Ingrid without anyone noticing."

Ford made a note. "Okay, we'll dig deeper. Brianna?"

"Got it." She opened a second file. "Derrick James. Age thirty-three. He comes from a large Toronto family, all overachievers. Dad a pastor, brother a pastor, sister a missionary in Uganda, another brother a doctor, and so on. He's a nurse and a physiotherapist. Wednesday afternoons he attends a class at U of T called 'Thought Processes among Elderly People and How Medication Affects Them.' Been in his current job three years. No police record. It's confirmed he was at his Wednesday class when it began and stayed after it was finished to talk to a few classmates."

Manziuk said, "So, unless he stabbed her on his way out just after 2:00, he's clear."

"He seems pretty unlikely to me," Ryan said.

"Agreed."

Brianna cleared her throat. "Scarlett Walker. Age forty-seven. Married at eighteen, divorced her husband a couple of years later. He was apparently abusive. One son, now an adult. She's worked as a cook in various places, each paying better than the last. No record. Got her present job five years ago when the place opened."

Manziuk added, "And Olive confirms that Scarlett was in the kitchen the whole time."

Ryan said, "Except Olive was out for a brief time to take towels to the laundry and go to the washroom."

"I wonder if Scarlett asked her to take the towels?"

"I'll make a note of it."

Brianna looked up. "Are you ready for the next one?"

Manziuk nodded.

"Olive Yeung. Age twenty. Lived at home until she got this job. Grandparents have a Chinese restaurant. She and her mother live with them. Parents divorced and father remarried. Three younger siblings also live with the mother and grandparents. She graduated with a practical nursing diploma this spring. Prior to this job she worked part-time at her family's hardware store and for six months as a chambermaid at a small hotel. Her younger brother has had a few run-ins with the police but nothing serious. He seems to have hung with the wrong crowd for a while but got out and is now at Sheridan College studying computer animation."

Manziuk nodded. "I'd say she's very low on the list."

Ryan added, "I'd say she isn't even on the list."

Brianna opened the next file. "Dr. Granger. Age fifty-two. He's been in private practice for twenty years. Came to Serenity Suites five years ago when it opened. One interesting note is that he was the Klassens' and the Davidsons' doctor already. Another very interesting note is that a couple of residents of Serenity Suites have sent complaints about him to the College of Physicians and Surgeons of Ontario in the last year. The complaints were dismissed."

Manziuk frowned. "Have them followed up."

Ford said, "Already happening."

"Good."

"We'll check Ms. Arlington, Mr. Wright, and the daily staff next."

Manziuk nodded. "Great! Let us know when you have something on them."

As they moved away, Ryan tapped her pen on her notebook. "So, aside from the question about Audra's abandoning her family, the only obvious question mark is about Dr. Granger and how competent he is."

"And maybe find out whose idea it was for Olive to take the towels to the laundry when she did."

They moved to another desk where a rather overweight man with greying hair and wire-rimmed glasses was working away on his keyboard.

Ford said, "Got a minute to update us, Tom?"

The man looked over and smiled. "Of course."

"Tom, good to see you," Manziuk said. "Constable Ryan, I don't know if you've met Sergeant Tom Bassinger. He's been on leave. He and I were rookies together."

"A long time ago," Tom grinned at Ryan. "Not sure if you'd have been born then."

"Maybe just." Ryan smiled back.

"And now they've got me at a desk. Which turns out to be a lot of fun."

Tom looked at his screen. "Gather round and I'll update you on the residents. So far, as we might have expected, all of them appear to be financially secure. And to be perfectly honest this is going to seem pretty dull.

"First of all the Kanes and Gerbrandts are where they're supposed to be. And who they're supposed to be. Nothing there to worry about.

"Next up is Kenneth Harper. He created quite a scandal when he tried to commit suicide some years ago. He was a minister in a Presbyterian church. His wife died from cancer, and apparently he fell apart. He left the church, started singing, and went on to achieve international success. He retired from touring this spring. But his agent said he's still doing some performing, mostly in Europe."

Manziuk added, "And the knife found next to the body was his."

Tom looked up in surprise. "So he's suspect number one?"

"No known motive. And he'd have to be stupid to use a knife people knew was his."

"So who could have stolen it?"

"That's what we need to determine."

Tom smiled. "Okay, next is Lyle Oakley. He's been acting since he was ten. Started with cereal commercials, then a couple of kids' TV shows. As an adult, he's what they call a character actor, not the leading man. Has done commercials, TV, movies, and plays. A few scandals but no arrests. Has an ex-wife much younger than himself and several kids still in school. He sees them once in a while. Has a reputation for being self-centred and doing just enough to get by, but those aren't crimes."

Ryan noted, "He went to the billiards room. He could theoretically have killed her on his way."

Manziuk said, "Possible, but we need a motive."

"Hilary Brooks. Born in British Guiana. Taken to England as a child. Became a ballet dancer. Lived in Holland and France. Moved to New York in her thirties. Married several times and divorced twice. Became a Canadian citizen twenty years ago while married to a Canadian producer. He died eight years ago. She married Grant Brooks last fall in Montreal. No children."

Manziuk said, "And no alibi. She was in her room alone except when Audra was there for a short time."

"But no motive," repeated Ryan.

"Right."

"Frank Klassen. He was a math professor at the University of Toronto. His wife, Violet, was a homemaker. One daughter. His first book was published in 1986. Violet had a cookbook published in 1990. A year later Frank stopped teaching. The books must have made a lot of money because they moved into a much more expensive house. He's had speeding tickets and a couple of minor accidents. Nothing fatal and never charged."

Ryan added, "His only possible motive is mercy killing, but that doesn't strike me as something he'd do. Maybe for his wife but not for someone else's."

Manziuk said, "Physically it would also be difficult if not impossible."

"Agreed."

"Patricia Klassen-Wallace is their only child. Age forty. Married for nineteen years. Husband is a computer programmer. Two children aged sixteen and thirteen. She was a journalist and is currently writing poetry and screenplays. No record."

Manziuk said, "At the bottom of the list."

"Ben Davidson hosted a popular radio talk show called *Ben's Room* for many years. He and his wife had five kids. She was a housewife. Happy marriage by all accounts. One of the kids was injured skiing when he was sixteen. Lost a leg. All their children are university educated, married, and seem to be doing well. Ben had lung cancer a few years ago and beat it."

Ryan said, "I can't see him doing this. Not *stabbing* her."

Manziuk looked away for a second. "But he's smart. He might know we'd never suspect him."

"True, but I still don't see it."

"He was in his room alone."

"No one saw him out of his room."

"But it's possible."

"Motive, yes. Method, no. Opportunity, possible."

Tom continued. "Mary Simmons. Children's singer. Never married. No scandals. Not even a parking ticket."

Manziuk said, "She had opportunity. She reads mysteries and watches them on TV. She'd know where the jugular vein is and how easy it would be to kill her that way. She knew Ingrid fell asleep there all the time."

Ryan added, "From what others said, she seemed excited by the idea of Ingrid's dying there."

Ford chipped in, "I'd put her as my number one suspect."

"Next we have Norm and Elizabeth Carlysle. Married forty-eight years. No children. Elizabeth is a jazz singer. Well-known. She has a few Juno Awards. She also has a reputation for fooling around as it were. Norm must be a pretty forgiving husband. Norm is famous in art circles. Speaking of which, I can't believe how much people pay for art." Tom turned to look at them. "Have you seen his paintings? One of them recently sold for two hundred and fifty thousand!"

Manziuk made a note. "We'll have to take a look at them."

"You can find some of them online, but I expect they're better up close." Tom swivelled around. "That's it for now, folks. We should have reports on the rest of them by morning."

Manziuk said, "Great, thanks. Talk to you later."

"If I find out anything super interesting, I'll let you know."

As they moved away, Ryan said to Manziuk, "I can't see a motive for either of the Carlysles. On the other hand, Norm was alone in their condo. He came into the common room claiming to be looking for Elizabeth, but she was in the recording studio right next door. Maybe he was anxious to have the body discovered? Or couldn't stay away?"

"If Elizabeth was in the recording studio, she had opportunity as well. But what would be the motive?"

Nikola sat strumming his guitar and thinking about what he'd offered to do. He had absolutely no idea how to approach Hilary. She rarely came out of her condo except for meals. And if he sat with her at a meal, everyone would talk. Plus, he didn't want anyone else to overhear the conversation.

He could just knock on her door and hope she'd let him in, but that would be awkward.

He seriously needed an angle. But for once his brain was stuck on stall. Unless…

Sixteen

Catarina and Nikola were the first residents to come into the dining room for dinner Thursday evening. They sat at their usual table.

As Hilary entered, Catarina used the voice that had reached with ease into the back rows of theatres. “Hilary Brooks, you are not going to sit there by yourself for one more meal. Either you will come and sit with us or we will come and sit with you. Which do you prefer? I myself believe this table is better, but either is fine.”

Hilary stood still staring at Catarina for a long moment, but took her usual chair.

“You prefer that table? Fine with me. Nikola, we move!” Catarina stood, made a show of picking up her plate, and glided over to sit next to Hilary.

Nikola followed in his wife’s wake and took the seat on Hilary’s other side. Olive quickly moved cutlery, napkins, glasses, and cups.

Still using her stage voice, Catarina said, “So! Now we find some things to talk about—the weather, our families, the lack of nice clothes for older women, our struggles to survive in the entertainment world. What topic do you prefer?”

Hilary looked from Catarina to Nikola and back again. Then, leaning toward Nikola, she whispered, “I don’t mind her sitting at my table, but if she’s going to talk nonstop, I might have to move.”

“You begin to interest me.” Catarina softened her voice. “Perhaps we will not make small talk after all but real talk.” She glanced around. “But not here.”

Hilary gave her an amused smile. "Perhaps."

"Shall we meet after dinner?

Hilary bowed acquiescence.

"In your condo or mine?"

"Yours," Hilary said. "That way I can leave the minute I get bored."

Manziuk and Ryan grabbed wraps at a nearby take-out restaurant, where he'd ignored Ryan's raised eyebrows when he'd ordered chicken and skipped fries. They were now in his office going over what they'd learned. Ford walked in. "I've got updates on three more suspects."

Manziuk said, "Let's hear it."

Ford sat down and opened his tablet. "First up is Naomi Arlington. Age thirty-one. Married and divorced twice. No children. She has a marketing management degree from Seneca College. Her previous jobs were in retail, including managing a couple of stores in shopping malls." He looked at up. "I'd say this job is a step up for her. I wonder how she got it. Hmmm. Oh wow! Can you believe this? Her uncle owns a condo on the sixth floor of Serenity Suites, and he's on the Residents Board. What do you bet he pulled a few strings?"

Manziuk said, "No police record?"

Ford shook his head. "A whole raft of parking tickets and a few speeding tickets. One minor accident where she was deemed at fault. That's it."

Ryan said, "And no one saw her on the floor after lunch, so she goes to the bottom of the list."

"Next is Catarina Rossi. Born in Italy. Her parents were Italian. Mother was an actress. Father was from a wealthy family. They emigrated to Canada, and he got into manufacturing and did very well. Catarina married at eighteen. Her first husband became a multimillionaire by the age of thirty. He died in a plane crash and left her very well off but with four young children. She'd had a little success as an actress in Canada, making it to Stratford. After her husband died she went to the US and became even more successful.

In 1975 when she was forty-three she married an Italian-born producer Giovanni Rossi, who lived in California. He died a little over three years ago, and eight months after his death she moved here."

"Not much contact with the other people in Serenity Suites over the years?"

"She and her husband knew Ben Davidson. So far as we know, that's it."

Manziuk said, "That makes sense. Because of his talk show, Ben knows a lot of people."

Ford looked at his tablet. "Now here's the really interesting one. We can't find Nikola Vincent. There are people with that name, but none of them are our Nikola. More important, there's been no marriage license given to Catarina in the last year and no marriage recorded."

Ryan raised her eyebrows. "Seriously?"

"My guess is that he's one of these gigolos who prey on older women. He'll either try to get her to let him invest her money or make her pay him off to get rid of him."

Ryan frowned. "Catarina told everyone they were married."

"Some confidence men go through a form of 'marriage' with women, but it's staged," Manziuk said.

"Why? If they're after money wouldn't they want the marriage to be legal?"

"Normally they're using an assumed name," Ford said. "Their goal is to get money from the woman and move on, leaving no trace."

"So do we tell Mrs. Rossi? Arrest him? Or should we try to figure out who he really is first?"

"At the very least we need someone in the lobby who can follow him if he goes out. Seeing where he goes might be the most useful thing anyway."

"Agreed," Manziuk said. "I'll get someone on it."

"But that doesn't give him a motive for killing Ingrid." Ryan shook her head. "Being a scumbag doesn't make him a murderer."

Ford stood. "Well, I'll go follow up on some things and leave you to figure out this one."

Manziuk drummed his fingers on his desk. "So we're still back at square one. No one gains financially by Ingrid's death. No one gains in any other way we can see, unless it's some variety of mercy killing. If it is, I don't really see Ben doing it. And I don't get the feeling anyone else was that emotionally attached to Ingrid. So why kill her? What are we missing?"

"You keep going back to Violet. Is there a motive for killing her?"

"Stop her cookbook?"

Ryan shook her head. "Trish said the publisher already has it and that she'll make sure it gets published."

"So what are we left with?"

"Maybe we need to brainstorm possible motives since we aren't finding any obvious ones?"

Manziuk sighed. "Okay, if Violet's death was natural, then we only have Ingrid's death to solve. The most obvious motive is a mercy killing because she was getting senile and needed to go to a nursing home."

"Which would implicate Ben."

"It could have been someone else. A close friend. Someone who felt he or she owed a lot to Ben. A staff member." He shook his head. "But I just don't see it. Your turn. What other motive could there be?"

"How about this? My aunt works with people who want to stay in their homes but need support. She's told me stories of people who, as they get older, lose their inhibitions. There are people who are always polite but suddenly become rude and obnoxious. Or someone who was always modest suddenly taking all their clothes off. Could it be that someone here has always been a respectable citizen but suddenly felt an impulse to hurt somebody?"

"I guess it's possible, but honestly I could see that more if Ingrid had done it instead of being the victim."

"Is there anyone else who's been showing signs of dementia? We didn't ask Audra or Dr. Granger about that."

"I guess it's a possibility. We might not be able to tell because we didn't know them before."

"Take Kenneth. He's only been there a short time. And he owned the knife. Let's say everything he told us was true, and he *was* thinking of committing suicide, but then something made him stab Ingrid instead. Maybe—I don't know—maybe he had a flashback and saw an enemy of some sort in front of him instead of Ingrid. It's happened before."

"I suppose it's possible he reacted to a drug of some sort. Hallucinated. We can check the list of medications for any that cause that sort of reaction."

"Okay." Ryan made a few notes, then looked up. "What about something from the past? Say Ben wouldn't have someone on his talk show twenty years ago and that's been on the person's mind ever since. Maybe someone blames Ben because he or she didn't become more successful because Ben didn't do a good interview or something. Or it could be personal. Maybe in spite of what she told us, Mary was always in love with Ben and she sees Ingrid has become a burden to him, so she gets rid of her, either to help him or because she thinks she'll be able to get him at last."

Manziuk gave her an appraising look. "Have you ever thought of writing novels?"

She frowned. "I'm just thinking of all possibilities."

"Well, you're doing a good job."

"When you brainstorm you're supposed to think of all possibilities and not evaluate them. So what if Violet's death wasn't natural?"

"Then the same person likely caused both deaths."

"So the question is, do we have a serial killer who's just getting started, or did one death lead to the other for a specific reason? Could Ingrid have been silenced because she saw who killed Violet? Or was Violet's the 'real' death and Ingrid's a red herring? Or maybe Ingrid was killed in order to draw attention to the fact Violet was murdered." She crossed her arm on the desk. "In a movie there'd be a third death to make it clear there's a murderer on the loose."

Manziuk tapped his index finger on the desk. "Maybe there was, and we missed it."

Ryan sat up. "Grant Brooks!"

"Why not? There are drugs that can induce a heart attack."

"Do you think Hilary would agree to have his body exhumed?"

Hilary spoke her name into the intercom, and the door to Catarina's condo opened. Catarina stood at the other end of the hallway.

Once the two women were seated in the sitting room and Nikola had served iced tea and was lounging on a recliner, Catarina said,

"Now to business." She leaned toward Hilary. "Is it true, as Nikola says, that you have been ordered to sell your condo and leave?"

Hilary took her time responding. "And how exactly did Nikola find this out?"

"Let's just say I sometimes overhear things," he said.

Hilary looked at the carpet for a moment, gathering her thoughts. "I see no reason not to tell you. Yes, I have been told in no uncertain terms by Ms. Arlington that I do not meet the qualifications for being here and I must leave. She's putting my condo up for sale this coming Monday, and I apparently have no choice in the matter. But as much as I dislike Ms. Arlington, I know she's only carrying out what the board has told her to do."

Nikola was frowning. "What did you tell her?"

"I told her I have no intention of moving, and that if she carried out her threat I will call my lawyer."

Catarina bit her lip. "This is not right."

"Help me understand," Nikola said. "*Why* is it that she says you don't qualify to be here?"

"My husband, Grant, bought the condo. As a producer, he met their qualifications. They say I don't and therefore can't stay."

"From what I understand," Catarina said, "you have been a dancer all your life. How then can they say you do not qualify?"

Hilary took a deep breath. "I was not in the Royal Ballet or any of the 'recognizable' dance companies."

"But you *were* a ballerina?" Nikola said.

"I was."

"Where then?"

"Do you really want the gory details?"

Catarina said, "Please. All we know is that you married Grant Brooks and came here with him. And to put all the cards on the table, as it were, it is rumoured that you married him for his money."

Hilary smiled. "Oh, yes, I know that's been said. All right. You may regret asking me. My parents immigrated to England from Guyana, which was then called British Guiana. I was born in London in 1938. When England declared war on Germany in 1939, my mother was so afraid that she returned to Guyana, taking my sister who was four and leaving me with my dad. We survived the war, and life went on. My sister and I kept in touch by letter. My mother wrote only sporadically, and she died when I was fourteen. My father then sponsored my sister to come to England."

"How sad. But I am glad you and your sister found one another."

"I did well in school but I loved dancing, and my father saw to it that I took ballet lessons. How he managed that, I don't know, because we were always poor. I did well as a dancer, but as I got older I realized that my only chance to become a professional dancer was to join a black ballet company. I did so, but of course that wasn't financially the best."

Catarina made a face. "Money! It gets in the way of so many things."

Hilary sat back and took a sip of her iced tea. "In 1958 England had what is called the Notting Hill race riots. They lasted several days. There were a number of attacks on immigrants from the West Indies in the area where we lived. Mobs of white people, mostly men, started attacking black people. Some used words, but others had sticks and knives. My father and my sister and I lived in the middle of the area where the riots were. It was a terrible time, and we were afraid for our lives. Bricks and bottles were thrown at us. Our windows were broken. It's a miracle no one was killed."

"I had not heard of these riots, but it shows that no one is immune. Any group of people can do ridiculously stupid things."

"Agreed. Anyway, my father and sister stayed in London, but I left. There were some black ballet companies in Holland, so I went there. Not long after I arrived, I met and married another dancer. I was twenty-two. He was also from England. In 1966 we divorced, and I moved to the United States, to New York. Over the years, I did dance with a few white ballet companies but only as part of the *corps de ballet*. It was never easy, and there were times I had to resort to jobs I didn't much like, such as exotic dancing, to keep a roof over my head and food on my table." Hilary stopped and looked around to see how the other two felt about her last statement.

"But of course," Catarina shrugged. "You did what you had to do."

"In 1974 I married a ballet choreographer from Montreal. He'd been working in New York, but soon we moved to Canada, and I eventually became a Canadian citizen. I danced until I was forty-five. Then I worked with my husband as a choreographer and a coach until his death in 1992. I kept working until 2008 when I turned seventy. A couple of years ago I met Grant Brooks at a party in Montreal. We kept in touch and last fall we married and then moved here."

Catarina sighed. "You have had an eventful life. But no children?"

Hilary shook her head. "I had two abortions in my early twenties. I couldn't let anything interfere with my dancing. One of my many regrets. And now I'm alone. My father died fifteen years ago, my sister five years ago. I've met her children, but I don't really know them. I've had many aches and pains, and arthritis led me to have knee replacements. And now you know everything about me." She leaned toward them. "What you must understand is that all of my experience as *prima ballerina* and the majority of my choreography was with black ballet companies."

"But I see no reason that should matter!"

Nikola had been leaning forward and listening intently. "What are some key roles you played as a dancer?"

"I danced as lead in *Giselle*, Odette in *Swan Lake*, Juliet in *Romeo and Juliet*, Clara in the *Nutcracker*, Nikiya in *La Byadere*, Swanhilda in *Coppelia*, Aurora in *Sleeping Beauty*, Titania in *A Midsummer Night's Dream*, Cinderella... But those were black companies, which never received the recognition of white ones. Even the Harlem Dance Theater in New York isn't universally known."

Catarina was frowning. "When you have danced all of these roles and more, how can anyone say you do not meet the qualifications for being here?"

Hilary's dark eyes met Catarina's blue ones. "I think the qualification I don't meet is that my skin is the wrong colour."

"Surely not in this day or in this country!"

Hilary raised her eyebrows.

Catarina rose and walked about the room, as she might when giving a monologue on centre stage. "You must understand, when you and Grant first moved in here, what I heard a little here and a little there is that you were an exotic dancer, even a stripper, and that you had somehow trapped Grant, and in a moment of weakness he married you. That is what I was told! And you and Grant kept to yourselves a great deal and said nothing to contradict it. And since his death you have been so quiet... Well, it is a terrible shame I did not know the truth!"

"So now what?" Nikola asked.

"Now we do something. First, who are these people who want you out? You said Ms. Smarty Pants Arlington is only their spokesperson. So who are the people we need to set straight?"

"The Residents Board."

"Very well. We will let this Residents Board know that they can't do this without a fight." Catarina paused, then nodded. "But first, we must have more people involved."

Hilary tilted her head to one side. "And how do we do that?"

"Leave that to me." Catarina said firmly.

Kenneth had long ago learned that when you had something you didn't want to do, the best thing was to just get it done. His first action was to address three business-sized envelopes to Katherine Clement, Kyle Harper, and Katie Harper-Dumont. Then he opened his laptop to the letter he'd written and printed for his children earlier in the week and read it.

> Dear Katherine, Kyle, and Katie,
>
> This letter is very hard to write. But please bear with me.
>
> It's been nearly twenty-three years since that day you found me dying in the study. They say that most people who try to commit suicide, but fail, rarely try again. It's true I've never again tried to do it, but that doesn't mean I haven't thought of it many, many times over the years.
>
> Recently I've been thinking about it again. And why everything went so wrong.
>
> I was never cut out to be a father. I hadn't even planned to get married. I wanted to focus on serving God and becoming the best pastor I could. But when I met your mother, it was, as they say, love at first sight. For the first and perhaps only time in my life, I followed my heart. So we married a year after I finished seminary. Soon after that, she told me she was expecting a baby. I knew she wanted a family, but for me it was all in the distant future.

In two short years I went from being a student in seminary to being a pastor of a church and a husband and a father. It was far too much, too fast. I was a scholar and reader. I had almost no training in dealing with people. I loved putting together my sermons and other teaching, but I wasn't prepared to counsel individuals or lead board meetings or deal with plans for the future. I floundered. And on top of that, to have a wife and child dependent on me!

Your mother helped as much as she could, but I didn't want her to realize how bad it was. When Katherine was born, of course your mother had to focus on her. I put all my energy into learning what I needed to know about being a pastor. And slowly I gained the respect of the people in the church and became more comfortable in my role as pastor.

By then we had Kyle, too. Just before Katie was born, I was called to a new larger church. So it continued, with your mother looking after you kids and the house and my needs, and me looking after the church to the best of my ability.

Your mother often urged me to spend more time with you. But there were always so many more urgent, seemingly more important, things for me to do. My own father was a busy pastor, and the only time he spoke to me was when I had done something wrong and my mother asked him to deal with me. So, I'm afraid that was my only role model.

But the fault lies with me, and perhaps a little with your mother. Her dad was also a busy pastor and she, too, had been mostly raised by her mother. But your Aunt Nora has likely explained that to you. We were both products of our environment.

When your mother died I suddenly had to look after not only the church but also three children who were hurting—all while I was feeling as if I'd been ripped open and my heart had been pulled from my chest.

I tried to kill myself, not because the pain was more than I could bear, but because I no longer felt I could trust God. And if I couldn't trust God, there was nothing left for me. I could no longer be a pastor, yet I had no other vocation. I had three young children who needed care and security and a home. And I felt I could give them none of this. For the first time in my life, I saw how futile it all was. How much I had invested in writing sermons that were in the end merely "sound and fury, signifying nothing." Yes, maybe people came back each week to listen to me, but did their lives change in any way because of what I said? Not that I knew of.

But more to the point, the one person who made me feel human was gone, and I couldn't believe a loving God would allow this to happen. In a moment of insanity, I hanged myself in my study, not even thinking that it would be my children who would find me—my children, who needed me more than anyone in this world has ever needed me, and who I failed yet again.

I gave your Aunt Nora permission to be your guardian, not because I didn't care what happened to you, but because I knew she could care for you far better than I ever could. And I left you so that you would be free of me and hopefully of all the reminders of your past life.

Ironically I rebuilt a sort of life singing songs that were meaningless to me. But the songs helped me pay for your care and gave me a way to keep going.

However, as I age, the opportunities for singing are slowing down and any joy I felt from singing and travelling has long disappeared. At this point, your need for me to provide for you financially is gone. (Although my will leaves you each a considerable amount that you can use as you please. Perhaps you can do some good with it. The irony is that it's far more than you would ever have seen had I remained a pastor.)

I know you were raised to believe there is a God. Your mother and your Aunt Nora shared that. Even your mother's impending death couldn't alter her faith. And I know you'll feel that my taking the easy way out so I don't have to deal with the pain of getting old and dying is not only a cop-out but a sin. However, I don't believe in God. I expect to fall into oblivion.

No heaven. No hell. Nothing. I don't want to dissuade you from your belief. Maybe you're right and I'll find myself in hell and regret it all.

If by chance I've misunderstood and there is a God who actually is loving, he has one final chance to prove it to me. I'm writing this letter on Monday, August 18th. I'll commit suicide by stabbing myself in the heart on Wednesday, August, 20th. So he has until then to show me I'm wrong. If you are reading this letter, then obviously I did not receive that proof.

Your delinquent father,

Kenneth Harper

Kenneth printed three copies of the letter, then folded and placed the copies in the envelopes. He had a new letter to write, but he'd have to do it tomorrow. Just making the decision to write it had left him exhausted.

At 10:30 Thursday night Paul was sitting in a chair in his living room with one of Frank's novels. Loretta was in a second chair with another of the books. They were both reading intently.

"This is kind of— Hmm," Loretta said.

"Kind of hmm?"

"Not sure what to call it. Maybe a guy book?"

"Yeah, I'd say it's similar to one of those women's romances where you know before you open the first page what's going to happen. In this case lots of action and swearing and sex but no depth."

Loretta put her book down. "You asked my opinion, so here it is. If you read books like this all the time, I'd be embarrassed to tell anyone. If you wrote them, I'd change my name."

"My original question was 'Are his books any different now from in the beginning?'"

"Judging from the first two I looked at, the earlier one might have had a few more redeeming factors. The characters seemed more developed. In the book published last year, the characters seem to be almost caricatures."

"You read enough to get that?"

She smiled. "No, I read some reviews on Amazon and compared them to what I've read and picked the reviews I agreed with. But it seems as if his books sell. And he had lots of four- and five-star reviews for *all* of his books, including the last ones. So if his writing skills *are* deteriorating, most of his readers haven't noticed."

Audra and Derrick were busy showing the security guard around the twentieth floor. They were shocked that Naomi had actually agreed to their request for Serenity Suites to hire someone to patrol the hallways at night.

The burly young man with the long blond ponytail already worked for Serenity Suites as a rotating guard on the below-ground shopping floor. He'd jumped at this opportunity, and he seemed determined to protect everyone to the best of his ability. He appeared to be in awe of his surroundings, muttering "Wow!" when they entered each area.

Naomi had said they could have him from 11:00 p.m. until 7:00 a.m. for one week, no more. Audra really hoped a week was enough time for the police to find the person Mary called 'the perp.'

At midnight Jacquie was sitting up in bed with one of Frank's novels. After reading the first chapter, she skimmed the rest of the book, reading bits here and there. She read the last chapter straight through, then threw the book on the floor in disgust. "Guy's got a weirdly warped mind!"

She was about to turn off the light when she realized that she hadn't checked her personal email account since that morning. Sure enough there was a message from Armando sent earlier that day.

> Hey, how are you doing, love? I hope your case is going well.
>
> We won the game tonight.

> I pitched 7 innings last night, and got the win. 118 pitches. Too many balls. But when I left the game, we were up by 2 runs, and the relief pitchers held them to only 1 more run.
>
> Are you thinking about Hawaii? I'd love to spend time with you. Lots of time.

Jacquie bit her lip as she read the message. Then she typed a quick reply congratulating him on the win but not mentioning Hawaii, turned off the light, and went right to sleep.

Trish was also sitting up in bed, holding a hardcover notebook with a rose on the front cover. She turned to the last page of writing, where she discovered an envelope taped to the adjoining page. After reading the words on the front of the envelope, she carefully removed it and opened it. As she read the letter, she shook her head and grabbed a tissue to wipe away the tears that had begun to fall. "No," she said softly. "Oh, no!"

She read the letter through two more times. Then she sat without moving for over half an hour, going over the details of her life in a swift panorama, examining everything she knew about her mother and trying to visualize her life from a strange new perspective.

She picked up the letter and read it one more time. Then, ignoring how late it was, she phoned her husband and read it to him. Together, they talked about what, if anything, she should do with the information.

Seventeen

Early Friday morning, Loretta set Paul's breakfast on the table and sat across from him. "I forgot to mention it last night, but Arlie's going to need to know soon if we want Woody's car."

"Do you think we should get it?"

"I do. And more important, so does Mike, although he's being very good in not bugging you about it."

"You're comfortable with the idea of having it in your name but sharing it with him?"

"Yes."

"And you really think he's responsible enough?"

"I do. And you do, too."

"Okay, tell Arlie we'll do it. But you'll need to take care of the paperwork. This case is taking every bit of energy and brain power I have."

"I honestly think Woody would be happy that Mike has his car. And maybe having it around will remind you of the good times you had with Woody."

"Maybe."

She let him finish eating before she asked, "How've you been the last couple of days? I haven't seen much of you because of your case."

"Fine." Tears came to Paul's eyes. "Okay, mostly fine. I guess the truth is, down deep I feel guilty. Woody and I were like twins. So why am I here and he's gone? His surgery went well. Why didn't he get a second chance?"

Loretta went to stand behind Paul's chair and put her arms around his neck. "Oh, honey, it's going to hurt for a long time."

Paul reached up to put his hands over hers. "Maybe I just need a change of scene. What I do can be so depressing. We're investigating the senseless death of an elderly woman. Maybe two deaths. If I didn't have this job, I wouldn't know that all this evil is out there."

"But, honey, it's exactly because you hate the evil that's out there that you do your job so well."

"Remember that getaway we talked about? Maybe we need to take it."

"You've got enough vacation days saved up."

"Yeah, let's book a week sometime in the fall."

"I'll start looking tomorrow for something we'll enjoy."

As Paul left the kitchen, his son Mike came down the stairs. "Dad, did Mom talk to you about getting the car? Arlie—"

Paul held up his hand. "Already taken care of. She's going to get the paperwork done today."

"Yee haw!"

"But it's going to be in your mom's name, and if you don't obey the rules you lose your driving privileges."

"Dad, I'll take good care of Woody's car. You know I will."

Paul smiled. "Yes, I believe you will."

"We going to a baseball game this weekend? You said you might be able to get tickets."

"I'll see what I can do."

"Sweet!" Mike started to go to the kitchen, then paused and turned back. "Dad, are you eating healthy?"

Paul stared at his son. "Not you, too!"

Mike looked away. "Well, I want you to be around for a while."

"I know, son." Paul reached over to grab Mike and envelop him in a bear hug. For a moment the two of them stood together, each with arms tight around the other. Then they broke apart, both embarrassed.

"I'll try to get those tickets." Paul opened the door to the garage. "And some time off."

Jacquie sat at the breakfast table that morning, looking at her often-tiresome aunt. Vida was a personal support worker who visited the homes of elderly or disabled people needing ongoing or short-term assistance to stay in their own homes. Her job involved everything from giving baths and doing personal grooming to feeding and helping them exercise. Some people Aunt Vida cared for were reasonably well off, like the people in Serenity Suites, but many weren't. Still, those without money needed help just as much as those with money, maybe even more.

As she got up from the table to leave, she walked behind Vida's chair, put her arms around aunt's shoulders, gave her a quick hug, and then left the room.

Three pairs of eyes stared after her in astonishment.

Manziuk and Ryan met in Manziuk's office at 7:30 to discuss their impressions of Frank's books. Ford joined them half an hour later. They were still comparing notes and working on a plan for the day when Benson walked in and perched on a corner of the desk.

"You look a bit frazzled," Ford said.

"That's an understatement."

"What's up?" Manziuk asked.

"I have reporters all over me; the mayor's office wants to know when we're going to make an arrest; and Naomi Arlington phones me every hour on the hour wanting to know what's happening. And you're giving me nothing!"

"I wish people would stop watching TV crime shows."

"You and me both."

Ryan said, "Can't you just explain that these things take time and leave it at that?"

Benson shook his head. "I wish. But we have to show ourselves to be approachable, and we have to demonstrate that we're doing everything we can, and yada yada."

"Well, I'm afraid we don't have much," Manziuk said. "Just tell them we're still investigating."

Benson sighed.

As Mary walked into the dining room for breakfast, Catarina called her name. Mary turned and stared. Though the two women were friendly enough, they'd never sat at a table together.

Catarina patted the chair beside her. "Please, sit here. I need to talk with you."

Mary stood rooted the floor for about thirty seconds, wondering what Catarina and her new husband were doing at Hilary's table. Then, with a shrug, she headed to the empty chair.

After breakfast, Mary and Lyle joined Catarina and Nikola in their sitting room.

"It's all very nice to say we're going to see to it that Hilary doesn't get evicted," Mary said, "but if wishes were horses, as my mother used to say, all beggars would ride." She leaned forward. "What exactly are we going to do?"

"My understanding," Catarina said, "is that the Residents Board wants her to leave."

"I suppose we could go and talk to them."

Nikola frowned. "Is there a board member from this floor?"

Mary looked down. "Frank."

"Then why don't we talk to him first?" Lyle asked.

Catarina shook her head. "Hilary said she *ha*s talked to him. Several times. He says it's out of his hands and there's nothing he can do."

Mary snorted. "What he means is there's nothing he *wants* to do. Frank is one of the ones who wants her out. I'd bet on it."

"I know what to do!" Catarina held up her hand. "A petition! If everyone else on the twentieth floor signs, Frank would be obligated to do something."

"You think so?" Nikola asked. "From what I've observed, Frank seems to march to his own drummer."

"You're right," Mary said. "Frank has always been as stubborn as a mule."

Catarina held out both her hands palms up. “So what can we do to fix this?”

“Get Frank voted off the board.”

Lyle shook his head. “Voting for the members of the Residents Board happens once a year. In June.”

Mary frowned. “And we only have until Monday.”

“What if we go over their heads to the owners of the building,” Lyle suggested. “The residents don’t own the building. There’s a corporation of some sort. Naomi gets paid by them.”

“That’s a good idea,” Nikola said. “Do you know the name of the corporation?”

Lyle shook his head. “Ms. Arlington and her predecessor are the only people I’ve ever dealt with, and I’ve been here for years.”

Mary nodded. “There’s nothing on the website or in the agreement I signed when I bought my condo. I’ve looked. It just says ‘Serenity Suites.’”

“Surely we can find out.” Catarina thought a moment. “Nikola, you said you were a bit bored lately. There’s a job for you. Find out who we should talk to.”

“I can try. But if it turns out to be a numbered company, it could be difficult.”

Catarina raised her eyebrows. “Start with Ms. Arlington. I’m sure if you use a little of your charm, she will tell you whatever you want to know.”

Mary and Lyle smiled at the look on Nikola’s face.

“Your wish is my command,” the younger man said. “I’ll see if I can make an appointment to talk to her.”

Lyle smiled. “I have a better idea on how to approach her.”

Shortly after 10:00, Ryan’s cellphone rang. Audra identified herself. “Detective Ryan, I thought I should contact you. Something has happened. Well, actually some*one*.”

“I’m listening.”

“There’s a man here who wants to see Violet. Normally, I’d have suggested he talk to Frank, but—he says he’s Violet’s son. Violet and Frank don’t *have* a son. What should I do?”

"Put him in the small office we've been using and keep him occupied until we arrive. We'll be right there."

When Manziuk and Ryan stepped out of the elevator twenty minutes later, they heard raised voices. Coming around the corner, they saw Frank sitting on his scooter at the door to the office they'd been using and shouting, "You'll answer to *me*! What right do you have coming here slandering the name of my wife?"

Derrick was standing on one side of Frank, Audra on the other side. Seeing the two detectives, Audra hurried over to them.

Derrick said, "Frank, please just go into your office. I'll come with you."

Frank glared at him. "I want that man out of here right this minute! Do you hear me?"

Audra said quietly, "Thank you for coming, Inspector. As you can see—"

In a calm voice, the man standing inside the office doorway said, "Mr. Klassen, I'm not here to cause trouble. Mrs. Klassen invited me to meet with her yesterday. When she didn't come and I didn't get a message from her, I decided to try to find her. I'm only in the city for a couple of days."

"You're a liar!" Frank yelled. "Get out of here!"

Manziuk looked with interest at this new man. "Sir, could you please take a seat in the office for now? We'll be right in." He turned to Frank. "Mr. Klassen, please go back to work and let us get to the bottom of this."

"I'm not going anywhere. I want you to arrest this man for trespassing and slander!"

Derrick put his hand on Frank's shoulder. "Mr. Klassen, let the police deal with this. Please."

Frank's face was red, and his voice hoarse with anger. "I don't want anyone to 'deal with it.' I want this liar kicked out of here! Don't you even give him the time of day!"

Ryan stepped forward and spoke in a low no-nonsense, voice. "Mr. Klassen, you know perfectly well we can't do that. We're going to talk to him, either here or at the police station. I know this is upsetting for you, but for now go to your office or to your condo. We'll come and speak with you as soon as we know what we're dealing with."

Frank sat breathing hard. Then he swore at them, jerked his scooter around, and headed down the hallway toward his condo.

Saying, "I'll try to settle him down," Derrick followed.

Audra ushered Manziuk and Ryan into the office. "I'll have Olive bring drinks. Do you need me?"

"No, thank you."

"Thank *you* for coming. It likely has nothing to do with your investigation, but I thought you should know. And then Frank had to choose that moment to come out of the restroom. I thought he was working in his office." She grimaced. "By now everyone on the floor has heard what was said."

The visitor gave the detectives a rueful smile. "Ms. Limson said she was calling the police, which I thought was a bit of overkill. But at this point, I'm glad to see you. I had no idea I was entering a hornet's nest. No idea whatsoever."

Manziuk shook the man's hand and introduced himself and Ryan. "I'm afraid I didn't get your name?"

"Jacob Sanderson. Call me Jake. This is a pretty classy place, eh?"

Manziuk nodded and sat down.

"Nice if you can afford it," Ryan said.

Jake laughed. "True."

Manziuk said, "So, Jake, can you explain what led you to come here today? From the beginning, please?"

"Well, sure. But first, can you answer one question for me. Where is Violet Klassen?"

"I'm afraid Violet died just over two weeks ago."

At the man's shocked expression, Ryan added, "She died peacefully in her sleep."

Jake shook his head. "I can't tell you how sorry I am to hear that. I was really looking forward to meeting her."

Manziuk said, "Can you tell us why you're here?"

"Of course. But first, let me give you some background. I live in British Columbia. My parents were originally from Ontario, but they moved to BC when I was ten. My dad was a GP. I followed in my dad's footsteps and became a doctor—except I chose pediatrics. I love kids. My wife and I have six of our own, four by birth and two by adoption. And there is the crux of my story. When I was eight years old, my parents told me I was adopted. It was never an issue. I loved them, and they loved me, and I always understood that somewhere there was another mother and father, but for some reason they hadn't been able to keep me. My parents did an excellent job of helping me see it had nothing to do with me but was the result of circumstances.

"A few years ago, more for my children's sake than my own, I decided to see if I could find out anything about my ancestry. I thought my birth parents would likely be dead by then so I wouldn't be bothering them. But I thought it might be good to know. And I guess I was rather curious.

"I contacted Parent Finders and through them the adoption services department in Ontario. They said they'd heard nothing from my birth mother and couldn't connect us without her permission. So that was that.

"A few months ago I got a letter from them saying my mother had contacted them and they could now connect us. So Violet and I sent some letters back and forth, and then we talked on the phone a few weeks ago and arranged to meet this morning at 9:15 at a little restaurant a few blocks from here. Only she didn't come. She'd mentioned that she lived here, so I decided to see if I could find her. And that's it."

He frowned. "She must have died just a day or two after our phone call." He suddenly looked at Manziuk and Ryan in a different way. "Wait a minute. Why *did* they call you when I showed up?"

Manziuk said, "Unfortunately there's been another death—a woman who was a friend of your mother's, but who didn't die of natural causes."

"And you're wondering if there's a connection?"

"That possibility has crossed our minds."

"I see. So did Violet die of natural causes?"

"We're considering exhuming her body and doing an autopsy."

"And does my appearance affect that?"

"It makes me all the more anxious to make it happen. Jake, did Violet tell you if she'd told anyone else about connecting with you?"

Jake shook his head. "I'm pretty sure she hadn't. She said she was married, but that her husband didn't know about me. And that he wasn't my father. I was born before they married."

"Did she tell you who your father was?"

"No, but she did say he was still alive and that when everyone found about me, it was going to cause a ruckus. That's what she said. A 'ruckus.' I did kind of get the impression that she intended for me to meet him while I was here, so I booked into a hotel for the weekend. Now you can answer a question for me. When will she be exhumed?"

"I'm going to talk to my boss about that in a few minutes. Soon, I hope."

"What about her husband? Just as Ms. Limson was bringing me here to wait, he came along. It seems he overheard enough to realize that Violet was my mother, so I told him the truth. She'd said to me 'when' everyone finds out, so I didn't think she planned to keep it a secret. But how unfortunate that her husband should learn about me that way. It's no wonder he was upset."

"The other thing that was no doubt upsetting him," Ryan said, "is that it's pretty clear who your father is."

Jake's face lit up. "You know my father?"

"We *think* we do." Manziuk shot a quelling look at Ryan. "We'll need to talk to him first and see if it's possible."

"Are you— You're not telling me he's here, are you?"

"Let's just say there's a man living here who's known your mother for many years, and you look a lot like him. Well, like he'd have looked twenty or so years ago."

Jake thought for a moment, then pulled a business card out of his wallet. "Look, I saw a coffee shop on the main level of this building. Why don't I get out of your way and go have a coffee, and you can let me know when it's a good time to come back? Or come and talk to me there if it's more convenient." He wrote on the back of the card and handed it to Ryan. "My cellphone number is on here, and I wrote the name of the hotel and my room number on the back. If I don't hear anything in the next hour or so, I'll go back there." He left the office, heading toward the elevator.

Manziuk nodded at Ryan, who followed and discreetly watched to make sure he got into the elevator and went down to the main floor. She returned to find Manziuk standing in the hallway. "So who should we talk to first?"

"Trish. Her life will be impacted by this as much as anyone's."

Derrick listened to Frank vent his anger for a good fifteen minutes before he calmed down enough for Derrick to speak. "Frank, he's talking to the police. If he isn't who he says he is, they'll deal with it."

"As if Violet could have had a child I didn't know about! Trish was born when Violet was forty years old. Did you know that? She'd been trying to get pregnant for almost twenty years. For this man to come here smearing her name and saying he's her son—I won't have it!"

Derrick placed his hands on either side of the scooter, his eyes focused on Frank's. "What are you going to do if it's true?"

"He's a liar."

"Frank, you're a writer. You know people's lives are complex. So what if it's true and Violet never told you? Maybe she was embarrassed. Maybe she was badly hurt. Can't you just for one minute think about her? Feel sorry for her that she never had the chance to meet her son? Maybe even feel sorry she felt she couldn't tell you?"

Frank glared at him. "You wouldn't say that if it were *your* wife. Why don't you think about how *I* feel, finding out my wife wasn't the person I thought she was?"

"Frank, I know you feel terrible about this."

"I don't feel terrible. I feel cheated!"

"What about your daughter? How do you think she's going to feel when she finds out?"

"Where is Trish?"

"I'll check." But his call to the guest suite was answered by Constable Kelly, who said Trish was with the police. Derrick hung up. "They'll let her know you want to talk to her."

Frank swore. "Is my daughter going to see that man?"

"Frank, if he is Violet's son, he's Trish's half-brother. If it were me, I'd want to see him."

"Well, if she talks to him behind my back, she's no daughter of mine!"

"Frank, please—"

"And you—! Get out of here this minute and never set foot in here again!" Frank raised himself slightly in the scooter, leaning toward Derrick. "In fact you might as well start packing, because your job here is going to be gone the minute I get in touch with the board. You're insubordinate and you think you know everything!"

"Mr. Klassen—"

"You heard me. Out!"

Shaking his head, Derrick left, intending to find Audra and suggest they get Dr. Granger to come and calm Frank down before his rage brought on a heart attack.

Manziuk and Ryan were in the guest suite, where Trish had been going through the last few bins with Kelly and Bixby. They took her into the kitchen to be private.

"How's it going?" Manziuk asked.

"We're almost done," Trish said. "All we have left are a bunch of photos from eighty or more years." She looked from Manziuk to Ryan. "What is it?"

"Trish, something very unexpected has come up. I'm not sure how to tell you this other than to come right out and say it. It looks as if your mother had a child before she married your father. A son."

Trish blanched. "How did you find out?"

"How did we find out? Then you knew?"

"Not until last night. Mom had a bin for each of her cookbooks, and we went through them, beginning with the most recent ones, thinking that if there was anything pertinent it would be there. Someone had asked me earlier if I remembered which bins were on the higher shelves, but I'd just pulled them out and hadn't noticed. But thinking about it now, I'm sure it was the older cookbook bins that were higher. I wish I'd remembered that before.

"Anyway, Constables Kelly and Bixby went home to get some sleep when we were halfway through the last of her cookbook bins, and I decided to finish it. Down on the bottom I discovered a notebook that seemed to be more recent than anything else we'd found. She talked about finding out she had cancer and a few personal things like that. And then, taped on one of the pages, I found a letter addressed to me. I wasn't sure whether to show it to you or not. I didn't think it could have anything to do with her death, or Ingrid's, but you'd asked me to let you know if I found anything puzzling or out of place in her possessions, so I was going to make a copy to give to you."

She took a small envelope from her pocket. "It's quite—well, astonishing. My mind is still whirling. It's a very sad letter." She held it out and sighed. "It explains so much about her."

Ryan and Manziuk looked at the envelope.

In clear printing, it said, "NOT TO BE OPENED BY ANYONE EXCEPT MY DAUGHTER TRISH KLASSEN-WALLACE, AND THEN ONLY IN THE EVENT OF MY DEATH."

Ryan opened it and read it aloud.

Wednesday, August 6, 2014

My darling Trish,

A big part of me wants to forget that what I am going tell you ever happened, or pretend it didn't. But it did, and even though it was long ago and no one else knows, I feel that I need to put it down someplace.

You need to know that I've lived with an overwhelming guilt. I can't not tell you, but I can't tell you to your face. You'll have to decide whether to tell your father or not. I can't.

So here I go.

They say when you have to take a bandage off, you should rip it off quickly. So I'll do that here.

Just after I turned 19, I had a baby. No, your dad wasn't the father. This was before I started going out with him.

I don't want to say who the baby's father was. He was a good man, and I felt it was my own fault that I got pregnant. He never knew. No one knew except my mother and my aunt.

I found out in the early spring, and my mother sent me to stay with my aunt for the summer and help with her children. My mother told my father that my aunt needed the help. I don't know if he believed her or not, but he never indicated anything else to me.

Near the end of summer, I wrote my friends to tell them my aunt needed me to stay longer, so I missed the fall term of college and started my second year in January.

The baby was born November 16th, and he was given to an adoption agency. I didn't want to give him a name or see him, but they made me choose a name. I named him Jake after my granddad (my mother's dad), who I loved very much. But of course that name would have been changed by the people who adopted him.

I didn't see him. My aunt did and said he was a perfectly healthy baby. My aunt never mentioned him again, and my cousins were too young to understand what was going on. My friends never guessed.

I'm trying to think what questions you might have. Knowing you, lots. I expect you'll want to know how it happened. Well, that was long before they had the pill. And I wouldn't have been taking it even if they did. I was a good Mennonite girl, and good girls didn't do such things.

And I didn't either. Much.

It was the boy's idea in the first place, not mine. But he didn't coerce me, and I didn't say no. In my mind, it was sort of just this one time—just to know what it's like. In all, it happened maybe three times.

After I realized I was pregnant, my first thought was to get married, but I knew that while I liked him as a friend, we really weren't suited to each other—not enough to make it a permanent relationship. So I broke up with him. He wasn't happy about that at the time, but later he realized it was the right decision. And I never for a minute regretted that part.

You'll want to know why I didn't keep the baby anyway. Single girls do it all the time now. Well, in those days, you just didn't. You hid the truth from as many people as possible and later you pretended it had never happened.

My mother had gone with me to the doctor and made all the arrangements with my aunt. But she never spoke to me about it, not even in the early days, other than to tell me where I was going to go and what to pack. She did tell me I was a fool. That I remember. That I was no better than a streetwalker. And that there was no need to consider anything other than having the baby and giving it up for adoption.

When I think about it now, it's kind of funny. It was 1953, and we were heading into the sixties with all the hippies and free love, but there was no glimmer of that in my world.

What else? The baby was born in the morning at about 10 o'clock. He weighed about 8 pounds, I think. Or close to that. I believe my aunt said he had blond hair. He was registered under my maiden name. So his name was Jake Toews.

Maybe you're wondering why, if I was able to have a son when I was 19, there were no other children except you. In the beginning, we wanted to have a family, but after I had four miscarriages, we stopped trying. I thought God was punishing me for the first one—for Jake. And, really, your dad was never much of a child person.

And then you came, right out of the blue, when I was 40. I honestly didn't know if you were a punishment or a gift. Both, perhaps.

I've never known how to tell you I love you. I was so afraid—I don't know what of—losing you, I guess. I suppose I thought if I didn't care too much, it wouldn't hurt if I lost you. But I did love you. Always. I do love you. Please believe that.

I read a book a few years ago that talked about the need to grieve, and I realized that I never grieved for Jake. I never grieved for me. How could I when I had to pretend it never happened?

I guess that's it. I don't really know why I wanted to tell you all this. Maybe you'll think more of me, maybe less.

I love you so much. I just wasn't very good at showing it.

Your mother,

Violet Klassen

P.S. Trish, I just this minute remembered something else. I only thought of it now because I realized I never really grieved about it either. I might write about it later. Or I might not. It's all in the past. It's the suicide of a person I knew. At least, they all said it was suicide. Only

I never believed it was. A few months ago, I heard something that made me even more positive it wasn't suicide. But it happened a long, long time ago, and wouldn't mean anything to anybody. Except...

Even now, I hate to think about it. But if it wasn't suicide, then what some people did was wrong. I'll have to decide if it makes sense to tell you more. I shouldn't have said this much. If I don't write more about it, just forget this. Years ago, I read the book "Crime and Punishment," and it helped me see that just because you think someone has gotten away with something, it may not be the case. God still knows, and the person still knows.

"So sad." Tears in her eyes, Ryan handed the letter to Manziuk.

Trish nodded. "My poor mother."

Manziuk said, "Do you know what that last part is about? Had you ever heard anything about a suicide?"

Trish shook her head. "No, I'm not aware of anyone in our immediate family who committed suicide, and I can't think of anyone else Mom might be referring to. Dad might know, I guess." She looked from Ryan to Manziuk and back again. "Wait a minute. You started this conversation by telling me that my mother had a son. How did *you* know?"

Ryan answered. "A man named Jake Sanderson came to Serenity Suites this morning looking for your mother."

Trish blanched. "His name is Jake?"

Manziuk nodded. "The other thing is that Jake is the image of a younger Norm Carlysle."

Trish turned white. "Oh, my."

"Jake told us he spoke to your mother by phone just days before her death and arranged to meet yesterday."

"I see." She took a deep breath. "If he finds out, my father will be very upset."

Ryan said, "I'm afraid he already knows. He was in the hallway when Jake came up and he overheard enough to figure it out. Plus, he saw Jake, and I've no doubt he saw the resemblance to Norm."

"I bet he's livid."

Manziuk looked at Ryan. "Call Ford and have him look for records of any suicides involving someone Violet might have known."

"Where should he start?

He thought for a moment. "Go back to when she was a young child."

As Ryan left the room, Trish said, "What now?"

"Do you want to meet Jake?" Manziuk asked.

"I may as well."

"He's waiting in a coffee shop on the main floor. Do you want to meet him there? And after that, perhaps you should go with Audra to talk to Norm? As far as we're aware, he doesn't know."

Trish took a deep breath. "Sure. Let's do it."

Manziuk phoned Jake and told him to expect Violet's daughter to meet him at the coffee shop. "Trish, I'll have Constable Bixby follow you down and keep an eye on you during the meeting, just in case. And we'll let Audra know what's going on."

"Thanks. You don't really suspect him of murdering my mother and Ingrid, do you?"

"No, but you have to admit his showing up like this is suspicious."

"Well, wish me luck. This is going to be very weird."

Manziuk and Ryan left Serenity Suites to go to the cemetery where Dr. Weaver and Special Constable Ford were supervising the exhumation of Violet Klassen's body. They'd begun at 6:00 that morning and hoped to have the body at the Forensic Services and Coroner's Complex by noon so that Dr. Weaver could begin his autopsy.

Eighteen

Frank reluctantly let Audra into his condo. "Is that imposter gone?"

"Frank, Dr. Granger happened to have a moment and wanted to see how you're doing. He's on his way up now."

"Is that liar gone?"

"If you mean the man who came here this morning, he's no longer on this floor."

"You're trying to trick me, aren't you? But you're not going to change my mind." Frank slammed his fist on the handlebar of his scooter. "All of you ganging up on me. I won't have it, do you hear?"

"Frank, please try to calm down."

"I'm not going to have a heart attack if that's what you think."

Audra had left the door slightly open for Dr. Granger to enter behind her. Now he stepped into the sitting room. "Frank, unless you have a medical degree I don't know about, I'm going to need to take your blood pressure just to be on the safe side."

"Do what you like. It's obvious I'm not going to get any writing done today. But don't think you can change my mind."

"I have no interest in changing your mind about anything. I'm simply concerned about your health. And I'm looking forward to the coffee and muffins Scarlett said she'd send in."

Dr. Granger looked at Audra. "I'm sure you have other things to do."

With a quick nod she left them.

Audra and Derrick were in the office when Trish entered a little after 2:30. Derrick looked up. “Did you just get back? How was it?”

“Okay, but I think I’m kind of in shock. I mean, I’m moving and talking, but part of me wonders if this is all a weird dream.”

“I don’t blame you.”

Audra turned to face her. “So how was the meeting?”

Trish dropped into a chair. “Jake appears to be a totally nice man. And after fifteen minutes, I felt as if I’d known him all my life.” Her eyes filled with tears. “It’s crazy, but I told him things I never could have said to either Mom or Dad. It felt just like I always imagined it would to have an older brother.”

“I’m so glad,” Audra said.

“And there’s no question he’s Norm’s son. Not only does he look like Norm, but he seems to have his easy-going nature and even some of the same mannerisms.”

“Could you see your mother in him, too?” Audra asked.

“Not as easily, but he seems to be very practical and businesslike, so I expect that came from Mom.”

“Are you ready to talk to Norm, or do you want to have a cup of tea first?”

“I left Jake waiting in the coffee shop, so I’d better go and talk to Norm now, assuming he’s here.”

“He is,” Derrick said. “Elizabeth, too.”

“What about my dad? How is he?”

“Dr. Granger got him to calm down,” Audra said. “He had a tray in his room at lunch time and then went back to work in his office.”

“Good. I won’t disturb him then.”

“Do you want me to go with you to talk to Norm?”

Trish nodded. “Please. I have no idea how this is going to go. Just give me a few minutes to go back to my suite and freshen up, and then I’ll come get you. Derrick, I’m counting on you to keep an eye out for Dad. If Norm agrees to see Jake, I’d like to get him up here without Dad’s noticing.”

Derrick grinned. “I’ll start by praying really hard that he stays in his office.”

Kenneth sat back and read through the letter that had taken him all morning and much of the afternoon to write.

Friday, August 22nd

Dear Katherine, Kyle, and Katie,

Please read the other letter first.

As you can see by the date on this letter, I'm still here. Something unexpected happened. A woman was murdered with my knife. I expect you've heard about it on the news. It's all made me think a great deal.

I now realize that a good deal of my problems all my life were caused by my own selfishness. All I could see was the hole your mother's death made in my life. I blamed God. But I now feel the problems I had were due to my being unable to cope. Selfishness? A lack of faith? A form of mental illness? Depression? A lack of support? Perhaps all of these things.

Whatever it was, I confess to you that I was wrong. Everything I did, first trying to kill myself and then deserting you, was wrong. Wrong for you, and wrong for me.

I have confessed this to God, and I believe he has forgiven me. One of the first Bible verses I learned was 1 John 1:9. "If we confess our sins, he is faithful and just to forgive us our sins, and to cleanse us from all unrighteousness."

My next step is to forgive myself. I'm working on that.

I don't tell you this to ask you to forgive me but rather because I know that my cowardice and selfishness affected you, and perhaps knowing what was going on in my life might help you deal with issues from your past that involve me. As well, since you have my genes, it's possible that you might one day find yourself in a similar situation.

I just want to add that in as much as I am able to love, I do love you all. Those first years with you and your mother were easily the best years of my life. I only wish I'd realized that at the time. At this moment, I feel as if I completely understand Ebenezer Scrooge, both in his own selfish bubble and after the bubble burst.

Let me assure you that I'm not looking for anything from you. However, I will presumably be sticking around for a while longer, so I'll be here should you ever wish to see me or talk.

Your father
Kenneth Harper

He printed three copies of the letter, then carefully folded them and put one in each of the envelopes containing the first letter. He sealed each one, added a stamp, and sat back.

He felt a sense of relief, but also a good deal of sadness. A voice somewhere in his mind said, *The past is the past. The future is still before you.* It had been a long, long time since he'd thought about having a future. For years it had been all he could do to get through each moment, to merely exist.

Audra spoke into the intercom, and the door opened. Trish walked in first and found an unsmiling Elizabeth standing in front of her. "Can I help you?"

"I was wondering if I could speak with Norm?"

"What about?"

"It—it's sort of personal."

"You want to talk to my husband and you don't want me to know?" Elizabeth's voice was cold and flat.

"It—it's about something that happened a long time ago. Something I discovered while looking through my mother's keepsakes."

"Well, you can tell both of us then. Norm and I have no secrets from each other."

Norm came out of the kitchen. "What is it, Liz?"

"Trish has something to tell us."

"I'll put the coffee on."

"Yes, I have a feeling we might need some."

Norm gave her a quizzical look but went back into the kitchen.

Trish sat on a blue microfibre sofa with Audra beside her. Elizabeth sat across from them on a matching loveseat and stretched out her slim legs. "Hurry up, Norm. They're bursting to tell us something. Probably something juicy."

When Norm came in, Audra jumped up and took the tray with four cups from him. "Let me help."

Norm sat next to his wife on the loveseat, and picked up the cup Audra had set down on the table beside him. "Now, what can we do you for?"

There was a brief silence. Trish took a quick sip of coffee, then took a deep breath. "Norm, as you know, I've been going through Mom's papers. I found a letter she left for me to find after her death. There was something in it that concerns you. I don't know if she intended to talk to you but didn't have the opportunity, or if she didn't know how to tell you. I assume that since she told me, she wanted you to know. In any case, I feel it's something she should have told you long, long ago."

Norm was frowning, his hands trembling. He glanced at Elizabeth and back at Trish. "Something your mother should have told me?"

"Yes."

Norm coughed, and a small amount of coffee spilled.

"Do be careful." Elizabeth wiped his pants with a tissue. "Get coffee on your pants if you must, but not on the furniture or carpet."

Using both hands, Norm carefully set his cup back on the table. Then he folded his hands in his lap. "All right. Can't spill anything now. What is it, Trish?"

"Norm, back in the summer of 1953, after finishing the first year of university, Mom spent the summer helping her aunt with her young children. She didn't start her second year until after Christmas for the second term."

Norm thought for a moment and then nodded. "Yes, that's right. Her aunt needed the help, and Violet needed to make money to pay her fees."

"No, Norm, her aunt really didn't need the help."

His eyebrows went up. "No?"

"No."

There was a long moment of silence. "Well, what then?" Elizabeth asked. "Unless you want to drag this out until we've died of boredom."

"Mom was pregnant when she left university. She had a baby that November. A boy. She named him Jake. Jake Toews."

"Well, how about that!" Elizabeth smiled. "So your goddess was human after all."

Norm didn't look at his wife. "Who—who was the father, Trish?"

"Mom didn't say. But we have reason to think it was you, Norm."

Elizabeth gave a short bark of laughter.

Norm coughed and turned red. "We—we only did it a couple of times. I never thought— Violet never said a word about it to me."

"Mom didn't want you to know. She thought you'd offer to marry her, and she didn't want to get married. She also didn't want to get an abortion. So her mother sent her to her aunt's to wait it out."

Norm clasped his hands together and looked down. "So the baby—it was all right?"

"Yes, the baby was adopted. Violet never saw him. I think she was afraid if she saw him she'd never be able to give him up."

Norm thought for a moment. "He'd be pretty old now. If he's still living."

"Sixty."

"Really? Sixty?"

Elizabeth yawned. "Well, of all the news you might have come to tell us, I must say this was never on my horizon. So you and Violet 'did it' a few times, eh, Norm? I wonder what Frank would think of this if he knew."

Norm turned quickly toward Trish. "*Does* he know?"

"I haven't told him. But I'm pretty sure he suspects."

Norm shook his head. "I don't want him to know. It's nothing to do with him. *Please* don't tell him. I beg you."

Elizabeth laughed.

Audra said, "I'm afraid it's too late for that, Norm. Jake is here. Violet had made an appointment to meet him this morning at a restaurant. He had no idea that she was dead so, when she didn't show up, he came here looking for her. She'd given him this address. Unfortunately Frank saw him, and I'm pretty sure he figured it out right away."

"Frank *knew* about the baby?"

Trish said, "No, but when a man shows up here telling everyone that he's looking for his birth mother, Violet Klassen, and that man is the spitting image of a man Dad has known all his life, I'm pretty sure he didn't need to be told anything."

Norm's eyes brightened. "He looks like me?"

"Poor man," Elizabeth smirked. "I hope he hasn't come to free-load off us."

"He's a pediatrician," Trish said. "I don't think he needs money."

Audra said, "Norm, he wants to know if you'd like to meet him."

"Of course I want to meet him." Norm's right hand was shaking uncontrollably. "Very much."

Audra smiled. "Good. He's waiting in the coffee shop on the main floor. I'll ask him to come up." She left the room.

There was a long silence, which Elizabeth finally broke. "I feel like I'm watching an episode of a daytime soap opera. A particularly maudlin one."

"Norm," Trish said, "do you want me to leave?"

Norm shook his head. "No, no. You're Violet's daughter. Why, he'd be your half-brother, wouldn't he?"

She nodded.

"Have you met him?"

"I just had lunch with him. But I only learned about his existence last night in a letter Mom left me. His showing up this morning is just—surreal."

"She never told me. Not one single word."

They sat in silence until the front door opened and Audra ushered Jake into the room. On seeing Norm, he laughed. "It's like looking at one of those pictures that shows you how you'll age in twenty years." He went toward Norm and held out his hand. "Jacob Sanderson. Everyone calls me Jake."

Norm rose from his chair. "Violet never told me one blessed thing. If she had, well, I never would have let her give you away." Tears spilled out of his eyes. "I never would have." Instead of taking Jake's hand, he wrapped his arms around him. Jake returned the hug.

After a while, Norm drew back. "This is my wife, Elizabeth. We never had any children."

"We never *wanted* children."

Norm looked at her but didn't speak.

Trish broke the awkward silence. "Norm, Jake is what Mom named him. Jake's parents kept that name."

Jake grinned. "That's right. Except they made the official name Jacob, because that looked better on certificates. But I've always been Jake. They felt keeping my name was the least they could do for the woman who'd had to let me go."

Norm shook his head. "You must have had great parents."

"They're the best. And there's no 'had' about it. I still have them. My parents are in their nineties, but they're still going strong. And I know they'd love to meet you." He turned back to Trish. "All of you."

"Sit down, sit down," Norm said. "Can I get you some coffee? Tea? A cold drink?"

"Thanks, but no. I'm fine. I will sit down though."

Norm sat, too. He placed one hand over the other as if to keep it still.

"So you're a doctor?" Elizabeth said.

"A pediatrician. And I love it. I can't think of anything more rewarding than helping children live better lives."

Audra stepped to the doorway. "I'll leave you. I'm so glad you've been able to connect. Call me if you need anything."

"Jake, can you stay for dinner?" Norm asked. "Can he, Audra?"

"Yes—or I'll take the three of you to a restaurant if you'd prefer."

"Well, that would be nice, too. But I'd like to introduce you to my friends."

"Yes," Elizabeth said. "I'm sure Frank in particular will be thrilled to meet him."

Trish stood up. "Perhaps I'd better go and talk to Dad."

Audra offered, "I'll come with you. But first we should let Scarlett know to set a place for Jake."

Nikola walked into the sitting room and Catarina, Mary, and Lyle all turned to look at him. Catarina raised an eyebrow. "Well?"

Her husband took his time choosing a chair and getting comfortable. "Instead of trying to make an appointment with Ms. Arlington, I took Mr. Oakley's advice and hung around the lobby near her office until she left for lunch. She chose a booth at a nearby restaurant. Since she seemed to be eating alone, I joined her. Bowled over by my charm, she gave me a few minutes of her valuable time."

Lyle laughed. "If I know anything from all my acting, it's that most women enjoy it when a handsome man pays attention to them." Catarina smiled. Mary frowned but didn't speak.

Nikola continued, "The gist of what she told me is that she does what the owners and the Residents Board asks her to do. When I said we'd like to talk to the owners of Serenity Suites, she told me I wouldn't get anywhere. She doesn't even know who the owners are herself. She only talks to a lawyer who gives her their instructions."

There were murmurs of frustration.

"She did tell me one interesting thing, though. She let it slip that Frank is the person who's been leading the charge to get Hilary evicted, and that he must have some kind of 'in' with the owners, because he seems to get whatever he wants."

"I knew it!" Mary said.

"What did she mean 'He gets whatever he wants'?" Catarina asked.

"Well, according to Naomi, the Residents Board makes recommendations to the corporation, and it seems that 'whatever Frank wants, Frank gets.'"

"He's not going to get away with this." Mary looked away. "You know I've always had a feeling he was racist, but it was only a suspicion, nothing I could ever have proved. Now I'm sure of it."

Catarina sat up straighter. "I have it! Since Frank is the representative for the residents on this floor, we must depose him. And since this is a democracy, we should begin with a petition."

"So you're saying we write up a petition to remove Frank because he's not representing the wishes of the residents on this floor?" Mary said.

Nikola frowned. "I hate to ask this, but—do you *know* that? I mean, did Frank ever ask for people's opinions on this?"

"He never asked for mine," Mary said.

"Nor mine," Catarina added.

Both women looked at Lyle, who coughed. "I might remember him making some comments I thought were a bit on the negative side, but I don't remember him ever asking my opinion."

"All right, then," Nikola said. "It might work."

"Mary," Catarina said, "you write it up. Then we will sign it and take it around to everyone except Frank."

"All right. But you'll have to help me figure out what to say."

Half an hour later, it was finished.

We, the undersigned, wish to revoke the presence of Frank Klassen on the Serenity Suites Residents Board since Frank has not represented the true wishes of the residents of the 20th floor. We wish to elect a new representative before any further decisions are made.

In particular, we protest the Board's attempts to evict Mrs. Hilary Brooks from her condo on the 20th floor.

We, the undersigned, are satisfied that Mrs. Brooks meets all the qualification of a resident of Serenity Suites according to the terms of the contract, and we believe the attempts to evict her led by Frank Klassen have been the result of his own prejudices. The other residents of the 20th floor do not support his wishes.

Mary Simmons

Catarina Rossi

Lyle Oakley

"Nikola, you sign it next."

"I think not."

"And why not?" Catarina glared at him, her hands on her hips.

"Because the condo is in *your* name, not mine. My signature could just be a distraction."

"He's got a point," Mary said.

Catarina reflected for a moment. "All right, I concede. So now, Mary, the two of us will go and get everyone to sign.

Lyle said, "You realize not everyone may want to sign this?"

"You think not?" Catarina gave it some consideration. "You are right. Some of them might need convincing."

"Can you start with someone easy?" Nikola said. "Who do you think will sign it without difficulty?"

"Ben," Mary said. "We should start with him."

Catarina nodded. "Excellent idea."

Nikola said, "His wife just died. I'm not sure—"

"According to Hilary, he and Grant were friends," Catarina said. "And of anyone here, she said he's been the kindest toward her."

"He'll sign," Mary said. "I'm sure."

"All right, we begin with Ben."

"And then Norm. He'll sign if Ben does. I don't know about Elizabeth though. She likes being perverse."

"Have no fear. I will deal with her."

"So that just leaves Ken. And that's everyone who's here right now."

"What about Hilary?" Lyle said. "Should she sign it?"

"No," Nikola said. "Not when it concerns her."

"I am ready," Catarina said. "Let us begin."

Ben walked through his condo by himself. He'd stayed at his son's house while they made funeral arrangements. Now they only had to wait until the police released Ingrid's body. Bruce had wanted Ben to stay with them longer, but once he knew that he was free to return to his condo, Ben stood firm in his decision to come back to Serenity Suites.

He knew perfectly well that any of his children would welcome him into their homes. One of his daughters had urged him to come and stay at her place, and he'd almost given in. But something held him back, and he'd held firm in declining her invitation. It wasn't that he didn't love his children and their families; but they were all busy with their lives, and he'd feel he was in the way, no matter what they said.

Right now, what he needed more than anything else was quiet and time to think. His life had just changed dramatically. He needed to consider what that meant. So he'd chosen to be here, in the place he'd called home for the past five years, among familiar sounds and faces.

Most important, he needed to explore the wave of relief that had come over him, unbidden, the night before, which was now making him feel so terribly guilty.

He was contemplating that guilt when his intercom sounded, and Mary and Catarina asked him to let them in for a few minutes.

At 3:00 Dr. Weaver began his autopsy on the body of Violet Klassen. Manziuk and Ryan watched him examine every inch of her skin with a powerful magnifying glass. After half an hour he motioned to them to come closer.

Dr. Weaver held up Violet's left hand and spread the index and middle fingers apart. He used his other hand to hold the magnifying glass in position so first Manziuk and then Ryan could look through it. "There are three needle marks. Very small and very faint. In the skin between the fingers of her left hand. This one is the easiest to see. Can you see it?"

Manziuk shook his head. "Not really."

Ryan said, "Yes, I see it. Right in the V of the fingers. It's tiny."

Manziuk sighed. "I guess I might need those reading glasses Loretta suggested."

Dr. Weaver laughed. "Might help." He put Violet's hand down. "I'm going to do some tests for drugs. I have a list of everything Ident found during their search, and we'll particularly look for those things that could have been injected easily and made her look as if she'd died in her sleep."

"But she's already been embalmed," Ryan said. "How…?"

"I should be able to get some vitreous fluid from her eyes. There's a good chance it won't be contaminated by the embalming fluid. We'll also check her organs." He shrugged. "It'll take some time to get all the tests results, but given the needle marks I found, I think we can proceed on the theory that her death wasn't from natural causes."

"What would most likely have been used?"

"Going purely on ease of use, based on the list of medications Ford found in the rooms there, my first choice would be insulin."

"The only insulin was in Ben and Ingrid's condo," Ryan said.

Her heart in her mouth, Trish spoke into the intercom at the door of her dad's office. "It's Trish, Dad. Will you let me in, please?"

The door opened, and Trish went inside, followed by Audra.

Frank was sitting at his desk; his face was red. "I know what you're up to," he shouted. "None of you care one bit about me!" He glared at Trish. "Your mother lied to me! Our whole married life, she lied to me!"

"Dad, this had nothing to do with you. Mom got pregnant long before she started dating you."

Frank hit the top of his desk with his fist. "I thought she was a virgin when we got married. She never said different. All those years acting like she was better than everybody else, and she was a whore and a liar!"

"Dad!"

"I don't want Violet and Norm's bastard in my home. He has no right to be here. And I want Norm out of here, too. I want him gone."

"Dad, you're being ridiculous."

He stared at her. "Oh, I am, am I? And why is that? Because I don't like finding out the woman I trusted lied to me? And that one of my best friends slept with my wife behind my back? And we have no idea how long it went on. How exactly does that make *me* ridiculous? And why did she tell you and not me? Huh? Why?"

PART IV

It used to be thought that the events that changed the world were things like big bombs, maniac politicians, huge earthquakes, or vast population movements, but it has now been realized that this is a very old-fashioned view held by people totally out of touch with modern thought. The things that really change the world, according to Chaos theory, are the tiny things. A butterfly flaps its wings in the Amazonian jungle, and subsequently a storm ravages half of Europe.

—NEIL GAIMAN, *Good Omens: The Nice and Accurate Prophecies of Agnes Nutter, Witch*

NINETEEN

Audra and Trish finally calmed Frank down enough so that he'd talk to them without shouting.

Audra hesitantly put her hand on his shoulder. "Frank, it must be terrible to find this out the way you did. And I don't blame you one bit for being angry with Violet. But can I tell you a couple of things you don't know?"

He glared at her, working his lips in a struggle to get them under control. At last he spat out, "What don't I know?"

"Violet didn't tell Norm either. He just found out a few minutes ago. In the letter she left, which she wanted Trish to find after her death, she said no one knew except her mother and her aunt. It sounded like she was afraid of what would happen if she told anyone."

"Especially her father," Trish added.

"He'd have thrown her out of the house." Frank glared at Trish. "And he'd have had every reason to."

"Dad, you need to read the letter she left."

"Well, she didn't *leave* me a letter."

"I'm sure she meant me to show it to you."

"Huh!" He turned to glare at Audra. "You said some *things* I don't know."

"The second thing is that Jake is a very nice man. I think you'll like him. He's a doctor, and he's got a mixture of Norm's charm and Violet's practicality. I'm sure he'd welcome you into his life just as much as he will Norm and Trish."

"I don't need anybody else in my life." His voice became petulant. "I have books I need to finish. Who knows how much time I have left. And thanks to all of you, I'm getting nothing done!"

"Dad, Norm wants to have Jake stay for dinner so he can meet everyone. But Jake wants to know that you're okay with it first. Will you please meet him?"

His bottom lip quivered. "Don't think I'm going to forgive your mother for not telling me."

"I'm going to give you her letter and let you read it. Then I'll ask him to come and see you. Okay?"

"Well, hurry up about it. My books don't write themselves, you know."

Audra stood in the doorway watching the residents gather for dinner. Frank had more or less said he wouldn't make a scene, so she and Derrick put two tables together to allow Trish and Frank to sit with Norm, Elizabeth, and Jake. Audra had her fingers crossed that all of them would be on their best behaviour—especially Frank and Elizabeth.

Norm saw Ben entering the room and called him over to introduce him to Jake. Ben handled it well, shaking hands and then giving Jake a hug, and sat at the empty space at their table.

When all were present, Norm stood up and coughed to get their attention. "Everyone, this is my son. Until this morning, I didn't even know he existed. His name is Dr. Jake Sanderson."

There was a scattering of applause and some whispering.

Norm led Jake to each table and made introductions. Then he went to the kitchen door and introduced Jake to Scarlett, Olive, and Derrick.

When they were seated again, Frank put both hands on the table and pulled himself up so he was leaning on the table.

Trish quickly stood up beside him. "Dad, what are you—?"

"Leave me alone! I want to say something. You needn't worry."

"All right. Let me help you stand."

After a moment of hesitation, he leaned against her instead of the table. "Some of you may have heard that Jake's mother was my wife, Violet. She never told me. So I was thunderstruck to find out. However, since it happened before we even started going out, it's nothing to do with me. I wish she'd told me, but since she didn't, I'll make the best of it. At least now when I'm gone, Trish won't be all alone. She'll have a half-brother."

As Frank sat down, everyone applauded. Then Scarlett and Olive came in with the plates, and everyone relaxed.

In the kitchen, Derrick whispered to Audra. "Can you believe Frank?"

She shook her head. "He knows how to put on a show."

"Since everyone is so friendly, it might be an idea to just make one large table tomorrow.

Audra smiled. "Don't push it."

Derrick laughed. Then he became more serious. "Oh, by the way, you've had a long day. You need to take some time off after dinner. Go do some of that shopping you said you needed to do. I can handle things tonight."

"Are you sure?"

"Positive. I'll call you if anything out of the norm comes up."

"Well, it might be nice to get out for a bit of fresh air."

"Go."

Manziuk and Ryan stopped at a restaurant for take-out roast chicken and vegetable dinners. Back at the car, Manziuk opened the passenger door. He hated not driving, but he'd realized that Ryan felt exactly the same, and he was determined to be fair. While Loretta preferred to have him drive—at least that's what she'd always said—he had no right to insist on driving when it was clear that Ryan liked to drive, too. He and Woody had always shared driving duties, so it only made sense to share them with Ryan.

As Ryan got into the driver's side of the car, her phone buzzed. Manziuk almost offered to drive so she could talk, but instead held his tongue and did up his seatbelt.

Ryan put her phone on speaker. It was Ford. "A young woman jumped from the Prince Edward Viaduct, now the Bloor Street Viaduct, in June 1952. Her name was Sharlene Bryce, and she was seventeen years old. According to the newspaper report, she'd recently learned that she was pregnant. Presumably that's why she killed herself."

Ryan asked, "Any connection to Violet?"

"The newspaper story indicates that Sharlene was a student at the high school Violet attended. They were the same age and in the same grade."

"That sounds promising."

"We'll keep digging, but so far it's the only suicide we've found that has a possible connection to Violet. Oh, there's one other very interesting thing. There's a picture of Sharlene. Looks like a school photo. She was black."

Manziuk and Ryan exchanged looks. "It's a long shot," Manziuk said, "but can you have somebody go down to records to see if the file from her investigation is still around? Since it was a suicide, there's a chance they kept it."

"Already on it. There was nothing in the computer so Fossey is looking through the hard copies now. Might take a while."

Ryan said, "We'll be right there." She started the car, backed out, and took off like they were fleeing for their lives. Manziuk restrained himself from commenting but made sure his seatbelt was good and tight.

Audra left Serenity Suites at 7:00, did a few errands, and quickly discovered that she had no heart for shopping. She wandered over to a park on the edge of the Serenity Suites property, where she sat in the middle of a bench to watch the water from a crystal fountain splash down on the rocks below.

What a crazy world it was when a respectable elderly lady could be murdered in such an ugly way on the twentieth floor of a luxury high-rise designed to meet all the needs of its residents, including safety. But then, what a crazy world it was when a supposedly fair judge could call a loving mother unfit and give her children to a father who only wanted them because their mother had tried to keep her family together instead of giving him a divorce the instant he asked for it. Life wasn't fair at all.

She made her brain stop going over things and forced it to pay attention to the shower of water from the fountain, wondering idly why the sound of moving water was so calming.

"A penny for your thoughts," a man's voice said. Audra turned to find Nikola standing behind her. He sat down beside her on the bench. "Or is it a nickel now?"

"What are you doing here?"

"I saw you leave and kind of hung around hoping to catch you before you went back inside."

She looked away.

"You're not on duty right now, so it's none of Naomi's business who you talk to."

Audra shook her head. "No, I can't talk to you."

He sat down beside her. "Well, *you* may not mind spending all your time with elderly people, but while I don't mind spending some time with Ben and Frank and Lyle and Mary and so forth, I'll go crazy if I can't also talk to younger people. And right now I don't know many. I've talked to Derrick a few times, but we have very little in common." He shrugged. "You're the only person in Serenity Suites who's just about my age and doesn't seem to have a busy social calendar herself."

"Where are you from?"

"Recently I've lived a lot in Europe."

"I don't understand how you met Catarina."

"We were both on a short holiday."

"And you married her after knowing her only a few days?"

"I knew who she was, of course."

"Oh, of course."

"She's a brilliant actress."

"Yes, I know."

"Very rich."

"Yes."

"And entertaining. She makes me laugh a lot."

"How wonderful for you."

"It's definitely a new lifestyle for me."

"Must be very enjoyable."

"Perhaps a little awkward."

She shot him a look.

He was watching her, an amused smile on his lips. "So do you want to walk for a bit? Maybe grab a coffee?"

Ready to say "no," she hesitated. *Why shouldn't I have a coffee if I want? In a couple of weeks, I'll be gone. Then it won't matter.* She got to her feet. "Why not."

Ford was waiting for Manziuk and Ryan at police headquarters. "One thing I forgot to mention earlier. Nikola Vincent had lunch with Naomi Arlington at a restaurant near Serenity Suites, which seems a bit odd. It was hard for Detective Patterson to hear their conversation, but she thinks they were talking about the board and Frank. By the way, she said the Arlington dame was quite taken with Nikola. She actually reached across the table to touch his hand and acted kind of 'come hither' if you get my drift. Or so Patterson said."

Ryan gave Manziuk a pleading look. "Are you sure we can't bring her in for questioning just to annoy her?"

Manziuk smiled and shook his head. "I'm not sure I understand your idea of fun."

She made a face.

Ford said, "I printed off the newspaper story of the suicide so you can see it."

It was a pathetically short summary of a person's life, positioned on the bottom right corner of the last page of the first section. It gave her name, age, school, the fact that she was in her last year of school and would have graduated soon, and the fact that she was pregnant. Cause of death was listed as suicide.

The black-and-white photo was grainy, but in spite of the poor quality, no one could miss the smile on her lips and the sparkle in her eyes.

"Pretty girl," Ford said.

Manziuk nodded. "She wasn't depressed in that picture."

"I guess finding out she was pregnant changed things."

Ryan didn't speak. Her eyes had spontaneously filled with tears, and she didn't trust her voice.

"So she went to the same school as Violet?" Manziuk asked Ford.

"Not only Violet but also Mary, Norm, Frank, and Ben."

Ford's phone buzzed. "Text from Patterson. Our boy Nikola has been busy today. He followed Audra Limson out of Serenity Suites and stayed about fifty feet behind her while she did some shopping. Then he approached her while she was sitting on a bench in a small park. After talking for a short while, they walked together for about ten minutes, went into a store where Audra bought a couple of books from the children's department, then walked some more. Right now they're sitting at a table in a coffee shop about ten blocks from Serenity Suites."

Manziuk whistled. "Interesting."

"I don't see that it has anything to with our case," Ryan said. "I mean, he's the perfect picture of a con man, and maybe we should warn her, but—" Ryan snapped her fingers. "I don't know why, but that just reminded me of something! Didn't Kelly say they were planning to go through Violet's photos today? Should we ask her if they found any with a black girl or woman in them?"

Manziuk nodded. "Good idea. Give her a call."

Ryan ended the call with Kelly. "She's at home. They went through the last of the bins tonight, which were basically photos. She said she recalls seeing maybe eight or ten older photos that had black women in them. They didn't isolate them, though, so she'd have to sort through to find them. She thinks it would take her less than half an hour to find them. She's supposed to be off-duty tomorrow, but she offered to go over to Serenity Suites at 9:00 in the morning after her husband gets back from an early swim practice with one of their kids."

"Tell her we'd appreciate that. Sharlene's been dead for over sixty years, so I guess we can wait another night. A few hours of sleep might not hurt us, either."

"Twelve hours of sleep would be even better."

Ford grinned. "I could almost, but not quite, curl up on the floor right here."

Fossey walked into the room and waved a thin manila file folder. "Got it!"

Ford laughed. "Oh, well, sleep is over-rated anyway. Yay, Brianna!"

A few minutes later, they were sifting through the contents of the folder, all that was left of the investigation into Sharlene's death.

Elizabeth sat watching her husband fiddle with the coffee maker for several minutes before asking, "What are you doing?"

"I don't know."

"It's been a long day. I'm going to bed soon."

"It was a nice day. Jake seems to be a fine person."

"Yes, a bit boring maybe, but certainly a model citizen."

"I didn't find him boring."

"I know. He takes after you."

"Thanks." He paused. "I can't believe Violet never told me."

"No doubt she was afraid you'd want to marry her if she did."

"Well, I hope I'd have done the right thing."

"And the right thing would have been marrying Violet?"

"Well, if she was having my baby…"

"I've known people who married because of that, and it didn't work out."

"I would have married her. If she'd told me."

"Why am I wondering whether or not I should be happy or sad that she didn't tell you?"

"You've never liked Violet."

"Speaking of Violet, Trish is leaving soon. You need to finish the picture you started and give it to her. Unless you want to keep it for yourself."

"I don't want to keep it! I told you. Every time I've tried to work on it, my hand shook so much I could barely hold the brush!"

"Apparently you weren't shaking while you were painting the other picture."

"I know that. I don't know why."

"You just don't want to let go of it. That's all."

Norm rounded on her, his face red. "Liz, shut up! I don't know why you always have to go on the way you do about Violet. Yes, I used to date her. And yes, I'd have offered to marry her if I'd known she was pregnant. But it was sixty years ago. Why can't you let it go? The poor woman's dead."

"You never let her go. You're always saying things like 'poor Violet.' Always being so polite to her. Thinking what she'd like."

"I always felt bad for her being married to Frank."

"She chose to marry him, Norm. Chose him when she could have had you. She got what she wanted."

"I didn't only feel bad for her because of that. Her parents were mean. I don't think they ever paid her a compliment. All they did was complain. And then her not being able to have a baby when she always wanted one—not until Trish came along, anyway."

"*I* never had a baby. Do you feel sorry for me?"

"You never wanted one." He gave her a puzzled look. "That's what you said. You said neither of us would make a good parent."

"And it was true. The way you forget about everything else when you're painting, you'd have forgotten you had a baby."

"And you wanted to enjoy life, not have to change diapers. That's what *you* said."

"That's what I said," she whispered.

Norm studied her. "It's a bit late to change your mind now, you know."

"I never said I'd changed my mind." Elizabeth turned away.

Neither spoke for several minutes.

"I'm going out for a while," she said at last. "Why don't you try to finish that painting so you can give it to Trish? If you don't, I might just throw it out one day."

Norm gave her a long look. "Liz, you didn't have anything to do with Violet's death, did you?"

As she turned to stare at him, the intercom sounded. Catarina was asking if she and Mary could talk to them for a few minutes.

After much thought and a good deal of pacing around his condo muttering to himself, Ben made a phone call. When his son Bruce answered, he said bluntly, "I need you to do something for me."

Manziuk, Ryan, and Ford went over the contents of Sharlene's pathetically thin file several times. There was nothing much in it. A short description of the investigation. Her birth and death certificates. A dozen black-and-white photos of her lying on the ground where she'd died. Another dozen shots of her before and during the autopsy.

The police had clearly seen Sharlene's death as a straightforward case of suicide. They'd spoken to her parents and her doctor. Searched her room looking for a note. Decided she'd been too upset to leave one. They apparently hadn't talked to her friends or tried to figure out who the baby's father was. Had basically taken her death at face value. The autopsy said she had died as a result of a fall. That was it.

"It's nearly 10:00," Manziuk said. "We might as well call it a night. Start fresh in the morning."

"What about Violet?" Ryan asked. "If she was given a drug of some sort as Dr. Weaver seems to think, what do we need to do?"

"I wish I knew. Maybe things will seem clearer in the morning."

"If it was insulin," Ryan said, "it points to Ben."

"It does," Manziuk said. "But I don't think we can assume."

"Maybe we need to solve a sixty-year-old murder before we can solve the recent one."

Hilary was in her bedroom deciding whether to get ready for bed and read for a while when the intercom sounded. "Hilary," Catarina's voice said, "Let us in!"

Hilary picked up her cane and headed down the hallway to the front door. Mary and Catarina were already inside, both of them smiling.

"Ta da!" Catarina held up a piece of paper.

Hilary tried to sound light and uncaring. "So you got a few signatures?"

"Not a few. All of them!" Mary beamed. "Norm and Elizabeth went out with Jake after dinner, but they finally came back. So we've talked to everyone."

Catarina giggled. "Well, all except Frank. We never asked him."

"I can't believe it."

"Here, read it for yourself."

Hilary quickly scanned the names. "You must have done a lot of arm twisting."

Mary shook her head. "Not a single arm was twisted. But I do have to say Catarina was wonderful. She explained the situation very honestly and convincingly, and they all signed."

"I'm amazed. I—I thought they'd all say no."

Catarina shook her head. "They would not dare. It would be acknowledging they are prejudiced. But even so, I do not think they would have said no in any case. They all seemed genuinely surprised. And now I will tell Nikola when I go home, but we must let Audra know at once."

Hilary tapped 2001 into the intercom. "We can let her know right now."

After a brief conversation with Audra, Catarina said, "We have done enough for today. Tomorrow we take our petition to the board."

"Before we do that, I'm going to tell Trish," Mary said.

Catarina shook her head. "But she is not a resident. She cannot vote."

"She needs to know her father is acting like a jerk."

"Are you sure she needs to know?" Hilary asked.

"Since she was tiny Trish has always looked up to her dad. She was what you'd call a daddy's girl. She and Violet never had much of a relationship. A good part of that was Violet's fault. I think maybe after all the miscarriages she was afraid to care too much when she finally had a living baby. So Frank became Trish's knight in shining armour.

"Even though it might hurt, I think she needs to know how her father has been acting. Especially now that Violet's gone. It might prepare her for worse to come as he gets older and perhaps more set in his ways. And just maybe she could get Frank to see reason so we don't even have to use the petition."

Trish was in her pyjamas, but had been awake reading. "You wanted to talk to me about something? Jake?"

"No, something else." Mary paused. "You're not going to like what I have to say."

"You'd better come in and sit down." Trish moved aside to let Mary enter. "What am I not going to like?"

"Your father has been acting like a total jerk."

Trish sighed. "I'm beginning to think that may not be unusual. What is it now?"

"You know Hilary Brooks?"

"Yes."

"He's been trying to get her evicted."

"Why would he do that?"

"I'm beginning to think it's because she's black. Do you have any reason to believe he's racist?"

Trish looked down. "I dated a guy who was Asian when I was in college, and Dad was, well, let's just say not too happy about it."

"So this doesn't surprise you?"

"It saddens me but, no, it doesn't surprise me."

"Your dad is the representative from this floor on the Residents Board. We've made up a petition to get him off the board because he's not representing our wishes. Everyone's signed it—all the residents who are here, anyway. The next step is to take it to the board. However, if Frank were to back off and tell the board he's changed his mind about Hilary and wants her to stay here, we'll consider tearing it up."

"Blackmail."

"You might call it that. Or extortion. I can never tell them apart."

"Why are you telling me?"

"Well, I wondered if you'd talk to him, or at least come with me to tell him. He might listen to you."

"You think?"

Trish paused at the door to Frank's condo. She knew he rarely went to bed before midnight, so she'd decided to tackle him that night and get it over with. And if she waited until morning, he'd be annoyed with her for keeping him from writing.

She'd decided to see him alone, partly because she was afraid he'd be rude to Mary and partly because she wanted to protect him as much as she could. He was still the dad she'd always loved, even though she'd begun to realize that the man she'd thought he was had probably never existed.

She steeled herself to speak into the intercom. "Dad, are you still up? May I talk to you for a few minutes?"

"Trish? What do you want now?"

She shut her eyes. *Not in a good mood.*

But the door opened. She went inside.

He was seated on his scooter in the kitchen, awkwardly pouring himself a cup of tea. "Your mother used to make this stupid herbal tea before we went to bed. I told her I didn't want it, but she made it anyway. Now I feel like I need it. Dratted woman. Do you want a cup?"

"Sure, if you have enough."

He put down the pot, and she took a cup from the cupboard.

"Can you get the cookies out of that cupboard?" He pointed.

She found a bag of plain sugar cookies and put some on a plate. Then she sat down at the kitchen table, with him near her on his scooter.

"I assume you want something," he said.

"I wondered how you were doing. It was a rather eventful day."

He snorted.

"Jake seems like a nice man."

"If you like that type."

"He's a lot like Norm, and you and Norm have been friends for nearly seventy-five years."

"Huh! Doesn't mean I like him."

She sat back. "Dad, how can you say that?"

"Well, it's true. He hung around Ben and me all those years like he was a puppy, but I'd just as soon he hadn't. He never got my hints to take off, and Ben was too nice to let me outright tell him we didn't really want him around." He sipped his tea. "Besides, we didn't see that much of him over the years. Now and then we'd get together, the six of us, that's all. Or we'd go golfing or something. I tell you, I've seen way more of him since we moved in here than I ever wanted to. And if I'd had to see this much of him over the years, I'd likely have strangled him. And if I'd known about him and your mother, well..." He took a cookie and bit into it. "Now this is a cookie I like. Not the least bit healthy. Just butter and sugar and eggs." He licked his lips.

Trish smiled. "Dad, you're impossible."

"Just being honest."

They drank tea and ate cookies in silence for a few minutes. "So what do you want? Are you leaving tomorrow?"

"Maybe. It kind of depends on what the police say."

"They'll never solve this. Somebody stabbed Ingrid without knowing what he was doing. Likely Kenneth. It was his knife, after all. And what do we know about him anyway? You can't go by what people tell you. And Ben told me he's been in Europe and Asia. Who knows what he did over there."

"Speaking of Europe, did you know Hilary was raised in England?

He narrowed his eyes. "What's that got to do with anything?"

"Why do you want her out of Serenity Suites?"

He frowned. "Where'd you hear that?"

"Why?"

"She doesn't belong here."

"Because?"

"She doesn't fit."

"Because?"

"She was some kind of dancer. And not a good kind."

"She was a ballerina."

"Huh!"

"She was, Dad."

"That's not what I heard."

"So you decided to railroad her out of here based on some rumour you'd heard? I don't buy that."

"She doesn't fit here."

"Because she's black, right?"

"Well, no one else on this floor is black."

"Except half the staff."

"That's different."

"So it's okay for black people to work for you but not to be treated as your equal?"

"That woman doesn't know her place. She acts like she's the Queen of England."

Trish rolled her eyes.

"She smells funny."

Trish just stared at him.

"She—she makes me uncomfortable."

"Dad, I can't believe this. You're an intelligent man. Your agent came here from Hong Kong. Your lawyer is East Indian. Why would you judge Hilary on the basis of her race?"

"I get along with plenty of people of different races. But I draw the line at living with them!"

"Well, unfortunately it's not only about you. The other residents of the twentieth floor have signed a petition asking for your removal as their representative on the Residents Board. However, if you convince the board to let Hilary stay, they'll tear up the petition."

Frank's face blanched, then reddened. He swore, first at the other residents and then at her.

"That won't get you anywhere, Dad."

He glared at her.

"Dad, give it up. Hilary's not going anywhere."

"We'll see about that. I'll have the owners throw her out."

"No one knows who the owners are."

"Oh, don't they?" Frank picked up his cellphone and punched in a number. He spoke into it. "Ben, we need to talk— Yes, I know it's late. How about tomorrow morning? I'll be up by 7:30— See you then."

He smiled at Trish, who was looking at him in amazement. "Now, we'll see who wins."

On her drive home from police headquarters, Jacquie had been going over the possible suspects for Ingrid Davidson's murder, hoping to see something that would break the case open. But as she parked her red Toyota Corolla next to her mother's three-year-old black Honda Civic, she was struck by a thought that had nothing at all to do with her job. Seeing the dark outline of the three-storey house she called home made her realize that being at Serenity Suites had given her a whole new perspective on living space. The people who built Serenity Suites had obviously analyzed the needs of elderly people and built with those needs first and foremost in their minds.

But why wait until you were old to create an environment that met your needs?

Their house was technically Gram's. She owned it. But it wasn't suitable for her needs. It was way too big for one person. And Gram was getting to the age where she'd benefit from some of the things in Serenity Suites. My goodness, when you thought about it, Gram was really acting as their unpaid housekeeper!

Jacquie took a deep breath.

Could they renovate the house to make it more suitable for the five women living there? Starting with Gram's needs, then the needs of Vida and Jacquie's mom, and finally her own needs, and those of Precious. She rolled her eyes. Precious had so many needs! But that was a challenge for another day.

It was clear where they should start. One full bathroom and a half bath for five women was beyond ridiculous!

Still in thought, Jacquie left her car and walked into the house to the sound of women shouting at each other. She shut her eyes for a moment, then slipped off her shoes and put them and her purse in their spots on the narrow bench in the hallway. She removed her belt and holster and carried them into the living room, where her mother, aunt, and cousin seemed to be trying to talk over each other, while Gram sat watching and shaking her head.

"Better put the gun away, Jacquie, or you might be tempted to use it," Gram said.

"I'm taking it up to my room. Thought I'd see what's going on here first."

"It's her fault." Noelle pointed at Precious.

"It is not!" Vida retorted. "It's your own fault."

"This is so unfair!" Precious shrieked.

Jacquie sighed. Using her no-nonsense police constable voice, she said, "All of you be quiet. Now one of you tell me what exactly is going on. Mom?"

"Precious used up all my water."

"Aunt Vida?"

"Your mother just up and started yelling at Precious for no good reason."

"Gram?"

Precious stamped her foot. "Why not ask me? I'm the one getting mistreated here."

"All right. Tell me. What's going on?"

"Your mother is blaming me because there's no hot water."

"That's it? You're going at each other like a gaggle of geese because of hot water? After all the times we've run out of hot water in the past?"

"Friday night is my night to have a relaxing bubble bath at the end of the week," Noelle said. "I've been doing it for years. So I go to run my bath and there's only cold water. And why? Because *she*—" Noelle pointed dramatically at Precious "—had to have a shower and wash her clothes so she could impress some guy she doesn't even know."

"I want to look nice."

"It's a blind date with some friend's cousin."

"My friend's boyfriend's cousin."

"The point is that it's *my* night for *my* bubble bath. You surely have other clothes you could wear. And maybe I don't even mind the shower so much, but you could have at least told me instead of letting me undress, light my candles, pour bubble bath oil in the tub, half-fill the tub with water, and then find out that the water was cold."

"I said I was sorry."

Aunt Vida stepped in. "Don't yell at my daughter, Noelle Ryan. Why should you get all the water every Friday night?"

Jacquie held up her hands. "Okay, everyone sit down."

Precious pouted. "I have a date. I'm already late."

"All right. You leave. But the rest of you—I'm going to take my gun upstairs and get into something more comfortable, and then I'm going to come down, and the four of us are going to talk. I wasn't going to say anything yet, but it's occurred to me that if we're all going to keep living together, we need to make some changes. Like get a big enough water heater, for instance. And another full bathroom."

"Should I warm up your dinner?" Gram asked meekly.

"No thanks, Gram. I had dinner earlier."

Precious put her hands on her hips. "So you're all going to talk about the house while I'm out?"

"That's right."

"That's not fair."

"Choose. Blind date or stay home with us and talk."

Jacquie headed for the stairs. She'd been exhausted when she'd walked in the front door, but now she felt exhilarated. This ought to be interesting.

Paul drove into the garage where Woody's car—now Loretta and Mike's car—was sitting. He got out of his elderly van. Yes, he desperately needed a new car. And he was going to get one. The moment he had a free hour or two. It was well past time for him to give in.

He looked over at the blue Honda Accord his partner had bought back in 2008. Woody had been so pleased with it. He'd said he felt like a king when he sat inside. It wasn't at all hard to imagine Woody sitting in the car. Or more likely sitting on the hood, the way he used to sit on Paul's desk.

Paul looked at his old van. It had served a purpose when the kids were younger, but that purpose was long gone now. Maybe that was it—he was reluctant to let it go because it meant letting go of that season of their lives.

"I'm going to get myself a new car, Woody," he said aloud. "It's past time. And I'm going to get one I like—not just whatever's the best deal. I might even get myself a red one, who knows? Been a long day, Woody. And you'd have complained that this case was the nuttiest ever. Or maybe the saddest. Whoever this person is, he's not normal at all. Probably thinks he's doing the right thing. We'll nail him soon. I sure hope so anyway. We have to get him behind bars. No telling what else he might decide to do. Or her, of course."

He paused for a second and made a face. "Oh, about Ryan. Maybe I'm just getting used to her, but I think this might actually work out. I'm kind of hoping she doesn't marry her pitcher and quit the force. I'd hate to have to break in yet another new partner. Seldon might even be right. The more freedom I give her, the better she gets. Well, I guess I'd better hit the sack. Tomorrow morning is going to come pretty quickly." He kicked a tire on his old green van. "Sorry, buddy, your time has come."

TWENTY

Although they'd all gone to bed late the night before, when Jacquie came down for breakfast Saturday morning, she found her mother and Aunt Vida sitting at Noelle's computer in the dining room-turned-office. Both wearing housecoats, they had their heads together in excited conversation.

Jacquie wandered into the kitchen where, as usual, her grandmother was making her breakfast. She kissed her cheek. "Morning, Gram." She motioned with her head toward the other room. "What's up?"

Her grandmother set a bowl of porridge on the table. "You've unleashed a hurricane is what's up. They're making a list of renovators to contact for an estimate."

"Ah, okay, I think. Are you all right with it?"

"I am."

"You don't mind having us all stay in your house?"

"No, I don't mind having you all here. But as you said last night, it's time this wasn't *my* house."

"I never said that."

"Sit down and eat your breakfast, child." Jacquie sat; her grandmother sat across from her. "No, but that's what it boils down to. And I'm fine with it. I loved what you said about each of us having our own bathroom and a sitting room with a little kitchenette. And if we can't do that in *this* house, I'm happy to sell it and find a house that will let us do it."

"You've lived here a long time."

"I have. But it's only a house, and a pretty inefficient one at that. I liked what you said about figuring out what we need and then making the house fit our needs instead of us just trying to made do with it as is. Makes complete sense."

"I'm glad you're not upset."

Gram narrowed her eyes. "Though I do wonder if you're sure you want to stay here with us. You and that baseball player were looking mighty comfortable with each other not many days ago."

Jacquie dropped her eyes. "Oh, him." She looked up to see her grandmother watching her with concern. "Well, uh, we—I guess *I've* decided I'm not ready for a serious relationship. I want to focus on my career for now. I'm just getting to where I want to be with the homicide department."

"If you were in love, something like that wouldn't stop you."

"Maybe not. And maybe I don't want to be in love."

Her grandmother laughed. "Child, you don't have a choice. When it's love, it just is. You'll find out. Some day."

"Ryan's not so bad, you know," Paul said to Loretta as they ate fluffy omelets filled with vegetables.

"Oh?"

"Yeah, we actually work together pretty well."

"That's good."

There was a long silence.

"I've taken to talking to Woody when I come home. In the garage of all places."

"To his car?"

"No, to Woody. Only now that his car's parked in the garage, it feels like he's there, sitting in it, listening."

Loretta smiled. "You'll let me know if he starts answering you, right?"

At 8:00 that morning, face red and eyes blazing with anger, Frank sped down the hallway on his scooter. His stomach was churning;

his heart was racing. His meeting with Ben hadn't gone at all the way he'd expected, and he was so angry he'd had to leave before he said something he'd later regret.

He'd have to think of another way to approach the problem. One thing he knew for certain was that if Hilary stayed here, it would be over his dead body.

At breakfast Saturday morning Hilary sat at her usual table. She was alone for only a minute before Catarina and Nikola arrived and sat with her. Shortly after that, Mary took the last chair. The four of them were talking about the weather and their plans for the day when Ben came in, stopped behind Hilary, and put his hand on her shoulder.

She turned to look up at him.

"Hilary, I can't say how sorry I am for what's been going on here. I had absolutely no idea until Mary and Catarina asked me to sign their petition last night. If there's anything else I can do to help, just let me know."

"Thank you, Ben."

"We'll talk more later." He moved to the next table and sat with Norm and Elizabeth.

Frank came in shortly after Ben. When Olive accidentally got in front of him, he snapped at her. His eyes narrowed as he noticed Mary sitting next to Catarina at the table with the Brooks woman.

He checked out the table on his other side, where Ben was sitting with Norm and Elizabeth. They'd expect him to sit with them, but he wasn't going to. He was tired of all three of them. Serve them right if he found other company.

He looked over at Lyle and Kenneth. He had no desire to sit with those two boring old men. Lyle only wanted to talk about himself, and Kenneth barely said anything. But it was that or sit at the empty table in the corner. Trish would expect him to sit with Lyle and Kenneth, so he would. But he'd rather sit alone.

It was past time for Trish to leave. She'd been helpful in the beginning, dealing with the funeral and the lawyer and Violet's things. But she'd hung around a lot longer than was necessary. Surely she must realize her place was with her young family! She almost seemed to be enjoying buddying up with the police during this investigation.

Frank moved his scooter to Lyle and Kenneth's table and, with Olive's help, took the seat next to Kenneth. He snapped at Olive again when she began to push his chair in too quickly.

As Olive brought a platter of food to the table, he turned toward her. "Where's my daughter? I thought she said she wasn't going home yet."

"I'm not sure. I'll ask Audra if she knows."

"Do that."

A few minutes later Olive stopped by to tell Frank that Trish was meeting someone for breakfast but would be back for lunch.

"Likely that interloper, Jake," he muttered. "She didn't ask me if I needed her."

Kenneth looked at him in amusement. "If you always treat her the way I've seen you do at meals here, I can only wonder why she'd want to be around you at all."

Frank glared at him. "I wouldn't be so quick to make fun of others if I were you. I heard it was your knife that stabbed poor Ingrid. I've a good mind to call the police commissioner and tell him they need to arrest the obvious suspect."

Kenneth raised his eyebrows. "Do as you please. I've nothing to hide."

Frank thrust out his lower lip and concentrated on his breakfast.

As the residents were beginning to think about leaving the dining room, Audra entered and announced, "The police have released the common room, and you're now free to use it." She quickly glanced at Frank. "Also, I just received an email from Ms. Arlington. She asked me to let everyone know that Mrs. Hilary Grant has been approved as a qualified resident and is welcome to stay here as long as she likes."

Amid the general outpouring of approval and a scattering of applause, Frank pushed his chair away from the table, and Olive hurried over to help him move to his scooter. He left the room without a word.

Everyone else stayed for longer than usual, enjoying extra cups of coffee and tea, celebrating their win over the nebulous *them* who had tried to evict Hilary.

Derrick whispered in Audra's ear, "Trust Naomi not to even have the decency to come and tell Hilary herself."

"We won. That's what's important."

Breakfast and morning walk over, Mary pushed her walker ahead of her into the common room where Lyle was already reading the newspaper. She sat down a few chairs away from him. "I don't know if I'll be able to get used to being in this room again."

"The chair is gone. I guess they couldn't get all the blood out. The floor looks clean."

"They had people in to clean it early this morning."

"Oh?"

"Audra told me." Mary opened her book.

Lyle put his paper down. "What do you think the police are doing now?"

"Investigating. Tying up all the loose ends."

"Whatever that means."

"Do you watch *CSI* and *NCIS* and *Criminal Minds* and—"

"No."

"Never?"

"Never had any interest in all that depressing stuff. I watch baseball games and things that matter."

"Oh, sports." She shook her head. "I watch all the police shows. I've always loved mysteries. And of course I read mysteries, too."

"Yes, I think by now we all know that." Lyle eyed the book on her lap. "Though I'm not sure how you can read one of those after what's happened here."

"These are make believe. They're just puzzles for my mind to work on."

Lyle frowned. "Do you think the police see murders that way? As puzzles to solve?"

Mary tilted her head in thought. "Could be. But it's a lot different when it's make believe in a book." She leaned forward and spoke more quietly. "Speaking of which, do you think Violet was murdered? First Violet and then Ingrid? It could have happened that way."

Lyle shuddered. "I sure hope not. One murder is bad enough. If it was two, then one of us might be next."

"Yes, that's what I expect."

Lyle stared at her in horror. "But there's no reason for anyone to go around killing us all off!"

Mary laughed. "There doesn't have to be a reason. I mean, it doesn't need to be logical to us. Murderers often think in odd ways. Like maybe they're doing us a favour. Like a nurse going around knocking off people who are dying so they don't have to feel more pain."

Lyle shivered. "All the talk these days about euthanasia scares the living daylights out of me. Not sure where this world is headed. First it's okay to kill babies just because they aren't born yet. Now some idiot is saying it's okay to kill babies if they aren't perfect when they're born. Soon it'll be okay to kill old people when they stop being useful or they take up too much space. Then it'll be anyone who isn't able to function whatever way *they* think is normal."

"There was a book about that. "*1984* I think? Or was it *Brave New World*? Been so long since I read them."

"Sounds like Hitler and other dictators to me. Well, if they don't find out who killed Ingrid soon, I'll be looking for another place to live. I'm not going to sit here waiting for someone to end my time." Lyle folded his newspaper into the side of his chair and left the room.

Mary watched him go. She could live happily enough without Lyle if he chose to leave. But with Ingrid and Violet gone, her biggest concern was that she might be next. And maybe it wouldn't make any difference where she was.

Audra left Serenity Suites right after breakfast. At Derrick's urging, she'd agreed to take her regular Saturday off and, as had been planned weeks before, take her sons to the new aquarium.

However, she was looking forward to the day with mixed emotions. Although she desperately wanted to see her boys, she was afraid they would be focused on trying to convince her to find a way to get custody of them from Giles.

She hoped she could get through the day without bursting into tears or promising something she'd find impossible to do.

Kenneth had decided to spend the day sorting through some of the boxes that had been packed up and left in storage since his wife died. While he knew that reading the letters and looking at old photos and other keepsakes wouldn't be easy, he felt he needed to do it to cleanse himself from the past and fully forgive himself.

Derrick had used a trolley to bring three boxes up from Kenneth's storage locker. He'd even told Kenneth to call him if he found it too difficult to face on his own.

By 9:45 Manziuk and Ryan were in the guest suite watching Kelly sort through the photos.

When they'd phoned Trish the night before, she said her mother had never mentioned a school friend who was black. She quickly agreed to let them sort through the photos while she went for breakfast with Jake.

So far they'd found six photos that included black women. Several were black-and-white photos of an older woman. A couple had a young girl in them. None of the women looked anything like the newspaper photo of Sharlene Bryce.

Suddenly Kelly held one up. "Ta da!"

Sure enough, the photo of six young people included a black girl who looked a lot like the one in the newspaper. The others bore a strong resemblance to Ben Davidson, Norm Carlysle, Violet Klassen, Mary Simmons, and Frank Klassen."

"So they *did* know her!" Ryan said.

"It might have been a bit more than just knowing her," Manziuk said. "Doesn't it look to you as if they're three couples going out for an evening? The boys are all wearing suits, and the women have on party dresses. Ben has his arm around Sharlene, Frank's is around Mary, and Norm's is around Violet."

"Is there anything on the back?"

"No. And no date anywhere. But it sure looks like them to me."

"Here's another photo with some writing on the back," Kelly said. "Violet and Mary at their high school graduation."

"That was in 1952." Ryan took the photo. "Their hair and general appearance look the same as in the other picture."

Manziuk noted, "1952 was the year Sharlene died."

"Could the baby have been Ben's?" Ryan asked.

"It's certainly a possibility."

"Who do we talk with first? Ben?"

Manziuk thought for a moment. "It would appear that we have four people who knew her—Frank, Ben, Norm, and Mary. I think I want to talk with Mary first. See what she has to say. And then talk to the others."

"There's also a very good chance this is a rabbit trail that has nothing to do with Ingrid's and Violet's deaths."

"It probably is, but right now we've got nothing much else."

Manziuk and Ryan found Mary in the common room, and the three of them went back to her condo. After they accepted her offer of lemonade, the three of them gathered around the table in her kitchen.

"What is it?" Mary asked. "I'd so like to be able to help."

Manziuk said, "Ms. Simmons, we need you to think back. Do you remember a woman named Sharlene Bryce?"

Mary frowned. "Sharlene? I don't think— Oh! You don't mean—? You can't!"

"You knew her when you were younger. Back in high school."

"Then, you *do* mean—" She looked at them in confusion. "I don't understand."

Ryan said gently, "Please just answer the question, Ms. Simmons. Perhaps this picture will help." Ryan held out the picture in its plastic covering.

Mary took it. "Oh, my heavens! I haven't thought of Sharlene in years and years. Yes, of course I remember her."

Manziuk said, "What can you tell us about her?"

Mary brought her hands up to cover her mouth and rocked forward on her elbows. "She died, you know. A terrible death."

"Can you help us understand the relationship between Sharlene and the rest of your group back then?"

Mary set the photo down. "I don't understand why you want to talk about that. It was so very long ago."

"Violet left a note that might possibly refer to Sharlene's death, suggesting that there might have been a question about it. We know from experience that events from the past can sometimes affect people's actions later on, even years after."

Mary pushed her glasses up and peered at him in confusion. "You think Ingrid's death had something to do with Sharlene?"

"It's more that we need to make sure it doesn't." He smiled. "Tell me, how well do you remember those days?"

"Sometimes I actually remember those days more clearly than I remember yesterday. Now that you've mentioned Sharlene's name, it's like you've opened a door in my brain, and a whole bunch of memories are clambering out."

Ryan said, "Can you tell us when you first met her?"

Mary clasped her hands together in her lap. "You're thinking about the fact that Sharlene was black and we weren't. And you're right. In those days we normally wouldn't have been friends. But Sharlene's mother worked as the housekeeper for Violet's parents. And they only lived a few streets from us in an apartment above a dry-cleaning shop. So the three of us were friends from when we were about four or five. Violet and Sharlene knew each other even longer, of course. Sharlene's mother brought her kids to work with her when they were too young to be in school."

Manziuk said, "When you say you were friends, what do you mean?"

"Well, we played together a lot. 'Hung out' as they might say today."

"And when did you get to know Ben and Norm and Frank?"

"When we were in grade one. Ben was in the same class as Violet and me, and Norm and Frank were in the same grade but in a different class. There was a boy, a big bully, who was in grade three. He liked picking on kids who were small, and back then Ben and Norm and Frank were all skinny and small. What you'd call nerds nowadays. None of them were all that interested in sports. And none of them had the foggiest idea how to fight a bully. Frank would have tried to defend himself if he thought he had no choice, and Ben might have tried to defend someone else. Norm would run away or try to fade into the scenery."

She laughed. "Violet and I, on the other hand, were little hellions, and that was part of why we clicked from the first day we met. If I wasn't in trouble, Violet was. My parents dealt with it quite well, even encouraged me to think for myself, but Violet's mother was a wuss, and her father was all about what people thought—a real stuffed shirt—so they were terribly embarrassed when she got into trouble. It wasn't long before they scared her into acting more like their idea of a lady, but she never changed inside. Just learned to hide her real self from just about everyone. I guess I learned the same thing. What they'd call being politically correct nowadays. We learned to say what they wanted, do what we wanted, and make sure they never knew the truth." She frowned. "Not that we ever did anything *really* wrong. We were too smart for that. I guess Violet learned that too well, didn't she? I mean with respect to Jake. She never even told *me* about him.

"Anyway, you asked me about meeting the guys. Well, one day when we were in grade one, Violet and I came on Frank and Ben being picked on by the big bully from grade three. It was just the one guy, so we decided to do something about it. We took him out with a few well-placed blows and one kick, and he ran off crying. Frank and Ben were both embarrassed and grateful, and they decided to reward us by taking us down to a nearby corner store for ice cream cones." She smiled. "You have to understand that in those days even little kids walked to school, and no one worried about where we were. Anyway, from that day on, the four of us were friends. And since Norm was also their friend, he automatically became our friend, too."

"Did Sharlene go to your school?" Ryan asked.

"No, but we still saw her after school and on weekends, and we stayed friends, off and on, right through elementary school." She grimaced. "Violet's parents didn't approve, you know. They didn't want Violet hanging out with their housekeeper's daughter. Violet didn't care. And *my* parents didn't care. So we usually went to my house. But when we were in grade six, Violet's parents fired Mrs. Bryce. I forget the reason they gave, but we knew it was so that Violet and Sharlene wouldn't have any reason to see each other any more. However, since we all still lived in the same general area, we kept seeing her. And then, of course, in grade nine we all went to the same high school."

Mary abruptly got up and went into the kitchen to get a glass of water. "Can I get you some more lemonade?" Manziuk and Ryan let her refill their glasses.

Mary sat back down. "You may not get it from her sad story, but Ben called Sharlene 'Butterfly Girl.' We—Violet and Ben and I anyway—loved having her around. I'm not so sure about Norm and Frank. Not that they said anything against her, but I never was sure how they felt." She fell silent.

"But I'm rambling on and on here. What you want to know about is what happened to her. It's hard to talk about, even now. Sometime near the end of grade eleven, we kind of started pairing up occasionally, me with Frank and Violet with Norm. Which meant Ben was at loose ends. He dated a few girls, but there was no one he wanted a second date with. But one day Ben showed up at a movie with Sharlene." She shook her head. "You have to understand, in those days that just wasn't done. For a white person to date a black person, I mean. Only happened once in a while, and the people who did it were looked down on.

"So we were all uncomfortable, Sharlene as much as anyone. But Ben was our friend, and Sharlene was our friend, so Violet and I decided we didn't care what other people thought and went along with it. And Frank and Norm kind of followed our lead.

"Of course, by the end of that evening, it was clear it wasn't going to be a one-date thing. Violet and I discussed it and decided we just wouldn't let Violet's parents know. It turned out Sharlene didn't want her parents to know either, because they'd think she was getting above herself. So the six of us did things together, kind of on the quiet for the sake of Violet's and Sharlene's parents. I was never sure about Ben's parents. He seemed to think they'd go along with it, but I wasn't convinced. It's one thing to talk about prejudice and racism being wrong as abstract issues and another thing to have someone in your family dating someone of another race." Mary sank into thought.

"And in the spring of your last year of school?" Manziuk prompted after a while. "Something happened?"

Mary hugged herself. "The first I knew was when Violet phoned early in the morning to tell me Sharlene was dead. Norm had called to let her know. It wasn't until it came out in the newspaper that we found out Sharlene had been pregnant. Sharlene hadn't told Violet or me." She stared at the far wall.

"Was Ben aware that she was pregnant before she died?"

Mary nodded. "He told us he knew and was going to marry her. He kept saying, over and over, that she should have trusted him to look after her. At the same time he blamed himself for getting her pregnant."

"Mary," Ryan said, "think hard about this. Did any of you—Ben, Violet, Frank, Norm, anyone else who knew her—wonder if her death might have not been suicide?"

Mary turned to stare at Ryan, her eyes growing wide. "Of course not. We all knew what had happened. In those days it was bad enough to be pregnant, but to be pregnant to a white man? Her parents would have been beside themselves."

"So you think she jumped because she was afraid to tell her parents?"

"Well, to be honest, I thought she did it to protect Ben. She knew better than any of us what it would have been like for him. In those days white people didn't marry black people. Why, my goodness, that was years before *Guess Who's Coming to Dinner* came out!"

"So you believed Sharlene was capable of committing suicide? Of making a decision to jump off that bridge and carrying it out?"

Mary frowned. "Well, she did, didn't she?"

Ryan pressed. "Before it happened, would you have believed she would do that?"

Mary looked at the top of her table for a long moment. Then she looked up. "Well, if you want the truth, no. Sharlene was afraid of heights. She actually hated having to walk over the bridge. Her family had moved across the valley a few months before her death. She kept going to the high school because she was about to graduate. Mostly she took a streetcar, but sometimes she had to walk over the bridge, and she hated it. Honestly, I'd have thought she'd have found another way to do it. Pills, even a gun. Something easier."

Manziuk said, "Could her death have been an accident?"

Mary gave him a puzzled look.

"I know the railings on the edge weren't very high in those days. Perhaps she was walking along near the railing, and someone came by on a bike and knocked her over."

"She'd have fallen on the ground then, not over the railing."

"Stranger things have happened."

Mary raised her eyebrows.

"Did anyone see her jump?" Ryan asked.

Mary shook her head. "Not as far as I know. The police asked for witnesses, but no one came forward." She bit her lip. "You have to understand that in those days Toronto was much whiter than it is today. People might not have noticed her *because* she was black. If that makes any sense to you."

"Yes, it does. Unfortunately. What about her parents? Did they accept that she'd jumped?"

"I think so. They were devastated. They blamed Ben, more for trifling with her when he had no intention of marrying her than for getting her pregnant. Of course he told them he *was* going to marry her, but I don't think they ever believed him."

"Do you think Sharlene's family would have thrown her out if she'd told them?"

Mary shook her head. "No, they were good people. They'd have maybe wanted her to give the baby up for adoption, but they'd have supported her. They were thrilled that she was going to be the first person in their family to go to university. And she had a scholarship, too. She had the highest marks in our class."

Manziuk asked, "How quickly did Ben get over her death?"

Mary frowned. "Not quickly at all. For a while we thought he might jump next, that's how upset he was. We decided someone had to be with him all the time. He had two older brothers, so they helped, too. When he realized what we were doing, he told us he wasn't going to do anything stupid. And he eventually got over it, but it was a long, long time. He didn't date anyone until third year university when he met Ingrid."

Ryan said, "I'm curious. When did Frank switch from dating you to dating Violet?"

"That happened in our second year of university. Norm and Violet broke up after Christmas, and Frank asked her out almost right away."

"Did that cause a rift in your friendship with Violet?"

"No, it wasn't her fault Frank liked her better than me. She hadn't done anything to steal him. She even called me after he asked her out to ask me what she should do. I told her if she wanted to date him to go ahead. I told her I might just try my luck with Norm."

"So Frank and Violet dated from then on?"

"And got married right after graduation."

"And Norm?"

Mary laughed. "I was just joking. I never made a play for Norm. He wasn't my type. He eventually found a girl who played the cello. A real sweetheart. We all loved her. Unfortunately she was badly injured in a boating accident a year after their marriage and died three years later. Norm eventually met Elizabeth and married her. I'm not sure that was ever a good match-up, but what do I know?"

Manziuk asked, "And you—did you ever marry?"

She shook her head. "To be honest, for a while I regretted breaking up with Frank. But it was kind of awkward since Violet was my best friend. So I told myself to get over it. And as I got older, I learned to value my independence, and I never found anyone I wanted to give it up for."

She looked at Ryan. "That may sound strange to you, but it's true. When you marry someone, from then on you always have to think about the other person or check with the other person. And it's worse if you're a woman. Back in those days most men thought women wanted to be shielded and given a strong shoulder to cry on, but I never did."

She shook her head again. "I had a couple of close calls, but I managed to avoid getting stuck the way most of my friends did."

She laughed. "I know that sounds terrible, but if I hadn't already come to see it before, living in such close quarters these last few years with Frank and Violet and Norm and Elizabeth would have cured me of any misconceptions I had."

"What about Ben and Ingrid?" Ryan asked.

Mary's face softened. "That's different. If I'd had any brains, I'd have gone after Ben the moment I got free of Frank, before he met Ingrid. But at the time he was still grieving for Sharlene. Anyway, Ingrid was perfect for him, and they had many happy years. If ever a man knew how to treat a woman, it was Ben. And that was true for Sharlene just as much as it was for Ingrid."

Her voice became very earnest. "He would have married her, you know. He was crazy about her, and we all knew it. And Sharlene wasn't so noble she'd have killed herself to save Ben from having to marry her. She was young and optimistic and just as much in love with him as he was with her."

Mary paused, a strange look crossing her face. "I can't believe I just said that. I—I've not thought about this for over sixty years."

She turned to Manziuk. "You asked me if I believe Sharlene jumped off that bridge. When I really think about it, I have no idea why she'd jump. She wasn't even remotely the kind of person who would panic. She was very practical, and she was an optimist, always seeing possibilities." She shook her head and took several deep breaths. "Back then it seemed so obvious. But thinking back, it doesn't make any sense. Sharlene wasn't a quitter, and she wasn't afraid to stand up for herself. Lord knows, she'd had to do it many times.

"So, if she killed herself, there must have been something else. Like maybe it really wasn't Ben's baby, and she knew he'd find out. Or maybe Ben lied to us about telling her he'd marry her. I don't know."

Manziuk said, "Did Violet believe Sharlene committed suicide?"

"I don't think either of us questioned what the police said." Mary sat forward on the chair. "But there wasn't much of an investigation. It was what they called an open-and-shut case. She was young and pregnant, and they decided right off that she killed herself in a fit of depression. The police never looked past that. Aside from a policeman who took our names and a few details, no one ever talked to me or to Violet in any depth."

Mary's eyes went from Manziuk to Ryan. "Tell me, what does Sharlene's death have to do with Ingrid's death? I really don't understand."

"Perhaps nothing," Manziuk said. "But the subject came up, and we have to follow every possible lead to make sure there's no chance it might be connected."

Ryan said, "We'll want to talk to Ben, Norm, and Frank, too, so please don't mention this conversation to anyone else until we've done that."

Mary nodded. "I haven't talked to anyone about it for decades. Not likely to start now."

"Do you know if Sharlene's family is still in the Toronto area?"

"Why, I—I don't. I went to the funeral—we all did—but I never had any more contact with any of them. I don't know if Ben did or not. I know they didn't want anything to do with him." She shook her head. "How strange to realize that I never even thought of them again."

The detectives found Derrick in the office.

"Just a quick question," Manziuk said. "Was Ingrid Davidson the only person on this floor who used insulin?"

"Yes, that's right."

"So no one else would have had insulin in their possession during the past few months?"

"No, just Ingrid."

"And you or Audra gave Ingrid her insulin?"

"Yes. What's this about?"

"Would you have noticed if some of the insulin and one or more needles were missing?"

"How much insulin?"

"Say three needles' worth."

"Syringes. So a full syringe?"

"Yes."

"So could someone have filled three syringes with insulin without Audra and me realizing it? Probably. I mean, it isn't as if we're tracking every millilitre the way you would if you were doing all the meds for everyone and writing down how much you'd used and so forth. We just gave Ingrid her insulin.

"There's a box of syringes in the medicine cabinet next to the bottle of insulin that's open. Unopened bottles are kept in a box at the back of a drawer in the bottom of the refrigerator. I think we'd have noticed if a bottle was missing but not if some insulin was gone from the opened bottle. As for syringes, they come a hundred in a box, so unless it was almost empty, we'd be unlikely to notice if three were missing." He looked from Ryan to Manziuk. "Why are you asking about this?"

"We're checking all sorts of things."

TWENTY-ONE

Manziuk and Ryan found Frank in his office. He wasn't happy to see them.

"First I have Violet and Norm's bastard dropped on me, and now you people show up. How do you expect me to get any writing done?"

Manziuk said, "Sorry to bother you, Mr. Klassen, but we have a few additional questions."

Frank heaved a sigh. "What is it now?"

Manziuk took the big easy chair across from Frank's desk. Ryan perched on the corner of the credenza. "We'd like to know what you remember about Sharlene Bryce."

Frank frowned. "Who?"

"Sharlene Bryce. You knew her years ago, in high school."

"I don't remember everyone I knew ten years ago, never mind back in high school."

"This might help your memory." Ryan handed him the photo.

With a show of reluctance he took it and sat staring at it. "I recognize myself and Violet. And the badly dressed girl must be Mary. She dresses the same as she did then—frumpy. And I assume the other young men are Norm and Ben, although neither one has an ounce of extra flesh on their bones. So the other girl—is that this Sharon you asked about?"

"Sharlene."

"Whatever you say. I don't remember her at all. She mustn't have been around long."

Ryan frowned. "You really expect us to believe you don't remember Sharlene Bryce? Even though you knew her from the time you were six or seven until the spring of the year you graduated?"

Frank stared at the picture. "Sharlene, you said?"

"She committed suicide by jumping off the Bloor Viaduct in the spring of 1952."

"Oh, her!" Frank dropped the photo onto his desk and brought his hands back into his lap. "Oh, now I remember. But I never had much to do with her, you know. She was Mary and Violet's friend, not mine. And Ben took her out a few times. But I never knew her that well. She just kind of tagged along with Violet and Mary, and they felt sorry for her and let her."

"What did you think when she committed suicide?" Manziuk asked.

"Well, I felt sorry for her, of course. But if she was going to play around, she should have thought about possible consequences first, shouldn't she?"

"Our understanding is that Ben was the father of her baby."

Frank looked down. "So he said, but I never believed it. I'm positive there were others."

"She went out with other guys as well as Ben?"

"I'm sure she did. You know what they're li—" His eyes darted from Manziuk to Ryan.

Ryan said, "What *who* are like, Mr. Klassen?"

Frank looked down. "You're just trying to trick me. I never noticed that Ben felt anything for her other than friendship. He treated her the same way he did Mary and Violet."

Ryan's eyes narrowed. "You didn't know Violet had a baby before she married you. So maybe you don't notice everything."

Frank gave her a dirty look.

"Were you surprised when Sharlene committed suicide? Did you wonder if it might have been something else, maybe an accident?"

"They said she'd jumped. That's all I knew." He frowned. "She died years ago. Why are you wasting my time asking about her? What's all this about?"

"In the letter where she talked about a son, your wife mentioned a suicide she didn't think was really a suicide. I thought you read it."

"As you might imagine, I was focused on the part about the son."

"I can understand that." Manziuk stood. "Well, we won't take up any more of your time. Thanks for answering our questions."

When they were in the hallway, Ryan turned toward her partner. "That man is insufferable!"

"You have steam coming out of your ears."

"I've never in my life met anyone so completely focused on himself. Not to mention so rude. Doesn't he know how he comes across?"

"I doubt it. My impression is that Violet wrapped him in cotton wool. What I can't figure out is why. Was she completely besotted by him even after close to sixty years of marriage?"

"I wouldn't survive a week around someone like him."

Manziuk looked at her quizzically. "And yet, if I may point out, you're dating a professional baseball pitcher."

She stared at him. "I don't get it."

"You do know that baseball pitchers as a group have the reputation of being some of the most self-absorbed people you'll ever meet."

She thought for a second, then nodded. "You may have a point."

Manziuk didn't allow himself to say anything, though inwardly he chided himself. *Whew! I need to watch it. Giving Ryan personal advice is nowhere in my job description.*

Ben sat on the edge of the chair and looked from Manziuk to Ryan and back again. "You have more questions?"

Manziuk said, "Our questions have to do with a woman named Sharlene Bryce. Do you remember her?"

Ben sat straighter. "What name did you just say?"

"Sharlene Bryce."

"I don't understand. Why are you asking me about her?"

"Is it true you knew a Sharlene Bryce many years ago?"

"Yes, of course I did. But that was years before I met Ingrid."

Ryan said, "We've seen the police report of Sharlene's death. I expect you knew she was pregnant?"

He frowned. "Of course I knew. It was my baby."

"Was her pregnancy the reason she committed suicide?"

Ben started to get up, but then settled back into his chair. "All right. If you want to talk about this, I'll assume you know what you're doing. But I haven't thought about it for years. Sharlene was my girlfriend. We were in high school. We were in love and we planned to get married one day. We were foolish, like so many young people are. Couldn't wait. We thought we were being careful, but near the end of May Sharlene told me she was going to have a baby. She said she didn't know what she was going to do. We were all planning to go to university.

"By 'we,' I mean her, me, Frank, Norm, Violet, and Mary. The six of us were a group, you see. Sharlene was the smartest of the bunch of us but also the poorest. Her dad worked as a porter on the trains, and her mother had been a housekeeper but was then a cook in a hotel. Sharlene had a full scholarship to go to university. The rest of us were what you'd call middle to upper class, I guess. Between our parents and part-time jobs, we had enough money to pay our way. Although I have to say Violet had the devil of a time convincing her parents to let her go. She was fortunate she had a partial scholarship, or her father likely never would have agreed. He saw no reason for women to be educated when all they were going to do was marry and have children, which was all he thought they *should* do. She finally convinced him to let her go into teaching, because that way what she learned would be useful when she had children of her own."

"So Sharlene's pregnancy was a problem for you."

He nodded. "I guess you'd say that. Some people would have found a way to get an abortion even though it was illegal, but Sharlene wasn't going to live her life knowing she'd sacrificed another life just to get out of the mess we'd made."

"And what did you say to that?"

"I guess a small part of me was sorry she thought that way because it complicated things. But honestly I don't think I could have gone along with her having an abortion even if she'd wanted one. I planned to marry her, and that was no way to begin our lives together. So I told her we'd get married sooner than we'd planned, and everything would be fine. I was living at home and had planned to stay there, but I decided to rent a small apartment near the university. I told her I could get a part-time job. She already had one working as a waitress. She said she'd be able to keep it for a while. One thing, though, I didn't want her to lose her scholarship."

"So what happened on the day she died?"

"She lived across the Don Valley, just off the Danforth. While I was walking her home, we started to argue. She said having the baby would mess up the year anyway, so she'd just get a job and skip university for now. Then she said they'd never let us get married—my parents or her parents. I told her if we had to, we'd elope and worry about what they said later. We could always go to western Canada where nobody knew us. Or to the United States. She said she'd think about it. I had a meeting with the debating team and I realized I was going to be late. She said for me to go, that she'd be fine. The last thing I said was for her not to worry, that I'd look after her." His voice broke.

"Take your time," Manziuk said.

Ben drank some water. "The next I knew was when Violet phoned me early the following morning to tell me Sharlene's mother had called her in hysterics asking if she knew where Sharlene was. I called Norm and Frank, and the three of us ran over to where I'd left her not far from the bridge, intending to follow the route she'd have taken to get to her house.

"As soon as we got to the bridge, we saw police cars. There seemed to be something happening in the valley. There were a lot of police milling around, and they tried to keep us away, but we found a way down, and I badgered them until they finally admitted it was a young woman. When they brought a purse they'd found near her, I identified it, and they let me through to see her." Tears filled his eyes. "It was horrible. They said she hadn't suffered—she'd died the second she hit the ground." He looked at them. "I was going to marry her. I really was. No one could have stopped me." He took a couple of deep breaths.

"Nowadays they use the expression 'love of my life.' Well, she was mine. I loved Ingrid, too, but I have to say I never loved her the way I loved Sharlene. I'd have given up everything for Sharlene." He took the tissues Ryan held out and wiped his eyes.

"For months I was so angry with her. I don't know if she did it because she didn't believe I'd look after her, or because she had some stupid idea of protecting me." He blew his nose. "All because of the colour of her skin and because her dad was a porter and her mother a cook. What did any of that matter? She was a brilliant, funny, amazing person, and we could have had the most wonderful life. But she—she never gave us a chance."

Manziuk asked, "You never suspected anything other than suicide?"

Ben looked startled. "Of course not. Why would I?"

"If I said we have a letter from someone who felt that Sharlene's death might not have been suicide, what would your reaction be?"

Ben glared at him. "If you think I'd have harmed a single hair on that girl's head, you're crazy!"

"What about someone else?"

"I don't— Who wrote this letter?"

"Violet."

Ben sat back, a perplexed look on his face. "Violet? I don't believe it. First of all, how would she know? She wasn't there. *No one* was there. And why would she write it in a note? Why wouldn't she just tell me? Or the police, if she had some reason to think that."

Another thought struck him. "Who did she send this letter to?"

"Mr. Davidson, we don't understand this either, but when Trish Klassen-Wallace was going through her mother's papers, she found a letter that was dated the morning of the day Violet died. She wanted Trish to get the letter after her death. There was an indication that she might have said more about it, but of course she never had the chance."

"This is mind-blowing, Inspector. I haven't thought of Sharlene for years. I mean, I've thought of her but as a sad memory. However, I never once questioned how she died. The police said it was suicide, so I assumed it was. What else could it have been?"

"Do you know if Sharlene's family is still in the Toronto area?"

"About six months after she died they moved to the Maritimes. Either New Brunswick or Nova Scotia. They found it too hard to have to go over the bridge all the time. And they had family out there. I didn't try to keep in touch because her parents blamed me."

Manziuk and Ryan found Norm and Elizabeth in their condo.

Elizabeth was holding her purse. "We're just going out, Inspector. We're meeting my husband's new son for lunch."

"This won't take long."

With a sigh, Elizabeth set her purse on a small table in the hallway and led the way into the sitting room.

"What's this about?" Norm asked. "Have you found out something to do with Ingrid's murder?"

"Not exactly," Ryan said. She showed him the picture Kelly had found and asked if he recognized the young woman with Ben.

"No, I don—" He slapped his forehead. "It's her!"

"Her?" Ryan said. "What do you mean?"

Norm peered more closely at the picture Ryan was holding. "It's the woman in my dream." He jumped up. "Come."

The others followed him to his studio.

"Is this Violet?" Manziuk pointed to a large canvas on an easel.

"Yes, it's for Trish. I finished it early this morning."

"Wow!" Ryan exclaimed. "You almost expect her to speak."

Elizabeth gave Ryan a funny look. "I wonder what she'd say."

Norm set another large canvas on another easel. He stood back. "That's her. That's Sharlene."

Ryan held up the photo. "Yes, that definitely looks like her."

"When and why did you paint this?" Manziuk asked Norm.

"I woke up one morning recently with her face in my mind, and I knew I had to paint it. I had no idea why, or who she was." He shrugged. "My memory isn't what it once was, you know."

"I'm not sure your memory was ever very good," Elizabeth said in her usual dry manner.

Manziuk was looking closely at the painting. "How recently? Since Ingrid died?"

Norm shook his head. "No, after Violet died. I tried to finish the painting of Violet that I'd begun, but I just couldn't. And I couldn't paint anything else either. Then I woke up one morning and had to come and paint this."

Elizabeth said. "It was the Saturday after Violet died. Remember? You were in here painting, and I wanted to go to a movie, but you wouldn't leave until you finished. I went to a movie by myself."

Norm was nodding. "Yes, that was it. I wanted to finish it before I lost the picture in my mind."

Elizabeth looked at Manziuk. "It was very unusual. He only paints people who pose for him. On rare occasions, he paints from a photograph if the person is dead. But he never paints people out of thin air."

"I had this dream, and she was in it. Her face. Just like this. When I woke up, I could still see her. For some reason I felt I needed to paint her. I have no explanation. Nothing like that has ever happened to me before."

Ryan held up the photo. "Do you remember when this picture was taken?"

"There was a dance at the school. Violet told her parents she was staying overnight at Mary's, or she'd never have been allowed to go."

"And a few weeks later Sharlene was dead."

Norm's face convulsed. "Yes."

"What can you tell us about her death?"

"She jumped from the bridge. It was horrible."

"Were you surprised?"

"Of course."

"What would you say," Manziuk said, "if we told you she might not have jumped?"

His face turned white. "What are you saying?"

"Violet left a note hinting that perhaps Sharlene didn't jump."

"I don't understand. How would Violet know? She wasn't there."

Ryan frowned. "How do you know she wasn't there?"

"What?"

"How do you know Violet wasn't there?"

"She'd have said something if she was. Besides, she was with her parents that night. Some kind of family thing."

"Where were you that night?" Manziuk asked.

"I was with Frank and Ben and Sharlene for a while. Then Ben and Sharlene left, and Frank and I hung out for a while until I had to go to home."

"Do you know anything about Sharlene's death, Norm?" Manziuk watched him carefully.

"No, of course not. Just that Ben was late for a meeting, so he left her on our side of the bridge. No one saw her jump. The police said so."

"So you're satisfied she committed suicide?" Ryan asked.

"I—I—that's what the police said. I assumed they knew."

"Just now when we came in, you said you were on your way out. Will you be gone long?"

"Most of the day.

"We might have more questions for you later."

"Well," Elizabeth said, "we won't run away. And I have a cellphone if you should decide you can't go another minute without talking to us."

As they left the Carlysles' condo, Ryan said, "He's a terrible liar."

Manziuk nodded. "Curious. Of the four of them he's the only one who appeared to be holding something back. I wonder what he knows that he didn't want to tell us."

"Should we pull him in for questioning? If we take him down to headquarters, he might crack."

Manziuk just looked at her. "Crack? Seriously?"

Ryan blushed. "Well, tell the truth."

"For all we know, there could have been something about that night that he didn't want to tell us in front of his wife. It might have had nothing to do with Sharlene's death."

"True."

"Let's let him stew about it. Talk to him again tomorrow. Without Elizabeth if necessary."

"She's what I think my mother would call a 'pill.'"

Manziuk looked at her.

"A genteel way of saying the 'b' word."

"Ah."

"So what do we do next? It sure seems that Sharlene must be the person Violet was referring to, but we're kind of at a dead end."

"I wonder if Ford has learned anything more. We still don't know who Nikola Vincent really is. Maybe—"

Ryan's cellphone buzzed. She put it on speaker phone, so they both could hear Trish.

"Constable, I feel like an echo, but I've just discovered something else that you should know. I just spoke to my parents' accountant. He didn't know anything about Mom's death until he got home from his holiday and listened to my voice messages. He told me something about Mom's investments that we didn't know."

"Can you give me the gist of it?"

"Yes. Do you remember the money from Mom's investment that seemed to come from a numbered company? He knows about it."

"Where are you?" Ryan asked.

"I just spent the morning with Jake. Norm and I are tag-teaming, so it's his turn now. I could meet you wherever you want."

After a quick discussion with Manziuk, Ryan said, "Could we meet you at the accountant's office?"

"He has a home office and said he'd be available at 1:00. I'll let him know to expect us."

Manziuk went into the office next to Frank's to make a personal phone call before leaving for the accountant's. Ryan wandered down the hallway and almost bumped into Derrick. "Oh, hi," he said. "Can I help you with something?"

"No, thanks. I was just looking around. We're thinking of doing some renovations to make our house more useful, and I was just thinking about what's necessary and what isn't. The whole concept of how this place is geared to the residents' needs got me thinking."

"Well, this is obviously bigger than a house, but if you think about what you want to do, you can extrapolate. For example, you need a place to sit with others and talk, a place to play a card or board game, a place to exercise, a place to be alone if you want, work space, and so forth."

"Right. So basically think about what you want to do and make sure there's a place for it?"

"Exactly. And it's going beyond the basics. I mean, every home has a kitchen, but some kitchens are pretty inconvenient because they don't fit the particular needs of the people who live there. So, for example, if you mostly use the microwave to heat stuff and have toast and coffee every morning, you need to make sure your toaster and coffee maker and microwave are right out where you can get them."

She was nodding. "Right."

"On the other hand, if you like to bake a lot, then your number one need might be a decent amount of clear counter space."

"Yeah."

"I think you said there are five women in your house?"

"Right."

"And not enough bathrooms?"

"Yes."

"So what you probably need to do is have a plumber come in and tell you what's possible. If it's an older home—"

"It is."

"Ah, then it's possible you'll need all new plumbing in order to add a bathroom.

"That sounds expensive."

"Might be. But you never know."

"I hadn't thought about things like that. The wiring is probably as old as the sea, too."

"But it's entirely possible to update it and add what you need, too."

"Well, we've started making our needs list. So I'll add plumbing and electricity to it."

"Don't forget to check the foundation, too."

"What could go wrong there?"

"Old things can crack or crumble. Especially if you start moving or adding walls."

"Is there anything you don't know?"

Derrick laughed. "My sister's husband is in construction, so I've learned a fair bit from hanging out with him."

"In Oshawa?"

"Yeah, but he has contacts in the city. He could probably recommend somebody for you to talk to. If you want somebody you can trust to give you an honest evaluation and estimate..." He hesitated. "I could maybe get him to have a look at it for you. Just to advise you on whether he thinks it would makes sense to renovate or not."

"Really?"

"Yeah. Maybe he and my sister could drive in and we could go for dinner or something afterwards. That's if— Well, you don't wear a ring, so I'm assuming you're not married, but you could be in a relationship, and if so that's fine. But on the off chance that you aren't, I was kind of wondering if you'd be interested in maybe going for dinner or coffee." He grinned. "That's a euphemism for getting to know each other better."

"I'm sort of in a relationship. But not an exclusive one. At least I don't think so."

"So should I ask Pieter if he'd have time to look at the house?"

"Can I get back to you on that? I should talk to the other inmates."

"Sure, that's fine. Here's my card."

"No need. You gave me your card yesterday. Here, I'll give you mine."

He winked. "I'll be in touch."

As she started to go back to meet Manziuk, he said, "So you don't want to tell me more about why you were asking about insulin?"

"Sorry. Just following up every possibility."

"You think Violet was killed, don't you? Three syringes of insulin could have done it."

"It's only a supposition. Please don't say anything to anyone."

"I won't."

Saturday was Scarlett's day off, but she'd left a cold lunch for Olive to serve.

The lunch crowd was small. Norm and Elizabeth were out with Jake. Catarina and Nikola had taken Hilary out with them.

At one table Lyle was explaining to Kenneth that he'd decided to go out for the afternoon before he went stir-crazy. And besides it was safer to be out than to be a sitting duck here.

Frank, Ben, and Mary sat at a second table making painful small talk. Finally Mary said, "Did the police call on you today?"

Ben nodded. Frank swore.

"I think they talked to me first," Mary said. "They asked me not to say anything. But if they talked to you, I guess it's okay. I assume they talked to Norm, too."

"I don't understand why they're bringing this up," Ben said.

"Apparently Violet wasn't sure it was suicide. She left a note or something about it."

"Violet knew nothing about it," Frank said. "She should have minded her own damn business."

Ben shook his head. "But what could Sharlene's death possibly have to do with Ingrid's?"

"Maybe it's a serial killer," Mary said.

"Don't be ridiculous," Frank said. "Serial killers don't leave sixty years between their crimes."

"Maybe Ingrid knew something," Mary said. "And the killer was afraid she'd spill it."

Ben frowned. "Ingrid didn't even know Sharlene."

"Do you think Sharlene was murdered?" Mary's eyes grew wide.

"Of course not," Frank snorted.

Ben shook his head.

Mary sighed. "I sure wish Violet had told me instead of just writing an obscure note."

Even though he'd eaten only a small part of his lunch, Ben stood up. "I'm not hungry. I'll see you later."

At the restaurant on top of the CN Tower, Hilary, Catarina, and Nikola ordered their lunch. Hilary leaned forward and whispered to Nikola, "Since we aren't at Serenity Suites and no one can hear us, do you think you and your stepmother can drop the pretense?"

Two pairs of eyes stared at her in surprise.

"I have no idea what you mean," Catarina said. "What pretense? Nikola is my husband."

"Oh, come now. I wasn't born yesterday."

Nikola stared at her. "How do you know?"

One corner of Hilary's mouth raised. "I recognized you immediately. I'm a big fan."

Catarina's eyes were huge. "And you said nothing?"

Hilary shrugged. "None of my business. I expect you had a good reason."

"Well, we did," Nikola said.

Catarina quickly glanced around to make sure no one could overhear. "He wanted to take a quiet vacation. This seemed to be the perfect spot."

"Not what *I'd* choose for a vacation spot." Hilary smiled.

"Are you really a fan of his?"

"I have most of his albums, and I've seen him live twice. That's why I recognized him in spite of his overly long hair, which I assume is a wig, and the beard. Of course, since his last name is not Vincent but Romano-Rossi, and his father was your husband, it was very easy to come to the conclusion that you're his stepmother. Plus Gulab told me you sleep in separate rooms."

"Ah, the staff." Catarina shrugged. "Always they know more than we want them to."

Hilary smiled.

"But you will not give away our secret, please! He wants to stay until the last day of his vacation time, which is not too far away. And besides, he has been useful."

"Agreed. But perhaps, before you leave, you might do a short concert for everyone. The acoustics in our theatre are excellent. I think we deserve that."

"Your wish is my command." Nikola bowed his head.

By 3:30 Saturday afternoon, Manziuk and Ryan had met with Trish and the accountant, contacted a forensic accountant to check into things further, and were back at police headquarters.

Trish had returned to Serenity Suites to finish packing and spend some time with her father. She was determined to leave for home the next day.

Ford met the two detectives with a smile. "Good to see you. We think we know who Nikola is. And you're not going to believe it!"

Manziuk said, "Please enlighten us."

Ford sat on the edge of the desk. "Okay, since Nikola obviously knew Catarina, I did some more research on her. Turns out she had four children with her first husband. But they're all older than Nikola appears to be, by more than ten years. However, after her first husband's death, when she was forty-seven she remarried. Her new husband had three children, the youngest of whom was four years old. He is now forty-two. And his name is Gabriel Alessandro Nikola Vincent Romano-Rossi.

Ryan said, "Wait! Did I hear Nikola Vincent in there?"

"I did."

"Photo confirmation?" said Manziuk.

Ford pulled out his tablet and did a quick search for a website. "Check it out."

"The hair is darker, shorter, and much better maintained, and the beard is absent, but I'd say that's him all right."

"It gets better."

Ryan frowned. "Better? In what way?"

"Gabriel Romano-Rossi is a world-famous composer and classical guitarist."

"You're kidding!"

"And a little digging tells us that no one has seen him for nearly a month. The official report is that he's taking a much-needed rest. No one has been able to find him. And since he's a big name, the paparazzi have been looking."

Ryan laughed. "Where better to rest than in a senior citizens' residence?"

"Oh, yeah, definitely!"

"I assume this takes him off our suspect list. I can't think of any motive he'd have to kill Ingrid."

Manziuk said, "We still need to talk to him."

"Right now he's on top of the CN Tower having lunch with his stepmother and Hilary Brooks. Patterson is quite enjoying himself."

"Okay, he'll keep."

"On that other matter, we have a contact in Nova Scotia following up on Sharlene's family."

"Good." Manziuk stretched. "I think I'm going to call it a day. I promised Mike we'd go to the Matrix game tonight unless there was an emergency, and I was able to get some good seats. We need to get the results from the tests on Violet to know what to look for. And we need to talk to Norm again, but I want to give him a bit of time to stew. The security guard at Serenity Suites is still on duty there tonight, right?"

"As far as I know."

"Okay, you get some R and R, too."

"Sounds good. My bed has been wondering if I moved. I'll be there if you need me."

Norm and Elizabeth spent Saturday afternoon showing Jake some of their favourite spots around Toronto. Since Jake's flight home to British Columbia was the following morning, Trish and Frank joined them at a restaurant for dinner Saturday night.

Jake had offered to delay his flight due to the murder investigation, but Trish convinced him it would be less stressful for her and Frank if he went home. She'd keep him up to date.

Paul and his son made it to the baseball game in time to grab foot-long hot dogs before going to their seats on the first-base side of the field.

Mike said, "Great seats, Dad! I'm so glad you could get away."

Paul sat back in satisfaction. He knew full well that having your seventeen-year-old son want to share a ball game with you was as good as it got. "Me too, Mike."

Jacquie was also at the game, sitting in the section reserved for wives and girlfriends of the players. Afterward she waited in the family area downstairs until Armando came out of the clubhouse.

She ran up to hug him. "Nice going! You're doing so well these days. No sign of the problems you had earlier this summer."

"Even I did not realize how much everything that was going on was affecting me. As Yogi Berra said, 'Ninety percent of this game is half-mental.'"

"I'm so glad you're back on track now."

"As am I. Of course," he smiled down at her, "it might have something to do with you."

They took a taxi to a nearby restaurant frequented by Matrix players and found a table in a corner. After they'd ordered and been served their drinks, Jacquie leaned forward. "Armando, I've been doing a lot of thinking in the last few days. Well, when I haven't been trying to solve a murder."

Armando laughed, and Jacquie did, too.

"You asked me to go to Hawaii. I'm afraid I'm going to have say no. I like you a lot, but I'm just not ready to make any kind of commitment right now."

Armando leaned across the table and took both her hands in his. "Jacqueline, it is okay. I am not asking you to only be with me."

She pulled her right hand back and stirred her iced tea. "Well, see, if I'm going to be in any kind of relationship beyond friendship, then I guess I prefer the old-fashioned way. The one that involves a ring and a church and the whole enchilada." Hastily she added, "Someday, I mean. Not now. I'm not ready to commit to anything right now."

"Jacquie, you know I care about you."

She looked down. "Armando, I—" Her words ended as he leaned across to kiss her nose.

"If you don't want to go to Hawaii, I understand. Maybe I don't need to go either. Maybe I will stay here in Toronto. Who knows, eh?"

She looked at him and sighed. "No, you should go with your friends. I don't want you to change because of me."

"Jacquie, what you said about not being ready to make a commitment. Do you mean that you aren't ready? Or do you mean you will not ever want to commit with me? Is there someone else?"

"Mostly the first. Not ready, period."

"Mostly? So there is someone else?"

She shook her head but didn't look at him. "No, not really. I just like to have things out in the open."

"Well, for now we are friends. Maybe a little more than friends." He frowned. "You know I have had relationships in the past that were more than that. I do not know about you."

"I've had a few relationships, but mostly I've been too busy with my job to get involved with anyone. And, since we're being honest, I guess I've never met anyone I cared about enough to want to make a commitment of any kind."

He sat back. "So, to have things in the open, we like each other, but neither of us is ready for what you called the 'old-fashioned way' with the ring and the church. So I think what we need to decide is whether that means we are both free to 'play the field,' as I have heard some say, or not."

Jacquie nodded. "I guess."

"So who is it you are wondering about?"

"I never said—" She saw the laughter in his eyes and sighed. "Okay, it's somebody I met on our case. A nurse. And it's nothing. He just— Well, he asked if I was in a relationship or if we could have coffee, and I wasn't sure how to answer him, and that reminded me about Hawaii and made me think we should talk."

"I see."

"It doesn't really matter. I barely even know him."

"No, no. It is all right. You are free to have coffee with him. As long as you go to dinner and a movie with me."

She laughed. "So you're not mad that I don't want to go to Hawaii? Or commit to more than friendship?"

Armando shrugged. "I am sad, of course. But I am not angry. However, you realize that if you are free to go for coffee with this nurse, I am free to go for coffee with someone I might meet."

She looked down. "I know."

He grinned. "Right now there is no one else I want to have coffee with."

She looked up and gave him a rueful smile.

He reached over to touch her cheek with the back of his hand. "You know, if we ever are to be in a committed relationship, I might have a problem with your job. You seem to meet too many interesting men on your cases."

TWENTY-TWO

Sunday morning Paul left the house while Loretta was still asleep. He felt guilty picking up coffee and a breakfast sandwich at a fast-food place, but he'd awakened early and, after lying awake for a while, decided that he'd be able to think better in his office. He needed to make sense of the convoluted mess this case had become.

There were so many rabbit trails. Nikola Vincent, for example. Chances were extremely unlikely that he had anything to do with either Violet's or Ingrid's death. And what about Sharlene Bryce? Was her suicide a red herring or a key clue?

The only thing he knew for sure was that Norm had lied, but about what he had no idea. Likely something personal that had nothing whatsoever to do with anything. Still, they needed to talk to him again.

But first Paul wanted to go over every single thing they knew one more time. And when Ryan got in, they'd go over it all again. And then—who knew?—maybe something would jump out at them.

Trish was up early, too. She'd offered to drive Jake to the airport. He'd said his goodbyes to everyone the night before and intended to take a taxi to the airport, but she'd insisted on driving him. Before they parted at the airport, he made her promise to bring her family to his home in British Columbia for a long visit.

Trish drove away from the airport, tears in her eyes as she realized that she wasn't an only child any more. She had a big brother, and he was everything she could have wanted.

All she had to do was go back to Serenity Suites and move her mother's bins and boxes into her van. Then she'd have lunch, say goodbye to her dad, and go home. She couldn't wait to see her husband and children. There was so much to tell them.

Manziuk and Ryan showed up at Serenity Suites at 10:00. They told Audra they were on the premises, then went to see Norm.

When Elizabeth let them into the condo, Norm was standing at the end of the hallway. His face turned white, and he began to tremble. "I told you everything I know yesterday."

"I'm sorry, Norm," Manziuk said, "but we thought you held a few things back."

"I don't know what you mean."

"Norm," Ryan said, "it means you're a lousy liar."

"You ought to treat your elders with more respect."

"Norm, yesterday you told us that you knew nothing about Sharlene's death."

"That's right." Norm's face was turning red.

"We can usually tell when someone's lying, Norm."

"They're right, Norm," Elizabeth said. "You don't lie very often, so you haven't had nearly enough practice. It's written all over your face. You might as well tell the truth."

Norm looked desperately around the room. His breathing grew faster.

"Would you prefer to talk to us without your wife present?" Ryan asked.

Norm looked at Elizabeth and shook his head.

"Take a couple of deep breaths," Manziuk said. "Let's sit down."

Norm looked down, took a deep breath, then another to calm himself. He took a seat in the living room, followed by the other three. Ryan spoke first. "Were you with Sharlene that night, Norm?"

He licked his lips a few times and nodded. "We were all together after classes ended. Violet had some family thing happening, and

Mary had a project she needed to finish for school, so they left. Frank and I left shortly after, but then Frank remembered something he wanted to ask Ben, so we went back." He turned his head to look toward a painting on the wall.

"It wasn't anything important. Just about going fishing the next morning. We followed the path they'd have taken to the bridge and found them a couple of blocks from it in a sort of park area. As we got close to them, we could tell they were arguing, and we heard a little bit about what they were saying. It was pretty clear they were talking about getting married and having a baby.

"They hadn't seen us, so we ducked behind some bushes. I tugged on Frank's shirt and motioned that we should leave, but he ignored me." Norm hung his head.

"We heard Ben say he was going to marry her and that everything would be fine. Then he must have looked at his watch because he said something about being late for his meeting with the debating team. Sharlene told him to go, so he kissed her and left.

"After a few minutes, Sharlene started walking toward the bridge. I wanted to leave, but Frank said, 'Come on. We need to help Ben out.' So I followed him."

Norm paused and wiped his palms on his pants. "You need to know that Sharlene didn't like heights. She hated walking across the bridge over the Don Valley. So Frank and I caught up with her and offered to walk across with her. We pretended we'd been looking for Ben and had just come up and seen her. But when we got halfway over the bridge, Frank told her we'd overheard their conversation and that she couldn't marry Ben. He said she'd have to get an abortion." Norm stopped. "I need something to drink."

Elizabeth went to the kitchen and came back with a glass of water.

Norm took a long drink. "Sharlene was horrified that we knew. Frank told her we'd help her get an abortion—that nobody else ever needed to know. Not even Ben. She said no, Ben wanted to marry her and he'd look after everything.

"I told Frank we should leave, that it was none of our business. Anyway I had chores to do for my dad, so I needed to get home. Frank said for me to go. That he'd see to it Sharlene got home. So I left." He looked from Ryan to Manziuk and back. "When I left, Sharlene was fine."

"So you went home?"

"Yes."

"The next morning when you found out Sharlene was dead, what did Frank say?"

"While Ben was talking to the police, I asked Frank what happened after I left the night before. He said Sharlene told him she really wanted to go to university, and she didn't want the baby, but Ben wanted to get married. Frank told her he'd help her get an abortion, and she said she'd do it. Then he walked the rest of the way across the bridge with her and left her on the other side. He figured that after he left, she must have realized what a mess she was in and gone back on the bridge and jumped. Frank and I both felt terrible. Honest! We felt we caused it by urging her to get the abortion."

"What did you and Frank tell the police?" Ryan said.

"They never talked to us."

"You could have gone to them and told them what happened."

"We were scared. We figured they might not believe us. And we knew Ben would be angry with us if he found out we'd talked to her after he left. So we never told anybody."

"You know, I believe I need some fresh air." Elizabeth picked up her purse and left the condo.

Mary was sitting in the guest suite with Trish, surrounded by stacked bins and luggage. Trish was holding to her decision to go home after lunch, no matter what. They were drinking tea and eating some muffins Scarlett had given Trish for her ride home.

Mary asked Trish in a roundabout way if she'd learned anything over the last few days.

Trish sighed. "Mary, I don't think I knew my parents at all."

"I wonder how much anyone knows their parents? I mean, you can never really know what they're like when they're young, or what they were like growing up. Although I guess some people don't change much over the years."

"Mom was fifty when I was ten, sixty when I was twenty. Not exactly girlfriend material. I used to envy my friends whose mothers were younger and fun to be with."

"In some ways, your mother was never young. You met your grandparents, didn't you?"

"Yes, but when I was ten they were in their mid-seventies. However, I know what you mean. I can't remember a time when they weren't complaining about something. Like they'd been cheated somehow. I'm not sure how to explain it."

"No need to explain it to me. I knew them, and they were always like that. Especially your grandfather. He seemed to think he'd been given the short end of the stick and the universe owed him something. And he took it out on the people around him, especially his wife and children."

"Not a happy family to grow up in."

"They provided the basics but nothing more. Your mother had to fight to get a party dress, to go on dates, to go to university. Every inch. And then she married Frank Klassen, a man who, as I look back now, is a lot like her father. A man who wanted to be the centre of his own little universe. And your mother, for the most part, went along with him."

"Mary, it seems as if my mother led two different lives. Outwardly she was a dutiful wife and mother and amateur writer of nice little cookbooks. But in her other life she was a bestselling author and a savvy businesswoman and investor. It's so strange for me to think of her that way. She hid it so well."

Mary stared at Trish. "What do you mean she was a bestselling author and a business woman? Violet had her cookbooks, but they were just a hobby."

"Promise me you won't say anything to my dad?"

"I promise. Over the years there are a lot of things I've never felt the need to tell Frank." She grinned. "And a few things I've refrained from telling him only because I knew it would hurt your mother."

"Mary, Mom's cookbooks make more money than Dad's books. And it looks as if Mom made even more money through investments."

"Are you sure?"

"Her accountant showed me the spreadsheets."

"I can't believe it."

"Mary, you never knew she'd had a baby when she was young, did you?"

"No."

"She knew how to keep secrets."

Mary looked at the floor. "I never kept secrets from her. Never thought she kept any from me."

"Mary, how close was Mom with Sharlene?"

"Very. Her mother was their housekeeper, and she brought Sharlene and Billy with her. So in a sense they were raised together."

"Billy?"

"Sharlene's younger brother." Mary put her hand to her cheek. "Oh, my! I haven't thought of him in so many years. He was the sweetest little boy. Always smiling."

"I wonder if he's still alive?"

"He likely grew up hating all of us. If not for Sharlene's friendship with us, she might still be alive."

"What else do you remember about Sharlene?"

"Let me think. She was the second youngest in her family. There were three or four older kids. I didn't know them that much. Billy was two or three years younger than Sharlene." She sighed. "Let me think. Sharlene's mama went to work for Violet's family when Violet was three or four years old. Her older kids were in school and after classes went to their apartment. The oldest would have been about twelve or so—old enough to look after the others. But Sharlene's mom kept the younger kids with her, and Sharlene and Violet often played together. Billy would have been one or two when I first met him.

"When Sharlene started school, she went to her own home after class on some days, but she also came to Violet's house or mine a couple of days a week. Mostly my house.

"We never went to Sharlene's house because that just wasn't done in those days. It was all right for Sharlene to come to our house, but our parents and hers, too, would have had a fit if we'd gone to her house."

"That's just so terribly sad."

"It was a different time. Funny how when you look back it's so easy to see how wrong some things were."

"That doesn't stop us from making similar mistakes in the present."

"I know." She paused a few moments in thought. "Anyway, until he started school, Mrs. Bryce had Billy with her. So we'd play with him when we were at Violet's house. And even after he started school, we'd sometimes include him. Neither Violet nor I had a younger sibling, so we all sort of treated him like a younger brother. And he never took advantage of that. He was a happy little kid but serious, always with his nose in a book." Mary shook her head. "I'd forgotten all about him. I guess when Sharlene died the way she did, I just blocked everything about her out of my mind."

"I wonder if Billy is still alive. If the police are asking questions about Sharlene, I'd think they'd want to talk to Billy or other members of her family."

"Do you think we can find him? Maybe on the Internet?"

"We can try." Trish went to her computer. "So I should look for Billy Bryce?"

"He might not have used Billy as an adult. Maybe Bill. I suppose his full name might have been William."

A few minutes later, Trish called Mary over to look at the screen. "Could this be him? The age seems right. But…?"

"Should we call the Inspector?"

At that moment the intercom buzzed, and Ryan's voice asked if they could come in.

Trish rushed to the door. "I was just going to phone you!"

Mary was standing behind Trish in the hallway. "We've got something to tell you. We might have found Sharlene's brother."

"Really?" Manziuk said. "We've started looking for her family, but I don't believe we've found them yet. How did you find him?"

"I just googled his name," Trish said. "We aren't a hundred percent sure it's him but maybe ninety-nine percent."

They spent several minutes looking at the photo and information on the man Trish and Mary had found.

"What do you think?" Mary asked. "I'm pretty sure that's Billy. Everything fits."

"We'll know soon enough." Manziuk went into the hall to phone Ford.

"You didn't come here because of Billy," Trish said to Ryan. "Why did you come?"

Ryan glanced toward the hall. "We actually came here to talk to someone else, but as we were leaving we got a call from the coroner with some new information. We need to talk to you about it."

"About Mom?"

Ryan nodded. "You might want to sit down."

Trish was about to say that wasn't necessary when she realized she was trembling. She sank down on the nearest chair.

"Should I leave?" Mary asked.

"Stay," Trish said.

Mary sat down on a loveseat, Ryan beside her.

Manziuk came back in and sat down on a chair across from Trish. "Trish, according to Dr. Weaver, the tests on your mother show a high level of insulin and a low level of C-peptide, which apparently are indications of an insulin overdose. It was likely administered in three doses between the fingers of her left hand. She had also taken or been given a common sedative, so she was likely in a deep sleep when the insulin was injected."

Tears trickled down Trish's cheeks. "Poor Mom. She didn't deserve that."

"We'll be treating your mother's death as a homicide."

"I—I guess I can't go home yet then?"

"Not right away. In addition to following up on how your mother was injected with insulin, I've scheduled a meeting for 2:00 this afternoon in Ben Davidson's condo, and I'd appreciate it if you could be there. It's about your mother's investments."

"Can I ask my husband to come here? He won't likely arrive in time, but I think I need him here."

"Of course."

At 2:00 that afternoon, Ben and Bruce Davidson, Trish, and Manziuk and Ryan were all seated around Ben's dining room table.

Manziuk spoke first. "Before we begin, I have to tell you that we're now treating Violet Klassen's death as a homicide."

Bruce's mouth dropped open.

Ben said simply, "How was it done?"

"She was injected with insulin, likely after being sedated."

"Insulin?"

"You exhumed the body?" Bruce asked.

"Yes."

Bruce glanced at Trish. "Who authorized it?"

"I did."

"Does your dad know?"

"Not yet."

Ben took a deep breath. "I must be missing something. Yesterday you asked me about Sharlene. Now you tell me Violet was murdered. I thought I was too old to be shocked, but this is beyond anything I've ever experienced." He leaned back in his chair and looked at Manziuk. "I assume the person who murdered Violet also murdered Ingrid?"

"That's our assumption unless proven otherwise."

"But what does Sharlene's death have to do with it?"

"Maybe nothing. We're just following up on every lead that's come up. At this point we don't have any new evidence to show that Sharlene didn't commit suicide as was determined at the time."

"I see. All right, let's get this meeting out of the way so you can focus on finding out who murdered my wife and my good friend."

Manziuk cleared his throat. "We've just discovered that the three of you own Serenity Suites."

Trish gasped. "What do you mean the three of us own Serenity Suites? Her accountant only said Mom had money invested in it."

Ben reached over to touch Trish's arm. "I'm so sorry. I had no idea until Inspector Manziuk spoke to me earlier this morning that your mother hadn't told you."

Bruce shifted uncomfortably in his seat. "We honestly had no reason to think our ownership of Serenity Suites had anything at all to do with Mom's death. As I said when we talked before, no one benefited financially. All of the information I gave you before included Serenity Suites as one of our holdings—I just didn't call it by name. Obviously we should have mentioned it earlier, but we were afraid it would be more of a red herring than anything."

"So," Manziuk said, "the Davidsons and the Klassens built Serenity Suites. But you didn't tell anyone?"

"That's correct," Bruce said. "We hid it because Dad and Mom and Frank and Violet were living here, and they didn't want the other residents or staff to know they were the owners."

"We wanted this to be our home," his father elaborated. "And the last thing we needed was for the other residents and the staff to treat us differently. Or, worse, to come to us with any problems or issues that arose."

"Yes, that makes perfect sense," Manziuk said. "So you're certain that none of the residents or staff, including Ms. Arlington, is aware of who the owners actually are?"

"Positive," Bruce said. Ben nodded.

"Unless I hear otherwise, I'll assume you're correct." Manziuk looked at Ben. "I'm curious. How did Serenity Suites begin?"

Ben cleared his throat. "About ten years ago Ingrid and I were out for dinner with Frank and Violet. I think it was Frank who mentioned an older man we all knew who'd moved into an expensive retirement home for seniors and hated it. His long list of complaints included the small spartan apartment that could hold only a few of his prized personal possessions; the fact that he had nothing in common with most of the other people in the residence, all of whom were strangers; and, his biggest complaint, the disturbing discovery that only a few of the other residents could even hold a normal conversation, never mind a stimulating one. We all agreed it might be a good idea to plan our old age before something happened and other people planned it for us.

"At the time we both owned large homes in the Bridle Path neighbourhood, and none of us had any interest in downsizing. However, we agreed that none of us wanted to settle for an existence like our friend's. Before we knew it, we were idly planning our ideal retirement residence. Just in fun, you know?

"About a year later I happened to hear about a prime piece of land that had just gone on the market in downtown Toronto. I don't even know why I did it, but I phoned Frank and said something like 'Should we go for it?' He said it seemed like a good idea to him. So we talked to our wives, and they agreed.

"Ingrid basically just told me to do whatever I thought was good. Violet was much more involved. She wanted costs and a plan of some sort before we did anything. So Bruce and I scrambled to talk to people who knew how to develop a project like this. When Violet was satisfied, we bought the land, formed a numbered corporation so no one knew who the owners were, and met with architects. When it was ready for people to move in, we established a Residents Board, which more or less runs the day-to-day operations.

"Either Frank or I have usually been on the Residents Board. Right now it's Frank."

"Our family already had a company Dad had started for producing shows and looking after a few other holdings," Bruce continued. "Dad was president until he was seventy-five, when he stepped down and I was elected company president. We all have shares in that company, so our half of any money made through Serenity Suites belongs to the whole family. Violet was our partner only in Serenity Suites, not in our other businesses."

"What do you mean *Mom* was your partner?" Trish asked. "What about Dad?"

Manziuk said, "Frank is a partner in name only. Is that true?"

Bruce looked at Ben. "Well, yes."

"Frank has always assumed *he* was the partner and that Violet did what he told her," Ben said. "But he had no more interest in the details than Ingrid did, and Violet was more than happy for him to go on thinking whatever he wanted. We went along with her wishes."

"So, as Violet's sole heir, Trish now owns Violet's share of Serenity Suites?"

"Yes."

"And Frank has no share in it?"

"Violet made it very clear to me that the money she used was her own, not Frank's. But that he wasn't to know that."

"Who is on the board of the corporation?" Manziuk asked.

Ben said. "Me, my children, Frank, and the lawyer who acts as our intermediary. Violet acted more as a secretary than anything. The board meets four times a year. We hire an administrator to look after the day-to-day operations, including hiring staff and looking after residents' moving in and out. That person is ultimately responsible to the corporation but also to a board made up of elected residents.

"Unfortunately, we let our previous administrator hire his replacement, Ms. Arlington, and we have some thoughts of making a change there."

"We're definitely making a change there," Bruce added.

"I should perhaps mention that Frank is very angry with me right now. He asked to meet with me yesterday morning before breakfast and was adamant that I have Hilary Brooks evicted from her condo. I told him in no uncertain terms that I wasn't doing anything of the sort and that she's welcome to stay as long as she wishes. I had no idea until Friday when I spoke with Mary and Catarina that the Residents Board under Frank's goading had been trying to force Hilary out. I've already had the lawyer Ms. Arlington reports to inform her that Hilary is staying."

Ryan said, "Do you know why Frank wanted her evicted?"

Ben shook his head. "He went on and on about how she isn't qualified to be here. I finally told him that, qualified or not, this is her home for as long as she wants to be here. He was livid. I finally had to ask him to leave before I called Derrick to come and throw him out. You can imagine how angry that made him."

"Why do you *think* he wants her evicted?"

"Frank is pretty much a letter-of-the-law kind of guy. I believe that in his mind she doesn't qualify. And maybe she doesn't. I don't know, but I don't care. She lost her husband with no warning at all just a few months ago. I have no intention of inflicting more hardship on her."

"Do you think her being black was part of it?"

Ben looked at her. "I suppose it's possible but I've never known Frank to be racist. I think it's more that he felt she didn't qualify. And quite possibly that he didn't like her on a personal basis. To be honest, there are a number of people on our floor Frank doesn't like—Catarina, Lyle, Elizabeth, probably more— but he can't evict any of them because they clearly qualify."

"All right," Manziuk said. "Thank you for being candid." He looked around the table. "My concern is to look at everything from the standpoint of whether or not any of this provides a motive for Ingrid's and Violet's deaths. Our first question is always 'Does anyone gain from this death?'"

Bruce said, "As I've said before, no. Dad, Mom, and each of their children have full shares, and each grandchild or great-grandchild has a half-share. We all receive an annual sum from the business if it's successful, which it has always been. The money for those who are under age goes into trust funds managed by their parents. With Mom's death, her share goes into the pot, and each person will get a little more. But none of us is in need. Not only Serenity Suites, but our other businesses as well, are all quite successful."

"Which leaves me," Trish said. "And I'm floored. I honestly had no idea that they owned Serenity Suites, never mind that Mom had left it to me. I can't prove it, but I'm telling the truth."

Bruce turned to her. "Is your family in financial need, Trish?"

"No, my husband and I both have good jobs. If we needed money, we'd only have to ask either my parents or my husband's. You're free to check our bank accounts." She looked down at the table. "I wasn't going to mention this but perhaps I should. After talking to the accountant, I've already begun the process of giving Jake an equal share in everything Mom left me." She smiled. "I know you're all thinking this gives him a motive or he came here hoping to get money. Neither is the case. He never asked me for a dime or hinted in any way that he needed money. But when we were talking—and we talked about a lot in a very short time—he happened to mention a medical clinic he's involved with. After I got back here, I did some checking and found the website. He and some other doctors have started a clinic in a third-world country where babies and young children have a high mortality rate. The only thing keeping them from expanding to other neighbouring countries is the need to raise more money. So I'm going to create a trust fund to give them money. I know without a doubt that Mom would want me to do that."

Bruce said, "Inspector, I think you can assume no one had a financial reason to murder either my mother or Violet. I can also assure you no one in my family, especially Dad, would have stabbed Mom in some misguided attempt at a mercy killing. And none of us had any reason to harm Violet. She was like an aunt. Which leaves what exactly?"

Ryan said, "I have another question. Everyone has said that Ingrid would have had to leave Serenity Suites because the rules don't allow people here who need full-time care. If you own the building, why not change the rules so that Ingrid would have been able to stay?"

Bruce said, "Frank and I both said the same thing." He motioned toward Ben. "But Dad refused, and Violet agreed with him."

Ben said, "We created it the way it is for a reason. I wasn't going to change it just to benefit myself. Violet actually suggested making one floor into a nursing home, and I believe that's being considered for the future. Or buying a building near here and remodelling it.

But it wouldn't have been possible to do either of those things soon enough for Ingrid."

"So Ingrid would have had to be moved out of here and into a nursing home?"

Bruce shook his head. "No, our plan was for Mom and Dad to move into my sister Shelley's house and to hire a couple of caregivers, so someone was always there to help."

"Your sister was fine with that?"

"It wasn't ideal but yes, Shelley and her husband were fine with it. And if that didn't work out or if Shell needed a break, there are five of us kids and a bunch of grandkids, and one of us would have taken them in." He smiled. "I realize you never met Mom and from what you've heard about her you'll probably have trouble understanding this, but she was an amazing person, and we all adored her." He glanced at Ben. "Dad, too. We owe them so much, and we can afford to get the help needed to take care of them."

Trish spoke. "I don't understand how this is helping us figure out who killed Ingrid or my mom. I don't believe that Ben did it, and I know I didn't. I wasn't even anywhere near here when Mom died." She frowned at Manziuk. "The problem is there doesn't seem to *be* a motive. So what are you going to do? You can't let this go unsolved."

"We won't," Manziuk said with an assurance he had no rational reason for feeling. "We're going to get to the bottom of this, no matter how long it takes. And no matter who is involved."

Twenty-Three

Frank looked up as Manziuk and Ryan walked into his office, followed by Trish. "I'm in the middle of a crucial scene and can't be bothered talking to you. You're never going to solve this anyway, so stop pretending you are."

"Mr. Klassen," Manziuk said, "we thought you should know that we've exhumed your wife's body and found evidence that she was injected with a massive dose of insulin before her death. Enough to kill her."

Frank's jaw dropped. "You what? I never gave my permission!"

"The coroner decided an autopsy was warranted. He had permission from the executor of your wife's will."

"It's all nonsense. Violet died of natural causes. Dr. Granger said so. So did the coroner."

"Once he had more information, the coroner changed his mind."

"I don't understand. Insulin?" Frank looked lost and confused. "Where did she get insulin?"

"It's very doubtful that your wife injected herself."

Trish went up to him. "Dad, I'm so sorry."

Frank was breathing hard. "You're saying someone murdered Violet? The same person who killed Ingrid?"

"That's what we suspect."

"But who would do that? Two defenseless women. I don't understand." His breathing was getting faster. "It's not possible." Tears began to flow down Frank's cheeks.

"Dad, why don't we go back to your condo and call Dr. Granger?"

Frank looked at his computer monitor. "I can't do this any more. Save it for me, please. And help me get on my scooter. I need to be alone. I need to think this through."

"Mr. Klassen," Manziuk said, "before you go, I have another question for you."

Trish frowned. "Inspector, does it have to be now?"

"I'm afraid I need to know. Mr. Klassen, Norm Carlysle says that you and he were with Sharlene Bryce on the day she died, after Ben left her to walk home alone across the bridge. Is that correct?"

"Norm said that?"

"Yes."

"We didn't hurt her."

"Norm says you tried to convince her to get an abortion."

"So what? It was the right thing to do."

"Ben was prepared to marry her."

"Ben!" Frank snorted. "Damn fool. He was an easy mark, even in those days. He'd had a bit of fun with the girl, but there was no need to marry her. It would have ruined his life. I wanted her to understand what it would be like. That's all. Told her I'd help her get an abortion or get the baby adopted if she preferred. She said she'd get an abortion if I'd help her. I made an appointment to meet her the next day. I left her and went home. I don't know why she jumped."

"Why didn't you tell the police you'd been with her?"

His voice rose in anger. "I might have if they'd asked me. I don't think they even talked to Ben beyond having him identify her, and that was only because he badgered them." He took another deep breath. "There was no point in rocking the boat. She jumped, just like they said. That's all that mattered."

"Don't you feel any regret?" Ryan said. "It was likely your badgering her to get an abortion that made her jump!"

"That's not true! She didn't want to have the baby. She wanted to go to university. She was happy that I'd offered to help her."

"And you knew how she could get an abortion?"

"As a matter of fact I did, Miss Smarty-Pants. A friend of mine went with his girlfriend when she got one a few months before. I knew I could get the name and address from him." Frank thrust out his lower lip. "I was trying to help both Sharlene and Ben. Neither of them wanted that baby. Sure, Ben was ready to do the honourable thing and sacrifice himself, but it would have destroyed both of their lives. Sharlene was going to get the abortion and then tell him she'd had a miscarriage.

"We had it all worked out. I don't know what happened after I left her. I've always assumed she talked to someone in her family after she got home, and they said something that made her jump. But I didn't tell the police. What good would it have done?" Frank was trembling.

"Inspector, Dad needs to lie down."

"All right." Manziuk looked at Frank. "I hope you've told us everything."

"I have no reason to lie."

Trish helped Frank move from his chair to his scooter. As he went past Manziuk, he looked him in the eye. "You find out who did that to my wife, Inspector. Or I'll see that you never work in this city again."

Manziuk and Ryan went to the office they'd used for their interviews. Ryan began to laugh. "I'm sorry, but where on earth did he get that last bit? Sounded like something straight out of a forties movie."

Manziuk just shook his head and sat down.

After a few minutes, Ryan looked over. "What are you doing?"

"Thinking."

"This case is getting crazier and crazier."

"So crazy that it's maybe going to soon start making sense." He stood up. "What else do we need to do while we're still here?"

"We haven't talked to Nikola yet."

"Right." Manziuk nodded. "Okay, let's see if he's around."

"Wait a minute. It's just about 3:00. They'll be having tea now."

"Okay, we'll wait until after that. Assuming he's here."

"I wonder what Scarlett made for tea today?"

Trish had Olive bring tea for her and Frank to his condo. The other residents and the staff were gathered for theirs in the dining room when Manziuk and Ryan came in and informed them that Violet's death was now being treated as a homicide but gave no further details. There was a buzz of conversation followed by several people wondering aloud if they should leave the next day, if not sooner.

As Nikola stood up to leave, Ryan quietly approached and asked him to come to their office. He said a few words to Catarina, then strode into the office and settled easily into the empty chair. "I understand you wish to speak with me?"

"That's right, Mr. Vincent," Manziuk said. "We have a few more questions."

"Nikola is fine. How can I help you?"

"Really?" Ryan raised her eyebrows.

Nikola looked at her in surprise.

"*Nikola*, is it?" Ryan tilted her head to one side and batted her eyes. "I thought it was usually Gabriel?"

His serious expression dissolved into a smile. "So you've scoped me out, have you?"

Manziuk said, "You admit your name is actually Gabriel Alessandro Nikola Vincent Romano-Rossi?"

"I do. But my family and friends shorten it to Gabri."

"And I also assume, since Mrs. Rossi is your stepmother, that you aren't her husband?"

He laughed. "Cat has been so kind as to let me hide here. Since we couldn't explain who I was without running the risk of drawing media attention, and because only a spouse is allowed to remain longer than a week or so, she thought of the fake marriage. Cat had decided she would enjoy my company. Actually I was surprised by her willingness to have me. I now believe it's because she's been used to living a much faster-paced life than she's lived here in the last while and she was somewhat bored. Having me here provided a diversion." His eyes twinkled. "Although recently she's begun complaining that I leave my guitars and other equipment all over the place, so the writing is on the wall for my departure."

"And you're in hiding because…?"

Gabri shrugged. "I had a need to get away from everyone and everything so that I could consider my life. Is it all I want it to be? Is there something I'm missing? And also to write some new music. I could think of nowhere else that I could go about freely without the need of bodyguards and other staff to protect my solitude. Of course, with them around me, I wouldn't be alone.

"I happened to mention my desire to Catarina, and she said, 'Why would the paparazzi think of looking for you in Canada, and in a place like Serenity Suites?' And so it has proved. I've been left completely alone here. This, alas, doesn't entirely please her. There was a time her marrying someone—anyone—would have been front-page news. When she said it wouldn't draw attention any more, I'm sure she was secretly hoping she was wrong."

Ryan crossed her arms and gave him a stern look. "Do you have anything more to tell us about Ingrid's murder? Anything you felt disinclined to mention because of your masquerade?"

He shook his head. "I'd never have hidden something from you because of our, as you say, masquerade. And I regret any expense you've had following up on me. I'll see that the police fund gets a donation. One question—is it possible to keep my identity a secret for a little longer? I'd hate for the paparazzi to descend on Serenity Suites right now. Or ever." He raised his eyebrows.

Ryan looked over at Manziuk, who replied. "If your identity has nothing to do with our investigation, I see no reason for us to tell anyone. But I advise you to let everyone know before you leave rather than have them find out after you're gone."

"Yes, that was always the plan. I have commitments beginning in September, so I can't be here much longer." He grinned. "Hilary has suggested I owe them a concert."

Manziuk frowned. "I thought you said no one else knows."

"I've told no one. However, she informed us yesterday that she recognized me when I first arrived. Apparently she's a big fan."

He got up and started toward the door, then paused. "Actually there's one small thing I happened to remember earlier today. I'm sure it's meaningless, but one day last week I saw Mr. Klassen walking from his office past this one to the bathroom next door."

There was a short silence. "Walking?" Manziuk echoed.

Ryan said, "Are you sure it was him?"

"Well, when I say walking, I may be exaggerating. He was moving slowly and holding onto the wall. I was a bit surprised because I thought he could only take a step or two without assistance, just on and off the scooter, but he was on his own. Of course he didn't have far to go, and I'm certain it means nothing. But I thought perhaps I should mention it."

Ryan found Derrick in the exercise room. "Don't you get time off?"

"Actually I was out for church this morning. Normally I'd be at my parents' house today visiting with family, but with the murder and all, Audra and I have both been sticking pretty close."

"Yeah, I guess it's pretty unsettling for everyone."

"That's an understatement." He cocked his head on one side. "Can I help with something?"

"I need to know how far Frank can walk."

Derrick frowned. "Well, he can certainly get off the scooter to move to his chair, his bed, the toilet, and so forth, but he hasn't been doing much walking lately."

"So if someone saw him going a few steps from his office to the bathroom two doors down, would that be unexpected?"

"*Did* someone see him?"

"Apparently," Ryan said.

"It's certainly possible. It's a pretty short distance. And some days he's in less pain than other days."

"What's his problem again?"

"Frank has osteoarthritis. It affects both his hip joints and his knees. Basically he's spent years sitting at a typewriter or computer and doing very little exercise, and his joints have suffered. It hurts him to walk, and if he fell he could easily break a bone because they're fairly brittle."

"What does he do for it?"

"A special diet. Some meds. I do massage and physio with him regularly. Usually in the mornings and evenings. I have him doing some easy Pilates and yoga. I get him in the pool twice a week. And I do get him to walk a bit, but with a railing on either side to hold onto. He also has painkillers if he needs them, and he's had several cortisone shots."

"So it's not that he can't walk; but it's painful."

Derrick frowned. "That, and he hasn't got a lot of strength. I doubt that he could walk very far."

"How long has he been using the scooter?"

"I can check if you like, but I believe it was delivered near the beginning of June. So roughly two and a half months. But why are you asking this?"

"We'd assumed he couldn't walk at all, so we thought we needed to check."

Audra sat at her desk wondering what would happen if they didn't discover the murderer quickly.

There was a knock on the partly open door. Hesitantly she said, "Come in."

Nikola entered the room. "Do you have a minute?"

"Yes, but I'm working."

"I know, but this can't wait. The police already know, as does Hilary, and I don't want anyone except me to tell you."

Audra frowned. *Has he come to confess? Surely the police wouldn't let him walk around free if he— What am I thinking? Of course he isn't the murderer. I couldn't feel this way about a murderer!*

Nikola came around her desk and leaned against the corner next to her. "Probably best if I start at the beginning. Have you ever heard of a man named Gabriel Romano-Rossi?"

Audra pushed her chair back a little, away from him, and shook her head. "No, I don't think so." She frowned. "Rossi is Catarina's last name."

"Right. Gabriel Romano-Rossi—whose full name is Gabriel Alessandro Nikola Vincent Romano-Rossi—is a musician. A guitar player and composer who performs all over the world."

"I—I don't understand." Her eyes narrowed. "Wait a minute. Are you saying *you're* this Gabriel person?"

He smiled. "See, you *do* understand. That's exactly what I'm saying. And further, the most important thing for you to know is that Catarina is my stepmother and not my wife. I was married a long time ago, for six happy years, but one day a drunk driver lost control and ended up killing three people and injuring four more. My wife was one of the ones who died. And the baby inside her died, too."

She put her hand out. "I'm so sorry."

As his fingers grasped hers, he said, "My life is very busy, and there are always people around me. I wanted to just disappear but, even if I were to find an island and bring only my own staff, I'd still be surrounded by people who see their only role in life as looking after me. And that can get very tiring. Some months ago I happened to mention this to Catarina. And then one day she proposed that I come here. But to truly come in disguise so that not one single person in the world knew where I was, I would not only need to wear a wig and grow a beard and dress in clothes I'd never normally wear, but we'd need to pretend to the people who lived here that we were married. And so I came, and it worked amazingly. No one found me."

Audra realized he was holding her hand and quickly withdrew it. "I see. At least I think I do. And I see why you wouldn't tell anyone. Even if you'd told me or Derrick or Naomi, you couldn't rely on our not mentioning it, even by accident." She thought for a moment. "Are you really so well-known? Why don't I know your name?"

He shrugged. "I play classical guitar. Not everyone is into that kind of music. But that isn't necessarily why you might know of me. You see, my father, Eduardo Rossi, owned property all over the world as well as several businesses. And I inherited most of it. So I'm what you might call very well-to-do."

"You mean rich?"

"*Very* rich."

"Oh."

"Does that bother you?"

"Why should it matter what I think?"

"I want to know. Does it bother you that I'm rich?"

"Why should it?" She shrugged. "Better to be rich than poor."

"I agree. And it also means we can hire the very best lawyers out there so that you can get custody of Gavin and Graham."

Audra shook her head. "I don't know what you're talking about."

"Audra, when I said I needed to get away to think, it was because I'd realized that my life had become meaningless. But being here has helped me so much more than I ever expected."

He stood and walked to the other side of the room, then back. He leaned forward, placing his hands on her desk and looked directly into her eyes. "After my wife died, it hurt so much that I decided I'd never let myself care that much about another person again. And for all those years, I didn't. So there was no more pain, but also there was no joy. With you there is joy, and if there's also more pain, then I'll deal with it. I no longer want to live without pain if it means living without love."

"But—you barely know me."

"I know you well enough to know that I can't leave here without a promise from you that we'll get to know each other a lot better. And that one day soon you'll consider becoming my wife."

Tears began flowing from Audra's eyes. "This—it's too much. I never dreamed—I thought you married Catarina for her money and you were trying to have me on the side. I wanted to hate you."

"But do you hate me?"

She whispered, "No. I've been so angry with myself. I ought to have hated you."

He laughed. "I tried very hard to make you *not* hate me."

"You don't know how hard it was." She looked down. "On the day Ingrid died I decided to resign from this job."

"Because of me?"

"Yes. I found it so hard to see you every day. And I was so angry with you for continuing to make a point of talking to me."

"Because you didn't want to talk to me?"

"Because you were Catarina's husband!"

"Ah, that was a crazy idea."

"No. If you hadn't done it, I'd never have met you. Nikola—no, that's not right. What should I call you?"

"My close friends call me Gabri. But Nikola is one of my names. Either is fine."

"Gabri?"

His eyes were laughing. "And may I call you Audra instead of Ms. Limson?"

"You know I'm Filipina?"

"Really? I hadn't noticed. I suppose your sons are, too."

"Mostly. Their father is part French."

"I'm mostly Italian. Is that a problem for you?" He held up his hands. "I promise I have no genes from Catarina. Not a one. She's only my stepmother."

"I love Catarina."

He laughed. “So do I, but you have to admit she can be a handful.”

“I—I don’t know what to say.”

“A simple ‘yes’ will be enough.”

“But my boys—”

“I love the idea of having a family.”

She looked down. “I was trying so hard not to even like you.”

“But…?”

“But I was failing so badly.”

“Then we’ll start fresh and get to know one another, with no secrets?”

She took a deep breath before raising her head to look at him. “Oh, yes!”

He smiled down at her. “Now we need to go and inform Cat. As you might expect, she wants to know immediately that you’re not mad at me.”

“I wish I knew where we were,” Ryan said on their way to the parking garage of Serenity Suites. “There are way too many options.”

Using his fingers, Manziuk said, “Are Violet’s and Ingrid’s deaths related? Did one cause the other? What, if anything, does Sharlene’s death have to do with the other women’s deaths? Did she commit suicide, or was she murdered?”

“And are we looking for one murderer, or two, or even three?”

“It’s hard to know which way to look at it. Do we start from Ingrid and work back, or from Sharlene and work forward? It’s like one of those abstract paintings that you have no idea which way is up.”

Ryan stopped cold. “The autopsy pictures!”

“What?”

“Your talking about paintings reminded me of the pictures of Sharlene. They’re like abstracts in a way. It’s hard to know what to look for with all the bruising and everything. But what if we were able to enhance them? Do you think there could be marks on her body that would show if she was pushed?”

“We need to find out. You drive, and I’ll call Ford and have him scan them and send them to Dr. Weaver. If anyone can find something useful in those pictures, it’s him.”

Ryan shut her car door. "Better let Dr. Weaver know they're coming."

"Wait a minute. Let's just grab some dinner at a restaurant near here and listen to the interview with Norm again. There was something I noticed that puzzled me, but I couldn't put my finger on it. I just realized what it was."

Elizabeth opened the door. "What do you want now?"

Ryan said, "I'm afraid we have some more questions for Norm."

"He's painting and doesn't like to be disturbed."

"This will only take a few minutes."

Elizabeth continued to stand in the doorway.

At the far end of the hallway, a door opened. "What is it Liz?"

She sighed and stepped back to allow Manziuk and Ryan enter. "The police want to talk to you yet again. You're becoming popular."

Norm came toward them. "Why are you here? I've already told you everything I know."

"We have a few additional questions."

Norm's face fell. "You'd better come into the sitting room."

When they were seated, Ryan asked, "Norm, when you told us about Sharlene and the bridge, you said that when you left Sharlene was alive and she was fine."

Norm nodded.

Ryan leaned forward. "Norm, we went over the last interview. You were very careful to say that she was fine when you left. And you told us what Frank said to you the next day. But we're wondering if you know more about what happened after you left the bridge. Did you see or hear something?"

The guilty look on his face gave her his answer.

Manziuk said, "Did you see something else, or did someone tell you what happened?"

Norm looked away, his eyes filled with tears. Elizabeth stared at him as if she'd never seen before. He walked over to the sitting room window, turned, and said in a gravelly voice, "When I left, they were in the middle of the bridge."

"What happened next?"

"When I was near the end of the bridge, I heard a sound that could have been a bird or maybe a cry. I turned and looked back, and I saw her—I saw her fly over the railing."

"Where was Frank, Norm?"

"He was standing there, and then he leaned over the railing to look down." Norm brought his hands up to cover his face and began sobbing uncontrollably.

Ryan grabbed a box of tissues and took several of them over to him.

"Norm," Manziuk said, "Frank threw her over the railing, didn't he?"

"No! He tried to stop her from jumping."

"Does Frank know you saw him?"

His voice was little more than a whisper. "Yes, I talked to him the next morning. While Ben was talking to the police. I told Frank I'd seen Sharlene fall, and he said he'd tried to stop her, but she'd been too quick for him. I wanted to tell the police, but he said if we told anyone we'd been there, we'd all be accused of murdering her. So we decided to just say we'd walked her to end of the bridge and left, and that she'd been fine when we last saw her. And everyone believed us." Norm bowed his head.

Elizabeth shook her head. "You're an even bigger fool that I thought you were."

"Will—will I go to jail?" Norm whispered. "I don't mind, you know. I deserve to go to jail. Anything rather than face Ben."

"Norm," Ryan said, "let me get this straight. Frank told you that Sharlene jumped and he tried to stop her?"

"Yes."

"Do you still believe that Frank tried to stop her?'

He nodded. "Of course I do."

"After you saw Frank standing alone on the bridge, what did you do?"

"I went down under the bridge and hid behind some trees."

"Why?"

"I didn't want Frank to see me."

"Why not? Were you afraid of him?"

"I felt sick. I didn't want to have to talk to anyone."

"And did Frank see you?"

"No."

"What happened next?"

"I waited for a long time to make sure he was gone. I couldn't—I didn't want to have to talk to anyone just then."

"What did you do after he was gone?"

"I—I decided I needed to make sure—make sure she was dead. If she was alive, I'd have gone for help."

"So you went down?"

"Yes. It wasn't hard. The first part was just going downhill, and then it was mostly walking on leaves and dead branches and grass. Mary was always reading mysteries, even back then, and so I knew to stay on the grass as much as possible so as not to leave footprints. It was muddy in some places so I had to be careful."

"What time would this have been?"

"Somewhere around eight o'clock."

"And how dark was it?"

"It was starting to be twilight, and there were shadows in the valley, but it was still pretty light."

"Were there other people on the bridge?"

He shook his head. "I didn't see anyone. And they'd have had to be looking over the railing to see me."

"So you went right to the body?"

"Yes."

"Did you touch her?"

"No."

"What did you do?"

"I stopped about six feet away. There was no point going further. She was on her back, with her head at a funny angle and her eyes open, and I knew she was dead. I had nightmares for years after that. I should have realized she'd never have survived the fall." Norm was trembling.

Elizabeth offered to make tea or coffee. Both Manziuk and Ryan accepted.

After they'd had tea, and the colour had come back into Norm's face, Manziuk took over the questioning. "Norm, what did you do after you realized Sharlene was dead?"

Norm picked at a thread on the arm of the chesterfield. "I started to get worried that somebody might see me so I decided to get out of there. I went out the same way I'd come in." He paused and looked away for a second.

"Was there something else?"

"I just remembered. When I turned to go back out of the valley, I saw something on the grass a couple of feet from me. I went over to check it out. It was Sharlene's necklace. One Ben had given her. She'd had it on that night. It must have broken as she fell."

"How close was the necklace to Sharlene?"

"It was about, oh, maybe eight or ten feet from the body, I'd think. Further from the bridge. Like she fell straight down and the necklace fell more in an arc."

"What did you do when you saw it?"

"I picked it up. I figured it might get lost. Or the police might keep it. I thought I owed it to Ben to look after it. I put it in my pocket. And then I got out of there as fast as I could."

"What did you do with the necklace? Did you give it to Ben?"

Norm stared at Manziuk. "I couldn't very well, could I? He'd have wanted to know where I got it and what I knew about her death."

"Why didn't you tell someone what had happened?"

"I wanted to. But while I was walking home, I realized I couldn't. I knew it had been an accident, but the police might not believe us. I didn't sleep all night. All I could think about was that she was lying out there and no one even knew. But nothing I said was going to help Sharlene at that point."

Ryan shook her head and shut her eyes. She just as suddenly opened them. "What happened to the necklace?"

"I hid it. And—" Norm shook his head. "You know, I haven't thought of it for years and years. I honestly have no idea what happened to it."

"What did it look like?" Elizabeth asked.

Norm turned to her, his face a study in perplexity. "It was a silver chain with a butterfly attached to it. The butterfly had some stones that sparkled like diamonds, but I'm sure they weren't." He turned back to Manziuk and Ryan. "I'm sorry. I don't remember what I did with it."

Elizabeth stood up. "You old fool," she said softly. "I thought you were bad now, but you were just as bad when you were younger."

Saying, "Wait here," she left the room.

Ryan trailed after her.

A few minutes later, they came back. Elizabeth was carrying an ancient cigar box in her hands. "We have what I call a keepsake trunk. My grandmother gave it to us when we were married. Over the years I've put in it any memorabilia that I wanted to keep. When Norm and I got married, I helped him go through his things. I looked inside this box and realized it was his memorabilia. One of the things was a broken necklace. I assumed it belonged to his first wife. I just put the whole box in my trunk, and it's been there ever since." She set the box on the coffee table and opened it.

Ryan put on a latex glove and reached in. Moments later she took out a wrinkled white handkerchief, opened it, and held up a chain. Attached to the chain was a butterfly with crystals in each wing. The silver was tarnished and dirty. Flakes of dried mud fell off.

"It's just the way I found it," Norm said. "I didn't want it, but I couldn't throw it out. So I put it in a box with some of my baseball cards and a few other keepsakes and forgot all about it."

"Those aren't diamonds, are they?" Manziuk asked.

"I'm sure they aren't," Elizabeth said. "They look like rhinestones to me. One of the stones is slightly chipped and there are a couple of scratches." Her lips twisted into a hint of a smile. "Don't worry, if I'd thought it was valuable, I'd have asked Norm about the necklace when I found it."

Ryan said, "Norm, when you saw Frank the next morning, did he have any bruises or scratches?"

He stared at her.

She repeated the question.

"I don't think so."

"The railing was low then, and they didn't put up the suicide barrier until much later. Did it ever occur to you that Frank might have pushed her over it?"

"No, never. I—he was my friend. I trusted him."

"And what about Ben? Wasn't *he* your friend?"

For the first time in the conversation, Norm's eyes sparked. "Don't you think I spent hours agonizing over this? But even if Frank *did* push her, I couldn't have stopped him. And I don't believe he did. If I'd told them Frank was with her, I would have messed up his life and maybe my own, too." He faced the three of them, his mouth quivering and his hands shaking. "Don't you think I'd have said something if it would have brought her back? But nothing was going to do that. And while I'm the first to admit Frank is an irritable old codger and he's never suffered fools gladly, I don't believe he'd ever intentionally hurt anyone."

"He's telling the truth," Elizabeth said. "He's the most gullible man I know."

Norm looked at her. "You really think I don't know about all your men?" He was trembling all over. "I let it go because I'd rather share you than lose you. If that makes me gullible, I guess I am."

Elizabeth stared at him. "You knew?" she whispered hoarsely.

"You always tired of them."

"I—I—"

"I didn't want you to tire of *me*." He looked away. "But right now I don't know if I care any more."

He looked at Manziuk. "Inspector, I'm sorry if I didn't do what I should have. I tried to do what seemed best. If you don't have any more questions, I'm going to lie down for a while." He left the room.

"Are you all right?" Ryan asked Elizabeth.

The older woman wrapped her arms around herself. "I hope so."

TWENTY-FOUR

At 9:00 that night Ryan and Manziuk met with Ford and Dr. Weaver.

There had been a dozen photos of Sharlene's unclothed body in the autopsy file. Dr. Weaver had blown the photos up and was now using his magnifying glass to go over every pixel. "I see a couple of things. It's difficult to see on the original photo, because it's black and white, and not only is her skin quite dark but her body is a mass of bruises. But on the enhanced photo you can clearly see a thin line across the middle of the back of her neck. Either something was put around her neck and pulled tight, or something that was already there, like a chain, was pulled from the front."

He used his magnifying glass to look at the other photos. "Yes," he said after a minute, "you can see that the thin line is absent at the front of her neck but present at the sides."

"These photos are entirely consistent with the theory that she was wearing a chain of some sort, and it was pulled tight or ripped right off her neck from the front. We can blow the photos up even more and measure the size of the marks on her neck against the chain you found, but I expect they'll fit." Dr. Weaver was still examining the photos. "But that doesn't explain how she fell to her death."

Ryan moved closer. "Do you see something else?"

"I do. Her body is so bruised it's virtually impossible to see it on the original photos, but when they're sharpened and blown up, it's a different story. It's a shame they didn't catch it when they did the autopsy, but unless you operate on the assumption that it might not have been suicide, there's a very good chance you'd miss the fact that some of the bruises differ from the others."

Manziuk said. "I don't see anything else."

Ford said, "Look again. Here and here and here. Use the magnifying glass."

After a few minutes, Ryan said, "I see them. That should give us all the evidence we need." She turned to Manziuk. "What do we do next?"

"It's unorthodox, but I think we call for a meeting of all the people involved in this case. Or, rather, these cases. Let's try to get everyone together at 9:00 tomorrow morning. I'll call Audra first and see if we can use the theatre there."

"What about the other thing we talked about?" Ford asked. "Should I get over there right away?"

"I'll call Audra to warn her you're coming. But it has to be done either after everyone's in bed or before they get up in the morning. I don't want to tip our hand."

Hilary looked at the clock. Just after 3:00 a.m. Not the time she wanted to start her Monday morning. She shut her eyes. Maybe she should get up and make herself some warm milk. Sometimes it helped her get back to sleep. But getting up was such a pain. Maybe if she just lay still for a while—

In the distance she heard a click that sounded like a door closing, and her eyes flashed open. It sounded like her front door. But no one had access. Audra and Derrick, but they wouldn't come into her place in the middle of the night. Not unless she called for them. The security guard in the hallway had the only master key. Could it be him? But why?

She almost called out, but stopped herself. Audra or Derrick would have said something. Anyone else shouldn't be here.

She moved her pillows to form a vertical line, pulled the duvet up over them, and then, as carefully as possible, rolled herself off the bed on the side away from the door, taking care to leave the duvet in place. Once on the floor she reached up to grab her cellphone from her night table and crawled on hands and knees to the foot of the bed. She peeked around it. All the time she was thinking that she was probably being ridiculously foolish. But two women were dead.

Footsteps were coming close. Either the person was being cautious or walking slowly for another reason.

She had no weapon. Her cane was leaning against the night table on the other side of the bed. She quickly sent Audra a short text message.

Help! Someone in my room.

Her bedroom door had been almost shut. She heard it opening and sensed someone walking into the room.

Hilary retreated back into the shadows along the end of her bed.

The movement was shuffling. Someone who didn't walk well? Mary shuffled sometimes, but only when she was wearing her fuzzy bedroom slippers.

Hilary scootched forward and peeked around the bottom of the bed, but the person must have moved further into the room, near the head of the bed.

There was a whooshing sound, and she felt the mattress jump. She knew in a flash what had happened. The person had taken her cane and used it to whack the pillow where her head should have been. Would have been, if she'd been asleep.

Another thud. Then a male voice shouted an annoyed, "What!"

She shivered. Her attacker had realized something was wrong. She would have to defend herself. But how?

She could hear the duvet being pulled back and the voice. "You thought you could defeat me, didn't you Sharlene?" She recognized the voice as Frank's. But what on earth was he talking about?

"I know why you're here, but you aren't going to win."

Hilary relaxed. Frank didn't worry her. Then she thought of Ingrid with the knife in her neck and shivered.

"If you really loved Ben, you'd leave. It will hurt him if you stay."

Mystified, Hilary spoke up. "Frank, what are you talking about?"

"You might as well give up. I always win."

Hilary felt her confidence surge back. "I survived the Notting Hill riots, you old fool. They gutted our house, all because of the colour of our skins, but that only made me stronger. And I survived dancing in seedy bars where you wouldn't have lasted five minutes.

So, yes, I think I can defeat you." Putting her hand on the edge of the bed, Hilary pulled herself to her feet just as the light went on.

Frank Klassen stood at the wall next to the light switch, her cane in his right hand and an evil grin on his lips. His eyes were cold and dead. "You think you can defeat me, don't you, Sharlene? Well, you're wrong."

Hilary came out from behind her bed. "What are you talking about?"

"You know what I'm talking about. You won't win."

"Frank, where's the security guard?"

He laughed. "I've been timing his rounds. He's somewhere near the exercise room right now. He won't be back here for ten minutes or more. He stops to have a smoke in the storage room." He took several shuffling steps toward her and raised the cane above his head.

Without taking her eyes off him, Hilary took a few steps away from the foot of the bed toward the door. He moved to cut off her route of escape. She backed away toward the bathroom. He countered, as if the two of them were linked.

"I know who you are. I've known it all along."

"I don't know what you're talking about, Frank."

"Just tell me you'll leave. I'll even help you pack."

"Frank, why don't you sit down, and I'll get you some help."

"You have to leave!" He lunged toward her, striking out with the cane. Hilary sidestepped, and he fell to his knees.

Seconds later, the security guard burst through the open door, Audra and Derrick right behind him. "Hilary," Audra cried out, "are you all right?"

"I'm fine. I knew you'd come."

Frank was struggling to get to his feet, a stream of obscenities flowing from his mouth.

Derrick came up behind Frank and put his arms around the older man to hold him, the security guard kicked the cane away from his outstretched hand, and Frank burst into tears.

Jacquie's cellphone buzzed at a few minutes before 3:30. She looked at her radio alarm clock and turned over, burying her face in the pillow. The phone buzzed again, and she shot up and grabbed for it. "Ryan here."

"Frank Klassen was caught a few minutes ago in Hilary's bedroom. He's now confined to his bedroom by the security guard.

"Seriously?"

"Audra just phoned. I'll see you there in half an hour."

"On my way."

At 9:00 Monday morning the residents and staff of the twentieth floor of Serenity Suites, along with Trish Klassen-Wallace, her husband, and Bruce Davidson, entered the theatre. Naomi Arlington and Dr. Granger took seats at the back of the room.

Frank, seated in a regular wheelchair, was pushed into the room by a burly police officer and helped into a chair at the end of the front row. A police officer sat on either side.

A few people looked shocked; others confused. They were all sneaking looks at Frank.

When he saw everyone was present, Manziuk went to the front of the room. "Because of the nature of this case, we felt it would be appropriate to address all of you together. I'll let Detective Constable Ryan begin."

Ryan stood up. "At 3:00 this morning Frank entered Hilary Brooks's bedroom. If not for the fact that Hilary hadn't been able to sleep and was very quick-witted, she might not be with us."

"She wasn't hurt," Frank stated. "The most you can charge me with is attempted assault."

"And breaking and entering."

His face turned red. "That's not true! I have my own master key. I own the bloody building; I can go wherever I like!"

Elizabeth gasped. "*You* own the building? Why you devious little man!"

"It's true." Frank looked at Ben. "Tell them!"

Ben sighed. "We built Serenity Suites together, the Klassens and my family. But we didn't want anyone to know."

"You people seem to be masters at keeping secrets," Elizabeth said. "First Jake and now this. Anything else?"

"That's what *we'd* like to know," Ryan said. "Specifically, Frank, we want to know what really happened to Sharlene Bryce."

Ben shook his head. "You know what happened. She jumped off what's now called the Bloor Street Viaduct. It was *my* fault. I should never have let her walk home alone."

"No, Ben." Norm stood up. "You had nothing to do with it."

"If I hadn't got her pregnant—"

"Ben, she knew you'd have looked after her. She trusted you. It was—"

"It was her family," Frank said. "They said something to her that night that made her go back and jump."

"That's interesting, Frank," Manziuk said. "We talked to Chief Justice William Bryce this morning. You might remember him as Sharlene's younger brother, Billy. He's very interested in knowing what we find out. He says his sister never came home after school that day. And he also said that he never for a single moment believed his sister committed suicide."

Norm was still standing. "I know what happened."

Frank shouted, "Norm, stay out of this!"

"No, I won't stay out of it!" Norm was trembling, and his face had become twisted. Slurring his words, he said, "Ben, Sharlene wasn't alone that night. We were with her. Frank and me. On the bridge."

Ben's body jerked. "You what?"

Mary stood up, a stunned look on her face, one hand held out. Catarina, who was sitting beside her, gently but firmly pulled her back down.

"Norm, shut up!" Frank hissed.

"We did it for your own good," Norm said to Ben.

"Norm's getting senile," Frank said. "He must have it mixed up with some other time."

"Norm might be a lot of things," Elizabeth said, "but senile isn't one of them."

Ben leaned toward Norm. "Tell me what you're talking about."

"We followed her and talked to her. Told her she couldn't let you throw away your life. Told her we'd help her get an abortion."

Ben jumped to his feet, glaring at Frank. "Why you meddling— You made her jump!"

"Ben," Mary said, "let Norm finish. I want to hear this, too."

"No, no," Norm said. "She was fine. She believed you. She kept saying, 'Ben said we'd be okay.'"

"If she was fine," Mary said, "how did she end up underneath the bridge?"

Norm looked down. "I told Frank we should leave her alone."

Ben shook his head. "How could you, Norm? How could you do that to me? To her?"

Norm was in tears. "I had chores to do for my dad. Frank wouldn't come, so I left him with her. And when I looked back, she'd jumped over the side. There was nothing I could have done." He whispered, "I did go down to her, but she was already dead."

Ben stared at him, then turned to Frank. "You were there when she jumped?"

"I tried to stop her from jumping but I wasn't fast enough. I was afraid the police might not believe me. That's why I didn't say anything." Frank's eyes were pleading. "You have to believe me. I never wanted anything bad to happen to her. I just didn't want you to wreck your life because of her."

"Is that true, Frank?" Manziuk asked. "Did you try to stop her from jumping?"

"Of course I did."

"Really?" Ryan said. "I don't think so."

Ben looked from Ryan to Manziuk. "What are you saying?"

"Sharlene Bryce didn't jump over the railing," Ryan continued. "And she didn't accidentally fall over it either. She was pushed. The coroner, Dr. Weaver, has examined the photos taken during her autopsy. He's willing to testify in court that you can see the imprint of a hand around her upper arm, the imprint of hands around her ankles, and bruises on her back from hitting the top of the railing before she fell."

Mary jumped up and walked toward Frank. "Frank Klassen, what did you do?"

"Nothing!"

"You pushed her over that bridge, didn't you? I've always thought you knew more than you let on, but I never believed you capable of something this despicable. You are the most selfish, most—most horrible—person I know." Her last words were garbled as she broke into tears.

Kenneth jumped up and went over to put his arms around her. She sobbed against him for a few minutes, then let him lead her back to her chair, where she collapsed, sobbing.

Ben was staring at Frank, shaking his head. "I—I don't believe it. How *could* you? Frank, how *could* you?"

"I'm so sorry, Ben." Norm used the backs of his hands to wipe the tears from his cheeks. "I thought—Frank said you'd be blacklisted from doing the things you wanted to do if you married her."

"And you really thought I'd have cared?"

Frank smiled. "You were always a dreamer and an optimist. Your life would have been turned upside down if you'd married her. All you had to do was convince her to have an abortion. Or give her a monthly cheque and let her raise the kid if that's what she wanted. But you had to do the honourable thing, no matter how stupid it was."

Ben was shaking his head. "I *loved* her. Frank, do you even know what love is?"

Frank's lips twisted into a hint of a smile. "I've always thought I did."

Ben's voice rose. "I think it was more that you didn't want to be known as the friend of someone who married a black woman."

"Ben, I'm so sorry," Norm whispered. "All we were doing was trying to get her to get an abortion so you didn't have to get married. That's all, I swear."

Elizabeth said, "Norm, shut up. This isn't about you."

"I—" He slumped over, his head in his hands.

"Well, Frank?" Manziuk said. "What happened between you and Sharlene after Norm left?"

"Nothing happened. I told her that Ben was wrong and marrying her would destroy him. I told her his family would disown him if he married her. That they wouldn't be able to find a decent place to live. That no one would hire him except for menial jobs. That all she had to do was get an abortion. And before I could stop her, she turned and jumped."

At this Ben rose to his feet, fists raised. Bruce quickly got up and put his arms around his father. "Dad, it's not worth it."

Breathing hard, Ben sat back down.

Manziuk said, "Mr. Klassen, I'm not buying it. I think what happened is that she said she was going to marry Ben, and you felt you had to stop her. I also think that at some point, you grabbed her arm, ripped off the necklace Ben had given her, and threw it."

"All right, yes. I threw the necklace over the railing. He'd been a fool to give it to her. She didn't deserve it. But that's *all* I did. If she was bruised, it was from the fall."

Ryan moved closer and stood so she could stare into his face. "Had you planned to push her over all along?"

He glared at her. "She was the most stubborn woman I'd ever met. She was talking about what they'd need for their apartment and how they'd manage, and she wouldn't even focus on what I was saying—how marrying her would hurt Ben's chances, and how they'd never have anything more than a room in a dingy boarding house. So I—I grabbed her by the arm to get her to pay attention to me, and I yanked off that necklace Ben had given her and I threw it as far as I could. Then I told her she might as well just tell Ben to jump over that railing because that's what marrying her would do to his life. And she started crying, but all she said was, 'Frank, you had no right to do that.' The look in her eyes told me she hadn't heard a word I'd said. She didn't care anything about Ben."

"What happened next?"

Frank looked down.

"Frank, there's a very clear bruise from a right hand on her upper left arm. There are also imprints of hands around her ankles. We can measure those marks against your hands. And there's a wide mark across her chest that we're pretty sure was the result of her hitting the railing after she was pushed. So you might as well tell us the truth."

Ben was shaking his head in disbelief.

Frank was breathing hard. "She wouldn't listen. She tried to leave, and she said, 'Don't think I won't tell Ben what you just did.'" His face puckered up. "She turned her back on me. She refused to listen to reason!"

He took a deep breath. "It was an accident. Over in an instant. Something made me look around, and there was no one else on the bridge. No cars and no people anywhere in sight. And without even knowing what I was doing, I'd shoved her toward the railing. She hit it, and while she was off-balance, I just grabbed her ankles and pushed her over." He looked around. "I didn't mean to do it. It just—she was just gone."

There was a long silence, broken only by Mary's sobs.

Her head leaning against her husband's shoulder, Trish said, "Did Mom know?"

"Of course not."

"In her letter she said something she'd overheard had made her wonder if a death had really been suicide. Did you say something to her about causing Sharlene's death?"

"Of course not! There was nothing to say."

"I'm guessing you did say something, Frank," Manziuk said. "Maybe without realizing you'd said it. I believe Trish said she was surprised to discover that she was the executor of her mother's will and that her mother's cookbooks and personal money were left to her. We can easily check with the lawyer to find out when Violet changed her will, but I'm willing to bet it was in the last few months, and that it was because of something you inadvertently said."

"It was an accident. A terrible accident."

"It was murder!" Ben looked at Manziuk. "Inspector, I hope you're going to arrest him."

Frank said, "It happened over fifty years ago. No way they can charge me now."

Ryan said, "Frank, you of all people ought to know there's no statute of limitations on murder."

"I didn't go there with intent to murder her."

"Maybe not. But it wasn't an accident."

"Manslaughter at most. And what would charging me get you? Nothing would change."

"All these years," Ben said, "I've thought you were my friend."

"I *am* your friend. Everything I did was for you."

"Excuse me," Mary said. "But what about Violet and Ingrid? Did Frank murder them, too?"

"Yes," Manziuk said.

"You're bluffing!" Frank yelled. "You have no evidence."

"You said yourself you had a master key," Manziuk said. "Your office is only a few steps from the door to the Davidsons' condo. You could have entered it at any time when you knew they were out and taken some of Ingrid's insulin and syringes. And the knife from Kenneth's condo, too."

"If I killed Ingrid, I'd have had blood on my clothes."

"Frank, if anyone knew how to get rid of bloodstains, it would be you. My guess is you wore long gloves, which you cut up in tiny pieces and flushed down the toilet."

"I ride a scooter. How do you think I would have done all that and not have someone notice me?"

"You could have gone out early during lunch, as you often do, saying you were going back to work on your book, and slipped down the hallway. You knew Violet's habits, so you could easily put sleeping pills in her orange juice. Since the container was in the garbage, there was likely only enough for one cup left. You might have even emptied some of it to make sure. Later, when you were certain she'd be asleep, you slipped in and injected the insulin.

"As for Ingrid, you could have gone to the common room, stabbed her, and been back in your office pretty quickly. You chose the day Derrick had his class so there'd be one less person to see you."

"You can't prove any of that. Someone would have seen me on my scooter. It's noisy."

"Ah, but you didn't use your scooter."

"What are you talking about?"

"Did you use your scooter to go to Hilary's condo last night?"

Frank blanched.

"Nikola saw you go from your office to the washroom one day last week. He said you used the wall for support. So, early this morning, we brought a team of people in to search for fingerprints. And sure enough, your prints are on the walls of the hallways going from your office to the Davidsons' condo, to Kenneth's condo, and to the common room. There are more on the hallways inside the Davidsons' and Kenneth's condos, and on the door of the medicine cabinet and the box of syringes in the Davidsons' bathroom. There are even some on a few of the chairs leading to where Ingrid was stabbed."

Ryan smiled at Frank. "You were so pleased with your little deception and so certain about your invincibility that it didn't even occur to you to wear gloves."

"Frank Klassen," Manziuk stated, "you're under arrest for the murders of Sharlene Bryce, Violet Klassen, and Ingrid Davidson, and the attempted murder of Hilary Brooks."

A struggling Frank was transferred from his chair to the wheelchair and held in place by a seatbelt.

As they began to push him out of the room, he shouted, "Everything I did was for you, Ben."

"For *me*?" Ben asked in disbelief.

"Everything."

"You knew I loved Sharlene. That I wanted to marry her."

"She was only going to bring you down. You'd never have had the opportunities you've had if you'd been tied to her."

"And you think I would have cared?"

"Maybe not right away, but at some point you'd have known what a mistake it was." Frank shook his head. "She was a fool! And stubborn as a mule. I even offered to pay for the abortion. But she said nothing would stop her from marrying you."

Ben's face contorted in pain. "And Ingrid? I suppose you killed *her* for me, too?"

"Of course I did! You were going to move out of Serenity Suites because of her! I had to stop you."

"And your own wife? Violet? How was that for me?"

"That—that was a mistake. When she told me about the cancer, she said she needed to make things right. I—I thought she was talking about Sharlene. I thought—I thought she suspected something." He looked toward the far wall and mumbled, "I guess maybe she was talking about her son."

"And Hilary? Why did you try so hard to get her to leave? And then attack her last night?"

"You're so blind!" Frank shouted, his face wreathed in anger. "You don't see what's right in front of your face! She's Sharlene come back to mess up your life. I had to protect you from her."

"Frank," Ryan said, "what about Grant Brooks? Did you have anything to do with his death?"

He looked at her in astonishment. "What are you talking about? Of course not. As long as *he* was here, Ben was safe from her."

Lyle shook his head. "Frank, you're crazy as a loon."

"I knew the moment I saw her that Hilary was Sharlene come back to life."

Ben stared at him. "Frank, even if it was, why did you think you needed to protect me from her?"

Frank's face twisted.

"Why, Frank?"

"Because—" Frank's face turned red, and his chest began to heave. "You thought those women loved you. But you were wrong. I loved you more than anyone. Violet knew. She knew you were the only one I've ever loved." Frank's words ended in a whisper.

As he took in the look of horror on Ben's face, he shut his eyes and let his head hang forward on his chest. "Get me out of here."

Manziuk nodded, and the officer who was pushing Frank's wheelchair moved on.

Ben stood watching, his mouth open and his eyes wide. Mary hurried over to put her arm around him and rest her head against his arm.

Norm turned to Elizabeth. Tears were running down his cheeks. He shook his head. "I always believed he tried to stop her."

After a moment of hesitation, his wife put her arm around him. "All those years you were protecting a madman."

Norm shook his head. "I never—"

"Let's go have tea. It'll make you feel better."

Elizabeth left with Norm but returned a few minutes later carrying the large painting of Sharlene. She held it out to Ben.

"Norm wants you to have this. He saw her face in a dream and painted it, but he didn't realize until yesterday whose face it was. Last night he added the necklace."

"I—I don't know what to say."

She hesitated. "Ben, Norm feels terrible. But you need to realize he honestly believed Frank tried to stop her from jumping, and that he and Frank would both be arrested if they said anything. He feels terrible for deceiving you."

She began to leave and then turned back. "And you might want to know that all these years, Norm had the necklace hidden away. The police took it as evidence, but Norm asked them to give it to you when it's released."

Ben gazed at the painting, tears filling his eyes. "It's a beautiful painting. She almost seems—alive. And I'll be grateful to have the necklace." His voice broke.

Slowly, he reached forward to trace the curve of Sharlene's cheek. "Thank Norm for me. Tell him I forgive him and I'll come and talk to him one of these days. But right now you need to understand I've not only lost Ingrid, but I feel as if I've lost Sharlene all over again."

EPILOGUE

Whatever affects one directly,
affects all indirectly.
I can never be what I ought to be
until you are what you ought to be.
This is the interrelated structure of reality.

—MARTIN LUTHER KING, JR.
"Letter from a Birmingham Jail"

The large bookstore on Yonge Street was crowded. A line of people snaked from a few feet inside the front door, down an aisle, and ended up at the back of the store where a large table was piled high with books.

On a high stool behind the table sat Scarlett Walker. She was dressed in a bright red wrap dress with three-quarter sleeves. Her hair was curled and glossy, free of the chef's hat she wore at Serenity Suites. She wore diamond earrings the residents of the twentieth floor had given her in celebration of the book's release. Her face was wreathed in smiles as she talked to people and signed cookbook after cookbook. A representative of the publisher sat beside her, opening each book to the title page so she only had to sign it and hand it to the waiting customer.

Mary was sitting in the coffee shop with Lyle, drinking herbal tea. "It's been a marvellous day. I just wish Violet was here to enjoy it."

Lyle nodded. His voice cracked slightly as he said, "Speaking of Violet, Mary, I have to apologize."

She gave him a puzzled look. "For what?"

"I—I have to confess that I thought it was you."

"Who was me?"

"I thought you killed them. Violet and Ingrid both."

She drew back, frowning in surprise. "Really?"

"Yes. I thought you were bored."

"So bored I started murdering people?"

"Well, you do read all those books about murder and watch all those nasty TV shows that just give people ideas. And you're always talking about it."

"I suppose."

"Anyway, I want to make it up to you. For even thinking it might have been you."

"Oh? How do you propose to do that?"

"I have a new role in a play. Just a small one. I'm the butler, you know, the old family retainer. And it's a mystery. How do you like that?"

"Well, it sounds good. But I don't see—"

"They're looking for an elderly woman to play the cook. I told my agent about you."

"Me?"

"It's only a few lines and some humming while you rattle pots and pans. And there's a small paycheque. It's something to do, you know, to get out."

"Oh, I could never do that. I've never liked being up in front of people."

"You'd be supporting cast, you know. Not alone on the stage. The audience would be watching the main actors."

Mary thought for a minute, then shook her head.

"You could do it, you know. You'd be perfect."

"Do you really think so?"

"I do."

"Well, maybe I'll consider it. It might get my mind off what's happened."

"Been a bit rough, hasn't it?"

"That's an understatement."

"Getting up on a stage isn't that hard, you know. I mean, you had to do it when you were singing."

"But that was for children. I never minded being up in front of children."

"Well, instead of picturing the audience as naked the way they always tell you, picture them as children."

As she considered the idea, she began to nod. "You know, maybe I could do that." She leaned toward him. "Do you have a copy of the script that I could read? Just to see if I like it."

Paul and Loretta Manziuk came through the front doors and took their place at the end of the line.

"Inspector Manziuk?"

Paul turned to find Ben Davidson at his elbow. After Paul had introduced him to Loretta, Ben said, "Scarlett asked us to watch for you. She didn't want you having to stand in line. A very busy and rewarding day. Violet would have hated every minute, but Scarlett is in her element. If you'll just follow me, I'll take you to her via the shortcut."

"Are you sure?"

"Absolutely. Detective Constable Ryan already has a copy." He pointed past Scarlett's table. "She and her grandmother and some other members of her family are over there talking to Derrick and Catarina."

"Is everyone from Serenity Suites here?"

"Oh, yes. It's a good day for all of us. We love Scarlett and we're so glad to see the cookbook published." He grinned. "That line hasn't become any shorter since she started signing an hour and a half ago. And people are still coming in."

"Good. So how is everyone coping?"

"Very well actually. Gabri cancelled a concert in London to be here this weekend. He and Audra just went with Trish and her husband to get their kids some ice cream. They'll be back shortly. Catarina has already picked the date for their wedding, and I believe Audra will soon have custody of her boys." Ben winked. "Money seems to speak, as they say—particularly to Audra's ex-husband's new wife, apparently—and Gabri is loaded. Derrick is going to take over as manager of the twentieth floor when Audra leaves, and we're all happy for him. And there's a new nurse coming next Monday to take Audra's place. Not that anyone ever could.

"Scarlett is teaching Olive to cook, so she can do some touring with her book.

"Oh, and Kenneth's younger daughter is here this weekend, too. He's over the moon that at least one of his children wants to get to know him better, and hopefully in time the others will give him a second chance, too."

"That's good to hear."

"Yes, but we've had a bit of a scandal, too. Dr. Granger's wife found out he was having an affair with Naomi Arlington, and is suing him for divorce. Naomi had already been fired, but he's leaving, too. I guess you never can tell." He sighed. "As for the rest of us, what can I say? I guess old people are pretty resilient."

"Are Norm and Elizabeth here?"

"No, they're in British Columbia visiting Jake. They've put their condo up for sale and plan to move to Victoria. They want a fresh start."

"That reminds me. I have something to give you. Since Frank is pleading guilty to all charges, it's been released." He held out a shiny silver butterfly on a chain. The rhinestones sparkled in the sunlight. "I took the liberty of getting it cleaned and repaired."

Ben took the necklace and held it up. "Thank you so much. I gave this to Sharlene a few weeks before she died. I wanted to give her something special so she'd know how I felt about her. When I saw this at a jewellery store, I knew at once that it was perfect, even though it took every cent I had. I'd always teased her about being like a butterfly—not only because she always wore bright colours, but because she was always flitting from one idea to the next." Tears came to his eyes. "Sharlene would have done wonderful things. And our baby… Such a tremendous waste." He took a deep breath. "But that's all in the past. Nothing more to be done about it now.

"Before I forget, I want to thank you for putting me in touch with Billy. He and his wife actually paid us a visit last week. I have to get used to calling him William." He shook his head. "Chief Justice William Bryce. He told me he listened to *Ben's Room* whenever he could but never tried to get in touch because he didn't want to remind me of the past. As if I ever forgot. Mary and I were so happy to find out how well he's done."

Hilary appeared next to Ben and slipped her arm around him. "Hello, Inspector. Nice to see you. Scarlett will be thrilled." Without waiting for a reply, she looked at Ben. "Are you ready? Kenneth wants to go and make sure everything is as requested."

She winked at Manziuk. "You're welcome to come if you like. We have a little surprise for Scarlett after this is over. The cookbook has already made the bestseller list, based on pre-orders, and the publishers have worked out a deal for Scarlett to audition for her own TV show! We've booked a restaurant for the celebration. Ben is the host; Kenneth and Mary are going to sing; Lyle and Catarina are doing a scene from Scarlett's favourite play; the Kanes and Gerbrandts are doing a skit; and Gabri is going to end it with a mini-concert. And who knows? I might even dance a few steps."

Ben slipped the butterfly necklace into the pocket of his suit jacket and smiled down at Hilary. "Yes, we do need to go. No time to waste." He reached out to shake Paul's hand. "I'm very glad to have met you, Inspector. And your partner, too. Superintendent Seldon told me I wouldn't be disappointed, and he was absolutely correct."

He started to leave with Hilary and then turned back. "By the way, I recall your mentioning that your parents were fans of my radio show. Perhaps you and your wife could bring them over some evening. I'd love to meet them."

ACKNOWLEDGEMENTS

Years ago, my mother lived for a year in a residence for seniors. Then she lived in two different nursing homes. Somewhere in there, I decided to set a mystery in a seniors' residence of some sort.

My husband, Les, had a friend who lived in a residence for seniors and frequently complained that only a few of the other people were worth trying to have a conversation with and several of them were mad at him. One day Les commented to me that what many elderly people need is an apartment with a housekeeper and three other competent elderly people, each with his or her own bedroom.

From those thoughts, plus a few visits to some nice condos, came Serenity Suites. But I still needed a plot.

One day I was walking along a sidewalk beside a busy road when it occurred to me how easy it would be to push the person next to me into oncoming traffic. We sometimes think it's difficult to commit murder. And "we" couldn't do it. But I don't believe it's difficult at all. Even children do it. I believe the really difficult thing is to restrain the impulse to lash out, whether in hot anger or cold rage. And that getting away with acting on such an impulse might lead to a lifetime of arrogance.

Thanks to Les who supports my writing to a ridiculous extent.

Thanks so much to Kent G. Laidlaw, owner of Canuckcare.com and formerly of the Halton Regional Police Service, who answered a number of questions about police procedure and what-ifs.

Thanks to Dr. Kevin Dautrement for his medical advice, and to the eleven other members of The Word Guild listserv who shared information from their personal medical history as well as from working with the elderly in various capacities.

While I appreciate all the help, I had to pick and choose what I used for my story, so any mistakes are solely my responsibility.

Thanks to all the members of The Word Guild who answered random questions, encouraged me to keep writing because they wanted to read the book, and prayed for me when things weren't going well.

Thanks to Audrey Dorsch for making me rethink scenes and kill off a few of my darlings.

Thanks to Elaine Freedman for her painstaking copy editing and encouragement.

Thanks to Mary Lou Cornish for catching a bunch of those little glitches that always get through when I make changes.

Thanks to Patricia Anne Elford, Janet Sketchley, Linda Hall, and Jayne Self who did a quick last-minute read and caught more little glitches. Everyone seems to notice different things!

Hopefully, between all the eyes, we got them all.

Thanks to the members of Crime Writers of Canada, Sisters in Crime, and the Writers Union of Canada who constantly challenge me by their accomplishments and support.

Finally, a huge thank you to all the readers who've kept asking me when the next Manziuk and Ryan mystery is coming out. I guess we'll be starting that process all over again, right?

J. A. MENZIES

While I'd hate to stumble on a real body under any circumstances, I have a thing about noticing the "perfect" locations for finding mythical bodies. In order not to waste this fascinating (and hopefully, unusual) skill, I decided to write mysteries.

Truth is, I've been reading mysteries since I first discovered Trixie Beldon (I owned every book). Later, I discovered and devoured the work of Erle Stanley Gardner, John Creasey, Agatha Christie, Georgette Heyer, Ngaio Marsh, Dorothy L. Sayers, Desmond Bagley, Raymond Chandler, Emma Lathen, Marjorie Allingham, and others far too numerous to list here.

I still go back and reread many of the authors of the British Golden Age—they're my comfort-books. I also read a variety of contemporary authors, including Donna Andrews, Louise Penny, Alan Bradley, Sue Grafton, Peter Robinson, Rick Blechta, Vicki Delany, P. D. James, Marcia Muller, and T. Jefferson Parker.

I'm a member of various writers' organizations, including Sisters in Crime and Crime Writers of Canada. I also teach workshops for writers. I especially enjoy sharing some of my secrets on developing plots. (One of my favorite reviews, from *Library Journal*, called me a "master of plotting.")

By the way, in real life, people know me as N. J. Lindquist. And my first two mysteries were actually published under that name. Afterwards, I decided that I really needed to separate the mysteries from my other books, so—better late than never (I hope)—I made my birth name (J. A. Menzies) my alter ego.

CONNECT WITH ME AT:

http://jamenzies.com/

Books & Stories by J. A. Menzies

Classic Mysteries in Contemporary Settings

Manziuk and Ryan Mysteries

Shaded Light: The Case of the Tactless Trophy Wife
Glitter of Diamonds: The Case of the Reckless Radio Host
Shadow of a Butterfly: The Case of the Harmless Old Woman

Short Stories

"The Case of the Sneezing Accountant: A Paul Manziuk & Jacquie Ryan Short Story"
"The Day Time Stood Still"
"They Can't Take That Away From Me"
"Revenge So Sweet"

How to Make an Author Happy

Writing a book is actually a lot of work.
Writing a **good** book is even more work.

If you've liked a book and would like to show your appreciation for the effort the writer put into it (thus encouraging said writer to write more), here are 4 ways to do it.

1. Write a review. Post your review on Amazon, Barnes and Noble, Goodreads, your blog, and/or anyplace else you frequent. It doesn't have to be long. A couple of sentences is enough. (Just remember not to give away the plot!) And tell the publisher or writer about your review. Even if you said a few negative things, it's okay.

2. Tell other people about the book. Better yet, buy some copies to give as gifts to other people you think would enjoy them.

3. Buy the writer's other books. Or get them from your library. You'll no doubt enjoy them as well.

4. Connect with the writer by signing up for his or her email updates or newsletter, and/or following on Twitter, FaceBook, or whatever other online connections you both have.

Trust me, the writer will appreciate it very much.

PUBLISHER

MurderWillOut Mysteries publishes whodunits set in Canada but written in the classic Golden Age style. It's an imprint of That's Life! Communications, a niche Canadian publisher.

murderwillout.com